MAIN

DEATH &
THE JUBILEE

DEATH &
THE JUBILEE

A Lord Francis Powerscourt Mystery

DAVID DICKINSON

CARROLL & GRAF PUBLISHERS
New York

Carroll & Graf Publishers
An imprint of Avalon Publishing Group, Inc.
161 William Street
NY 10038-2607
www.carrollandgraf.com

First Carroll & Graf edition 2003

First published in the UK by Constable,
an imprint of Constable & Robinson Ltd 2003

ISBN 0-7867-1110-8

Printed and bound in the EU

For Lizzie

Prologue

London 1896

One nondescript room at the top of the War Office in London had become the nerve centre of the British Empire. It had two small windows that looked out over the rooftops of the capital, a threadbare carpet, a fading portrait of Queen Victoria over a mean fireplace, a battered desk and an ink-stained table.

But these cramped quarters were the focal point for one of the greatest movements of military personnel the world had ever seen. Tens of thousands of soldiers and cavalrymen were to sail across the globe on orders despatched from this bureaucratic command post.

This was the Planning Headquarters for the Jubilee Parade in honour of Victoria the Queen Empress on her Diamond Jubilee on 22nd June 1897, now a year and a quarter away. This was to be the grandest parade the world had ever seen, grander even than Roman triumphs through the eternal city two thousand years before. No captured chieftains or Oriental despots in chains were needed to adorn this procession. These were Victoria's subjects, to be carried across the red-coloured map that marked the glory of her Empire. Hussars from Canada and carabiniers from Natal had to be transported, Hong Kong Chinese Police, Cypriot Zaptiehs, Dyak head-hunters from North Borneo, Malays and Hausas, Sinhalese and Maoris, Indian lancers and Cape Mounted Rifles, cavalrymen from New South Wales and Jamaicans resplendent in white gaiters. Fifty thousand troops were to march through London to a Service of Thanksgiving at St Paul's, a splash, an explosion of colour on the dull grey buildings of the capital, a heady and intoxicating draught of romance for the million citizens expected to wonder at their passing.

1

General Hugo Arbuthnot was the man in charge of this huge enterprise. He had been a soldier all his life, a life spent in the mundane details of military planning and administration. Not for him the glory of the cavalry charge or the heroic defences of the British Army in adversity. His campaigns were fought not with the sword but with pen and ink, fought on paper in committee meetings and the interminable boredom of staff work. From this unpromising terrain he had created an empire all his own. If some dashing general was faced with a complicated logistic problem he felt was beneath his talents, Arbuthnot was the man. If the Army wanted a vast feat of organizational complexity, Arbuthnot was the man. Above all, he was known as having a safe pair of hands.

But there was one cross he had to bear, as he repeatedly told his wife in their tidy house in Hampshire, the lawn always neatly trimmed, the roses punctually pruned, on his return from the daily grappling with shipping lines and the near insoluble problem of camel feed on requisitioned steamers. General Arbuthnot was also in charge of security on Jubilee Day. Security, he used to say, was not something, like cases of rifles or ammunition, that could be nailed down. It was slippery. It was elusive. And some of the people he had to deal with on the issue of security were, he felt, decidedly slippery, decidedly elusive.

This morning Arbuthnot had convened a meeting in his office of some of the key elements in the Whitehall jungle whose views had to be consulted. On his left sat the Honourable St John Flaherty of the Foreign Office, an exquisitely dressed young man whose diplomatic reticence was marred by a fabulous gold watch. Flaherty was renowned in diplomatic circles for the quality of his prose and the regularity of his affairs with diplomatic wives. On Arbuthnot's right sat a harassed-looking Assistant Commissioner from the Metropolitan Police. Furthest away was Dominic Knox of the Irish Office, a short and wiry man with a small beard and a secret passion for the gaming tables. Knox had no official job title but wandered through the bureaucratic maze as a senior member of the Secretariat in Dublin Castle. Everyone round General Arbuthnot's table knew that this was the foremost expert in Britain on terrorism, subversion and intelligence gathering in Ireland.

'Perhaps, Mr Flaherty, you could enlighten us with the views of the Foreign Office?' General Arbuthnot had little time for the Foreign Office, a talking shop full of milksops in his view.

'Thank you, General, thank you.' Flaherty smiled a conde-

2

scending smile. 'I could burden you with the reports we have collected from our embassies round the world, gentlemen.' Flaherty waved at a pile of cables in his folder as if it were a bad hand at whist. 'But I won't. The key fact is this, gentlemen. Assassinations since the time of Julius Caesar and before have always been home-grown affairs. Brutus and Cassius stabbed their fellow Roman on the Ides of March. Roman assassinates Roman. John Wilkes Booth shot his President Abraham Lincoln at the theatre in Washington. American assassinates American. Russians blew up their Tsar Alexander as he drove through St Petersburg in his carriage fifteen years ago. Russian assassinates Russian. In some parts of the Balkans and the Middle East, I believe, more rulers are assassinated than actually die in their beds.

'In short, the most likely person to try to assassinate Queen Victoria or let off a bomb is an inhabitant of these islands, a Briton trying to assassinate a Briton. Madmen and fanatics from anywhere in the world cannot be ruled out of course, but you cannot legislate for the insane.'

'Quite so,' said the General, looking up from the notes he had just made. 'Let me now turn to the position of the Metropolitan Police. Mr Taylor.'

William Taylor, Assistant Commissioner, felt slightly out of place. He brushed his remaining hairs back across his forehead. He was a practical policeman. He had risen through the ranks from mundane police stations in Clerkenwell and Southwark, Hoxton and Hammersmith. It would be his task to issue the public order notices, to prepare the plans of his force for the maintenance of order on the day of the procession. The historical sweep of the Foreign Office world view left him cold.

'Our position, General, is quite simple. We have increased our penetration of the various subversive societies that operate in and around the capital. You will recall that we were allotted extra monies for the purpose. We are still working on our security strategy for the week or so surrounding the Jubilee. At one point we considered banning the public from the roofs of all the high buildings along the route of the parade to St Paul's Cathedral, but the Home Office believe it would be politically impossible.'

William Taylor winced slightly as he remembered the response of the Home Office Minister. 'Completely, totally and utterly impossible! Impossible! We are meant to be celebrating the glory and power of the British Empire! Are we so frightened that we have to have a flat-footed constable on every rooftop looking for assassins? What would they do if they saw one? Blow their whistles?'

'For the time being, General,' Taylor went on, 'we watch and wait. We are in very close touch with our colleagues from the Irish Office, as you know.'

A telephone was ringing insistently in the room next door. Noises of the great world beyond the windows infiltrated the War Office, clocks tolling, the rumble of traffic, the shouts of the delivery men. General Arbuthnot looked briefly at his favourite picture. It showed an enormous military parade at Aldershot, ranks of troops stretching without end towards a pale blue horizon. Not a button, not a plume was out of place. That was as it should be. General Arbuthnot had organized the parade.

'Knox,' the General said suddenly, 'you may be the last person to speak, but I am sure we all believe that your intelligence may be the most serious.'

'Thank you, General.' Dominic Knox knew that the General did not care for him. He did not care for the General. Knox looked as if he might have been a priest or a philosophy don. Years of reading through the ambiguities of intelligence reports, of second or third or even fourth guessing the words and actions of his opponents had left him with severe doubts about the accuracy of language, written or spoken.

'I am sorry to have to disappoint you, gentlemen. The only honest answer I can bring to this meeting about the level of threat from Ireland on Jubilee Day is that we do not know. We do not know what new groups may have formed over there by next year. Undoubtedly there is a small section of Irish opinion which would dearly like to assassinate Queen Victoria.'

The Army, the Foreign Office and the Metropolitan Police looked shocked as if Knox had just blasphemed at Holy Communion in Westminster Abbey.

'We have our intelligence systems in place. We should hear of any such plan inside forty-eight hours. But the Irish are very cunning. They may have made their plans some years ago. They may have planted the would-be assassin in a safe job in London already. He may be going about his lawful business even as we sit here this morning, a waiter in a club or a servant in a grand house somewhere along the route perhaps, watching and waiting for the parade itself when he will reveal himself in his true colours. It may be that we have to investigate all those who have come to London in the last two years.

'I am sorry that I cannot bring more hopeful news. But I would be betraying my duty if I did not tell you how we see the position. There is over a year to go before Her Majesty sets out from Buckingham Palace en route to St Paul's. We shall be watching the threat from Ireland on an hourly basis until then. Hour by hour, if not minute by minute.'

Berlin 1896

'Only in war can a nation become a true nation. Only common great deeds for the Idea of a Fatherland will hold a nation together. Social selfishness, the wishes of individuals, all must yield. The individual must forget himself and become part of the totality; he must realize how insignificant his life is compared with the whole. The State is not an Academy of Art, or of Commerce. It is Power!'

Five hundred pairs of eyes were riveted on an old man at a lectern. Once more the audience in the Auditorium Maximum of the Friedrich Wilhelm University in Berlin rose to their feet. They cheered, they stamped their boots, they waved their hats in the air. Heinrich von Treitschke, the Professor of History, was old now. People said he was dying. His delivery was not couched in the musical cadences of some of the other professors whose eloquence could never pack the lecture halls like he could; it was harsh, and as his deafness increased he shouted in a rough monotone like a man trying to speak in a storm.

'If a State realizes that it can, by way of its power and moral strength, lay claim to more than it possesses, it turns to the only means of achieving this, namely the force of arms. It is absurd to regard the conquest of another province or another country as theft or as a crime. It is sufficient to ask how the vanquished nation may best be absorbed in the superior culture.'

Von Treitschke had been giving these lectures on German politics and history for over twenty years. His audience was composed not merely of university students, but of bankers, businessmen, journalists, army cadets from the garrisons of Berlin and Potsdam. For many of them, who attended week after week and year after year, the message of the ancient historian, his hair white, his face lined, his expression fierce as he preached the love of the Fatherland, had become more important than that of any preacher they might hear in the churches of the capital. The body and blood

5

of Christ had been replaced with the bodies and the blood of Germany. Here was a true Prussian prophet in his final years leading his people out of the wilderness into the promised Fatherland.

'When we look . . .' the old man paused and stared defiantly at the lecture hall and his disciples, 'when we look at the lessons of our great past towards our glorious future, what do we find? We find that Germany's greatest enemy lies not to the east in Mother Russia, but in the west! Yes, in the west! Our greatest enemy is an island! An island whose arrogance and presumption has too long denied our great Fatherland its place in the sun, its historical role at the heart of world power.'

Standing by the entrance was a tall thin young man called Manfred von Munster whose face had all the ardour and faith of the congregation. But his eyes were fixed on an even younger man who sat in the second row and whose eyes were burning with passion. He took notes in a small black book and he was first to stamp his feet, to roar on the devotion of the faithful. Von Munster had attended every one of Treitschke's lectures for the past ten years. For him they were not just a confirmation of his creed, a communion with other believers. They were a recruiting ground.

'They have a song, these English,' the Professor was shouting now as he built towards his peroration. 'They call it "Rule Britannia, Britannia rule the waves." That has gone on for too long. England, with its decadent and effete aristocracy, its complacent and avaricious merchants who have used the Royal Navy to build up their trade and commerce across the globe, its slovenly and unhealthy workers, this England has been allowed to rule for far too long. One day, my fellow countrymen, when we have built our strength on sea as well as land, one day it will be Germany's destiny to replace these sordid shopkeepers in the ranks of the world powers. No more Rule Britannia!'

The audience were on their feet, throwing notebooks, hats, pens, hands into the air. 'Treitschke! Treitschke!' they shouted as though it were a battle cry. 'Treitschke! Treitschke!'

The old man held up his hand to quell the noise. He looked, thought Munster, like Moses on the mountain top, about to descend with the tablets of stone to his unworthy people.

'My friends! My friends! Forgive me! I have not yet finished my lecture.'

6

In an instant the audience went quiet. They did not sit down, but remained on their feet to hear the last words of the master.

'No more Rule Britannia . . .' Treitschke paused. Silence had fallen over his students as though a cloud had blocked out the sun. He stared at his audience, scanning their faces row by row. 'Rule Germania! Rule Germania!'

The cheers rolled out round the auditorium. Professor von Treitschke departed the stage slowly, leaning on a stick, declining all offers of assistance. The strength seemed to flow out of him now his lecture was over. He looked like any other old man, close to death perhaps, walking back alone to his apartment after the day's chores were done.

But for von Munster the day's work was only just beginning. He struck up a conversation with the young man in the second row as they struggled through the crowd leaving the university into a freezing Berlin.

'Forgive me, please. Haven't I seen you at the lectures before?'

'You have.' The young man's face glowed with pride. 'I have attended every single lecture this term. Isn't it a pity that they are nearly over?'

Von Munster laughed. He knew the young man had attended every lecture. He had watched him every time, looking not at Treitschke's face but at his companion and his growing devotion to the cause of a greater Germany. This was part of his job. Now, von Munster felt sure, he could bring another disciple into the fold.

'Have you time for a quick cup of coffee? It seems colder than usual today.' Munster spoke in his friendliest voice.

'If it is quick,' the young man said. 'I have to get back.'

'I was wondering,' von Munster began as they sat in the back of the coffee house, 'if you would like to be more closely associated with the Professor and his ideas. But, forgive me, how very rude, I don't even know your name!'

'My name is Karl,' the young man smiled, 'Karl Schmidt. I come from Hamburg. But tell me more about the Professor and his ideas. Are there more lectures I could go to? Or is it true that von Treitschke is dying?'

'I believe he may be nearing the end, but his message will live on,' replied Munster, lighting a small cigar. He looked carefully round the café, making sure that in their little alcove by the fire, they were truly alone. Pictures of German soldiers lined the walls.

'It's not a question of more lectures, alas. Would there were more where we could be inspired by the passion of the master. No.' He leaned forward suddenly, stirring his coffee very slowly as he spoke. 'There is a society devoted to his ideals.' He looked Karl Schmidt directly in the eye. 'It is a secret society.'

'Oh,' said Schmidt, feeling alarmed suddenly. His mother had warned him about the secret societies in the universities and the army regiments, terrible places, she had said, devoted to duelling and strange rituals like Black Masses and the worship of the dead. She had made Karl promise that he would never, never, have anything to do with these dens of vice. 'What kind of secret society?' he asked, his pale blue eyes troubled in the cigar smoke.

'Oh, it's not what you might think!' Munster laughed. 'We don't go in for drinking our blood mixed with wine, or ceremonies with black candles or anything of that sort.' He leaned back in his chair, as though he were insulted by the younger man's hesitation. 'It's much more serious than that.'

He paused. Long experience had taught him to make the secret society seem as important as possible.

'How do you mean?' The young man was leaning forward in his chair now.

'Well, we believe that von Treitschke's message is far too important to be sullied with the pranks and the games university students and army cadets play, far too important.'

He paused to see if his message was getting through. It was.

'But how do you join? What is the purpose of the society? What is it called?' Karl Schmidt sounded as though he would sign on the spot.

'I will tell you the name of the society in a moment. Its recruits have to satisfy four senior members that they will do everything to follow von Treitschke's teaching and to advance the cause of Germany. Not just in their relations with their friends and family. It isn't like joining a religious group or a church. It's much more important than that. It may be that their place in life gives them special opportunities to further the cause. Every new member has to swear an oath to do that. Then we sing our hymn, our Te Deum, our Ave Maria. Can you guess what it is?'

The young man shook his head.

'I'm sure you would get it if you had time to think. It is "The Song of the Black Eagle" which von Treitschke himself composed after France declared war on Prussia in 1870.' Munster began to hum softly.

'Come sons of Germany,
Show your martial might . . .'

Karl Schmidt joined in, smiling with pride.

'Forward to the battlefleld,
Forward to Glory.
At the sign of the Black Eagle
Germany shall rise again.'

'Hush,' said Munster, 'we mustn't get carried away, even with the Treitschke song. The society is called the Black Eagle. Every new member receives a ring like this one so he can recognize other members if necessary.'

He pulled a silver ring off his finger. It had no inscription on it. Karl Schmidt looked puzzled.

'Look on the inside. If you look carefully you will see a very small black eagle, just waiting on the inside, waiting to fly away in the cause of a greater Germany.'

The young man sighed. Munster waited. It was for Schmidt to make the next move. 'I think – no, I am sure,' he said, 'that I would like to join. But I am not sure how I can be of service.'

'You never know who may or may not be able to serve,' said Munster severely. 'That is for the senior members to decide. Sometimes people may have to wait for years before they find themselves in a position to do their duty. But tell me, what is your profession? Are you a student here at the university?'

'I wish I was,' said Karl sadly. 'I'm a clerk at the Potsdamer Bank just round the corner.'

'You work in a bank? You know how the banking business works?' Von Munster sounded eager, very eager.

'I don't know all of it yet,' said Karl Schmidt apologetically, 'but I am learning. And my English is quite good now. The bank pays for me to go to evening classes.'

'My friend, my friend,' Munster was smiling now and seized the young man's hand, 'tonight or tomorrow we shall introduce you into the society. We shall all sing "The Song of the Black Eagle" together. Singing it together, the new recruit and the senior members, that is very important. And then, in a little while, it may be that we have some very important work for you. Work of which von Treitschke himself would be proud!'

9

'Work here in Berlin? Inside the Potsdamer Bank?' Karl looked puzzled again.

'No, not in Berlin' said Munster. He sounded very serious indeed. 'In London.'

Part One

Ordeal by Water

1

They came across London Bridge like an army on the march, regiments of men and a few platoons of women, swept forward by the press behind them. They were a sullen army, an army going to a siege perhaps, or a battle they didn't think they could win. Behind them the roar of the steam engines and the shrieking of whistles heralded the arrival of reinforcements as train after train deposited its carriages into the station.

To the left and right of the army was the river, two hundred and fifty yards wide at this point, full of ships from every corner of the world. Shouts of the lightermen and the sailors added to the noise. Ahead lay their destination, the City of London, which swallowed up nearly three hundred thousand people every day in its eternal quest for business. Junior clerks with shiny black coats and frayed collars dreamed of better days to come. Stockbrokers with perfectly fitting frock-coats hoped for fresh commissions and extravagant customers. Merchants in all the strange substances the City dealt in, cork and vanilla, lead spelter and tallow, linseed oil and bristles, prayed that prices would get firmer.

All this silent army were coming to worship at the twin gods of the City, Money and the Market. Money was cold. Money was the yellow cakes of gold in the vaults of the Bank of England a couple of hundred yards ahead of them. Money was the bills of exchange the bankers and merchants had despatched across the five continents, the fine wrapping paper that enclosed English domination of the world's trade. Money was to be counted in banking halls and insurance companies and discount houses, the daily traffic measured out line by line and figure by figure in the great ledgers which stored its passing.

The Market was different. If Money was cold, the Market was

13

mercurial. She was like a spirit that flew across Leadenhall Street and Crooked Friars, across Bishopsgate and Bengal Court, turning in the air and changing her mind as she travelled across her City. Some older heads in the great banking houses said she could be like a volcano, erupting with terrible force to shake the very foundations of finance. There were many who claimed to know the Market's moods, when she would change her mind, when she would grow sullen and petulant, when she would dance in delight across the Stock Exchange and bring sudden wealth with floods of speculation about gold or diamonds found in distant parts of the world. The optimists believed the Market was always going to smile on them. She did not. The cautious and the prudent believed she was a fickle mistress, never to be wholly trusted. Their fortunes might have grown more slowly than the optimists, but they were never wiped out.

A sudden scream cut through the silent meditations of the marching army. Towards the further bank a tall young man was yelling and pointing to something in the water, his face unnaturally white against the black of his clothes.

'There! Look there, for the love of God!'

He pointed at something bobbing about in the water, bumping against the side of one of the ships moored on the City side of the river. Behind the young man there was a hurrying forward as the slow march transformed itself into double quick time. 'Look! It's a body, by the side of the ship, there!'

All around him brokers and merchants and commission agents pushed forward to peer into the water. Two sailors of foreign extraction appeared on deck and stared uncomprehendingly at the crowd.

'There's a corpse in the river! There's a corpse in the river!' The phrase spread quickly back across the bridge. Within three minutes word would reach the incoming passengers in London Bridge station. Within five minutes it would flash past Wellington's statue and reach the portals of the Royal Exchange.

The tall young man stretched even further forward towards the murky waters of the Thames.

'Oh, my God!' he shouted. He fell backwards into the crowd and fainted away into the amazed arms of a fat and prosperous old gentleman who was surprised at how light he was.

The young man was the first to see that the body had no head, and that the hands had been cut off. A grisly stump of neck,

14

clotted yellow and black, was inching its way towards the further shore.

Murder had come to the City at half-past eight on a Thursday morning.

Throughout the day rumour was King. Rumour, of course, was usually King in the temples of finance: rumours of revolutions and defaults in South America, rumours of unrest and instability in Russia, and, most frequent and most unsettling of all, rumours of changes in interest rates. But on this day one question and one question only dominated all conversations. Who was the dead man? Where had he come from? Why did he have no head and no hands? At lunchtime in the chop houses and the private dining rooms it reached its crescendo.

The tall thin young man, Albert Morris, was a hero for twenty-four hours. Revived by brandy and water in the partners' room of the private banking house where he earned his daily bread, he told his story over and over again. He told it to his colleagues, he told it to his friends, he told it eagerly to the newspapermen who laid siege to his bank until he was delivered up to them.

The first rumour, believed to have come originally from the Baltic Exchange, was that the corpse was a Russian princeling, a relative of the Tsar himself, murdered by those foul revolutionaries, the body transported from St Petersburg to London and thrown over the side. The head, said the Baltic Exchange, had been removed so the Russian authorities would never know he had been murdered, thus forestalling any of those fearful reprisals for which the Tsar's secret police were famous.

Nonsense, came the counter-rumour from one of the great discount houses. The corpse was not a Russian, he was French. He was a wine merchant from Burgundy who had been carrying on an affair with another man's wife. The cuckolded husband, the discount house version went on fancifully, unable to avail himself of the service of the official guillotine, had chopped off the head which had looked at his wife and the hands which had caressed her body. The corpse had been packed in with a consignment of Burgundy's finest and thrown into the river.

The last, and most ominous, rumour came from Home Rails on the Stock Exchange. This was the rumour that struck most terror into the small, but growing, female population of the City. Jack the

Ripper is back, claimed Home Rails. They nearly caught him when he went for all those loose women in the East End. Now he's going for men. This is only the beginning. More decapitated males were to be expected, dumped in the docks or carried upstream towards Westminster. Beware the Ripper!

The man charged, for now, with the responsibility of finding out the truth about the headless and handless corpse was sitting in his tiny office at Cannon Street police station. He was suffering, he knew, from his normal feelings of irritation and anger as he looked at his younger colleague.

Inspector William Burroughs was in his late forties. He was a stocky man with a small rather straggly moustache and tired brown eyes. Earlier in his career he had been involved in a successful murder investigation, and the reputation of being good with cases involving sudden death had stuck with him. But Burroughs knew that had been a fluke. An unexpected confession had solved the crime, not his detective skills. He had told his wife this many times, and as many times she had instructed him not to tell his superiors.

There are men who look good in uniform, men who carry it off well, men who can appear like peacocks on parade. Burroughs was not one of those. There always seemed to be a button undone, trousers not sitting properly, a tie adrift at the neck. His sergeant, on the other hand, always looked immaculate, like his bloody mother had washed and ironed him five minutes before, as Burroughs liked to tell himself. Sergeant Cork was still gleaming in his pristine state at half-past twelve on the morning when the body was found.

A couple of sailors had propelled the corpse gently towards the riverbank with a boathook. Inspector Burroughs had supervised the landing, blankets at the ready to cover the dead man. He had ridden with it to the morgue at St Bartholomew's Hospital and delivered it into the care of the doctors. They had promised him a preliminary report by the end of the day.

'We should be able to tell you how long he had been in the water, maybe how long ago he was killed,' the young doctor had assured him. 'Please don't expect us to be able to help you with any clues as to who he might have been.'

'Right, Sergeant Cork,' said Burroughs, 'we may as well start somewhere. I want you to go round or telephone all the police stations in the area and see if they have any missing persons on file.

'And there's one very unfortunate thing about this case, I can tell you. Very unfortunate. Just think what the newspapers are going to make of it. Headless man floating by London Bridge. Not just no head, no hands either. They'll be all over it for weeks. And if the poor bloody police can't find out who the man was, then we'll be for it too. Look at those incompetent detectives, the journalists will say, they can't even solve a murder right in the heart of the City. The newspapers will be out for our blood.'

'Are we sure it was a murder, sir?' Sergeant Cork had never been involved in such a prestigious inquiry before.

'You don't suppose he cut his head off when he had no hands left, do you? Or do you think he cut off his head first and then sawed his wrists off himself?'

'I'm sure you're right sir.' Cork hastened to the telephone room. 'I'll get started on these inquiries.'

And please, please, the Inspector thought to himself, just once, get yourself a bit untidy.

2

Lord Francis Powerscourt had turned into a horse. He was trotting slowly along his hall in Markham Square in Chelsea, making clip-clop noises with his tongue and his back teeth. He had practised these in his bath and tested them out to his own satisfaction on his wife Lady Lucy.

'Clip-clop, Clip-clop,' said Powerscourt, negotiating his way past a Regency table outside the dining room. Now, he knew, was the time for a strategic decision. Should he go into the dining room and make a round of the chairs, pausing possibly to look at the grass outside the window? Or should he essay the more dangerous, but possibly more entertaining journey up the stairs to the first or the second or even the third floor?

Lord Francis Powerscourt was one of the most successful detectives in England. He had learned his craft in Army Intelligence in India and transferred the skills learnt there to solving murders and mysteries at home. He was in his forties now, the black curly hair still intact, the blue eyes continuing to inspect the world with the same detachment and irony as before.

'Hold on tight, hold on very tight,' said Powerscourt, as he began a slow ascent of the stairs. He could feel two small hands hanging on very tightly to his collar. Thomas Powerscourt was four years old, born a year after his parents' wedding in 1892. Wandering about upstairs was Thomas's sister, Olivia, who could now tell the world that she was two.

On the wide first-floor landing Powerscourt broke into a trot.

'Faster, Papa, faster!' cried the little boy, beating on his shoulder with a small determined fist. 'Faster, horse, faster!'

The horse was growing weary now and anxious for the human consolations of tea and biscuits downstairs. Coming down,

Powerscourt remembered, was always a more dangerous man-oeuvre than going up. His passenger was in danger of falling down right over his head and tumbling head over heels to the marble floor below. After a slow, almost funereal trot down the stairs, Powerscourt speeded up along the hall just as the doorbell rang. The maid opened the door before he could resume his human form. He found himself staring into a pair of very brightly polished black boots. Above the boots were sharply pressed trousers. Above the trousers was a uniform jacket resplendent with shining buttons. Above the jacket were a pair of enormous moustaches and a helmet. A policeman's helmet.

'Good morning, sir. Would you be Lord Francis Powerscourt?' said the thin slit underneath the moustaches.

'I would, Constable, I would.' Powerscourt laughed happily. 'Forgive me while I return to human form.'

Thomas Powerscourt began to cry, quietly at first and then with huge quaking sobs that racked his little frame.

'What's the matter, Thomas?' said his father, smiling an apologetic parental smile at the constable. 'What's the matter?'

Thomas was not telling. His face was wet with tears and a small wet hand rubbed against his father's trousers.

'They can take on for no reason at all,' began the constable, about to relate the story of the three children of his wife's sister who bolted the minute he entered the room.

'He's a p'liceman,' said Thomas accurately, pointing a grubby finger at the representative of law and order.

'That's right, Thomas. The gentleman here is a policeman.'

'P'licemen catch bad people and put them in prison,' sobbed the boy.

Suddenly Powerscourt could sense the anxiety, but before he could speak his son was holding desperately on to his trousers and shouting as loud as he could.

'P'liceman won't take my Papa away!' He held on as if his life, or Powerscourt's life, depended on it.

Powerscourt bent down and picked him up. The constable coughed apologetically. 'I have a message from the Commissioner,' he began.

The little boy clung ever tighter to his father's neck, tears trickling down a collar that had been immaculate but a few minutes before. The Commissioner seemed to Thomas to be an even bigger, even more hostile form of policeman trying to take his Papa away to the cells or to prison. He didn't know what a Commissioner was, but it sounded pretty frightening to Thomas.

The constable ploughed bravely on. 'He would like to see you at once, sir,' he said. 'He would like to give you a cup of tea and then he will send you straight back again. I think he wants to take your advice.'

Powerscourt smiled. 'Thank you, Constable. I have often met with the Commissioner, or rather with his predecessor. I should be delighted to come with you.'

Lady Lucy appeared suddenly by his side. 'Good morning, Constable,' she said with her most graceful smile. 'So Francis is going to take tea with the Commissioner? I'm sure that will be delightful. And, Francis, you can tell Thomas and me all about it when you get back.'

She whisked Thomas away from his father's shoulder and began whispering to the little boy. As Powerscourt and the constable closed the door, Thomas was able to manage a small but tear-free wave.

Forty miles away an old man and a pony were waiting outside the stables of the great house. Samuel Parker had worked in these stables for nearly fifty years. He had risen in a series of slow promotions from apprentice under-groom to Head of Stables. His employers had given him a little cottage on the estate to have until he died. But today Samuel was a very worried man.

The house was almost closed down. The younger members had gone back to their great house in Mayfair, leaving the old man and his sister alone on the top floor, except for some servants in the basement. Every day, at ten o'clock in the morning, Old Mr Harrison would come to meet Samuel and the pony by the stables. Together they would make a circuit of the lake. Sometimes the old man would bring letters or papers from the bank with him to read on the way. Then Samuel would strap a small portable chair and table on to the pony and they would wait while their master attended to his business.

Samuel could just remember the family who lived in the great house before Old Mr Harrison bought it thirty-five years ago. The sons had gambled away the family money, the house and the estates all had to be sold, and the Harrisons, originally German bankers in Hamburg and Frankfurt, had moved in. Three generations of them lived in the house now: Carl Harrison known as Old Mr Harrison, his sister Augusta Harrison, known as Miss Harrison, his son Mr Frederick Harrison and his great-nephew, Charles Harrison, Young Mr Harrison as they were known to the servants.

Old Mr Harrison loved the lake and the two-mile walk that ran around its borders. There were strange grottoes and classical temples, funny buildings as Samuel thought of them, dotted around it and sometimes Old Mr Harrison would spend a lot of time inside these Roman buildings, looking at the statues or reading his correspondence beneath some pagan god.

Samuel Parker thought Old Mr Harrison had been worried recently. For the past few months his correspondence had been coming from foreign parts, from Bremen and Berlin, from Paris and Munich and Cologne. He had written a lot of letters too, perched at his table in the temple, a thick cape protecting him from the winds that whipped the waters of the lake and tore the leaves from the trees. And – this was what alarmed Samuel more than anything else – Old Mr Harrison had asked Samuel to post the letters he wrote down by the lake, as if he didn't want anybody in the big house to know who he was writing to.

The lake would be wreathed in mist this morning, Samuel knew, the great trees and the classical temples swirling in and out of sight like things glimpsed in nightmares. Samuel thought there were strange spirits living around it, older than the house, older than the village, older than the ancient church, older possibly than Christianity itself. Maybe the Druids or the pagan gods had dwelt there long ago, now living uneasily with the worldly deities of Rome.

It was twenty days, maybe more, since Old Mr Harrison had come for his morning ride, walking stiffly down the drive from the house, leaning on his stick. Samuel had lost count. Sometimes they would go round the lake twice or even three times in one day when the weather was good and the sun shone on the water, reflections of pillars and pediments dancing on the surface of the lake. The old pony knew something was wrong. It gazed sadly at the ground, raising a hoof from time to time to paw at the gravel.

Even Samuel's wife Martha, so crippled now that she could scarcely manage the hundred yards to the church to lay the flowers on Sundays, could not remember how long it was since Old Mr Harrison had disappeared.

'He'll have gone to London to see the rest of them, to be sure,' she would say anxiously, raking over the embers in the fire. But she didn't sound as though she believed it.

'None of the servants in the big house say he's gone to London. And how would he get there? He couldn't walk to the station, could he, not the way he is. I've taken Old Mr Harrison to and from that train every time he's gone anywhere for over thirty years. And I haven't taken him to the station, have I?'

'No, you haven't, Samuel.'

At half-past ten, after half an hour of waiting, Samuel took the pony back to its stall. He gave it some water. 'He's not coming today, either. Another day has gone,' he said to the pony.

As he walked down the path to his cottage Samuel Parker wondered for the hundredth time if he should tell anyone about his vanished master. But he wasn't sure who to tell. And he knew Old Mr Harrison would not want him to raise the alarm. 'You can't trust anybody these days,' Samuel remembered the old man muttering to himself after a long day with his correspondence by the lake, 'not even your own flesh and blood.'

Lord Francis Powerscourt was feeling curious as he made his way across London to the Commissioner's office. Maybe another case was going to begin. Ever since he was a small boy growing up in Ireland he had been fascinated by riddles and puzzles. He had devoted much of his adult life to solving mysteries and murders, codes and cryptograms in Kashmir and Afghanistan and the summer capital of the Raj at Simla during his time in the Army. He had solved a gruesome series of murders in the wine business at Oporto in Portugal where the victims were dumped in barrels of port, their flesh turned purple by the viscous liquor, and a long catalogue of murders in Britain and Ireland. His most important case had come five years before when he had solved the mystery of the strange death of Prince Eddy, the wastrel eldest son of the Prince of Wales.

Sir William Spence, Commissioner of the Metropolitan Police, rose to meet Powerscourt in his office at Scotland Yard.

'Lord Powerscourt, how very kind of you to come.'

'As you know, Sir William, I am in debt to your service and its officers for help rendered me in the past more than I can say.'

This was true. In two of his previous cases Powerscourt had received invaluable help from the police force of the capital. On the last occasion the Commissioner had treated Powerscourt to a magnificent dinner at his club where they had consumed two bottles of the finest claret in the cellars and the old man had told him terrifying tales of army life on the North West Frontier forty years before.

'Let me come straight to the point.' Sir William's moustaches were not quite as formidable as those of his constable, but they were still substantial. Powerscourt wondered if moustache cultivation was now obligatory for all those in police uniform. 'You will have seen the newspaper coverage of the body found in the Thames.'

'One could scarcely avoid it,' said Powerscourt. 'It has dominated the papers every day since the unfortunate discovery itself.'

'Most of what you read is made up, of course. The newspaper gentlemen enjoy themselves most when there are no facts at all to be reported, apart from the body itself. I sometimes think how easy it must be to be one of these reporters, making up the most fantastic stories out of your head and then presenting them as the very latest news.'

Sir William shook his head at the sins of the reporters. 'But let me ask you this, Lord Powerscourt. Have you any idea of how many people have come forward to claim the corpse? To say that it is a long-lost member of their family?'

'I have no idea, Sir William.' Powerscourt noticed that the four great maps of London, North South East and West, still adorned the office walls. And he observed that, as before, the East End was covered with small red circles denoting the most recent crimes.

'So far we have had over one hundred and fifty.' Sir William nodded to a pile of correspondence spilling out of a file on his desk. 'Would you believe it? We have kept that figure well out of the newspapers, of course. If they were to print it, we would be deluged under a flood of more claims. Some of them may be genuine, families where the parent or grandparent has disappeared and they would like the reassurance of being able to bury him. But even then there is something greedy about them, as if the urge to wipe away the social disgrace caused by the disappearance could be washed away by a proper funeral. But the others. . . .' Sir William paused and looked directly at Powerscourt.

'Insurance claims?' asked Powerscourt with a smile. 'Claims that need a body or a proper death certificate to satisfy the insurance companies?'

'You have it, Lord Powerscourt. Your powers are as strong as ever, I see. The attraction with these insurance claims is, of course, the money payable on the death of the subject of the policy. Without a body there can be no claim. So now we have the entry of the bounty hunters. We have one claim from a wealthy widow whose husband ran off twenty years ago but left her in possession of policies on his life. The widow is certain' – Sir William reached for a letter from his file – 'that the corpse by London Bridge is that of her vanished spouse. "Once I read the accounts in the papers," Mrs Willoughby of Highgate writes, "I knew that it was Alfred come back at last, albeit in unfortunate circumstances. It would be the last act of a sorrowing widow to come and identify the body, however harrowing that might be. I believe I owe it to Alfred's memory to perform this final act of piety from the living towards the dead".'

Sir William looked up with a ghost of a smile disturbing his moustaches. 'That might or might not be satisfactory. But then Mrs Willoughby rather gives the game away. "I believe it is customary in these circumstances for the next of kin to be given a copy of the death certificate so it can be forwarded to the appropriate authorities and the insurance companies."'

'Insurance companies plural?' said Powerscourt quickly. 'Was she going to cash him in twice, or even three times?'

'We cannot tell.' The Commissioner shrugged his shoulders. 'But we do know this. We could have positive identifications of that corpse one hundred and fifty times over, and not one of them would be right. Not one.'

'You don't mean to say that you know who the corpse is, or rather was?' Powerscourt was leaning forward in his chair, his mind racing through the possibilities of the case.

'No, we don't. But don't you see how difficult our position is? Here are all these widows and orphans desperate to identify the body as their Alfred or Uncle Richard or Grandfather Matthew. Soon they will start writing to the papers saying the heartless police have refused to let them identify their loved ones. The longer the mystery remains a mystery the more hostile public opinion will become, the greater the pressure to open the floodgates and allow these bounty hunters to claim their prize. Unless we know who the dead man is, we cannot refuse them.'

'What can I do to help?' said Powerscourt, anxious to offer his services. 'I mean to say, I cannot see how I could be of service, but I am more than willing to try.'

'Lord Powerscourt, how very kind of you.' The Commissioner fingered his moustaches. 'And forgive me for burdening you with our troubles. Let me tell you what we do know that has not appeared in the newspapers and has not been made up.'

Once more the Commissioner reached down to the mass of papers on his desk. 'This is what the medical men who have examined the body have to say. All the usual disclaimers, of course, three paragraphs of them. Why can't these people ever tell you anything straight?'

He frowned as he read through the circumspection of the medical profession.

'They believe the man was between seventy-five and eighty years old, though they could, of course, be wrong. They believe he may have been killed by a bullet wound to the head, though as we have no head, they may be right in their caution on that score. They believe he had been dead for a period of two to four weeks before ending up in the Thames. Though they could, of course, be wrong. And here, Lord Powerscourt, is the only useful thing they have to say. They believe that he was not poor, or destitute. Quite the contrary. Examination of the stomach and other organs gives reason to believe that the dead man may have been comfortably off at least, if not rich. I presume they worked out that he hadn't been living on tripe and onions. When I talked to these doctors they said that although they wouldn't like to put it down on paper, they thought he was a rich old man. Mind you, that's probably another reason why somebody wanted to kill him off.' Sir William nodded grimly at his file of one hundred and fifty bounty hunters.

'I don't suppose the internal organs indicate how many life assurance policies he had,' said Powerscourt, wondering if his flippancy was out of place.

'Very good.' The Commissioner laughed a laugh that turned into a strange braying noise at the end. 'This is what we would like you to do for us, Lord Powerscourt. You move in the best society. You have connections with the aristocracy, with the City of London where our unfortunate cadaver made his last resting place. Could you put out discreet inquiries about anybody who might have gone missing, anybody who has just disappeared? These people are not very likely to come to us as their first port of call. They would much more likely come to you. But if you could help us, the Metropolitan Police would be in your debt. We must clear this matter up as quickly as possibly.'

'I can assure you,' Powerscourt replied, 'that nobody has made any approaches to me, none at all. But I shall be only too pleased to help.'

As he left the Commissioner's office Powerscourt paused briefly by the map of the East End. He noticed a fresh-looking circle which appeared to have been added in the last few days.

It was right across London Bridge.

3

'Isn't this fine, Richard, isn't it just fine!' Sophie Williams danced a little jig, oblivious to the strict looks of the sober locals, all dressed up in their Sunday best and on their way to church.

'It is,' replied Richard, slightly embarrassed at Sophie's exuberance. 'If we hurry on, we should see the river quite soon.' He sounded anxious to escape from the citizens of Twickenham.

The young people had travelled to Twickenham by train and planned to walk along the river to Hampton Court. They had considered bringing their bicycles but Richard was not sure how suitable the roads and paths would be for two-wheeled traffic and he had an irrational fear of punctures.

Sophie Williams was twenty-one years old. She worked as a teacher in an elementary school by day and as a devoted campaigner for the suffragist cause by night. She was tall and slim with liquid blue eyes and wore her independence like a badge.

'There is Eel Pie Island, Sophie. Should you like an eel pie for tea on our way home?'

'I've only had eel pie once in my life,' said Sophie. 'I think it was by the sea somewhere when I was small and it didn't agree with me. Maybe I should try again!'

They struck out boldly along the river path. A steamer from London was approaching the island, clouds of steam rising from its twin funnels and important hoots from its siren. The passengers stared eagerly at the sight of their landing stage and a faint cheer sounded across the March morning. There was a bright sun but a stiff breeze which blew the Thames into tiny waves that rippled against the banks.

Richard Martin was twenty-two years old. He was a slim, studious-looking young man with masses of curly brown hair. He lived with his widowed mother and worked as a clerk in Harrison's Bank in the City. Richard had been there for five years now, studying at home in his spare time to improve his knowledge of commerce and banking. He went to evening classes to learn French and hoped to move on to German soon – Harrison's had wide connections with other houses and merchants in Hamburg and Frankfurt and Berlin.

'I've just got another three pupils in my class,' said Sophie, as they struck out towards Teddington Lock. Richard had not known Sophie for very long but already he felt that he had a close acquaintance with the pupils in her care and the other two teachers in her school.

'How many have you got now?' he asked, keen to reduce matters to the safety of numbers. Richard had always been very proficient at numbers, equations, mathematical calculations that were invaluable to his work in the City.

'Forty-seven,' said Sophie. 'Forty-seven six-year-olds.'

'Do you think you should be paid according to the numbers of pupils you have?' said Richard, looking for a formula in wide application in the Square Mile.

'Nonsense, absolute nonsense.' Sophie laughed. 'I'd be perfectly happy to have fifty or sixty, particularly if they were all as well behaved as some of them. Little Mary Jones and Matilda Sharp are as good as gold. I wish I could say the same about some of the boys.'

Richard suspected, but he would never have dared say it, that the girls, potential voters all, might receive favourable treatment in Miss Williams' class. Overhead a group of seagulls crying out against the wind hurried on towards the rich pickings of Teddington Lock.

'That's the one they call the coffin lock,' said Richard, pointing to a deep tomb of a lock with water many feet below the river. 'And that huge one there, the barge lock, can take a steam tug and six barges at the same time.'

He wondered if some of the produce shipped in and out of London and financed by bills of exchange underwritten by his bank passed through this very lock.

'Just think of it, Sophie, somebody might send wool for America from the Cotswolds through here. And it would be paid for at each end through the bank!'

Sophie didn't seem very excited at the thought. 'You're a romantic, Richard,' she said, 'a true romantic. For some people it's poetry or music, for you it's bills of exchange! But come on, if we don't hurry up we'll never get to Hampton Court at all.'

Richard was quite upset at being called a romantic. He didn't feel romantic about locks. But he knew he felt very romantic about Sophie. She had a toss of her head that turned his heart every time he saw it. But he didn't know if Sophie had any room for romance in her soul. She was so filled with the righteousness of the cause of women that she seemed to have no time for anything else.

'You don't want to have anything to do with girls like that, Richard,' his mother had said to him when he told her of his new friend who lived at the far end of the street. 'They don't know how to care for a man. They'd probably rather be men, running round in those strange pantaloons and smoking cigarettes and wanting the vote for Parliament. Whoever heard of such a thing. Your father wouldn't have let any of them in the house.'

'But she's very pretty, Mother, very pretty indeed.'

'They don't care about things like that, those new women,' said his mother, a lifetime of scorn whipped into the phrase 'new women'. 'They're not interested in finding a nice young man and settling down properly.'

His own new woman was striding ahead of him along the path. Richard hurried to catch up. 'Wait for me, Sophie,' he cried, breaking into a trot.

She turned and smiled. 'That makes a nice change, Richard. Men asking for women to wait so they can catch up!'

She turned and, as if contradicting her own words, she ran off down the path, calling back as she went, 'Can't catch me! Can't catch me! That's what they say in the playground!'

Eventually he did catch her and there ahead of them was the Tudor front of Hampton Court Palace, with the King's Beasts on guard around the entrance gate.

'Cardinal Wolsey, wasn't it?' panted Richard. 'It was built by Cardinal Wolsey in fifteen hundred and something or other?'

'It was built by Cardinal Wolsey,' said Sophie, moving effortlessly into teacher and suffragist mode in a single sentence. 'Then he had to give it to Henry the Eighth. I expect he maltreated some of his wives down here. What right did he have to cut their heads off just because they wouldn't give him another male to maltreat another generation of women? It's dreadful. Just because men have the power they think they can abuse women as though they were cats or dogs or something like that.'

29

Richard groaned inwardly. He hadn't made the connection between Hampton Court and the suffragist cause when he proposed this expedition. Now he suspected this tirade could go on all afternoon.

'Really, it's all so unfair,' said Sophie, looking, to the young man, impossibly attractive as her eyes flashed with indignation. 'I have to go to a meeting of the Women's Franchise League this evening. I shall remind everybody of how we are surrounded, even in our history, especially in our history, by the great injustices done to women by men. There is talk of another petition for the suffrage. This time we shall get more signatories than ever before.'

Richard stared at her hopelessly, helplessly. If she felt like that about men, he wondered to himself for the hundredth time, how could she ever engage her emotions with one? Was conventional love incompatible with her views? Was his mother right all along?

'Come along, Sophie, you can keep talking as we go along. What do you say to one of those pies on Eel Pie Island?'

In a gesture that lit up his heart like a sudden flash of lightning, she squeezed his arm briefly and ran ahead. 'I'd love one of those pies, Richard. Can't catch me!'

Every day the reluctant army made its way across London Bridge. Every day the slaves of Money and the Market went to their temple in the City by steam railway, on foot, by bus, by underground railway, by horse and carriage.

On Monday the rumour might be that there had been further finds of gold in the Rand. On Wednesday it might be that there was a great loan to be floated for a railway to link the remotest parts of Russia. On Friday it might be the flotation of another great manufacturing interest, the shares guaranteed to reach levels well above par in a day or so for those wise or foolish enough to buy them well in advance.

But of the identity of the corpse floating in the river there was no information. The popular papers printed stories on the body until even their over-fertile imaginations ran out. The procession of bounty hunters continued to make their way to the police offices, protesting their certainty of the corpse's identity and barely concealing their greed for the gold of the insurance companies.

Powerscourt, as requested by the Commissioner, had put the word about Mayfair and Belgravia. Lady Lucy, a veteran of such missions now, had invented a story of an aunt of hers in the Highlands who had disappeared one winter day and not been found for a month, when her corpse was found floating in a swollen stream, grossly disfigured. She worked conversations round to this story all across her considerable acquaintance, but she caught nothing. Powerscourt's sisters, pressed reluctantly into service, did their best but failed.

Only William Burke, Powerscourt's financier brother- in-law, held out a faint glimmer of hope.

'I've known men disappear for quite a long time – the pressure of debt, the fear of being hammered on the Exchange,' he had said thoughtfully to Powerscourt in his club, savouring a glass of their finest claret. 'I've known even more who should have disappeared and saved their fortunes while they could. But it seems a bit extreme to arrange to have your head cut off as well, unless there was some question of inheritance.'

Sometimes the police were hopeful. Occasionally they would find what they felt were genuine cases of lost or disappeared persons. Constables would be despatched to houses in Muswell Hill or Mortlake, Camden Town or Catford, to make inquiries. Always the disappearance seemed to be genuine, but the height or the age was wrong. The body itself remained in splendid isolation in the refrigerated mortuary of St Bartholomew's Hospital, watched over by a couple of porters and a flock of unruly medical students.

And then, on a blustery Monday evening in April, at ten o'clock at night, there was an imperious knock on the door of the Powerscourts' house in Markham Square. Lady Lucy was deep in *Jude the Obscure*. Powerscourt had fallen asleep by the fire, dreaming of cricket matches and late cuts in the summer months ahead.

'Mr William Burke, my lord, my lady,' said the footman.

A rather weary financier strode into the room and fell gratefully into an armchair by the fire.

'I have just returned from the Continent. I'm on my way home to see Mary and the children, if any of them are still awake.'

'Some tea? A glass of wine? Maybe even some lemonade to quench your thirst?' Lady Lucy was quick to offer comfort to the traveller.

'What a capital suggestion that lemonade is, Lady Lucy. Those trains are very dusty. Lemonade would be just the thing.'

'Francis, you remember the corpse in the river, the body by London Bridge? Well, I think I may have some news but I am not sure. I have been to Germany on business, to Berlin, that frightful city, so very Prussian,' Burke shook his head, 'and to Frankfurt and to one or two other places. The only person of my acquaintance who fitted the description of the corpse – Oh, thank you so very much.'

Burke paused to drink deeply of his lemonade.

'That is uncommon good for a weary traveller,' he said to Lady Lucy with a smile. 'Maybe we could make something of it in the way of business. Where was I?' He looked round suddenly as if he wasn't sure if he was in Frankfurt or Chelsea.

'Ah yes, the only person of my acquaintance who fitted the description of Francis' body was Old Mr Harrison of Harrison's Bank. I think he was christened Carl-Heinz but he came to be known over here as Carl and he was certainly the right age.'

'How old would you say he was, William?' asked Powerscourt.

'Probably over eighty. Maybe well into his eighties. I made discreet inquiries in the City – you cannot imagine what impact it could have on a private bank's standing if its founder had been found floating in the Thames without his head – and the word came back that he was in Germany, either Frankfurt or Berlin.

'Now . . .' He paused to smile again at Lady Lucy, thinking that five years of marriage had made her even prettier than when he had first met her. '. . . it might seem odd for a man of that age to go off to Germany at this time of year – in a few months it would be different – but he was always a tough and resourceful old bird. However,' Burke leaned forward and looked Lady Lucy full in the eye, 'I made more discreet inquiries when I was in Germany. I said I'd heard he was in town, would he care for lunch or dinner, that sort of message. But everywhere the answer was the same. Carl Harrison was not in Frankfurt. Carl Harrison was not in Berlin. Carl Harrison was not and had not been in Hamburg. I must have been misinformed. So.' He rose and clicked his heels together in the German fashion and bowed. 'No Old Harrison in Germany. No Old Harrison in London. But why should they say he was in Berlin when he wasn't? Over to you, Francis.'

Powerscourt was looking at his fingertips, rubbing them slowly together. But it was Lady Lucy who spoke.

'Could he not have gone somewhere else, William? The Italian

Lakes, or somewhere on the Rhine, perhaps. It would be so dreadful if this corpse was that poor old man.'

'I don't think he was poor.' Burke laughed cheerfully, a man reputed to be able to value the top men in the City to the nearest ten thousand pounds. 'Certainly not poor.'

'No matter how rich you are you shouldn't have to end up like that. If it *was* Old Mr Harrison,' said Lady Lucy, defending the rights of the dead.

'I'm not sure how to proceed,' said Powerscourt. 'It's unlikely that further inquiries in the City will make any progress. Maybe somebody should scout around their house in the country – Oxfordshire, did you say it was, William?'

'It is,' said Burke, resuming the mantle of business. 'But please be very careful, very discreet. The Harrisons may know that I was behind the inquiries made in Lombard Street. Word will surely reach them that I made further inquiries in Germany. We need to be very careful indeed.

'And I must be off home. Thank you so much for the lemonade. You won't forget that you are coming to me for the weekend in the country, to be there at the installation of my new vicar? I never realized that when I bought the house and the land I bought an incumbency as well!' William Burke laughed in the joy of his own prosperity. 'You have to read a lesson, Francis, you will recall. And I've got the Bishop coming as well. Publish it not in the streets of Gath, as the parsons say,' Burke smiled at his hosts, 'but I saved his whole diocese from bankruptcy three years ago. But that's another story.'

With that William Burke, financier and man of property, departed into the night. 'Francis,' said Lady Lucy, 'come back, come back.'

Powerscourt had disappeared into his own thoughts. Lady Lucy was used to it by now. She smiled at her husband as he stared into the dying fire.

'Sorry, Lucy. I was only wondering what to do. I think we need somebody to work their way in towards the Harrison house, the village, the neighbours, the postman, that sort of thing.'

'I know who you are going to send.' Lady Lucy leaned against his shoulder and put her arm round his waist. 'You're going to send Johnny Fitzgerald, aren't you? Well, you just tell him to be careful. That other time he was nearly killed because of you, and that was in the depths of Northamptonshire. I don't see why Oxfordshire should be any safer for him.'

Lady Lucy remembered the emaciated best man at their wedding, policemen guarding the doors, a wounded Fitzgerald strapped up like a mummy, almost fainting as he stood by the altar.

Powerscourt smiled at his wife, remembering Johnny Fitzgerald's speech as best man at their wedding. 'We'll take care, Lucy. Very great care.'

4

'Clarendon Park is a nabob's seat, East India Company money,' William Burke said to Powerscourt, pointing to his Palladian mansion not far from Marlow. They were waiting for their families as the women made last-minute adjustments to hats and children before the short walk to the small church for the installation of the new vicar. 'It was built by a fellow called Francis Hodge who made a fortune in India and came home to retire in peace by the Thames. But things didn't quite work out the way he thought.'

'What went wrong?' asked Powerscourt, slightly nervous, as ever, at the prospect of having to read the lesson.

'The poor man – well, he was fairly poor by the end – got impeached for greed and corruption in the East, rather like Warren Hastings. There were huge lawyers' bills. Hodge had to go up to Westminster for months on end to answer questions from sanctimonious MPs and watch the value of his shares in the East India Company falling like a stone. At one point, I believe, they dropped fifty thousand in a week.'

Powerscourt could see the appeal of such a house, its fortunes so closely linked to the City of London.

'Don't you worry,' said Powerscourt, 'that some of the uncertainty might rub off on to your own affairs, William? Daily appearances before some Commons committee? Radical lawyer MPs quizzing you about your affairs?'

'No,' said William Burke emphatically. He laughed.

As they sat in the little church, pews filled with tenants and family, Powerscourt was wondering about his sisters. They loved each other dearly, of course, but there was always an element of competition between them. Eleanor, the youngest, had certainly married the most handsome husband, but he had very little money.

Mary, the middle sister, had made a very prudent marriage to William Burke. Rosalind, the eldest, seemed to have won the marriage stakes by her alliance with Lord Pembridge, an aristocrat with a great deal of money and fine houses in St James's Square and in Hampshire. But over the weekend he had noticed a certain smugness, an air of quiet but unmistakable triumph about Mary. It showed in the way she almost patronized her elder sister, showing off the glories of her new house, wondering aloud about how many servants and gardeners they would need to employ. And Rosalind, for once, looked as though she felt her position as the most successful of the sisters, the Queen Bee of her own little hive, was under threat.

As he rose to read his lesson Powerscourt cast a careful glance at his family to make sure the children were behaving.

'The First Lesson,' he began in his clear tenor voice, 'is taken from the twenty-first Chapter of the Gospel according to St Matthew.

'"And Jesus went into the temple of God, and cast out all them that sold and bought in the temple, and overthrew the tables of the moneychangers, and the seats of them that sold doves."'

The new vicar, a red-headed man in his middle thirties, was looking serious. The Bishop, splendid in his purple robes, looked as if he was falling sleep. Powerscourt wondered, for the sixth or seventh time since he had entered the church, how the Bishop could have almost brought his diocese to bankruptcy. Had he fallen asleep in those apparently tedious meetings of the diocesan finance sub-committees? Had he invested the church collections unwisely on the Exchange?

'"And he said unto them, It is written, My house shall be called the house of prayer; but ye have made it a den of thieves."'

There was a very faint creak as the door opened and a late arrival slipped quietly into a pew at the back and opened his prayer book. The newcomer winked at Powerscourt. It was Johnny Fitzgerald.

'"And the blind and the lame came to him in the temple: and he healed them."

'Here endeth the First Lesson.'

Powerscourt had grown up with Lord Johnny Fitzgerald in Ireland. They had served together in Army Intelligence in India. On a number of occasions they had saved each other's lives. Johnny had been Powerscourt's best man at both his weddings.

'I have come to make my report, Francis.' Fitzgerald gave a mock salute to his former superior officer as they walked through William Burke's woods towards the Thames below. 'You remember you said I had to approach the matter very carefully and very slowly? Well, I did, I just hope I didn't exceed my powers at the end.'

'You're not suggesting you might have disobeyed orders, Johnny?' asked Powerscourt with a smile.

'I was thinking of it more like Nelson with his blind eye. Copenhagen, was it, or the Nile? A temporary lapse for the greater good of the cause.'

'I'm sure I should hear your report before passing any judgement, Johnny.'

'Right,' Fitzgerald bent down and picked up a stout branch to serve as a walking stick. 'My story begins in Wallingford, the King's Arms in Wallingford to be precise. I booked myself in there for a couple of days. Fine beer they have there, Francis, very fine beer with a fruity sort of taste to it. My story was that I left England some years before to be a banker in Boston in America.'

'I don't think bankers drink a lot of the local beer, Johnny, even if it is fruity. They're sober, respectable sort of people,' said Powerscourt, kicking a couple of pine cones out of their path.

'American bankers are very different from English ones. They're more open, more hospitable sort of characters. Anyway, I said I had been to London on banking business and then to Germany. I said I was looking for Old Mr Harrison who had taught me all I knew about banking twenty years ago when they had their offices in Bishopsgate. I checked out their old address with William, you see.'

'And what did the regulars at the King's Arms have to say about the old gentleman?' asked Powerscourt.

'Not a lot, most of them. The House of Harrison is a couple of miles away, at least, quite close to the river. Very respectable family, very hard-working, very good people to work for. They said I might get more news of him at the Blackwater Arms, a sort of family pub, like Mr Burke's family church, on the edge of the estate. It makes much more sense to have a pub rather than a church, don't you think, Francis?'

'I'm sure – no, I'm certain,' said Powerscourt, 'that you're better qualified to be a landlord than a vicar, Johnny.'

'They all said,' Fitzgerald went on, 'the natives in those parts, that Old Mr Harrison wasn't at home, that he hadn't been seen for a while. I was just about to go to bed when a very wizened old man called me into a corner. He fished about in his pockets and then he pulled out a piece of newspaper. It was an account of the discovery of the headless man by London Bridge. "See you here, young man," he croaked at me, waving his piece of paper, "see you here. This dead body, floating in the Thames down there in London, that be Old Mr Harrison. Mark my words. It's Old Mr Harrison." Then he folded the paper as if it was a ten pound note and returned it to his pocket. "What on earth makes you think that, sir?" I said to the old scarecrow. "Jeremiah Cokestone sees things. Jeremiah Cokestone hears things. In the night or at first light before the sun has risen." He spoke as if he was the Delphic oracle itself, I tell you. Then he downed his beer, almost a full glass, Francis, in a single pull, and he shuffled off into the night.'

They had reached the edge of the river now. On the far side a few boats were setting out for a Sunday trip along the Thames. Behind them a stiff breeze was rustling through the trees.

'The next day,' Johnny Fitzgerald tried skimming a couple of stones across the water, 'I went to see the vicar. And there I had one of the most uplifting experiences of my life. I shall always remember it.'

'You were converted.' Powerscourt looked suitably grave. 'You saw the light. You repented of the error of your ways.'

'I did not. But the vicar's wife gave me some of her elderberry wine. '95 she said it was, one of her better years. God knows what the bad years must taste like, Francis.' Fitzgerald grimaced at the memory. 'I cannot describe the taste. It was horrible, so sweet it made you feel sick. Christ.'

A successful skim of about ten hops began to restore his spirits.

'The vicar knew the family, of course. He hadn't seen anything of Old Mr Harrison for a while. But he recommended me to another elderly citizen, one Samuel Parker, chief man for the horses at the Harrison house. I could just see Mrs Vicar about to pour me some more of that elderberry tincture, so I got out as fast as I could.'

'We'd better be getting back to the house, Johnny.' Powerscourt remembered the family proprieties. 'We mustn't be late for Sunday lunch with a Bishop to carve the joint. What happened with Mr Parker?'

Fitzgerald sent a final stone skimming into the middle of the

Thames, nearly hitting a pleasure boat on its way downstream. Then he turned to stare intently at a bird that had just fled from a clump of trees on their left.

'Mother of God, Francis, was that a kestrel? Damn, I can't see it any more. Mr Parker took me down to the lake, a fabulous place, full of temples and statues of gods and a waterfall and stuff. He said he was desperately worried, that he didn't know what to do. When I told him I'd been in Germany and that Old Mr Harrison wasn't there he got even more worried. He went very pale when I told him that, white as a sheet in fact. "He's not in London. He's not in Germany. He's not here. So where is he?" he said quietly. Then it transpired that he too had seen the newspaper cutting about the body in the river. He hadn't wanted to tell his wife, so he'd bottled it all up.

'"There's only one thing you can do," I said to him. "You must report it to the police."He said he'd been thinking about that, but hadn't liked to. Surely it was the job of the other members of the family to do that. "Maybe they don't know," I said to him. "Anyway they're down in London. The policeman is only up the road."'

'So that very afternoon I drove him over to the police station where he reported that Old Mr Harrison was missing. Then I drove him back to his wife. Did I do wrong in getting him to the police station, Francis?'

Powerscourt paused. The elegant façade of the Burke house was just coming into view through the trees.

'I think you were right, Johnny. The police have been inundated with people claiming the body. We just have to alert them to take this one seriously. Maybe the family doctor or one of the members of the family could identify him without the head. He certainly fits the doctors' description of the corpse being a rich old man.'

'Do you think the corpse is Old Mr Harrison?'

'I do, actually, or I think I do,' said Powerscourt. 'But I'm very worried about why the rest of the family have done nothing.'

'Maybe the entire Harrison family killed him off and don't want to be found out.'

'Maybe they know he's dead but they want to keep it secret.'

'Bet you whatever you like,' said Fitzgerald, quickening his pace as they approached the front door, 'that the body in the Thames was Old Mr Harrison. Now then, do you suppose William has laid on anything good to drink with the Bishop here and all? I need something to cleanse my palate after that elderberry wine. Christ, Francis, I can still taste it now. A bottle of Gevrey-Chambertin perhaps, a touch of Pomerol?'

5

Five men shuffled uneasily into a small office at St Bartholomew's Hospital. On ordinary days senior doctors used it to pass on bad news to the relatives of their patients, news of the ones who had passed away, the ones who were doomed to pass away quite soon, the ones who would never recover. Long melancholy usage had given the room an aura of sorrow all its own. On one wall hung a portrait of Queen Victoria at her first Jubilee, a small but defiant representative of monarchical continuity, on the other an iconic painting of Florence Nightingale, looking like a saint rather than a nurse. Even her skills would not be enough to save the lives of those whose fate was discussed in here.

This morning the room had been taken over by the Metropolitan Police. Two of its representatives stood uneasily at one end of the long table in the middle of the room. Inspector Burroughs felt that one part of his mission had been accomplished; he picked uneasily at his tie, hoping it had not detached itself from its collar to roam freely around the top of his shirt. Sergeant Cork stood rigidly to attention, looking, Burroughs thought sourly, like a recruitment poster for the force he served. Dr James Compton had come up to town for the day from Oxfordshire. He had attended on Old Mr Harrison for many years. Mr Frederick Harrison, eldest son of Old Mr Harrison, had abandoned his counting house for the more disturbing quarters of the hospital and its morgue. Dr Peter Mclvor, the custodian of the body for St Bart's, the man responsible for preserving it in some sort of order until it could be identified, made up the final member of the party.

Normally it would have taken ten days or more for a report from an obscure Oxfordshire village about a suspected missing person to reach the Metropolitan Police. This time the process had been accelerated by the normal processes being reversed. The police, alerted by Powerscourt, acting on Johnny Fitzgerald's report, had gone looking for Samuel Parker's account of his fears, delivered to an elderly and rather deaf constable in the village of Wallingford.

The inspection of the corpse had been brief. McIvor had moved it into a small ante-room where it had more dignity than in its usual resting place, in which it was surrounded by other cadavers earmarked for dissection by the doctors and their medical students. The two doctors had examined it closely. The body had been turned on to its side, then rolled right over. The doctors muttered to each other about the processes of muscular decay and the impact on the skin of prolonged exposure to the polluted waters of the Thames. Frederick Harrison had merely looked at two places on the body, an area of the upper back and the lower part of the left leg. He shivered slightly at what he saw.

'Gentlemen,' said Inspector Burroughs uneasily, 'pray let us be seated.' Sergeant Cork thought he sounded like a vicar asking his congregation to take their pews.

'I have here some forms – regulation forms,' he added quickly, 'which may have to be filled in. But first, I must ask you some questions.'

He looked at Frederick Harrison.

'Do you, Frederick Harrison, of Harrison's Bank in the City of London, confirm that the body you have seen this morning is that of your father, Carl Harrison, of Blackwater, Oxfordshire?'

Outside, a group of medical students sounded as if they were playing a game of rugby in the corridor. Frederick Harrison looked directly at the policeman.

'I do.'

Burroughs turned his attention to Dr Compton who was stroking his moustaches. 'Do you, Dr James Compton of Wallingford, confirm that the body you have seen this morning is that of your patient, Carl Harrison, of Blackwater, Oxfordshire?'

'I do,' said the doctor, 'and let me say for the record – ' Sergeant Cork was writing busily in his police notebook – 'what convinced me. A small mole on the upper left back had given me concern for some time. It was identical to the one on the body we have just seen. And there were a number of scars on the lower left leg, sustained in a fall from a horse some three years ago. The scars did not heal properly – they seldom do in a man of his age – and required a lot of attention. I was sorry, gentlemen, to have to

42

inspect my own handiwork this morning. I have no doubt, no doubt, at all, that the body is that of Carl Harrison. May his soul rest in peace.'

'May he rest in peace indeed.' Inspector Burroughs echoed the doctor's words. 'Could I ask you gentlemen to sign these regulation forms I have with me, two of identification, and one of witness to the event.'

Under the watchful eyes of Florence Nightingale the three men signed. The body in the river was no longer a nameless corpse. Scandal and rumour threatened to sweep the City of London once more. Carl Harrison, founder and paterfamilias of one of the City's leading banks, had been identified as the headless man floating uncertainly by London Bridge.

The St Bartholomew's doctor returned to his patients. The two policemen marched off to Cannon Street police station to report their findings. Dr Compton returned to Wallingford with a heavy heart.

Frederick Harrison took a cab to his offices in the City. His concern, and it was a very real concern, was less with the fate of his father than with the future of his bank. He, Frederick Harrison, was now the senior partner in the enterprise. He had, of course, been with the bank for many years but nominal control, the biggest shareholding in the bank, had rested with his father. Until his brother Willi's death the year before, it was Willi, not Frederick, who had been the dominant voice in the bank's affairs. Frederick was of a nervous disposition, alarmed by having to take decisions, fearful of their consequences afterwards. He was not, by temperament, a banker at all. And now, after this terrible news, he worried about the future of the bank he had never wanted to control.

Confidence, the old man had told them so many times they no longer took any notice, confidence can take decades to acquire, but it can be lost in a day, even in a morning, even in an hour. Confidence was the glue that held the many different elements of the City together. Confidence in Harrison's Bank could be gone before the bank closed its doors this very afternoon.

Harrison knew that rumour could destroy everything his father had built up. 'Terrible pity about Old Mr Harrison,' one whispered condolence would go to a colleague, 'but do you think we should withdraw our funds at once, just in case?' 'I've just heard,' the next rumour would whirl round the narrow streets and alleyways, that So and So are withdrawing their funds from Harrison's. We must mourn for Old Mr Harrison, of course, but shouldn't we look to our deposits with them?' And the echoing rumour, flying back at breakneck speed, 'Old Mr Harrison was the body in the river. There's a run on Harrison's Bank. We must get in now before it's too late.'

Frederick knew that there was more than enough in the bank to cover all their liabilities many times over. But he was not sure how quickly he could lay his hands on it if the Gadarene swine came hurtling through his doors, all demanding their money at once.

As he walked up the stairs to the partners' room, he thought of closing the bank for the day as a mark of respect to his father. But that would be a rare move in the City, and could give time for the rumours to spread even faster. The gain of a day could result in a catastrophe the following morning. Frederick looked at his watch. It was a quarter to eleven. The first news would hit the streets before lunchtime. He had five hours to save his bank.

As he paced around the long partners' room, furnished with the regulation red sofa and armchairs, a roaring fire beneath a handsome fireplace, portraits of Harrisons past and present on the walls, a row of working desks by the windows, he could think of only one precedent to guide him. Barings, the terrible fall of Barings some seven years before that had shaken the City to its foundations, brought on by imprudent lending to Latin America. He remembered his father recounting in hushed tones the emergency meetings in the Bank of England, Harrison's themselves pledging two hundred thousand pounds to the rescue fund to maintain the reputation of the City of London. Surely the Governor, the Governor of the Bank of England, held the key to this crisis as he had held the key to the last. Should he go and call on the Governor in his handsome offices in Threadneedle Street? He looked at his watch again. A quarter to twelve. By the time he got there it might be too late. If he was seen calling on the Governor, it could be seen as a sign of weakness, of desperation even. Rumour would say that the bank was insolvent and was begging for emergency funds from the Bank of England.

Was there another way? There must be. He looked up at his ancestors on the walls. The streets outside were filled with the normal racket of rushing people, omnibuses, hawkers peddling the latest in new umbrellas and top hats. Calm, Frederick, calm, he said to himself, remembering another of his father's prescripts. 'Calm in banking is everything, however shrill the surrounding voices. Calm preserves, panic destroys.'

Frederick Harrison was a tall man, plump bordering on fat. He prided himself on his dress sense, always smart but always one or two steps behind the latest fashion craze to adorn the persons of the jobbers and the brokers. Then a different prescript came to his help. He could not go to the Bank. But the Bank might come to him. A visit in the early afternoon from the Governor, come to express his condolences and indirectly to affirm his confidence in the bank, that might serve his purpose.

He sat at his desk by the window and wrote a short note to the Governor. He knew that any sign of weakness would be misinterpreted, but that he must find some way of bringing the Governor to Harrison's.

'It is with deep regret,' he began, 'that I write to inform you of the death of my father, Carl Harrison. His was the corpse found floating in the Thames some weeks ago. I know that you worked closely with my father in the past and that you would wish to be informed of his tragic demise with all due speed. Naturally all the members of his family are prostrated by the news, and, in particular, by the strange circumstances of his demise.'

Now came the difficult bit. Frederick scratched his forehead and rested his pen on the tip of a finely waxed moustache. If he said that the bank would continue as before, that could raise a question mark over its ability to do so.

'As you know,' he went on, his handsome copperplate flowing across the page, 'our house has prospered mightily under my father's guidance and we shall continue to run it in the same fashion in honour of his memory. I do hope we shall have the honour of a visit from you in the near future, as you have so often honoured us in the past.'

Frederick read his note through three times. He summoned a messenger and told him to take the letter to the Bank of England as fast as he could.

Even as the boy began running through the City streets, dodging in and out of the traffic, one hand holding on to his hat, the other clutching the envelope, rumour was on the move again. Dead bodies in these parts usually meant failure, men taking their own lives because they knew they could not meet their obligations. Fear of shame and ostracism drove many to suicide. Earlier that year

Barney Barnato, himself the darling of the Kaffir Circus, founder of his very own bank to advance exploration and promote successful speculation on the Rand, had jumped into the sea on a voyage between South Africa and London, his fortune and his misdeeds carried to the bottom of the ocean.

'That body in the river was Old Mr Harrison.'

'Impossible!'

'It's true! The police identified him this morning!'

'There must be something wrong with the house! People don't get murdered if business is in good hands!'

'How much money do we have with Harrison's? Can we get it back?'

'Harrison's are bankrupt.'

'Harrison's are finished. It's going to be the biggest scandal since Barings! Withdraw!'

Even in the City there is a little respect for the dead. Men felt that maybe they should wait a while before sorting out their positions. Old Mr Harrison had been a widely respected man. His good reputation held the vultures off for a little while. They decided not to act at half-past twelve. They would wait until three.

The Governor of the Bank of England was a small plump man with a neatly trimmed beard. He was not, strictly speaking, a banker at all. Junius Berry had made his name and his fortune as a successful tea merchant. He had been on the Council of the Bank of England before being elevated to the Governorship a year before.

His position was a curious one. No formal powers attached to his office. No Act of Parliament defined and circumscribed his position and his function. Legally, he had no functions at all. He was a schoolmaster without a cane, a policeman without a uniform, a judge with no prisons to incarcerate those he sentenced. But he could cajole. He could whisper. If circumstances made it necessary, he could even wink. He could let things be known. He could bring people together. In a word he had authority, acknowledged sometimes reluctantly, sometimes petulantly by the unruly tribe he moved among. Keep on the good side of the Governor, and it would do you no harm, men said. Cross the Bank of England and it could break you.

Something of these thoughts about his position crossed Junius Berry's mind late that morning. He grasped the importance of Harrison's note instantly. He could call on the bank tomorrow or the next day, but he suspected Harrison might find that too late. He could call now, but that would be too soon. Very well. He checked his engagements for the day. He was due at lunch with the Council of Foreign Bond Holders very shortly. On his way back, at half-past two, he would call on Frederick Harrison.

As he ate his lobster, the Governor was told, as his predecessors had been told many times before, that conditions in the market were bad, that many of the foreign governments appeared to have little intention of paying the interest, let alone repaying the capital, on their borrowings; that the situation was so severe in some quarters that gentlemen living and working in the City of London were liable to lose their fortunes; that pressure must be brought to bear on the Prime Minister and the Cabinet to send in the Royal Navy to make the foreigners see sense, and, if that proved impossible, to seize some assets in the countries concerned to ensure that gentlemen living and working in the City of London could continue to do so in the manner to which they had become accustomed.

The Governor listened gravely. Like his predecessors, he promised to take serious account of their concerns. Like his predecessors, he did absolutely nothing. 'It's always the same,' Junius Berry said to himself as he walked to Harrison's Bank. 'They feel they have to protect their backs in case things should go wrong and some wretched government abroad defaults on its debt. They can tell their members that they raised the matter with the Governor – what more could they do? It's a ritual dance, a quadrille, played out at least once a year.'

At half-past two precisely the Governor arrived at Harrison's Bank. At two thirty-one Richard Martin, trembling with the responsibility of ushering such an Olympian figure up the stairs, showed him into the partners' room. At two forty-five, the Governor and Frederick Harrison shook hands on the doorstep, pausing for polite conversation for a couple of minutes so the passers-by could spread the word around the City. 'Very friendly exchange of views.' 'Most affable meeting.' 'Can't be anything wrong with Harrison's if the Governor himself pays a call.'

And so the vultures rose once more into the City sky, circling above the Thames and the Monument in search of other prey.

6

A ripple of excitement and satisfaction flowed through the clerks in Harrison's Bank. The Governor had called! He had stayed for a full eighteen minutes! For they had counted the seconds as diligently as they counted the figures in the house's ledgers. The senior clerk let them have their moment of glory and then called them back to business.

In the partners' room, Frederick Harrison was holding a meeting with his other two partners, the former senior clerk Mr Williamson, and his nephew Charles Harrison. 'I am not satisfied with these policemen,' he said, standing in front of his ornate fireplace. 'I do not believe they will be able to find out how my father died. You did not see them,' he went on, glancing at his colleagues in turn. 'A miserable-looking pair. An inspector called Burroughs whose clothes didn't fit, and a sergeant called Cork who looked as if he was just out of school. Burroughs and Cork, they sound like a firm of undertakers in Clerkenwell.'

Like many in his profession, Frederick Harrison set great store by appearances. He believed firmly in the divine right of the upper classes. He did not think that these two policemen were fit to make inquiries about his family. He felt that their proper place in any Harrison household would be downstairs in the servants' hall or supervising the gardens.

'What are you going to do, Uncle?' asked Charles Harrison, trying to conceal a smile. He thought his uncle was a most terrible snob but he would never dare to say so in public. Charles Harrison was a tall slim man in his middle thirties. He had an oval face with grey eyes that turned to black when he was angry. But the most remarkable thing about him was his redness. He had red hair. He had bushy reddish-brown eyebrows that met above his nose. He had a reddish brown moustache and a reddish brown beard trimmed to a sharp point. At school his colouring gave rise to the unremarkable nickname of Foxy and there was indeed something vulpine about Charles Harrison. He looked like a predator, but a predator who would not be captured however many hounds and huntsmen set off in pursuit.

'I am going to find a private investigator to look into matters,' said Frederick Harrison. 'Of course the police must continue what they are doing, plodding about the countryside no doubt, frightening the servants at Blackwater, writing things down in their little notebooks. But I am going to find somebody better qualified for the post. I shall go to my clubs and make inquiries. In fact,' and he moved away from the fire towards the stand which held his coat and umbrella, 'I am going to start right away.'

Frederick Harrison asked three people he trusted to search for his investigator. One was a well-known banker with political connections. One was a landowner and MP in the Conservative interest. One – the most surprising choice – was the editor of a weekly newspaper whom he had known as a young man.

They, in their turn, made their inquiries. By the time they all reported, exactly one week later, an extraordinary variety of people had been consulted: two retired generals, one former Prime Minister, four Cabinet Ministers and a number of senior civil servants with connections in the world of law and order right across the country. The most original consultations were made by the newspaper editor. As well as two Cabinet Ministers he had asked the governors of two prisons, known to be packed with the most serious criminals, to take discreet soundings of their inmates.

Frederick Harrison summarized their findings in a memorandum which he gave to his two colleagues in a special partners' meeting at the bank.

'You will see that we have three candidates to choose from,' he said, sounding as if they were discussing a prospective new partner for the bank.

'Candidate A – I have left the names until later in case any of you has heard of any of these people – operates mainly in the North of England. He has been involved in a number of cases involving commercial fraud and has saved his clients considerable sums of money. There is no suggestion that he has made any investigations involving murder but he is very well spoken of, a man who knows business and commerce well, even if he has seen them with a jaundiced eye.'

He looked up at his two colleagues. Williamson, the former senior clerk, was scratching his nose, a sure sign that he was concentrating hard.

'Candidate B,' Frederick Harrison went on, 'has been involved in the investigation of a number of serious crimes, including robbery and murder. He has usually managed to secure the return of stolen jewellery or paintings to their rightful owners. My informants believe that he has been involved with one murder, if not more. But he is said to be eager to publicize his successes to advertise for more business in the future.'

'Is he a full-time investigator who earns his crust through the payments made by his clients?' asked Williamson incredulously.

'He is, Williamson. Such is the proliferation of crime in these times that it is apparently perfectly possible for a man to make a very respectable living in this field.'

'Who would have thought it,' said Williamson, shaking his head, 'who would have thought it?'

'Candidate C is a former officer in Army Intelligence in India. He has been involved in a number of murders and serious crimes in London and the Home Counties. He has friends in high places. He is said to be a man of great discretion and very considerable professional ability. But he has no knowledge of banking.'

The discussion took its course. Williamson was very firmly against Candidate B.

'If we are going to employ a man who will trumpet his mission about the place, it would never do. Discretion, we must have discretion.'

Charles Harrison was equally firmly against Candidate A.

'This fellow may know his way around the mills of Yorkshire and the cotton towns of Lancashire,' he said dismissively, 'but surely he would never do in the City.'

'We do not know, or at least we do not know until somebody begins their investigations, that the murder had anything to do with the City,' said his uncle, browsing through the letters of his informants.

'If we employ Candidate C, won't we have to spend our time explaining our business to him?' said Williamson, who seemed to favour hiring nobody at all. 'That could waste a lot of the bank's valuable time.'

'Let me tell you what I think,' said Frederick Harrison, eager to sum up before the meeting degenerated into discussions about trivia. I believe Candidate A lacks the right experience for our purposes. I believe Candidate B may be a competent investigator, but his love of publicity makes him totally unsuitable. I believe we must choose Candidate C – and that, I should tell you, is also the verdict of the vast majority of opinions canvassed.'

Frederick Harrison did not say that the hardened criminals in Her Majesty's prisons, to a man, had said that the investigator they would most fear was Candidate C. Frederick Harrison did throw one name into the ring: 'Lord Rosebery says he is the best man in the kingdom for this sort of work.'

The name of a former Prime Minister, a man connected through marriage with some of the great princes of the City, a man known to have very considerable investments of his own, had great influence with Williamson.

'Rosebery said so, did he now,' he muttered to himself 'Rosebery.'

Frederick Harrison chose his moment.

'Could I ask you, gentlemen, to concur with me in the choice of Candidate C?'

All agreed, Williamson nodding furiously, Charles Harrison looking suddenly apprehensive.

'Might I ask, Uncle,' he said quietly, 'if we could now know the name of Candidate C?'

'Of course,' Frederick Harrison smiled. 'I am going to write to him directly. I shall ask him to call on us at ten o'clock tomorrow morning. Candidate C, gentlemen, is Lord Francis Powerscourt.'

At half-past ten that evening Lord Francis Powerscourt was taking tea with his sister Mary in Berkeley Square.

'William will be back any moment, Francis,' she said. 'You must be very anxious to see him tonight.' She peered at her brother as if she suspected he might be in some sort of money trouble. You could never tell with Francis. 'Lucy and the children are well?'

'Splendid, splendid, thank you,' said Powerscourt. 'I should tell you,' he smiled broadly at his sister as if he had been reading her mind, 'I need to consult William on a matter of business, something to do with my work.'

Mary looked slightly disappointed. There was a banging of the front door, sounds of a coat and hat being hung up and a William Burke in evening dress burst into the room.

'Good evening, my dear. Francis, how nice to see you. Even at this hour. I think I know why you have called. Mary, will you excuse us?'

Safely ensconced in his comfortable study, William Burke helped himself to a large cigar.

'People have been asking about you, Francis, all over the City and elsewhere too, I believe.' He began the lengthy process of lighting his cigar.

'Did you discover who they were, William?'

'I did not. But I can make a pretty good guess. Have you recently had any dealings with Harrison's Bank?'

'I think you are in the wrong profession, William,' said Powerscourt, laughing. 'This very evening I received a note asking me to call on Harrison's Bank at ten o'clock tomorrow morning. I came to ask you for a quick description of the bank, the nature of its business and what you know of the partners in the house.'

Burke paused and took a long draw on his cigar, looking directly at Powerscourt as he did so. Above the fireplace portraits of Mary and his children stared down from their frames, reminding him even in here of his family obligations.

'Right, Francis. I will try to give you the broad picture. Harrison's Bank. I think we should begin with Bismarck. Don't look so surprised. Just consider the number of different states in Germany before unification in the 1870s – big ones like Prussia, lots and lots of smaller ones like Hanover and Hesse, Coburg and Würtemburg. In the old Germany Frankfurt was full of small banking houses doing good business managing their rulers' money and dealing in foreign exchange and so on between these little principalities. Once they were united and once they had a single currency, the opportunities for bankers decreased. Some moved to Berlin. Some moved to Vienna, some to New York. But a number came to London. Like the Harrisons – they still have family connections with banks in Germany, I believe, but their principal centre is now London.'

Burke paused, deciding where to go next.

'There had been German banks in London before this, of course, so it wasn't virgin territory for them. Some backed the winner in the Napoleonic Wars and found richer pickings with the conquerors. Old Mr Harrison, as he was known, the headless man in the river, brought them here and established them as a considerable force in the City.'

'Do they still have links with Germany?' asked Powerscourt.

'They do,' Burke replied. 'Like most of the German houses in the City the sons are educated in Germany. Often they begin their careers in Frankfurt or Berlin or Hamburg before coming back to London. And the German ethos is still strong.'

'What do you mean by that?' asked Powerscourt.

'They work much harder than we do for a start. Most of the clerks in the houses in the City work forty to fifty hours a week. The German ones work sixty or even seventy hours and they are all expected to be fluent in a couple of other languages as well.'

'What is their particular speciality, William?'

'Forgive me,' said Burke, annoyed with himself suddenly. 'I am not making the position clear.' He tapped on his cigar as if collecting his thoughts. Powerscourt waited.

'There are in fact two Harrison's Banks. Harrison's City – I forget the full name – deals in the City of London, acceptances, issuing loans, the normal sort of thing. Harrison's Private is in the West End and looks after the money of the wealthy, like Adams or Coutts. They do a lot of work with charities too, I believe.'

'Why did they break into two?' asked Powerscourt.

'I think there's a perfectly innocent explanation for that. In Germany the two banking functions, a city bank and a private bank, could have been combined into one. In London we do things differently. Mr Lothar Harrison – he must be a cousin of the Frederick who runs Harrison's City – lives in Eastbourne and another cousin called Leopold lives in Cornwall, just across the bay from Plymouth, in a place called Cawsand. They run the private bank.'

'Do you think,' said Powerscourt, 'that the split could have anything to do with the murder, William?'

'That's definitely your department, Francis, ' said Burke. 'I just stick with the money.'

Powerscourt laughed. 'You stick with the money, please. But tell me more about Harrison's City.'

'They deal in most of the traditional banking areas of London. They are strong on foreign loans and have been very successful in that field. They run a profitable arbitrage business too, said to be making them a mint of money.'

'Arbitrage? What, pray, is Arbitrage?' Powerscourt felt like a new boy at school with only a week to learn all the rules.

'Sorry, Francis, I should have explained. Arbitrage depends on exploiting tiny price differentials in different markets. It could only be done with the telegraph sending constantly updated information. Let me put it at its simplest. Suppose you see that Ohio and Continental Railroad stock can be bought for one hundred pounds in New York and sold for one hundred and one and a fifteenth in London. There is your opportunity. If you are prepared to invest considerable sums into these transactions, you can make a lot of money.'

Powerscourt groaned inwardly at his ignorance of the intricate workings of the City of London. Maybe he would have to come to regular tutorials with his brother-in-law.

'But there is one fact, I think,' Burke went on, 'more important than all of these. I had forgotten it until yesterday when these people inquiring about you reminded me of it.'

Burke rose from his chair and paced about his study. His house was very quiet now, wife and children retired to the upper floors.

'Death is no stranger to the House of Harrison, Francis. You could almost say they were cursed. The family tree goes like this. Carl Harrison, Old Mr Harrison of Harrison's City, the man found floating by London Bridge, had two brothers and one sister. One brother died in Frankfurt, I believe. His two sons, Leopold and Lothar, as I said, now run the private bank here in London. The other brother had nothing to do with the bank but his grandson Charles is now a rising force in Harrison's City. Carl Harrison had two sons, Willi and Frederick. Willi was the elder son. He built up Harrison's City after his father retired. The younger brother Frederick played a minor role in the bank's affairs. They say he did not have the drive of his brother.'

Powerscourt suspected that the Harrison family tree was going to be almost as complicated as Lady Lucy's.

'What happened to Willi?' Powerscourt suddenly wondered if there might be two strange deaths waiting for him the next morning.

'Willi was drowned. Or at least everybody presumes he was drowned. He went sailing off Cowes in his little yacht about eighteen months ago. Willi was a very experienced sailor. But he never came back. The boat was never found. The body was never found. Some of the sailing experts in the City said it was impossible, that Willi and his little boat had disappeared like that. Some men suspected foul play. But there was never any evidence . . .'

William Burke left his sentence hanging in the air.

'Two deaths in the same family in a year and a half. One body never found, another one floating by London Bridge.' Powerscourt looked sombre. 'And the young man, Charles Harrison, now, you say, a rising force in Harrison's City. The old man was his great-uncle, and his four uncles ran the two banks between them. Is that right?'

Burke nodded.

'Why did he join the City bank rather than the private bank, William?'

Burke tapped some ash into his fireplace.

'They say he is very ambitious, that he wanted a larger stage to play on than the safe quarters of private banking. I believe he had a miserable childhood. His mother ran off with a Polish count, his father drank himself to death and Charles was shuffled round the other members of his family. I've heard that none of them ever wanted him, but they felt they had to bring him up.'

Burke looked at his watch suddenly as if he wanted to retire.

'One last thing, Francis,' he said, looking carefully at his brother-in-law. 'I was asked if you were the man to investigate.' Burke remembered the hasty conversation on the steps of the Royal Exchange. 'I said that as your brother-in-law I couldn't possibly make any recommendations. But speaking off the record I said you were the most brilliant man in England for this kind of work. Pray God I haven't sent you into some terrible danger.'

'I am concerned with one aspect of the Curse of the House of Harrison.' Powerscourt was thinking fast, planning already the moves he might make in this investigation. 'Let us suppose, just for the sake of argument, that the death of Willi was not an accident. Whatever the motive, the murderer has not got what he wants. So now Old Mr Harrison goes to join his son in the bankers' heaven, an Elysian Field of profitable loans and successful arbitrage, perhaps. But what if the murderer has still not got what he wanted, William? What happens then?'

'You don't mean – ' Burke began.

'I do. I mean precisely that. There may be a terrible threat, a terrible danger, to the remaining Harrisons. But whether it comes from inside or outside the bank, I cannot tell.'

7

The park was nearly empty now. A stiff breeze, driving hard through the trees, had sent most of the walkers home to Sunday evening tea or Sunday evening service. But for Richard Martin and Sophie Williams, this was how they liked it. During the week they met rarely, Sophie often busy with her suffragist activities and Richard reluctant to face the censure of his mother.

'Where do you think you are going now, Richard?' she would say, sometimes tracking him down as he tried to escape through the small back door. 'You're not creeping out to meet that girl again, are you? Haven't I warned you about her before? What would your poor father say if he knew that his son was leaving his mother all alone in our little house to carry on with that young woman?'

Richard suspected that his father would have wished him luck in the pursuit of such a pretty girl as Sophie Williams, but he never said so. It was easier, as well as more dutiful, to follow her wishes.

But Sundays, he felt, Sundays were his own, the only day completely clear of his work in the City. And on Sundays his mother was often busy on church business. Anyway, he thought, she wouldn't be able to imagine anybody flirting with a member of the opposite sex on the Sabbath.

So here they were, in the park a few streets from their homes, Richard and his Sophie, as they often were at this time on a Sunday.

'Richard,' said Sophie eagerly 'you must tell me all about what's been going on at your bank. Fancy a dead man turning up in such a respectable place!'

'Well,' Richard said quickly, 'he didn't exactly turn up at the bank itself.' He had a sudden vision of the headless corpse walking up the stairs and taking a seat in the partners' room on the first floor. 'He was found in the river some time ago. It was just the news that it was Old Mr Harrison that arrived this week. But, think of this, Sophie. I have met the Governor of the Bank of England!'

'You haven't! Is he more important than the Lord Mayor? Does he have a cat like Dick Whittington?'

'He is the most important man in the City, Sophie. He has influence over everything. Everything. And I had to show him upstairs to Mr Frederick. "How do you do, young man," he said to me very civilly on the staircase.'

'One day, when women have the vote and true equality, those banks and counting houses will not be run entirely by men.'

Richard groaned internally as the tale of his triumph was turned into another attack on the wickedness of male society.

'There are women working there already, Sophie,' he said, trying to deflect her.

'Oh, I know. I have met some of them at meetings. But they are only allowed in humble positions, operating the typing machines and junior clerking, that sort of thing. They're not going to be important.'

Sophie's eyes danced with passion as she preached her gospel. Richard looked at the vivacity, the animation of her, and he knew more than ever that he was in love with her.

'But tell me,' said Sophie, returning once more to Harrison's Bank, 'how did they take it? The partners, I mean. Were they very upset?'

'Well, no, I don't think they were,' said Richard, moving off the path briefly as two very large dogs chased each other across the park, pursued by the shouts of their owners. 'I think Mr Williamson, the partner who used to be the senior clerk, was the most upset of all.'

'But he wasn't even a relation!' Sophie turned to him, shocked at the inhumanity of bankers.

'Well, I think Mr Frederick – the one who's senior partner now was worried in case there was going to be a run on the bank. That's why he asked the Governor to call.'

Few matters in City offices escaped the notice of the junior staff. Gossip ran just as freely and just as widely inside the offices as it did on the streets and in the chop houses.

'And the young Mr Harrison, Charles, he just seemed to be cross about the whole business. Maybe he was so angry with whoever had done such dreadful things to his great-uncle.'

57

'Did you get to see the body, Richard?' asked Sophie, turning ghoulish, something she would undoubtedly have discouraged in her pupils. 'Was it very horrid?'

'No, I did not, Sophie,' Richard laughed. 'I'm afraid I can't satisfy your curiosity there.'

'And will the bank continue to prosper? Surely things aren't any different? Mr Frederick has been in charge for some time.'

Although she didn't like to say so, Sophie was suddenly worried about Richard's future.

'In theory, you are right, Sophie,' the young man replied, unaware of the girl's concerns. 'But in practice, I am not so sure. Most of the really important decisions were referred to the old man since Willi Harrison died. Many's the time we have lost money, or not made as much as we might have done, while we waited for a reply to telegrams and messages to Blackwater. On one occasion, when the telegraph was broken, we lost fifteen thousand pounds.'

In spite of his youth and inexperience, Richard Martin had a sharp banking brain. He had watched and learnt a lot in his five years at Harrison's and studying for his banking exams. 'I just don't know what's going to happen. I just don't know.'

Sophie knew little of the City. But she was sad to see Richard so sombre.

'Can I ask you a favour?' she said, looking at him directly.

'Of course,' said Richard, his heart beating a little faster.

'I have to go for an interview with the headmistress on Thursday afternoon. I don't know what she wants to see me about but I'm a bit worried. Could I see you in the evening, just to let you know what happened?'

'Yes, of course,' said Richard. He wondered how he could deceive his mother. Maybe he could tell her he would have to work late at the office. Maybe he would be able to leave early on Thursday. 'You're not in trouble, are you Sophie? They couldn't be unhappy with your teaching, your children are all doing so well.'

'I don't know what it is about. Maybe it isn't serious. But she did give me a very strange look last week.'

'Look,' said Richard, 'I'll see you in that coffee house opposite Liverpool Street station at five o'clock. I'm sure they'll let me go a bit early if I tell them it's important.'

As they set off, Sophie was worried about Richard's bank and her own interview. But Richard was feeling strangely elated. If she asked for this special meeting, didn't it mean that she must care for him a little bit?

They buried Old Mr Harrison on a bright spring morning, the little church at Blackwater filled to overflowing with servants and tenants and local people as well as a number of visitors come from London to pay their last respects. His coffin was carried down from the house past the lake he loved, the sunlight dancing on the water and lighting up the classical buildings that shared his secrets. He was to lie in the new Harrison Chapel, next to his eldest son.

Some days later Lord Francis Powerscourt was walking up the drive to call on Old Mr Harrison's sister, the oldest surviving member of the family.

'She's well into her eighties,' Frederick Harrison had told him at his morning meeting in the bank's offices in the City. 'She can still see, she can still hear most of the time, but her mind is liable to wander. It's as though parts of her brain get detached from the main instrument, then they rejoin it a little later.'

Johnny Fitzgerald had been despatched to Cowes to make inquiries about Willi Harrison, the eldest son who had perished in the boating accident. Powerscourt wasn't sure how much would be remembered about the event, well over a year after the tragedy, or how much would have been exaggerated with time. But he needed to know if his brother-in-law's information was correct.

He was shown through a handsome entrance hall, a cube of some thirty feet, full of paintings of the family. He thought he recognized Frederick in younger days, seated on a handsome horse, surveying his park.

Old Miss Augusta Harrison was waiting for him in the salon, a fine room with an ornate ceiling and views of the gardens beyond. She's shrinking, Powerscourt thought, as she welcomed him formally to Blackwater. Every year she must be smaller than the one before.

'And how can I help you, Lord Powerscourt?' she said slowly, showing him to a chair by the marble mantelpiece.

'I am very grateful to you for seeing me at such a difficult time,' Powerscourt began, thinking that the mourning black reminded him of Queen Victoria. 'I would just like to ask you some questions about your brother.'

'That would have been when we lived in Frankfurt,' she said

slowly. Powerscourt wondered if she had never really mastered English and was slipping in and out of German in her mind. She paused and looked at Powerscourt suspiciously. 'What did you want to know about my brother?' She returned to normality. 'I don't know anything about the bank.' She shook her head. 'I never did and I don't suppose I'm going to start now.'

'I wanted to know how he spent his time when he was down here, you know, how he passed the time,' said Powerscourt, looking at a Roman statue of a Vestal Virgin in the corner of the room.

'Do you speak German, Lord Powerscourt? I find everything easier in German.' The old lady seemed to be pleading with him, her gnarled hands rubbing together in her nervousness.

'I'm afraid I don't, Miss Harrison. My wife does, but she is not with me today. But take your time, please, I have no wish to hurry you.' He smiled.

'The trees are beginning to come out in the park,' the old lady said. 'I always like it here in the spring. It's not as good as the Rhine, nowhere is more beautiful than the Rhine in the spring.'

Powerscourt wondered about the ratio between connection and wandering in her mind. It seemed to be about half and half. He felt he couldn't in all decency stay much more than an hour. He wondered if he would get any information at all.

'I was wondering,' he said in his gentlest voice, 'how he spent his time when he was down here, your brother.'

'Carl lived very quietly when he was down here. He loved walking in the gardens and by the lake. It must have been in '35 or '36 that Father took us to Garda,' she went on, her mind slipping out of gear once more. 'Carl used to take me rowing in a boat.'

'Was he worried at all in the last year or so?' Powerscourt cut in quickly, trying to bring her back.

'Anybody involved in banking has reasons to worry, that's what Father used to say. Worries all the time. I think he was worried about something, yes. There were such dances in Garda,' she went on, a faint smile playing across her withered lips, 'and all the young men looked so handsome. Sometimes they would build a platform out on to the water so you could dance on top of the lake. Not any more, not any more . . .' she was muttering now, shaking her white head sadly from side to side.

'What do you think he was worried about?' Powerscourt tried again.

'And the mountains!' She was happier now, her eyes bright with the memories inside her head. 'The mountains were so beautiful. And you could walk up into them for such a long way. Carl used to take me up to look at the flowers. He was so worried that he went to Germany quite a lot in the last year. He went several times. On Saturdays we used to take a family party to row out down the lake and stop at some of the little villages by the waterside. Sometimes we would take tea in them. They had very good cakes. Do you know the cakes in the Lakes, Lord Powerscourt?'

'I do,' Powerscourt lied, 'very fine cakes they are too. Where did your brother go when he went to Germany?'

'I sometimes wish we had never left, you know, that we'd never come all the way from Frankfurt to London. Carl said business would be better here than it was in Germany. Frankfurt and Berlin are such fine cities, don't you think, Lord Powerscourt?'

'Very fine.' Powerscourt felt faint stirrings of irritation creeping over him. 'Was that where Carl went? To Frankfurt and Berlin?'

'So big now, they say, Berlin. And getting bigger all the time,' the old lady went on. 'Carl said he could hardly recognize it. Great big buildings for the Parliament and things. It wasn't like that when we were young.'

'Why was he going to Frankfurt and Berlin? Was it a holiday?' Powerscourt was finding politeness increasingly difficult.

'You never can take a holiday from a bank, Father used to say. There was something wrong at the bank. Even when you are away you take the worries with you, even to somewhere as beautiful as the Lakes. Poor Father.'

'Did Carl think there was something wrong at the bank? Something wrong at his bank in the City?' Powerscourt was struggling now to hide his irritation.

'Father used to say the only time a banker could ever feel at peace was when they put him in his grave.' Old Miss Harrison stared defiantly at Powerscourt. 'Well, Carl is there too now. I hope he's found some peace there. He said there was precious little peace left to him in his last years.'

'Was it Carl saying that, or your father? About precious little peace?' Powerscourt realized that he wanted to shake her but he knew it would be hopeless.

'Father was buried in that big church in the middle of Frankfurt. So many people there, such a fine service. It rained too, I remember, even though it was early summer. Not as bad as the rain here. I can hear it upstairs, you know, rattling on my window and making noises on the roof. There are very strange noises on the roof sometimes. They seem to have stopped now.'

'What was Carl worried about?' I'm on my last throw now, Powerscourt thought to himself, I can't take much more of this.

'Mother's buried there too,' the old woman said to him, 'in the same church, just eight months later. She never really recovered, you know. They say that sorrow brought it on. Do you think that can be true, Lord Powerscourt? If sorrow could kill us there wouldn't be so many people left in the world, would there?'

'Indeed,' said Powerscourt. 'Was it the bank that Carl was worried about?'

'Always worries in a bank, Father used to say. Always worries, yes. Worries. All the time.'

'Did Carl say what it was that worried him about the bank?'

'Always worries in a Bank, Father used to say . . .'

Powerscourt wondered if the old lady was better in the mornings. Probably she was. Maybe he would ask Lady Lucy to come and speak to her in German. Will I end up like that, he asked himself, my mind meandering round the past like a stream making its way to the sea? He thought he would rather be dead.

There were only two facts he could take away with him, the confirmation of what Fitzgerald had told him about the trips to Germany and the knowledge that Old Mr Harrison had been worried about the bank. At the very back of his mind he had filed away what she had said about the noises on the roof, terrible noises that the rain could not have made. But something else could have made the noises. A body perhaps, being pulled along above a household meant to be asleep, a body due to be decapitated in the woods, a body destined to be dumped in the river, a body destined to be found many miles away bumping alongside a ship moored by London Bridge.

As he walked the two hundred yards to the head groom's cottage Powerscourt wondered if Samuel Parker would be better in the mornings too. The light was fading fast now. He could see the church clearly on his left and below that, partly hidden by the trees, the faint outline of Blackwater lake.

'Do come in, Lord Powerscourt, please.' Samuel Parker met him at the door. He was in his seventies now, but still tall and upright in his bearing. Years of work in the open air had turned his face brown to match his eyes. 'Mabel isn't here just now. She's over at the church helping with the flowers and making sure the place is tidy.' He showed Powerscourt a chair by the fire. Blackwater logs burned brightly in the Blackwater grate. The walls were covered with pictures and sketches of horses.

'Are these splendid animals ones that have passed through your hands over the years, Mr Parker?' Start with what they know best, Powerscourt reminded himself, wondering if he had adopted completely the wrong tone with the old lady in the big house.

'They are, Lord Powerscourt, all of them. Those three just to your right were all born in the same year. Aeneas, Anchises and Achilles, they were. Old Mr Harrison always gave them names from the past and we had a different letter of the alphabet for each year. One year we had Caesar, Cassius and Cleopatra. Old Mr Harrison used to say to me, "We've got to watch these horses this year, Samuel. The original Cassius went in for stabbing Caesar to death in some great building in Rome and before that Caesar had been carrying on with that Cleopatra woman in Egypt." It always used to make him laugh, that, even when he was telling me for the twentieth time.'

'Was Achilles very fast, Mr Parker?' Powerscourt saw that the horses were a splendid introduction to Samuel Parker's world. He had, after all, spent his entire life with them.

'Achilles fast, Lord Powerscourt? Fast? That he was not. Oh no. He should have been with a name like that, but he was a slow creature, very slow. Very good-natured, mind you.'

'We used to have some splendid horses in the Army, Mr Parker, really magnificent.' Powerscourt thought that Samuel Parker might have served in the Army as a young man. A lot of the grooms had learnt their trade in the Royal Horse Artillery or the Transport Divisions.

'Was you in the Army, my lord? I wanted to join when I was young but my mam wouldn't let me. You've got a good steady job here, she used to say, no point in joining up to get killed in foreign parts. I don't know but she might have been right. But did you see the world, my lord?'

'Well, I spent some years in India,' said Powerscourt, 'up in the north, near the border with Afghanistan. I was working in Army Intelligence.'

'Was you now, Lord Powerscourt!' Samuel Parker leaned

63

forward in his chair. 'I would have loved to have gone to some of those places and seen some of those wild natives, dervishes and hottentots or whatever they were called. Did you meet some strange foreigners, Lord Powerscourt?'

Powerscourt smiled. 'I did, Mr Parker. Some of the tribesmen up there tried to kill me. They were very wild. They were very fond of their horses, though.'

'Were there great mountains, Lord Powerscourt, with snow on them all the year round?'

Powerscourt thought he could detect the heart of a traveller beating strongly in Samuel Parker, who had spent his entire life in the calm and order of the Oxfordshire countryside.

'The mountains, Mr Parker, are huge. Huge. Nearly thirty thousand feet, some of them, with snow covering the peaks even at the height of summer. I have a book of photographs of the great mountains at home. I shall bring it for you next time I come.'

Samuel Parker's honest face lit up with pleasure. 'That would be so kind, Lord Powerscourt. But I fear we are getting away from our business here. Mr Frederick said you wanted to talk to me about Old Mr Harrison.'

'I do. Perhaps you could just tell me about his time here, how he spent his days, what your own dealings with him were. Take your time, Mr Parker, take your time.'

'Well,' replied Samuel Parker, trying to arrange his memories into some sort of order for a man who had seen the great mountains of the Himalayas and had a book to prove it. 'Old Mr Harrison, he'd been living here most of the time for about the last ten years or so. Some of the time he was in London, sometimes he was abroad. For the bank, you understand.'

He paused. Powerscourt said nothing.

'My duties had to do with him and the horses. Ten years ago he would ride about the country quite a lot, on Caesar or Anchises – he was always very fond of Anchises. Then, these last few years or so, he was only able to make the journey from the house round the lake. He liked to go round it every day. "It looks different every single day of the year, Samuel," he used to say to me, "and I want to see it changing."'

For a moment Samuel Parker vanished into his memories.

'Then, about a year or two ago, something changed. He wasn't as well as he had been after his accident. It hurt his leg something terrible, that accident, he had to keep on going back to the doctor.

I blame that Cleopatra myself, she always was an obstinate beast with a mind of her own. After that, he would ride very slowly, sometimes on a pony. And this was different too.'

Samuel Parker scratched his head and put some more logs on the fire.

'He began bringing work with him. Letters he had received, papers from the bank, I shouldn't wonder. You haven't seen those temples by the lake yet, Lord Powerscourt, have you?'

Powerscourt shook his head.

'Sometimes he would work in there at his papers. We had a folding table we used to bring and he would work away, writing letters and things inside one of those temples. Sometimes he would give me letters to post for him. He got very slow towards the end, Lord Powerscourt. He was old and his leg was bad but I'm sure his mind still worked faster than his feet if you follow me.'

Samuel Parker stopped. Powerscourt waited. Perhaps there was more to come. Perhaps Samuel Parker had exhausted his memories.

'That is very interesting,' he said at length, 'and admirably told. Perhaps I could just ask you about one or two things, Mr Parker?'

'Of course you can, my lord. I was never very good at long speeches, if you follow me.'

'Can you remember exactly when he began to bring his work down to the lake?'

Samuel Parker looked into his fire. He shook his head slowly. 'I don't think I can, my lord. All I can remember is that it was about the time we began to hear about the plans for this new Jubilee up in London. Mabel reminded me of that the other day. She is very fond of things like Jubilees, my lord. I took her all the way up to London for that other one in '87. She can remember all the details to this day, can Mabel. I don't suppose either of us will get there for this one though. Mabel's legs wouldn't be up to it, so they wouldn't.'

'And when Old Mr Harrison took his papers down to the lake,' Powerscourt sounded his most innocent, 'do you suppose he left some of them behind sometimes? In one of the temples or somewhere like that?'

'I'd never thought about that, my lord.' Parker fell silent for a moment. 'Come to think of it, he could have done, I suppose. Sometimes he didn't seem to have as many of these papers going back as he did going down, if you follow me.'

'And would you know,' Powerscourt was looking at him

intently as the night finally closed in outside, 'where exactly he left them?'

'Do you mean, my lord, that they might be still there, these papers?'

'I do, Mr Parker.'

'God bless my soul, Lord Powerscourt, if you'll pardon the expression. I'd never have thought of that. I suppose they might be.' He scratched his head again as if unsure what to believe.

'And the letters, Mr Parker,' Powerscourt went on, 'the ones he gave you to post. Did you think that was unusual, asking you to take charge of them rather than leaving them in the big house for the servants to send off?'

'I thought it was unusual at first, my lord. Then I sort of got used to it. Mabel used to think Old Mr Harrison was making secret investments somewhere abroad.'

'Were the letters for abroad?' asked Powerscourt.

'Why, yes, I suppose they were. Mostly to Germany, Frankfurt, I remember, and Berlin, wherever that is. And some for a place called Hamburg. Mabel looked that one up in a map at the library.'

Powerscourt wondered if he had a rival in the detection business in Mrs Parker, obviously an assiduous researcher.

'Did he bring letters with him down to the lake?' Powerscourt went on. 'Letters that might have come from these foreign places?'

'I think he might have, my lord.' Samuel Parker scratched his head. 'I do seem to remember that sometimes they weren't opened. And they had foreign stamps on them. Mabel does like to look at a foreign stamp.'

Powerscourt wondered again about the precise role played by Mrs Mabel Parker in her husband's affairs but he let it pass.

'Could I make a suggestion, Mr Parker?' Powerscourt was already planning another visit to Blackwater House. 'I have to come back here again very soon, to talk to the people in the big house, you understand. Perhaps we could go on the same walk round the lake you used to take with Old Mr Harrison. Sometimes revisiting the places helps bring back more memories. Not that you haven't remembered very well already.'

Powerscourt smiled a smile of congratulation.

'There is just one other thing, my lord,' said Parker. 'You're not the first gentleman to have been round here asking questions about Old Mr Harrison. There was another gentleman round here the other day.'

Samuel Parker paused again.

'He was a very curious gentleman, my lord. I thought he was almost too curious. Very friendly, of course, but I wouldn't have said he was as discreet as yourself.'

Powerscourt rejoiced at this description of Johnny Fitzgerald. Not as discreet as himself, he liked that. He would tell Lady Lucy about it this evening. But as he set off for his train back to London one question above all others troubled him.

Why had Old Mr Harrison taken his business down to the lake? Why had he posted his foreign correspondence in this unusual way? Was it normal banker's caution? Was it merely the whim, the foible of a very old man? Or did he think he was being spied on inside the drawing rooms and the bedrooms of Blackwater House?

8

Powerscourt found he had company on his return to Markham Square. Johnny Fitzgerald was doing him the honour of sampling the latest delivery to the Powerscourt cellars below.

'I was just saying to Lady Lucy, Francis,' Fitzgerald began without the least hint of apology, 'that you need to sample some of this stuff once it arrives. They might have sent you the wrong year or the feebler stuff from the wrong side of the hill.' Powerscourt kissed his wife and turned to his friend.

'And what does this early test show, Johnny?' He picked up a bottle from the table and noted that two others appeared to have been carried up for inspection.

'I'm glad to say that you've done well with this one. This Chablis is very good, flinty I believe is the word they use in the trade. I'm afraid I may not have the time to sample those two over there as I have to buy dinner for a man I know in the City. On your business, Francis, Fitzgeralds never sleep.'

Lady Lucy laughed.

'But I must tell you what I found out when I was down south inquiring about boating accidents, Francis.'

Powerscourt stretched out in his favourite red leather armchair and poured himself a small glass of wine. 'You don't mind, Johnny, if I just try a glass of my own wine in my own chair in my own house, do you?'

Fitzgerald waved expansively from the fireplace. 'Help yourself, Francis, help yourself. This is Liberty Hall.'

'So what have you discovered down south?'

'Well,' said Fitzgerald, looking serious now, 'the first thing to report is that every year the Harrisons take a house near Cowes on the Isle of Wight. A huge house it is too, right on the water with a tennis court at the back and a little jetty at the front where you could keep small yachts. Harrisons from all Europe turn up at this place, Francis. Some of them come to watch the races in Cowes Week. I shouldn't wonder if the German ones are cheering for the bloody Kaiser rather than the right side.'

'How many members of the family are there exactly, Johnny?' asked Powerscourt.

'There could be up to fifty of them at a time,' said Fitzgerald, squinting into his wine glass, 'or so my informant told me. But the accident, Francis, the accident. Nobody down there likes to talk about it at all, I don't know why. One old seafarer told me it would bring bad luck all round. But a number of the locals don't think it could have been an accident at all. You can see that they think, though they wouldn't quite say it, that there was foul play.'

'What sort of foul play?' said Powerscourt, unlacing his boots and turning his feet towards the fire.

'That's the thing, Francis. I got hold of the people in the boat-yard at Cowes that used to look after the boat and they just couldn't believe it. A different man in another boatyard told me about how you could nobble a boat rather like you nobble a horse. There are so many ways that boat could have been fixed, not that I understood most of them. The most likely was to make a small leak shortly before your victims went out for their sail. The water would come in gradually and nobody would notice. By the time the water came through the floor it would almost certainly be too late. And if you were on your own, you would be hard pressed to bale out and sail the bloody boat at the same time. Or that's what my man said. So you see, Francis, somebody could have fixed the boat. But it could have been anybody.' Fitzgerald shrugged his shoulders.

'An English Harrison, a German Harrison, an Austrian Harrison – that's just the beginning,' said Powerscourt, running through his knowledge of the number of different branches of the family.

'What's more,' said Johnny Fitzgerald, 'all that part of the coast is overrun with people in the summer. Nobody would have paid any attention to anybody tinkering about in the inside of a boat. Half the bloody island is doing the same thing.'

Two men were waiting for a third by the side of the lake at Glendalough, thirty miles south-west of Dublin. They were shielded from sight by the trees but they commanded a clear view of the path that led down from the village and the hotel.

'He's half an hour late now,' said Thomas Docherty, the younger man.

'We'll give him another fifteen minutes or so,' replied Michael Byrne. Both men were whispering even though they were the only people to be seen on the fringes of the lake. Both were leaders of small revolutionary bands pledged to the overthrow of English rule in Ireland. Both lived in fear of their lives from the authorities, their secret files in Dublin Castle augmented daily by the reports of the informants, handsomely subsidized at the British Exchequer's expense.

They heard the third man before they saw him, his footsteps crunching on the path. Behind them small waves were lapping the surface of the lake. The water was still dark blue, fading into black with the coming of the night.

'Should we go and let him know we're here?' whispered Docherty.

'He knows. He knows exactly where we are going to be. Don't move. I don't think we were followed here but you cannot be too careful.'

The three conspirators had chosen Glendalough for its innocence. Any trip there could be excused as a visit to one of the ancient seats of Irish learning, the fifth-century tower further up the hill still visible like a beacon against the Wicklow hills, a light-house placed by God to illuminate the journeys of his people. Even a clandestine conspiratorial assembly like this could be excused by the need to pray at the lakeside. And Glendalough had a further advantage. It was a largely Protestant village, its loyalty rewarded by the visit some years before of the Prince of Wales himself with a large party of friends. It was one of the most unlikely places in Ireland for a Catholic conspiracy to be launched.

'God be with you, Michael Byrne. God be with you, Thomas Docherty.' Fergus Finn, the last arrival, made his apologies. Docherty worked on the railways, Byrne was a schoolteacher and Finn was a clerk in a solicitor's office in Dublin.

'Let's get down to it,' said Byrne, the acknowledged leader of the group. They sat on the damp grass beneath the trees, even more invisible to any watchers from Dublin Castle. Behind them the water lapped as it had done for thousands of years. The circle of hills around Glendalough, the glen of the two lakes, was black.

'This Jubilee. Two months from now,' Byrne went on. 'Should we make a noise in Dublin or in London?'

The others knew perfectly well what he meant by noise, an assassination, a bomb, a terrorist outrage that would bring their cause on to the front pages of all the countries of the known world.

'London,' said Finn. 'There will be enormous crowds there. Surely it would be easy to send a couple of our people in without the police knowing. They couldn't possibly vet every single citizen arriving in the city. It's beyond reason.'

'Dublin,' said Docherty. 'Sure, it has to be Dublin. However big the crowds are over there, it would still be impossible to get away. Whether it's a bomb or a bullet we are thinking of, the man doing it would be seized by the Londoners themselves. In Dublin there's more chance of getting our man away, of being able to hide him decently afterwards.'

'But it wouldn't have the same impact in Dublin as it would in London.' Finn was making his point emphatically, punching his right fist into his left palm as if he were addressing a public meeting. 'Think of all those troops from across the Empire marching through the city. Think of the crowds hanging off every balcony, sitting in their stands in Piccadilly, lining the rooftops to get a better view. And then an incident somewhere just away from the main parade, a great explosion. That would make them sit up a bit. It would be grand, wouldn't it?'

Docherty was not impressed. 'You'd never get away,' he said dismissively. 'They may all be watching the parade but there will still be thousands of them milling about the streets, trying to get as close as they can. A good bomb in Dublin would do just as well. Michael Byrne, what is your opinion on the matter?'

Byrne paused before he replied. He pulled a small branch from the tree above him and peeled the twigs off one by one as he made his points.

'I think it should be a bomb. We've got four lads just discharged with good records from the Royal Engineers. They've served all over the place and they know all there is to know about making bombs. Two of them have settled in Hammersmith, not far from the bridge. Two more have come back to Dublin and they're living beyond the brewery.'

He paused. A sudden gust of wind ruffled the surface of the lake and sighed its way around the trees that guarded its presence.

'I think it has to be Dublin,' he said finally. 'It will be easier to

71

organize in our own city. A bomb early in the morning of Jubilee Day. There must be some bloody statue we could blow up. Then the Castle people will be worried all day in case there are more to come. Maybe even in London. I think that is going to be our best plan.'

He held his hand to his lips suddenly.

'What was that noise?' he said ever so softly. Three pairs of ears bent to one side, straining for the noise of policemen on the march, soldiers on patrol. Behind them the lake continued to murmur, the roar of the waterfall on the other side occasionally breaking through.

'Nothing, Michael, it was just the wind in the trees,' said Finn, rather loudly.

'We're all too jumpy. Even here.' Byrne began demolishing another branch. 'There have been too many arrests in the last six months. Too many of them the right people too. I think we should go. Could you both draw up some possible targets before the next meeting on the beach at Greystones?'

Finn and Docherty left at five-minute intervals to return to their homes. Byrne heard their steps gradually fading on the path back to the village. He turned and looked at the dark waters of the lake. For months now he had suspected that Finn was an informer. He had set the meeting up as a trap. All informers were encouraged to press for the most extreme action, to provoke the terrorists to the most violent measures. He had learnt this from two members of his own organization whom he had encouraged to sell their services to Dublin Castle. The information he obtained from their instructions was invaluable; the payments the two men received strengthened the terrorists' arsenal. Within two days, he thought, possibly three, news of this meeting would have reached the authorities. He hoped they would believe what Finn had to tell them.

For Michael Byrne, implacable opponent of English rule, rated by his enemies as the cleverest foe they had, intended to make a noise in London all along.

He knelt down to the water's edge and splashed his face. He made the sign of the cross. He tapped his jacket pocket to make sure his pipe was inside. Then, like the others, he left the lake to make his plans.

9

Lady Lucy Powerscourt had been practising her German for some days.

'Don't worry too much if there are pauses while you turn the English into German in your head,' her husband had told her. 'Old Miss Harrison wanders in and out of the last fifty years, so a second or two here and there won't make any difference.'

She began with the rituals of sympathy. 'I was so sorry to hear about your brother's death, Miss Harrison,' she said very properly, sitting in the same chair in the same salon that her husband had sat in the week before.

'Death comes for us all,' the old lady said firmly, 'maybe it will come for me very soon. Nobody can escape it in the end.'

'I'm sure you will be with us for a long time,' said Lady Lucy brightly. 'You look remarkably well to me.'

The old lady smiled a thin smile. The lines on her face suddenly multiplied as she did so, running down in crooked lines from the corner of her mouth.

'I believe you wished to talk to me about my brother.' The old lady looked up at Lady Lucy. 'I find it so much easier to talk in German. You speak it very well, my dear. When we came here I found it so very difficult to learn English. Such an illogical language, English.'

Lady Lucy remembered her husband's advice to her as their carriage rolled up the curving driveway of Blackwater House. 'The most important thing, Lucy, is to get her on to her brother and his worries as soon as you possibly can. If you go in for the normal pleasantries her mind will have left before you get to the business. There is not a moment to be lost.'

'My husband tells me that your brother was worried about something in the weeks before he died.' Lady Lucy leant forward to make sure Miss Harrison could hear her. She wished she had a notebook. Now she understood why all those policemen were forever writing things down.

'Yes, he was worried.' The old lady paused, staring at a classical landscape on her wall. 'Always worries in the bank, Father used to say. Always worries.'

Lady Lucy remembered Francis' account of their first meeting, repeated virtually word for word in the drawing room in Markham Square, Francis changing seats for the different characters in the little drama, laughing at himself as he neared the end of his little play. This mantra, always worries, had cropped up over and over again. Oh dear, oh dear, Lady Lucy thought to herself. Don't say her mind is going to start wandering already. I couldn't bear to tell Francis I'd failed him.

At that moment her husband was greeting Samuel Parker just outside the door of his little cottage.

'I've brought you that book of photographs, Mr Parker, the one I mentioned last time. The book with the photographs of the mountains in it. Look at this one here. It's extraordinary.'

The two men gazed in awe at a photograph of the high Himalayas, taken some way off, but their snow-capped peaks looked majestic, the two tribesmen in the foreground like ants on the ground.

'Thank you so much, my lord.' Samuel Parker took the book with great reverence, 'I shall look at it later if I may. But come, I promised to take you round the lake and all the places where Old Mr Harrison stopped off.'

Parker suddenly disappeared back into his cottage. He returned with a large ring with a number of different keys on it, each one labelled in stiff awkward capitals.

'The keys, my lord. I always had to bring the keys with me. For the buildings and that.'

The two men set off down the path. In front of them was the lake, bright in the morning sunlight. Across the water a classical temple stood improbably in the middle of the view. To their left was a fine stone bridge – Palladian again, thought Powerscourt. Verona, or was it Vicenza where he had seen its like before?

'So you would be walking, Mr Parker,' said Powerscourt, slowing his pace to that of that of the old man. 'Old Mr Harrison would be on his pony with his portable table and his papers. Tell me, did you always have keys to the buildings? I mean, were they always locked up in the past?'

'They were not, my lord.' Samuel Parker was indignant. 'Old Mr Harrison only had the locks put on them in the last couple of years.'

'Did he say why, Mr Parker?' Powerscourt was looking curious.

'He did not, my lord. But the man who made them said to me afterwards that they was mighty strong locks. You'd think the old man had the Crown jewels inside them old temples rather than a couple of mouldy statues, he used to say to me. He's still there. Harold Webster, my lord, up at the big house, the man who fitted them.'

They had reached the path that ran round the lake, disappearing out of sight from time to time as it curved round the water's edge. A couple of rooks greeted their arrival, striking out over the water to the woods beyond.

'Which way do we go here, Mr Parker?' asked Powerscourt.

'Well, my lord, we can go left or we can go right as you can see. I never knew which way the old gentleman wanted to go until we got here. But I think at this time of year we would have turned right.'

Soon the flowering chestnuts and the rhododendrons would paint the path with colour. This morning they walked on, the old man leading, through green conifers and huge oaks.

'Did he talk to you much along the way, Mr Parker?' asked Powerscourt, noting that the classical temple had suddenly disappeared from view.

'He didn't talk to me, my lord. He talked to himself sometimes though. In German usually, I think, sometimes in some other language.'

'What was that?'

'I don't rightly know, my lord.' Samuel Parker shook his head. 'I never had any time to learn any of those foreign languages at school. I found it hard enough learning how to spell this one. But Mabel thought it might have been Yiddish.'

'How on earth did she know that? Does Mabel know Yiddish, Mr Parker?' Powerscourt marvelled again at the detective powers of Mrs Parker.

'Mabel speak Yiddish, my lord? Never a word of it. I think the vicar told her. He'd heard Old Mr Harrison talking to himself too. Yiddish, the vicar said, or maybe some other language beginning with an A. Arabian? Aramaic? I can't remember.'

They were now approaching another temple, not previously visible on the walk. It was quite a small temple with a portico of four Doric columns and an imposing inscription over the door. '*Procul, o procul este, profani*', the message warned. Powerscourt had sudden memories of translating the *Aeneid* at school, watched over by an unforgiving master. Be gone, be gone, you uninitiated persons, he said to himself. It's the Sybil speaking in Book Six, just as Aeneas was about to begin his descent into the underworld to meet his father and hear the story of the founding of Rome, a perilous journey from which few travellers returned. As he stood at the door while Samuel Parker fiddled with his bunch of keys, Powerscourt wondered if he too was entering some private underworld of the Harrisons where filial respect was marked out, not with piety and messages from the Sibyls, but with the bodies of the dead.

'What was he worried about, Miss Harrison?' Lady Lucy was looking concerned, hoping against hope that the old lady hadn't lost her mind again.

'He never told me very much, Lady Powerscourt. I tried to remember, after your husband called the time before. Germany, I think, it had to do with Germany. It's not the same now it's all one. I remember all those little states we used to have before that dreadful old Bismarck got his way and bundled them all up together like a big parcel.'

The old lady stopped suddenly and smiled a vacant smile. She's going, she's going, thought Lady Lucy. 'Was that why he went to Germany in the last years? Was he looking for whatever it was that troubled him?'

'Berlin,' the old lady said definitely. 'I know he went there. On business for the bank, he said. Frankfurt. He went there too. Berlin is full of soldiers now, marching up and down all the time, as if they want to fight somebody. That's what he said.'

'And did he have letters from Germany too?'

'Letters, letters?' said the old lady wildly, looking round as if the post had not been delivered that morning. 'Letters . . .' Old Miss Harrison was lost again. 'Father used to check we had learnt our letters when we were very small. Letters are very important, my children, he used to say, nearly as important in this world as numbers. That's what he used to say.'

'I'm sure he was right,' said Lady Lucy diplomatically. 'Did your brother have correspondents in Germany?'

'All our letters were handed out every morning by the butler at the end of breakfast. We children were so excited when we had letters of our own. I used to look at the stamps and the postmarks.' She nodded as if confirming the educational value of the postal services. 'He did have letters from Germany, my brother,' she went on, 'I remember the postmarks. Hamburg, Bremen, Berlin, Frankfurt, one from Munich with a beautiful stamp on it. Mountains, I think. Do they have mountains near Munich?'

Lady Lucy assured her that they did.

'Did he ever talk to you about his worries at all?' she continued, stressing 'at all' as if she thought it impossible that the two old people could have shared a house without sharing their fears.

'He talked in his sleep sometimes, he did. When he was sitting by the fire, just where you are now. After supper, he would usually fall asleep and sometimes he would mutter to himself in his sleep. I can't sleep much now at night. I can get off all right, but then I keep waking up again. Mother never could sleep at all at the end, you know. One of the doctors said if she'd slept better she wouldn't have been gone so soon after Father passed on. She wouldn't have gone so soon. That's what he said.'

'And what,' asked Lady Lucy quietly, praying for one last lucid moment, 'did he say to himself in his sleep by the fire after supper?'

'They call this one the Temple of Flora, my lord,' said Samuel Parker, ushering him inside. The air was damp. Spiders were taking over the left-hand wall of the little temple, their webs cascading down the walls. There were a couple of busts of ancient heroes and two sturdy seats, almost benches, on either side.

'Did Old Mr Harrison ever stop here,' asked Powerscourt, looking carefully at the statues, 'to read his papers or to write?'

'Only very rarely, my lord. Very rarely.' Samuel Parker was shaking his head, the wisps of his grey beard waving in symmetry. 'Once or twice he did, perhaps. One day I do remember him stopping in here and me bringing in his little table off the pony.'

'Can you remember how long ago that was? Did he seem to be in a great hurry to get started that day?' Powerscourt was looking carefully at the busts, Marcus Aurelius on the left, he thought, Alexander the Great on the right.

'I think he was, my lord. In a hurry, I mean. And I think that would have been last summer. I remember it was very hot, even though it was early in the morning.'

They set off again, the path turning now uphill towards the tree-lined hills, now down towards the water's edge. Sometimes another temple could be seen across the lake, sitting proudly on its semi-circle of turf. Sometimes it disappeared, lost among the bushes and the trees.

'I presume, Mr Parker,' said Powerscourt, 'that the garden was designed a long time ago, long before the Harrisons came here?'

'It was, my lord. It was created in the seventeen hundreds, I think. But Old Mr Harrison knew all about it. He used to quote to me in Latin sometimes out of his head. He read all about the building of it in the library up in the big house.'

They passed through a grotto, where a statue of a river god pointed the way forwards and a marble maiden slumbered on her bed of rock while the water dripped on all around her.

'I don't suppose Mr Harrison did much work here,' said Powerscourt cheerfully, as he bumped his head on a rocky outcrop, the bottoms of his trousers watered by the local deities.

'Not in there, my lord. But just a few yards up the road is what they call The Cottage. He worked a lot in there.'

The lake frontage was open at this point, with wide views across the water. A kingfisher, brilliant in blue, shot across the water at astonishing speed. On the hills above the lake the birds were singing happily, making occasional forays to forage at the water's edge.

The Cottage was laid out like a small summerhouse, converted only a couple of years before.

'In here,' Samuel Parker wrestled with his keys again, 'there is a table by the window as you can see. Sometimes I would wait for an hour or so while he wrote things or pottered about. Quite often he would break off in the middle of something and go and stare at the water, just by that tree over there. Then he would go back inside. The pony always liked to stop here. The grass is quite lush round this part.' What on earth was the old man writing down here? thought Powerscourt. Who was he writing to? Did these peaceful pursuits lead to his death? What was he looking for? Of one thing he was certain. Long before he came on the scene somebody else had embarked on a journey of discovery. The old man had been here before him. But of the nature of his quest, or his success or failure, he had, for the present, no idea.

'It must have been very peaceful for him here,' he said, smiling gently at Samuel Parker.

'It was, my lord, it certainly was. Now, there's one last place he used to work and then we'll have done the full circuit. It's the Pantheon next, my lord.'

So that was what the temple reminded him of. Powerscourt knew he had seen it somewhere before. It had been on a trip to Rome with Lucy for a wedding anniversary. The Pantheon. The pagan gods of Rome had transplanted themselves from the banks of the Tiber to a new home in the depths of Oxfordshire.

'Sometimes he would talk in German, sometimes in Yiddish.' The old lady was concentrating hard, as if she knew her time was limited. Lady Lucy wondered if Francis would want her to take a crash course in Yiddish. She rather hoped not. She waited. She thought Miss Harrison's mind was about to take off on one of its own private journeys once more.

'Secret societies, secret societies,' the old lady was whispering now. 'Why do people want to have secret societies, my dear? Father used to complain about them at the universities. He said they were terrible organizations devoted to duelling and drinking and that sort of thing,'

She stopped, lost in thought. Lady Lucy tried to head her off before she disappeared.

'Here, or in Germany?' she said in her most matter-of-fact voice.

'He knew they were in Germany. Oh yes.' The old lady was very definite suddenly. 'He knew that. Do you know what they say about getting old, my dear?'

Lady Lucy shook her head.

'They say that you can remember things that happened fifty years ago but you can't remember what happened yesterday. He didn't know if they were in England as well as in Germany. That's what my brother said in his sleep. Father got so upset about these secret societies because his best friend's son was left with a terrible duelling scar, right down one side of his face. Such a handsome boy he used to be before that.'

She drew a line from just below her ear to the side of her wrinkled mouth. Lady Lucy wondered if she had been in love with this handsome boy, all those years ago.

'Did he ever say what the secret society was for? What its purpose was?'

'No good will come of it, Father used to say,' Miss Harrison went on, 'no good at all. You don't want to go round stirring up hatred. That boy with the scar, look what happened to him after all that fighting. The girls would never look at him after that. What a shame, Father used to say. Duelling finished his future, poor boy.'

Lady Lucy longed to ask if Miss Harrison had been in love with him before his terrible scar. But she pressed on. Francis would never forgive her if she encouraged the love stories of the old lady from sixty years before.

'Did he ever say what the secret society was for?' she asked, remembering Francis' description of how he had wanted to shake Miss Harrison into sense as the interview went on.

'It's a secret brotherhood. It's a secret bloody brotherhood. I remember him shouting that once, not so very long ago. We'd had goose for supper. We used to have goose sometimes for Christmas when I was a little girl. Sometimes there were so many of us that we had two or even three. I can remember the smell, you know, of those geese cooking in the oven. It used to spread all over the house. Father loved carving goose. I remember him saying once with the great carving knife in his hand that he should have been a surgeon rather than a banker. Then he could have carved away all day.' Miss Harrison laughed a tinny laugh.

Lady Lucy smiled sympathetically. 'Is there anything else you can remember, Miss Harrison? Anything else of what he used to say in his sleep?' She tried another tack. 'Just imagine that he's sitting here now, in this chair, after supper, just the two of you. The fire is burning in the grate. It's dark outside. The curtains are drawn. It's very quiet. Gradually he falls asleep.' Lady Lucy slowly closed her eyes. 'Perhaps he begins to snore. Then suddenly he speaks. He mutters in his sleep, your brother. What is he saying?' She let her head fall on to her shoulder.

The old lady puckered her face as if she was a small child confronted with a nasty piece of mental arithmetic. Then she too closed her eyes.

Lady Lucy waited, eyes closed. When she peeped out of them she saw that her device had failed. The old lady's eyes had closed too. Her breathing grew slow and regular. Just at the point when she might have been about to tell the whole story, Miss Augusta Harrison had fallen asleep.

Six Corinthian columns flanked by a couple of ancient statues gazed out across the lake. This must have been the centrepiece of the whole place, thought Powerscourt, wondering not for the first time about the strange mind of the man who had designed these fabulous gardens, a mind where the ancient myths of Greece and Rome and the poetry of Virgil seemed to have been more important than the eighteenth-century world he actually inhabited. Powerscourt thought he would have liked to meet the mind, if it could be summoned forth from the springs and grottoes it had left behind.

The pony trotted happily down to the water's edge to munch the grass. Samuel Parker was fiddling with his bunch of keys.

'Did Mr Harrison rest under these columns in the summer? It must be nice and cool then.' Powerscourt could see the little temple, with its columns, dome and assorted statuary, in some Roman landscape of the Campagna, providing welcome relief from the sweltering sun. In England, he reflected prosaically, you could always shelter from the showers.

'He used to, my lord,' said Samuel Parker. 'Then I think he got worried about being overlooked, so he used to go inside. This was one of his favourite places to do his writing.'

Parker had opened the great doors and was wrestling with the key to an iron grille that protected the sculpture inside. Facing the lake was a marble statue of Hercules, flanked by Diana, goddess of hunting, Ceres, goddess of nature and harvest, and – more ominously – Isis, mistress of the dark mysteries of the underworld. Powerscourt inspected them carefully, trying and failing to remember all seven labours of Hercules.

'He'd leave the doors open, my lord,' Samuel Parker was placing himself exactly where he remembered the table being, 'and then he could look out at the lake when he wanted. Sometimes I'd wait for an hour or more just outside while he was writing away in here.'

'Did Hercules mean anything special to him?' asked Powerscourt, rubbing his hand over the surface of the statue to see if it might be hollow, if there might be some pressure from the hand which might open up a hidden chamber inside the marble.

'Hercules was very stupid, my lord,' said Samuel Parker, gazing out at the lake like his master.

'Was he? Why do you say that?' replied a puzzled Powerscourt.

'He could never do anything right. None of them beginning with H, Hannibal, Helen, Hercules, ever had any brains at all.'

Powerscourt could see that Helen might have been all beauty and no brains, but Hannibal? Surely the wily Carthaginian had destroyed a couple of Roman armies?

'Are you sure?' Powerscourt was inspecting Diana's flanks now, running his hand around the marble curves of her hips.

'Sorry, my lord. They were horses, Hercules and the others. I wasn't talking about the statues.'

Powerscourt laughed. 'Tell me, Mr Parker, if your master wanted to hide some of his documents, do you think he could have left them in here?'

Samuel Parker scratched his head. He took some time to answer.

'I suppose he could, my lord. But I have no idea at all where he might have hidden them. This would be a queer place to go hiding bits of paper.'

'That's just what might have appealed to him, the fact that nobody would expect it. But I have no more idea than you have of where it might be.' Powerscourt was feeling his way round Ceres' feet, in case some hidden spring might answer to his touch. The marble was cold to his fingers. It was smooth. But it had no message for him.

Lady Lucy sat very quietly in her chair. Far off in the gardens outside she could hear the sounds of grass being cut, the cheerful cries of the gardeners, the tolling of a distant bell.

She wondered if Miss Harrison, like her brother, talked in her sleep. Some of the years seemed to have fallen from her face, smoother now than when she was awake. Sometimes the old lady turned, as if she was dreaming. Her mouth fell open. Then she spoke.

'Secret societies,' she said in a firm voice. She stopped. 'In Germany. Maybe here. Conspiracy at the bank.'

Lady Lucy wondered if she was repeating what her brother used to say as he sat in his chair by the fireside in the evenings when he was still alive.

Suddenly old Miss Harrison sat upright in her chair. She was still fast asleep.

'That poor boy,' she said. 'Poor Karl. What a terrible scar.'

She dropped back in her chair. Lady Lucy hardly dared to move. She looked around the room, its tables cluttered with paintings and photographs of past Harrisons. She wondered if there was a likeness of Karl, hiding his shame somewhere in a dark corner. She couldn't find one.

Then Miss Harrison woke up.

'Always troubles in a bank, that's what Father used to say, always troubles.' She looked defiantly at Lady Lucy.

'Of course, Miss Harrison, how right you are. There are always troubles in a bank.'

'There's just one last temple, my lord,' said Samuel Parker, 'but Old Mr Harrison didn't go there. The path was very steep and he was worried he might fall.'

'Then I think we'll give it a miss today.' Powerscourt's mind was racing round the ancient myths and pagan gods that populated the lake, Aeneas travelling to the underworld to meet his dead father, Hercules cleaning the Augean stables, Isis presiding over her shadowy kingdom in the realms below.

To their right now was another lake, slightly lower than the one they had crossed, with a waterfall running into it.

'No ancient temples down there,' said Powerscourt, pointing down to the lower stretch of water.

'No, there aren't, my lord. I think we've got quite enough up here.'

'Tell me, Mr Parker,' said Powerscourt as they approached the Parker cottage once again, 'where do you keep your keys? The ones you use to open all the temples.'

'Why, my lord, they live on a big hook on the back of the front door. That's where all the keys are, with a special ring for each one. You'd be surprised how many different bunches of keys you need to get around this place.'

'And how easy would it be . . .' Powerscourt turned for a last look at the circuit of the lake, two Pantheons, reflection and reality, sitting peacefully on their semicircle of grass. 'How easy would it be for somebody to come and borrow them without your knowing?'

Samuel Parker stopped in his tracks. The pony made restive movements, anxious to return to her stall.

'I've never thought about that.' He paused to give the pony a reassuring stroke. 'I suppose it would be easy, if the person knew I would be out most of the day. And Mabel's going deaf, so she is, though she'd never admit it. Been going deaf for most of the past two years she has. Doctor says there's nothing he can do.'

Powerscourt thanked Parker for their morning expedition. 'It has been most useful, Mr Parker. I have to return again in a couple of days or so. Maybe I could borrow your keys and go for another inspection of the lake.'

He's looking for something, Samuel Parker said to himself as Powerscourt strode off up the hill past the church. He thinks there may be some of Old Mr Harrison's writings hidden away round the lake. I hope he finds them, he went on, hanging up his keys on the front door. But then again, maybe it would be better if he didn't.

10

General Hugo Arbuthnot looked angrily at his watch. Five minutes past eleven, and the meeting due to start at eleven o'clock sharp. If there was one thing guaranteed to put the General in a bad mood it was unpunctuality, particularly when the planning of Her Majesty's Diamond Jubilee, now only two months away, was at stake.

William Taylor, the representative of the Metropolitan Police, was already in his place at the table in Arbuthnot's headquarters in the War Office. At least the police could be trusted to maintain order and discipline.

There was a sudden rushing up the corridor. Dominic Knox, the representative of the Irish Office, burst through the door and made his apologies, a couple of files held aloft in his left hand.

'My apologies, General,' he panted. 'My most sincere apologies. We have had fresh information from Dublin.'

As Knox took his seat and shuffled with his papers, Arbuthnot wondered if the man from the Irish Office was beginning to adopt the customs and habits of the people he was meant to superintend. Going native in Ireland, he felt, would involve precisely this kind of behaviour, a lack of punctuality, a general inattention to business.

'Mr Knox.' Arbuthnot's voice was cold. 'Is your information from Dublin important?'

'Important enough to warrant my being late for the meeting?' said Knox with a laugh. Privately he despised Arbuthnot for being stupid. 'Yes, I believe it is. I believe it gives us all, especially my friend Mr Taylor of the Metropolitan Police, a great deal to think about.'

'Perhaps you would like to enlighten us then?' Arbuthnot was tapping his pen up and down on the table to mask his irritation.

'Quite simply, it is this. Four days ago a group of the most determined and dangerous nationalists held a secret meeting outside Dublin. Their purpose was to resolve on the nature of the disturbances they wished to cause at the time of the Jubilee.'

'Criminal acts, criminal acts,' muttered the General.

'Criminal acts, indeed, General.' Knox nodded at his superior. 'These three men were choosing whether to perpetrate an outrage in Dublin or in London in honour of the occasion. There were arguments on both sides. A bomb is the favoured method of causing the disturbance. I understand that there was some measure of disagreement about the site. In the end, London was deemed too dangerous for the particular terrorist to make his escape. So they have decided to make their protest in Dublin.'

'Does that mean we can regard London as being safe from Irish subversives at the time of the parade?' William Taylor, the policeman, was quick to see the implications for the manpower and deployment of his forces.

General Arbuthnot looked hopeful, as if one cross was about to be removed from his shoulders. 'Surely,' he said, 'we would be safe in making that assumption. That is, if your information is to be believed.' He looked at Knox suspiciously.

Dominic Knox looked at them both carefully. 'I wish I could share your optimism,' he said finally. 'You see, these may be the three most important terrorist leaders in the country. But there could be more we know nothing of. And there is something else.' He paused and looked at the General. 'Forgive me for being cautious. But it is such a game of bluff and counterbluff where this intelligence is concerned. One of those at the meeting is on our payroll, and I can tell you he does not come cheap. Somehow the more you pay them, the more you want to believe what they say. But my point is this. The senior member of the trio, a schoolteacher called Byrne, is the leader of this group and easily the most intelligent. He may suspect the truth about our informer, that the man is in the pay of Dublin Castle.'

'You mean the information may be false?' said William Taylor, quick to see the implications of Knox's difficulties. They had come across similar problems with informants in the East End.

'Exactly,' said Knox.

'But what does this mean for our planning, gentlemen?' General Arbuthnot felt himself growing irritated once more. He remembered briefly that his doctor had warned him about it. 'What precautions are we to take?'

'It means,' said Knox ruefully, 'as so often in Ireland, that black is white and white is black, or orange is green and green is orange. It could be that Byrne may have apparently decided to do one thing. But in fact, he intends to do the opposite.'

'What do you mean? What is the plain truth behind your riddles, Mr Knox?' The General was growing more petulant by the minute.

'What it means, although I cannot be sure, is that this man Byrne wants us to believe that a bomb is going to be planted in Dublin. But in fact, he may intend to put a bomb in London. Or a gunman. That could be what he intended to do all along.'

'Let me try to sum up what we know so far.' Lord Francis Powerscourt had summoned a council of war to the house in Markham Square. Lady Lucy was sitting by the fire, glancing from time to time at the notes she had taken of her morning conversation with old Miss Harrison. Johnny Fitzgerald was inspecting a bottle of Sancerre with great care. William Burke, fresh from his day's labour in the City of London, was beginning the complicated process of lighting a large cigar. A grey Powerscourt cat, recently acquired at the request of the Powerscourt children, was asleep at her master's feet as he leant on the mantelpiece.

'About eighteen months ago Old Mr Harrison begins to act strangely. We know it was eighteen months ago because Samuel Parker said it was about the time the publicity began for this Jubilee. He starts to take his correspondence out of the house to read by the lake. He begins to send his letters abroad through the good offices of Parker rather than through the usual channels in the big house. And he begins to talk about conspiracies and secret societies to his sister. Lucy.'

Lady Lucy had been watching her husband's long slim fingers as they checked out the points he wished to make. She was remembering the first time she had noticed them, at a dinner party some five years before.

'Yes, Francis.' She came back to the present with a little private smile for him. 'Old Mr Harrison talked about secret societies, secret societies in Germany that might have links here. He talked about conspiracies, probably involving the bank. He was worried about the future of the bank. If you distil what Miss Harrison said while she had possession of her wits, that's about it.'

'Let me play devil's advocate with that lot,' said Johnny Fitzgerald, putting down his glass. 'She's potty. Her mind is wandering all over the place. You can't believe a word of any of it. He's potty too, the late Mr Harrison, gone paranoid in his old age, imagining conspiracies and secret societies all over the place. If they didn't have money the two old people would have been locked up in an asylum by now. All we have is the deranged fantasies of a couple of eighty-year-olds. None of it is worth bothering with.' He filled his glass with Sancerre and took a restorative gulp. 'I'm not saying I believe all that, but I'm sure that's what a lawyer or a judge would say about the old pair.'

'William, can you cast any light on this matter?' Powerscourt turned to his brother-in-law, who was enjoying the first fruits of his Havana.

'All I can say,' said William Burke, 'is that there was no evidence at all that Old Mr Harrison was losing his wits. None at all. I talked to a man in foreign loans only the other day who had had dealings with him two months or so before he died. He said he was sound as a bell, that his brain was as sharp as ever.'

'But couldn't he have seemed to be perfectly sound in the City,' Fitzgerald was being contrary again, 'but actually out of his mind the rest of the time? I've known people say that I'm not the same when I've taken a glass or six or seven as I am when I'm sober. Couldn't it be like that?'

'Surely only a doctor could answer that.' Lady Lucy now had the cat asleep on her lap. 'I'm sure Miss Harrison was sane when she talked about her brother's worries. It wasn't that she was inventing things, just that her memory had slipped its moorings, if you see what I mean.'

Powerscourt ran his hand along the marble fireplace. The touch took him back to the strange statues at Blackwater, maybe hiding or pointing the way to the secrets of Old Mr Harrison and his anxieties.

'Let's look at it this way,' he said. 'Let's suppose everything we know is true. Let's try to make some sense of it all.'

Here come those fingers again, Lady Lucy said to herself, watching once more as they marked out the points her husband wished to make.

'Eighteen months ago, something starts going wrong at the bank.

88

Old Mr Harrison is worried. Not long after that his eldest son is drowned in mysterious circumstances. That could be murder. Old Mr Harrison takes fright. He doesn't want to read his letters in the house in case he is being watched. He takes his correspondence down to the lake instead. Some news from Germany alarms him. He goes back to the cities and financial centres he knew as a boy. When he comes back he is even more worried. Whatever he knows, it is too much. He is murdered too. I was sure he was looking for something on his walks by the lake, I don't know why, but I felt it very strongly. And there's all this talk of conspiracy involving the bank. What kind of conspiracy could that be, William?'

Burke was looking very alarmed. 'Something has just struck me, Francis, something very grave indeed. Are the lives of Frederick and Charles Harrison safe, if what you say is true? Should we warn them that they may be in danger?'

'They may be in more danger from each other than they are from any outside parties,' said Johnny Fitzgerald.

'I have thought about that, William,' said Powerscourt. 'Heaven help me if I am wrong, but I do not feel we have enough to go on to issue such a warning. We could be laughed at as scaremongers.'

'I hope you're right.' Burke sounded doubtful. 'I'm not sure about conspiracies involving the bank either. I know our critics say that the whole of the City is a vast conspiracy devoted to the ruination of the widow and the orphan, but I don't think they are right.'

'What kind of conspiracies might banks get up to, William?' asked Johnny Fitzgerald cheerfully.

'Well, there have been all sorts of conspiracies this century.' William Burke liked talking about the City's history. It reminded him that he belonged to a glorious past. 'You could conspire to defraud your investors by issuing foreign loans to countries where there is no hope of the money ever being repaid. God knows we've seen enough of those. Then there are the phoney prospectuses for share issues with outlandish names like the Great African Gold and Diamond Mining Corporation. The speculators think they are going to get rich from mining but the only people who get rich are the ones who took their money in the first place. Railways in exotic locations – they're usually good for a quick fraud. For some reason perfectly respectable citizens are almost always willing to invest in railways. Do you know there was even a company floated many years back to recover the valuables left behind by the Children of Israel at the parting of the Red Sea? The promoters claimed they were going to use Malaysian divers to recover the gold and treasure left behind on the seabed.'

'Great God!' said Powerscourt, laughing at the absurdity. 'Did the investors get rich, William?'

'The investors got poor, Francis. Some of them lost all they had, I believe. But I cannot see Harrison's Bank becoming involved in any of these activities. Their reputation would have been destroyed overnight.'

'You don't think,' said Lady Lucy, venturing boldly into this male world, 'that the conspiracy was a conspiracy to kill members of Harrison's Bank, do you? That way Young Mr Harrison and Old Mr Harrison were both killed as part of this conspiracy. That's what Old Mr Harrison was worried about.'

'You could be right,' said her husband. 'But where do the secret societies come in? Were members of the secret society doing the killing?'

'Surely you could say,' Fitzgerald was gazing sadly at an empty bottle, 'that the dismemberment of the corpse could have been part of some secret society ritual, some private kind of initiation rite?'

'I don't recall seeing reports that the Elbe and the Rhine are occasionally blocked to traffic owing to the prevalence of headless corpses,' said Powerscourt. 'Even the Lorelei weren't up to that.'

The Powerscourt cat had woken up and padded hopefully towards William Burke and his cigar smoke.

'Good Lord, Francis. Does this animal like cigars? She must be very advanced.' Burke looked at his new friend with astonishment.

'I'm afraid she does, William.' Lady Lucy smiled at her brother-in-law. 'But her favourite place in the house is the cupboard where all the children's clothes are kept. We're going to have to make it catproof.'

Powerscourt had abandoned his fireplace and was walking restlessly up and down the room, his mind far away.

'This is what I think we should do. I have to say I am not very sure of any of it. Johnny, I think you should go to Berlin. Didn't the young Harrison go to university there, William?'

'He did indeed,' said Burke, 'the Friedrich Wilhelm University, the city's finest, they say.'

'You want me to find out about secret societies, I presume, Francis?' Johnny Fitzgerald was looking very serious now.

'How is your German, Johnny?' asked Powerscourt.

'Well, I was once more or less fluent in German. I expect it'll come back. But I'm not going to tell them that,' his friend replied with a grin.

'They drink an awful lot of beer and schnapps and things over there,' said Lady Lucy with a smile. 'Do you think you'll be able to cope?'

'I expect I'll manage,' said Fitzgerald 'Maybe I need to get into practice, though, Lady Lucy. Would you be having any more of this Sancerre? All in the line of duty now, you understand.'

Powerscourt turned to the smoke-wreathed figure of William Burke.

'William, can I ask you to make more detailed inquiries about Harrison's Bank? The nature of their business, the shape of their finances, anything that could give us a clue as to what the conspiracy might be. Is there any chance that you could smuggle a man inside, a clerk or somebody like that? Somebody who could provide real inside information?'

'It would be risky, I think.' Burke inspected his cigar. 'They are very tight, these German houses. They employ their own fellow countrymen whenever they can. And if it were found out, my own reputation would be floating in the river too.'

'For myself,' said Powerscourt, 'I am going to continue my investigations into the old man's activities at Blackwater. I cannot get that lake and those statues out of my head. Somewhere, somehow, I am certain the old man hid some of his papers down there. But there are so many clues, Hercules, Aeneas, river gods, Diana, Isis, the whole place is like a gigantic puzzle. I am going to begin in the National Gallery.'

'Why the National Gallery?' asked Lady Lucy, remembering a previous visit there with her husband and hoping she might accompany him this time.

'It's the layout of those temples. I'm sure the man who built the mythical garden had been looking at paintings by Poussin, or Claude, maybe even both. Something in the paintings may give us a clue.'

'Francis.' Johnny Fitzgerald was looking very sombre. 'I shall set out for Berlin straight away. I may have to be there for some time. And I make you a prediction.' He looked at all three of them in turn as though he had second sight rather than a second bottle. 'I bet you that by the time I come back, there will be one fewer Harrison in this world. Another one will have gone to meet his maker in mysterious circumstances. But I'm not sure I could tell which one.'

Richard Martin was waiting for Sophie Williams in the coffee shop opposite Liverpool Street station. It was half-past five in the afternoon and the place would be closing soon. Outside the fog was getting thicker. It was ebb tide in the City of London. The army of occupation that had marched in that morning, as it did every morning, was in retreat now, slightly more cheerful as the foot-soldiers hurried towards the trains and the buses that would take them home.

Richard loved the coffee shops. He loved their history, the fact that so many of the great institutions of finance had their origins in places like this, the Jonathan's and Garroway's of a hundred and fifty years before that had given birth to Lloyd's and the Royal Exchange and the Stock Exchange itself. Coffee from the East Indies had lubricated, oiled, stimulated the growth of the City of London.

A gust of wind and slivers of fog rushed through the door, quickly followed by Sophie.

'Richard, oh Richard, I am so sorry I'm late.'

Richard Martin would have waited for the rest of his life for Sophie. In his darker moments he feared he might have to.

'Don't worry, Sophie, let me get you some coffee. You look cold.'

'I'm angry rather than cold,' she said, peeling off her gloves and laying them on the table. 'I've had that meeting with the head-mistress.'

'And what did she say?'

Sophie paused while a black-coated waiter deposited a cup of coffee beside her. Richard had made his one cup last for forty-five minutes and didn't intend to order any more if he could help it.

'She said . . .' Sophie looked close to tears. 'She said there had been complaints about me.' She paused and looked for her hand-kerchief.

'Hold on, Sophie, don't get upset.' Richard wondered if he should hold her hand or put an arm round her shoulder. Maybe the place was too public for that. 'What sort of complaints? Who was complaining? Surely they weren't complaining about your teaching? Everybody knows you're a fantastic teacher. The whole area knows that.'

Sophie managed a weak smile. 'The complaints weren't about my teaching. She said – Mrs White, that is – she said there had been complaints about my work for the women's movement.'

Sophie was looking defiant now.

'And what did you say?' asked Richard, indignant on Sophie's behalf. 'Surely it's none of her business what you do outside school hours?'

'She said there had been complaints from two sets of parents. She wouldn't tell me who they were. They want me removed from my job, these parents. They said they didn't want their children being taught these ludicrous notions.'

'What did you say to that, Sophie?' Richard was looking very carefully at her hands. He thought they looked very soft.

'I said I thought it was absurd,' said Sophie. 'I said I had never, never, referred to my beliefs in my teaching. Never. That wouldn't be right. If all teachers were allowed to indoctrinate their pupils with their own beliefs, it would be terrible. I'm going to find out who these parents are, mind you. I think I shall ask the children.'

'You can't do that.'

'Why not? You can't tell me what to do in my own school.' Sophie was indignant, her eyes flashing. 'What do you know about it?'

'I don't know about your school at all, Sophie. Only what you tell me.' In his heart Richard felt he knew a great deal about the school. 'But if you ask the children, however you do it, they'll all go back home and tell their parents. More of them may get involved. The whole business could get more difficult than it already is.'

Sophie looked at him. She thought that Richard was maybe wiser than he looked.

'More important, Sophie,' the young man went on, 'what did she say she was going to do about it?'

'She said that she was going to listen to what I had to say and then she was going to consider it. Mrs White doesn't like taking decisions in a hurry.'

'But your job is safe in the meantime? There's no question about that?' asked Richard.

'Yes, it is. I suppose that's good news.'

'I tell you what I think she'll do, Sophie. She'll talk again to these parents and try to calm them down. She'll make it clear to them that the choice of staff in the school must rest with her and not with

93

the parents. Otherwise it would be chaos. She'll probably say that she has made you promise that you won't preach the suffragist cause in the classroom. She'll probably make you promise that all over again. Then it'll all be over.'

Sophie looked at him carefully. Then she laughed.

'Richard,' she said, 'I thought you spent your whole time in the bank adding things up and putting them in ledgers. But they seem to be teaching you a bit of wisdom as well!'

'All kinds of human affairs pass through the banks, Sophie.' Richard felt older than his twenty-two years. 'Births, marriages, deaths, and most of the complicated bits in between.'

'And what has been happening in your bank, Richard?' Sophie seemed happier now. 'Is everybody still alive? No more bodies floating in the Thames?'

'We're still alive, but only just.' Richard Martin looked worried. 'Nobody's looking for any new business. The place is just ticking over. But there are some very strange things happening. I think I have been as worried about them as I have about your interview with the headmistress.'

'Were you worried about me?' said Sophie with a smile.

'Of course I was. I don't think I can say anything about what's going on in Harrison's Bank just yet. We're meant to be very discreet, we bankers.'

For the past ten minutes the waiter had been dusting the neighbouring tables, pulling down the blinds, sweeping the floor.

'I think they want us to go, Sophie. I'll see you home.'

'Are you very worried about what's going on in the bank?' asked Sophie, drawn irresistibly towards a secret.

'I am, yes,' said Richard, helping her into her coat, his hands lingering fractionally longer around her shoulders than they needed to. 'But I'll just have to wait and see what happens.'

So they joined the hurrying throng on its way home through the fog, home to loved ones, home to families, home to rest before another day in the Great City. Sophie was feeling rather proud of her Richard for being so sensible. Richard was watching the swing of her hips. He was wondering if now, with the light so bad and so many people about, if now might be the moment to hold her hand. Just in case she got lost, he said to himself.

The gravestone was granite. On top of it perched two black eagles, carved in marble to survey the city of Berlin. The epitaph was simple.

Here lies Heinrich von Treitschke. For forty years he served in the University of Berlin, instructing his students in the lessons of the past, and teaching that the history of his people points the way toward a more glorious future. In life he was revered. In death he will not be forgotten. Here lies a great German.

Even nine months after his death the flowers were piled high on top of the grave. A local florist, noting the appeal of this particular tomb, had opened an extra stall just inside the cemetery.

Both men standing there had attended the funeral, as the old historian was laid to rest with full military honours, the route from the church to his final resting place lined with hussars and guards, the slow beat of the drum punctuating his last journey.

'Even now, Karl, the people still flock to pay tribute to his memory.' Manfred von Munster, chief recruiter for the secret society set up to honour Treitschke's teachings, held his hat in his hands.

'They say in the banks,' said Karl Schmidt, one of von Munster's most recent recruits, 'that they are going to name a street or a square after him.'

'That would be splendid, a fitting memorial. But come, I have news for you today from the society.' Von Munster spoke reverently about the society. 'They are very pleased with your work,' he went on. 'The Potsdamer Bank are very pleased indeed.'

'I am delighted to hear it,' said Karl.

'But now,' said von Munster, gazing round the cemetery to make sure they were not observed, 'is the time for you to take the next step. You must leave the Potsdamer Bank very soon.'

'Leave?' said the young man anxiously. 'I thought you said they were pleased with my work.'

'Oh, they are.' Von Munster rubbed his hands together. 'They're so pleased that they are more than willing to take you back once you have accomplished your mission.'

'Is this the journey to England of which you spoke before?'

'It is,' said von Munster firmly. 'You are to travel to London and make your way to Harrison's Bank in the City of London. A position has been reserved for you there.'

'And what must I do when I reach London?' asked Karl,

delighted that his services were required at last. He had begun to wonder if the secret society was just a talking shop.

'You must wait until you get there. You will receive your instructions in London. That is all I am allowed to tell you at present.'

As they made their way past the long rows of graves, some marked with the Iron Cross denoting military service, Karl had one last question to ask.

'Manfred, can you answer this question for me?' Von Munster smiled. 'I will try as best I can.'

'You said I was doing well in the Potsdamer Bank, and that they will have me back once this mission is over. How do you know all that? Do you have members of the society inside the Potsdamer Bank who keep you informed?'

Von Munster put his arm around the young man's shoulder.

'Karl, I should not be telling you this. But, yes, we do have members in the Potsdamer Bank. We are increasing our membership. Soon we will have members in all the most important institutions in Germany.'

11

Powerscourt was thinking about family feuds as the early train carried him south-west to Cornwall for his rendezvous with Leopold Harrison, senior partner in Harrison's Private Bank, nephew to the man found floating by London Bridge. He knew that William Burke had said there were no rumours of a family feud in the splitting of Harrison's Bank, but he was still curious. Could a feud, which led to the bank dividing into two, be responsible for the Curse on the House of Harrison? Professionally, Powerscourt quite liked family feuds, they could last so long that perfectly unintelligible crimes could be explained by terrible internal wars a generation or two before.

The Greeks had been pretty good at family feuds, he reflected, until the Italians came along and took the prize. As his train rolled through the innocent Hampshire countryside he remembered the curse of the house of Atreus, the infamous feast laid on in Mycenae by Atreus for his brother Thyestes. Cubes of white meat bubble in a large bronze cauldron. Atreus offers one or two specially tasty morsels to Thyestes. Thyestes eats them. At the end of the banquet Atreus' servant brings in a plate crammed with human hands and feet. Only then does Thyestes realize that he has been eating the flesh of his own children. Revenge, hatred, murder, rape follow through the family for generations. Powerscourt had tried to count how many had perished from this one feud in his schooldays. He had given up when he reached seventeen. However ferocious a Harrison feud might have been he didn't think it could be as bad as that, even if headless corpses with their hands cut off could have come straight out of Aeschylus.

Cawsand was one of a pair of pretty villages four or five miles by sea from Plymouth but a long way round by land. The sea curved in to form one little bay, Kingsand, swung out again into a rocky promontory, then turned back into the other little bay of Cawsand. Powerscourt's cab deposited him in the small main square of Cawsand. The public house, the Smugglers, bore witness to the past of the inhabitants. The Harrison house was called Trehannoc, just up the twisting street that led from the square and the tiny beach. The houses were small and pretty, late eighteenth century or early in this one, Powerscourt thought, looking with admiration at the sea views they must command. He wondered if prize money from the long sea war against Napoleon had paid for them. Prize money, the lubricant of greed added to the fires of patriotism, had made the Royal Navy a terrifying force; captured privateers, caught trying to beat the blockade of France with sugar from the West Indies or coffee from Brazil, French men of war won in battle and sold off to His Majesty's Treasury, could have paid for these little houses. Lieutenants, climbing slowly through the numbers from fourth to first, helped on their way by the death toll in battle, could have spent a comfortable retirement here, walking along the coastal paths, inspecting the ships that passed by on their way in and out of Plymouth. Rich captains and admirals, he remembered, who took the lion's share of the spoils, would not have settled here. They bought their way into the country gentry with substantial estates in Devon and Hampshire.

Trehannoc was not a very handsome house. A black door, a nondescript window looked over the winding street. Leopold Harrison opened the door. He was a short tubby man in his late forties or early fifties.

'You must be Powerscourt. Come in, please.'

He was wearing a suit that looked as though it came from one of London's finest tailors and should have been walking along Lombard Street or Piccadilly rather than the twisting lanes of Cornwall. His shoes gleamed. His hair was immaculate.

Harrison brought Powerscourt along a passageway, past a dining room where he spotted a fine Regency dining table and chairs, into a drawing room that looked out over the sea. Then Powerscourt understood. The house was built back to front. Trehannoc stood at the apex of the promontory that ran between the twin villages. The front door was really the entrance on the little slipway on the rocks below. When you sat down in the corner of the room, all you could see was the ocean. In winter, Powerscourt realized, the spray from the storms must come right up to the top of the windows, encrusting them with salt.

Powerscourt could sense the tubby little man recoiling from him as they sat in the twin leather armchairs, looking out towards the grey waters where the Spanish Armada had passed by long ago. Maybe he's wearing that suit as a defence.

'Lord Powerscourt,' Harrison spoke in clipped tones, 'the family have insisted that I should see you. How can I be of assistance?'

Powerscourt thought he should begin with expressions of sympathy. Then he could spring his surprise.

'Naturally, Mr Harrison, I am very sorry about the terrible death of your uncle. I have been asked to investigate the matter.'

'The death has nothing to do with me,' said Harrison quickly, distancing himself from his family. 'I was here in Cornwall at the time.'

'Of course,' said Powerscourt, smiling sympathetically. 'Tell me about the family feud.'

There was a silence. Leopold Harrison turned rather red. His paunch seemed to expand with indignation. A little way out to sea, beyond the window, Powerscourt spotted a triumphant cormorant rise to the surface, a small fish wriggling in its beak.

'It was a very long time ago. It wasn't really a feud. That's all I wish to say.' Leopold Harrison sounded guilty.

'Most family feuds go back a long way,' Powerscourt said gently, wondering if he was about to be thrown out into the street. 'But they may still be relevant, even today.'

He waited. Harrison had a superb collection of paintings of sea battles on his walls, Powerscourt noticed, guns blazing, rigging falling into the sea, ships blown up in terrible explosions of red and black as their magazines took a direct hit. In happier times he could have spent a long time looking at them.

'It was a very long time ago. I repeat, that's all I wish to say.'

Powerscourt wondered if fear would work on Leopold Harrison. 'I have to tell you, Mr Harrison, that so far there has been little progress in this inquiry. The murderer or murderers may strike again. They might strike anywhere. Cornwall is not so very far away these days.'

The cormorant rose to the surface again. This time it had caught nothing.

'I do not see how those matters can have any bearing on the terrible killing,' said Harrison. 'I will tell you one thing and one thing only.'

He thinks I will go away with one small crumb of information, Powerscourt said to himself. He wondered what his morsel would be.

'It had to do with . . .' Harrison paused. He was finding this very difficult. 'It had to do with a woman,' he said finally. He said the word as though it were something terrible like bankruptcy or mental illness. He was panting slightly as if the word woman made him out of breath.

'Who was the woman?' Powerscourt asked very quietly, wondering if a latterday Medea or Clytemnestra was about to land in Cawsand Bay.

'I cannot say. I have promised not to say. Please.'

Please leave me alone, he's asking to be left in peace, Powerscourt said to himself. I'll just try one more question and then I'll stop. 'Did the events surrounding this woman take place here, or in Frankfurt?'

'Both,' said the little man bleakly, as if he had just broken all the promises he had ever made.

'Thank you for that, Mr Harrison. Could you tell me if the feud had anything to with the two separate branches of the bank being formed?'

There was another pause. A small sailing boat drifted past the windows. The sea murmured on against the rocks.

'It did and it didn't,' said Harrison. 'Please, please don't ask me any more about that feud. It makes me so upset. Promise me that,' he said weakly, 'and I'll tell you anything about the bank.'

Powerscourt wondered briefly if he could now have access to the financial secrets of the great of England, the debts of Cabinet Ministers, the real wealth of the new millionaires, the payments made by the aristocrats to their mistresses in Biarritz or Paris. He desisted.

'All I need to know is why there are two separate parts of the bank. Leaving aside the feud, of course.'

Leopold Harrison was looking happier now. 'It's very simple, really, Lord Powerscourt. It all depends on how you want to make your money.'

Powerscourt looked confused. The little man's cheeks were returning to their normal colour. The hands were stroking his stomach in a satisfied fashion, as if he had just eaten a very good dinner.

'How is that?' said Powerscourt.

'I like money. I am devoted to it.' Powerscourt thought he could hear greed in Leopold Harrison's voice. 'This house here may not seem very much, but I have a house in Chester Square. I have a villa in the hills just north of Nice near Grasse. Do you know Grasse, Lord Powerscourt?'

100

'Fragonard's birthplace?' asked Powerscourt. He couldn't see Leopold Harrison on a swing, surrounded by the tributes of love and the foliage of desire.

'Fragonard. Exactly,' said Harrison. 'I have a couple of them in the hall of my villa. But let me return to money and banking. There are two kinds of banking at present, Lord Powerscourt. Harrison's City, the parent firm of my own, deals in financial instruments. They trade in bills of exchange. They launch risky foreign loans. They lend money to governments. All of this is complicated and very hazardous. You could be wiped out in a moment. Barings were very nearly wiped out seven years ago. It took the City of London years to recover.'

'So what do you do?' asked Powerscourt.

'We lend people money,' said Harrison happily. 'We take in money from one lot of people as deposits. We pay them as little interest as we can. Then we lend it out to other people. We charge them as much interest as we can get away with. That's all.'

'But surely,' said Powerscourt, 'the people you lend it to could go broke or refuse to repay it, just like those foreign governments sometimes do?'

Leopold Harrison laughed. He patted Powerscourt on the shoulder like an uncle with a favourite nephew.

'Not so, Lord Powerscourt. Security, that's the key, security. Let me put it very simply. Suppose you want to borrow ten thousand pounds from me. Fine, I say. But I must have some security for a loan. You have a house somewhere worth ten thousand pounds? You do? Excellent. Just let me have the deeds of ownership, a mere formality you understand, and then you can have the loan. Would you like the money all at once?'

'What happens then if I don't pay you back?'

Harrison roared with laughter. 'Simple. We sell your house. We get the ten thousand pounds back. We have had such interest as you may have paid, and the arrangement fee for giving you the loan in the first place. You may lose, Lord Powerscourt. We cannot. It's all so simple!'

The cormorant was back in the swell beyond the windows. It seemed to be choking on a fish that looked too big to swallow. The cormorant was doing its best.

'Do you find it hard, selling off your customers' assets?' Powerscourt was sure he knew the answer.

'No, I do not.' Harrison laughed again. 'It is your choice as the customer, not mine. You want the money, you pay the price. And most of our customers repay their loans in the normal way, without anything having to be sold at all.'

Leopold Harrison sounded as though he preferred the less prudent ones.

Powerscourt thought he would try one last parting shot. He smiled happily at the little man.

'Just one question about the woman in the feud. Is she still alive?'

The atmosphere changed very suddenly. Powerscourt felt cold even though the sun had come out and Cawsand Bay was bathed in sunlight.

'She is alive,' Harrison snarled. 'I have had enough of your questions. Will you please leave now.'

Harrison rose to his feet and showed Powerscourt the door. As he walked through the narrow streets of the village he wished he had been able to ask one more question. Where was she, this cause of the Harrison feud? Was she in Germany? Was she in England? Was she – he looked back incredulously at the house he had just left – was she in Cawsand, hiding on the upper floors?

William Burke sat alone at the head of the great table in the boardroom of his bank in Bishopsgate. Another decision had been taken. He and the four colleagues who had just departed had decided to buy another small bank to increase the spread of their own branches. His bank, he sometimes thought, was like a spider or a squid, tentacles reaching out from the City of London to wrap themselves over other enterprises right across London and the Home Counties.

William Burke often thanked his God that he belonged to a joint stock bank, owned and run on behalf of its shareholders. The beauty of the joint stock bank, in his view, was that it enjoyed limited liability, unlike the private bankers where the partners were personally liable for any losses. The old names of the City, the Couttses, the Hoares, the Adams, might sneer at the joint stock bankers for living on their deposits rather than on their wits. But if a private bank failed, the partners faced financial annihilation – houses, pictures, racehorses, land would all have to be sold. Cautious, conservative, even boring his bank might be, but its owners could never meet such a fate.

And the joint stock banks had a further advantage in his view. All private banks were plagued by the problem of the succession. It was rather like the monarchy, he felt. A good and prudent heir could ensure the stability of throne or bank. A bad one, a spendthrift or a fool could bring the whole institution to its knees.

As he waited for his next appointment, Burke glanced round the great boardroom. It was as familiar to him now as his own drawing room at home. The long mahogany table was polished daily till it was almost a mirror in which he could observe the expressions of his colleagues. The walls were lined with pictures of banks and bankers, counting houses and the Bank of England. Lorenzo de Medici stared down on his successors, sandwiched between a view of the opening of the Victoria Dock and a reproduction Canaletto of the Thames by Somerset House. Lorenzo had met the same fate in the end as so many of his successors, imprudent lending with insufficient security, the crime of all crimes in Burke's private register of banking sins.

There was a knock at the door.

'Come in, come in,' Burke called cheerfully.

'Mr Clarke, Mr Burke.'

The head porter closed the doors carefully behind him. His footsteps faded away in the marble hall outside.

Burke had remembered Powerscourt suggesting the possibility of his infiltrating somebody into Harrison's Bank. That he had refused to do in case his own position was compromised. Burke had even considered buying Harrison's Bank outright but he felt it might bring down his own. So he had asked the senior clerk to find him the brightest, most charming young man his bank employed in the City. Advancing towards him with a nervous smile was one James Clarke, highly recommended by all who knew him.

'Clarke,' said Burke, rising to his feet, 'come and sit down. You can be a director for fifteen minutes!' He waved at the well-padded seat beside him. 'Mr Bagshaw, our senior clerk, tells me you have been with us for five years.'

'That's right, sir.' James Clarke was a tall slim young man, clean shaven, with a mop of brown curly hair. He had no idea why he had been summoned to the presence, if not of God, then at least one of his senior partners.

'And how do you find us? Do you think you will enjoy the business of banking?'

Burke was resolved to take the mettle of the young man for himself rather than rely on the word of his subordinates, however reliable.

'I do enjoy it, sir,' James Clarke said, 'I've always liked figures and arithmetic, ever since I was a little boy.'

Burke smiled at the young man with his best uncle's smile, friendly but a little firm. 'And what do you think the most important qualities are for a banker? Not necessarily in one of your age, but a mature banker, a banker of consequence.'

The young man didn't know it, but on this answer depended the fate of the interview. James Clarke thought of the books he had read, the sections on interest rates, on foreign lending, on the theory and practice of bookkeeping. He didn't think the answer lay in their lifeless prose.

'Well, sir,' he looked thoughtfully at his superior, 'I don't think it has to do with figures, the record keeping and all those things. I mean,' he hurried forward, aware that he might have been seen to deny much of his own work in the bank, 'those things are important but I think it has more to do with judgement. Especially judgement about people so you don't put the bank's money in the wrong place. And discretion, so that people will trust you. And remembering that the money you deal with is not your own.'

Burke clapped him hard on the shoulder. 'Capital, Clarke, capital! I couldn't have put it better myself! Now then, I want to ask you to do something for me. I have to tell you that it does not have directly to do with our bank. It is more of a private matter, but it is of the greatest importance. Before I tell you what it is, I must ask you to promise not to tell a single soul, not even your own family, about it.'

James Clarke wondered what on earth was going on. Had the old man been losing money on the side? Had he lost his fortune on the Exchange?

Burke sensed the unease coming from the young man. 'Believe me,' he said, 'it is nothing illegal I would have you do. It may seem perfectly innocent at this stage. Nothing may ever come of it. But I regard it as very important.'

The young man smiled. This could be rather a lark, a private adventure all of his own.

'Of course I will help, sir. And I promise I won't tell a single soul. What would you like me to do?'

William Burke rose from his chair and walked quickly to the great window above the street. Below him the hawkers and the telegraph boys, the messengers and the carriages continued the daily dance of the toiling City.

'I want you to make friends with somebody of your own age in Harrison's Bank. Somebody in the same position. You know Harrison's Bank, of course?'

The young man nodded. Old Mr Harrison's death, the cynics said,

104

had done what no advertising campaign or publicity spree in the newspapers could have ever achieved. It had made Harrison's Bank universally known down to the last costermonger in the City of London.

'Yes, I know the bank, sir. I don't know anybody who works there. But I am sure I could manage it. Is that all you want me to do? Just to make a friend of someone who works there?'

'It is for the present,' Burke was going to take things step by step, 'but when you have got to know this young man, could you let me know at once? At once, I say. It is a matter of great importance.'

On his journey back to London Powerscourt was wondering about the Harrison feud. Did that hold the key to the mystery?

As his train drew out of Exeter St David's station, he thought about going away with Lucy when this case was finished. Two or three times a year he took Lucy on a Journey into the Unknown, as he called them. He would tell her six weeks or more in advance so she could make her plans. But he never told her where they were going. Lady Lucy would use a whole variety of ruses to discover their destination before they departed. 'Hot or cold, Francis?' was the most obvious one to which he always gave some sort of an answer in case their holiday was ruined by Lucy having the wrong clothes. 'Should I be reading Balzac or Dante, do you think, Francis?' 'Will we be needing any art history books for the journey?' 'I just happen to be going to the milliner's today, Francis. What sort of hat would be appropriate for the trip?' And Powerscourt would smile his most enigmatic smile and leave the room.

Eighteen months before, they had gone to Florence. Powerscourt had threatened to blindfold her at the railway stations on the way so she could not read what might be their final destination. He remembered taking her to the cathedral and telling her about the murder.

'Honestly, Francis,' she had laughed at him, 'do you have to bring your occupation away with you on holiday? Could you have solved the murder easily?'

He had led her up to the front of Florence's cathedral, the inside bigger than a football pitch. 'Imagine it, Lucy,' he whispered, taking her arm and holding her tight. 'It is Sunday, 26th April 1478. It is High Mass, the most sacred point of the week. Up there near the altar are the Archbishop and the priests. The smell of the incense is very thick. The candles are gleaming on the altar. All around us are the

Florentines. Imagine they have walked out of the frescoes in the churches of the city and make up the worshippers today, the bent old men, the sober bankers, the dashing young blades, the pious wives. There was trouble brewing in the city, Lucy.'

Bankers, money and murder, he said to himself, the same lethal cocktail that I am investigating today. He told her how the Medici had done something almost unheard of; they had refused the Pope a loan, perhaps because he owed them so much already. A rival Florentine family, the Pazzi, had lent the Pontiff what he wanted. The Pazzi were trying to replace the Medici as the most powerful family in Florence.

'Nobody knows exactly when the murderers struck. Sometimes they killed people in churches when they bent their heads in prayer, giving a better target for the sword or the knife. On this Sunday some say the attack was triggered by the ringing of the Sanctus bell, others that it was during the Agnus Dei, others again that it was the words *Ite missa est*. The conspirators stabbed Lorenzo de Medici's brother Giuliano to death. They tried to make a start on Lorenzo but he jumped over the wooden rail into the choir and made his escape.'

'How long did it take Francesco di Powerscorto to find the assassins?' said Lady Lucy, gazing up at her husband.

'I don't think Francesco was ever summoned to investigate.' Powerscourt smiled. 'By the next day the Pazzi conspirators were hanging from the windows of the Palazzo Vecchio in the main square down the street. They say the crowds were very taken by the red stockings of Archbishop Salviati kicking in the air before he passed on.'

Lady Lucy shuddered. He remembered the two of them drinking coffee on the terrace of their hotel as evening turned into night over Florence. In front of them the muddy waters of the Arno gurgled noisily on their tortuous route to the sea. On the far side the Palazzo Pitti loomed large against the dark sky and San Miniato del Monte sat perfectly still, white and green and ghostly, on its hilltop above the city. Behind, not immediately visible from where they sat, the domes of San Lorenzo and the cathedral kept guard over the treasures beneath them.

Lady Lucy was talking about the two Davids they had seen on their visit.

'I don't think there is any comparison, Francis, I really don't. One is black and one is white – well, it was white when it was created. Donatello's is life-size in its black marble, Michelangelo's is huge, a Colossus in marble.

'Did you look closely at the Donatello, Francis, or were you still thinking about assassins? It was so beautiful, so graceful, so much a tribute to the glory of the male form. If you had leant forward to touch the skin – I almost wanted to stroke it – I'm sure it would have felt warm. Maybe the boy David would have smiled. I'm sure he would have liked people stroking him. And the face, it's almost the face of a girl, it's so beautiful.'

'Do I take it, Lucy,' said Powerscourt, looking solemnly into those blue eyes, 'that you prefer it to the Michelangelo?'

'I do, I do.' Lady Lucy was passionate. 'Of course the Michelangelo is impressive, it's so big. But it's much more about politics than about male beauty, I'm sure. It was commissioned by the city fathers to give glory to their little state. So Michelangelo made them this enormous thing, symbolizing the victory of Republican Florence over her latest batch of enemies, whoever they were at the time. Michelangelo's David is about the victory of Republican virtue over tyranny. Donatello's is about the victory of beauty over ugliness, youth over age – that slain Goliath looks about twenty years older, down at the bottom of the statue – maybe even of art over time. Did Donatello think that people would come to look at what he had done four hundred and fifty years later? I don't know, I just think he wanted to create the most exquisite young man in the world. Beauty is Truth, Truth Beauty, four centuries before Keats.'

She stopped. A wandering owl hooted over the rooftops of Florence. The bridges over the river looked mysterious in the dark.

'But come, Francis,' said Lucy, rising quickly from her seat. 'I want to show you something about the Michelangelo. Come along.'

She took them to the Piazza del Duomo, Brunelleschi's dome towering above them, the green marble of the exterior cold to the touch.

'Right, Francis. It's a summer evening in May, 1504 I think. From the workshops of the cathedral here a group of men are pulling something out on to the street. There are about forty of them. Waiting for the something is a very strange contraption indeed, a group of greased beams, with heavy ropes attached to them. It must have been nearly dark when they pulled Michelangelo's David out of the workshops and hauled it upright and secured it to the beams. Most of the statue was encased in a wooden frame. Only the head was visible at the top.

'The next morning, I think, they began to pull it on its final journey. Imagine the excitement, Francis. Most of the children in Florence must have come to stare at the Giant in a wooden frame. Maybe it gave them nightmares. The old people who lived round about must have looked out of their windows watching, fascinated, as the statue inched its way forward down the street. The forty men must have been like galley slaves, all pulling together on the cry of the foreman. Maybe Michelangelo himself was there, watching carefully in case it fell over. Maybe he helped to pull it, we don't know. Strangers to Florence must have been amazed – did these mad people pull huge objects on greased beams inch by painful inch around their city every day?'

Lady Lucy paused. Then she shuffled slowly forward.

'Shuffle, Francis, shuffle. Imagine you're one of the galley slaves, your back aching, your heart despondent as you realize how slow progress is. By the end of the first day they had come about fifty yards down the Via de Calzaioli to the junction with the Via del Tosinghi here. There are about another two hundred and fifty yards to go. I imagine the forty workers must have enjoyed their glass of Chianti or whatever it was at the end of the day. Keep shuffling, Francis.'

Lady Lucy shuffled her way down the street very slowly, holding firmly on to her husband's arm.

'We don't know if the Giant shook or nearly fell over on its journey. Imagine Michelangelo at that moment. Here is his masterpiece – and he is very sure it is a masterpiece – en route to its final resting place. The beams hit a rock perhaps. The men pull the wrong way. The Giant topples inside its wooden frame. It is about to disappear from history for ever, smashed into hundreds of pieces of marble on the hard streets of Florence. It would have broken his heart. He might never have been the same again.'

'But it didn't fall, Lucy, did it?' Powerscourt had shuffled his way to the edge of the Piazza della Signoria.

'No, it didn't.' Lady Lucy laughed. 'It took four days, imagine the four days of pulling that huge weight for the galley slaves, to reach here. And there it is. Or rather its replica is.'

A recent copy of Michelangelo's David looked down on them proudly from its great height. There was nobody left in the square. Behind the Neptune Fountain other statues kept a night watch over the Piazza.

Powerscourt held Lady Lucy very tight.

'Please may I kiss you just here?' he asked very quietly. 'It's always appealed to me. It's the spot where they burnt Savonarola at the stake.'

'Francis, you are quite incorrigible. I despair of you, I really do.'

Lady Lucy raised her face and the moon came out behind Brunelleschi's dome.

Powerscourt had an enjoyable but fruitless visit to the National Gallery. The Claudes and the Poussins had been elegant, they had been charming, they had been enigmatic. But although he had seen the shapes of most of the buildings at Blackwater in their canvases, an Aeneas at Delos here, a Landscape with the marriage of Isaac and Rebeccah there, he was no further forward. Maybe I'll have to read the whole of the bloody *Aeneid*, he said to himself as he returned to Markham Square.

He found Lady Lucy, weeping in the drawing room as though her heart would break.

'Lucy, Lucy, my love.' He took her in his arms and held her tight. 'What's the matter, my love? Are the children all right? They're not ill, are they?'

Lady Lucy shook her head through her tears. 'They're fine, Francis. They're absolutely fine.' She wept on.

'Has somebody died, Lucy? Someone in your family?'

'No, Francis, it's not that.'

Powerscourt waited for the tears to cease. He caressed her hair and whispered into her ear that he loved her very much.

She began to calm down. She dried her eyes and sat down on the sofa, tearstained eyes and cheeks gazing up at Powerscourt.

'It's just that we're so lucky, Francis. We've got money, we've got nice houses, we've got lovely healthy children.'

Powerscourt held her hand. He waited. Lady Lucy tried to straighten her hair.

'It's this family, Francis. They're having such a terrible time. Sorry, I'm not making myself very clear.' She dabbed at her eyes again. Powerscourt waited.

'You know our church organizes visits to the poor in Fulham and Hammersmith, just a couple of miles away from here?'

Powerscourt nodded.

'You know there are all these terrible books nowadays about the condition of the poor and the labouring classes, Francis. Well, I have tried to read them. My mind goes blank with all those statistics, those huge numbers rolling out across the pages. I keep telling myself I should finish them but I can't. But I have been going to see one particular family, Francis. I do what I can for them, clothes, food, money.'

Lady Lucy stopped as if her mind had left Chelsea and gone back to some tenement in Fulham.

'They're called Farrell, Francis. They have five children. The last one died in childbirth. Now the baby is ill, so very ill they think he is going to die too. He's got this terrible fever, little Peter, he's so small and so hot all the time, they can't get him cool at all.'

'Where do they live, Lucy?' asked Powerscourt quietly.

'Their flat is fine, Francis. It's at World's End in one of those blocks the charities have put up to house the respectable poor so they don't have to live in squalor. The other children are thin, terribly thin. I don't think the husband earns very much money. But think how dreadful it would be if little Peter died. It would break the mother's heart.'

Powerscourt knew she was thinking of Robert and Thomas and little Olivia, Robert at school, the two younger ones having their afternoon rest upstairs.

'You must go again tomorrow, Lucy, and bring them money for the doctor,' said Powerscourt.

'I must,' Lady Lucy replied, more cheerful now at the prospect of useful activity. 'I shall go tomorrow. You don't mind, Francis, do you?'

'Mind?' said her husband gently. 'The only thing I would mind, Lucy, after all you've told me, is if you didn't go tomorrow.'

Part Two

Ordeal by Fire

12

Lord Francis Powerscourt was tossing in his bed in Markham Square. Beside him Lady Lucy slept peacefully, one arm thrown lightly across her husband's shoulder. Powerscourt was in Blackwater again, inside the little temple by the lake, the Pantheon. The light was fading fast. Suddenly he heard the iron gates shut with a terrible clang. Outside them the two great wooden doors closed as well. Powerscourt did not have the keys. The only light came from the top of the cupola. He was looking at the statues who were now his companions, Hercules and Diana, Isis and Ceres.

Then the whole temple began to fall, with ever-increasing speed. It fell as though there was a special shaft to carry it down to the hidden bowels of the earth. *Procul, o procul este, profani.* He remembered the inscription on the Temple of Flora, the Sibyl's warning to the unsanctified in the *Aeneid* to keep clear of the entrance to the underworld. The temple was still shooting down, the flicker of light now reduced to a pinprick far far above.

As suddenly as it had fallen, the temple stopped. The iron gates swung open. The wooden doors followed. A ghostly light shone through the dead trees and the withered bushes that made up the new landscape. Wisps of fog floated by in the gloom. I'm in the underworld, Powerscourt said to himself. Soon I shall meet the boatman Charon, his eyes alive with flame, who ferries the bodies across the river of the dead. Here in the shadows I shall meet pallid disease, dejected age, fear, the terrible spectres Death and Decline, War and Lunatic Discord with the bloodstained ribbons in her snaky hair.

There was a loud and persistent knocking. Powerscourt wondered if the bodies of the unburied, doomed for all eternity to wait on the wrong side of Charon's river, were beating on the side of his boat. The knocking grew louder. Powerscourt now felt sure that the noise was not caused by the unburied, but was a message from one of the other monsters of the underworld, the flaming Chimaera with her terrifying hiss, Briareus with a hundred arms.

Lady Lucy was shaking him violently on the shoulder.

'Francis, Francis darling, you're not dead, are you?'

'I'm not dead, Lucy. I was in a dream. I was in the underworld.'

'Well, you're not in the underworld now, Francis. There's somebody knocking at the front door. They've been at it for about five minutes while you were down below.'

'What time is it?' whispered Powerscourt, fastening his dressing gown and looking in vain for his slippers.

'It's a quarter to six. Can't you get a move on?'

Powerscourt fled down two flights of stairs to his front door. As he opened it he found himself looking at the broad back of an officer of the Metropolitan Police.

'Lord Powerscourt, sir?' The back turned round. 'I have a message for you from the Commissioner's office, sir.'

'Come inside, man, come inside.' Powerscourt struggled with a lamp in his hall. He ripped open the white envelope.

'Dear Lord Powerscourt,' he read, 'there are reports coming in of a terrible fire at Blackwater. We have no more information at this point. I know the Commissioner would have wanted you to be informed as soon as possible. Arthur Stone, Assistant to the Commissioner.'

'My God. Oh, my God,' Powerscourt said very quietly. 'This is terrible news. May I ask you to take a short message back to the Commissioner for me, young man? I won't keep you a moment.'

'What is the matter, Francis? Good morning, Constable.' Lady Lucy appeared unperturbed by her early morning visitor. From the floors above came the noises of younger Powerscourts greeting the new day a little earlier than usual.

'There's been a fire at Blackwater, Lucy,' said Powerscourt. 'The Commissioner wanted to let me know.' He was writing furiously. He shoved his note into a dark brown envelope and handed it to the constable. 'Could you make sure that the Commissioner receives this as soon as possible? Thank you so much.'

The constable made his apologies once again and departed into the cold morning air, fog drifting among the trees in the square.

'Dear Commissioner,' Powerscourt had written, 'thank you so much for the news about the fire at Blackwater. I am more apprehensive than I can say. Pray God there has been no loss of life. Could you please arrange for the foremost fire investigator in London and the Home Counties to be sent to Blackwater without delay? Yours in haste, Powerscourt.'

'Lucy,' said Powerscourt, running up his stairs to get dressed, 'I must get to Blackwater immediately. I dread to think what I will find when I get there. Could you follow me a little later on? I hope old Miss Harrison is still alive. It might be a good time to talk to her.'

Paddington station had been crowded, sacks of mail being unloaded down the platforms, early morning arrivals hastening to their place of work. Sitting in a corner seat in his train to Wallingford, Powerscourt was exceedingly angry. Not with the twist of fate that had led to the blaze at Blackwater, not with the unusually early start to his day. He was angry with himself.

Only last week, he reminded himself, I was thinking of warning the remaining Harrisons that their lives might be in danger, that they should consider removing themselves to a place of greater safety. I didn't do it. Now one or two or three of them may be dead. And I could have stopped it. Pray to God there are no more funerals.

The Thames could be seen now out of his window, neat cottages lining its sides, early morning river traffic toiling upstream. He thought of his last encounter with the Commissioner in his great office with the maps of London.

'Officially, Lord Powerscourt, our inquiries into the death of Old Mr Harrison are proceeding. Proceeding quietly but methodically, I should say, if asked. In fact, we have almost closed the case down. Manpower is limited. We know that you are still at work. Do you think, Lord Powerscourt, that we have heard the end of this affair?'

'I'm afraid I do not,' had been Powerscourt's reply. He told the Commissioner of his fears, of the mysterious death at sea, of the sense of foreboding he had about the whole case.

'Rest assured, Lord Powerscourt,' had been the Commissioner's final words, 'that we shall keep our eyes and ears open for you. Any assistance you require, all you have to do is to ask.'

Samuel Parker was waiting at the station with a small carriage and a couple of horses. To his intense irritation Powerscourt found himself wondering what letter of the alphabet started their names. H for Hephaistos, god of fire perhaps? Better not to ask.

'Lord Powerscourt,' said Parker, 'I wasn't expecting you here this morning. I thought Mr Charles was to be on the train. Did you see him at all on your journey?'

'Good morning, Mr Parker,' said Powerscourt, shaking him gravely by the hand. 'I did not see Mr Charles Harrison on that train at all. It was almost empty. Would you have time to take me back to the house before the next one arrives?'

'Of course, sir,' said Parker, showing Powerscourt into the little carriage. Streams of travellers were waiting on the opposite platform to catch the next express to London. A distant roar announced the arrival of another train, smoke drifting back across the station.

'What news, Mr Parker?' said Powerscourt. 'I heard there had been a fire but no more than that. What can you tell me?'

'Well, sir, it's all very confusing. There's firemen all over the place, and policemen, and doctors too. Then there's all kinds of locals with nothing better to do who have come to stare at the ruins. I don't as yet know exactly what happened, sir.'

'Ruins, Mr Parker, did you say ruins? Is Blackwater burnt down completely?'

'No, it's not, not completely, my lord,' said Samuel Parker, his eyes firmly fixed on the road ahead, 'but it looks as if over half of it is. Those firemen won't let anybody into the house at all.'

'Was anybody injured?'

'We don't know that either, sir.' Parker shook his head. 'Them firemen won't say. Old Miss Harrison, now, she's all right. Jones the butler carried her out of the ruins and she's resting in our little cottage. She's in a terrible state. She seems able to speak in German and nothing else. Mabel's doing her best. The doctor is with her now.'

'Was there anybody else there?' Powerscourt was desperate for news of the living and the dead. 'Anybody who didn't get out?'

'Well, my lord . . .' Parker had turned the little carriage into the main drive up to the house. All around were the signs of England in the spring, the green fields, the trees in bloom, the ever-present sound of the birds. Then Powerscourt saw the sad remains of Blackwater House. Over half of the front of the house was blackened. Thin wisps of smoke could still be seen rising from the upper floors. Firemen on great ladders were plying their hosepipes through the ruined windows.

'Mr Frederick,' Parker went on, 'we think Mr Frederick was in the house. We haven't seen him at all. Mr Charles was here yesterday evening but he left to go to London. Nobody's seen Mr Frederick this morning at all.'

Powerscourt felt sick. If Frederick Harrison had perished in the inferno he would feel personally responsible for his death. It was as if the house was cursed, and he, Powerscourt, had failed to prevent the latest attack of the furies.

'And what exactly do you think you're doing?' a voice bellowed at him from inside the charred remains of the entrance hall. 'We've got enough problems round here without strangers tramping around the place and getting in the way. Be off with you.'

A weary policeman advanced slowly into the sunlight, his face blackened, dark bloodstains on his jacket.

Procul, o procul este, profani, Powerscourt thought to himself. Keep away, keep away, unpurified ones. The inscription on the Temple of Flora come to life in an Oxfordshire police inspector.

'I'm terribly sorry,' said Powerscourt warily, 'my name is Powerscourt. I am a private investigator. I have some business with the family here. I came to find out what I could.'

'And I'm the Queen of Sheba or Dido on her pyre in Carthage,' said the Inspector, who liked to borrow the classics from his local library. 'Be off with you, I say. We've got work to do here.'

A loud crash from the upper floors announced the collapse of more of the timberwork of Blackwater House.

'I'm terribly sorry, Inspector, I really am,' said Powerscourt, 'perhaps I could show you the message I received from the Metropolitan Police Commissioner's office this morning.'

Powerscourt thanked God that he had stuffed the letter into his breast pocket rather than leave it on his hall table at home. He thanked God that the assistant had put both the time and the date on his message.

The Inspector eyed it suspiciously. He began to wonder if he had made a terrible mistake. Visions of some stern reprimand for hindering the friends of the Commissioner of the Metropolitan Police flashed through his mind. One of his colleagues had been demoted from inspector to constable for being rude to a duchess he hadn't recognized. The Commissioner's writ didn't extend to Oxfordshire, of course, but he was still the most powerful policeman in the land.

The Inspector looked at Powerscourt dubiously. Powerscourt gazed calmly back, remembering the firm stare required for unruly privates in the army.

'I have met most of the members of the family here,' he said quietly. 'They asked me to look into the death of Old Mr Harrison, the body found floating in the Thames by London Bridge.'

Every policeman in Britain had wondered about that case. He's not at all impressed by my uniform, the Inspector thought to himself. Pretty self-contained customer, this one. Maybe he is who he says he is. The strain of the last few hours was beginning to tell. He wiped his brow, managing to leave thin lines of blood across his forehead as he did so.

'Wilson is my name,' he said finally, 'Inspector Arthur Wilson of the Oxfordshire constabulary.'

Powerscourt shook him warmly by the hand. 'Look here, Inspector,' he said, 'I don't wish to get in the way of your work. You must talk to me when you have the time, not before. I have only one question for you. Were there any fatalities in this fire?'

Only a policeman or a private investigator, Inspector Wilson felt sure, would ask that question at a time like this.

'I'm afraid I don't know, Lord Powerscourt,' he replied, remembering that the letter was addressed to a Lord rather than a mere Mister Powerscourt. 'Me and my sergeant have only been here for a couple of hours. The fire brigade won't let anybody into the upper floors at all. They say it's too dangerous. They're crawling about up there on ladders and planks laid out across the floorboards. So many of them have been destroyed. I did hear the Chief Fire Officer say that there was probably one fatality, but he didn't say who it was.'

'I see, Inspector. Thank you so much. Perhaps you would be kind enough to let the Chief Fire Officer know I am here and that I would like to speak to him. But only when he has the time. I do not wish to interrupt his vital work for one second. Or yours, for that matter.'

Inspector Wilson disappeared inside the house. Powerscourt stood back from the house and surveyed the damage. Blackwater was composed of a central block, built in the style of a Palladian villa, with a library wing added on the south side and a picture gallery to the north. There was a basement and two rows of windows on each floor. The fire seemed to have spent most of its force on the north wing. All the windows had gone. There were holes in the roof. As Powerscourt walked round the house to the west front at the rear he peered cautiously into the picture gallery. The walls were stripped down to the plasterwork or even the original brick. The paintings themselves seemed to have been burnt to nothing. Great piles of ash and rubble lay on the floor. Above he could hear the shouts and the swearing of the firemen as they threaded their way across the floorboards. From time to time there would be a great crash as more timbers fell to the ground.

The sightseers drifted off as the morning wore on. Powerscourt sat on a seat in the west front garden and contemplated the Curse on the House of Harrison. Murders he was used to in his profession, men and women killed in the heat of passion or with the cold calculation he found so frightening. Always, in his experience, there was a motive. Somebody had a reason for killing somebody else. But the Harrison case seemed so different. He had yet to find any sign of a motive at all.

Just before midday he returned to the main entrance. There was a lot of shouting from the inside. As he peered into the remains of the entrance hall he could see two firemen, standing on ladders laid across the upper floor, lowering something wrapped in a blanket and tied firmly to a plank of wood.

'Steady, there, steady,' said the voice above.

'We're ready down here,' said Inspector Wilson and his colleague, waiting to receive the package.

For one moment the fireman at the top of the stairs let go of his rope too quickly. The package swung down at an angle of forty-five degrees and looked as though it might fall into the rubble below.

'Christ almighty, Bert,' said a voice above, 'can't you hold the bloody thing steady, for God's sake?'

'Sorry, sir,' said Bert, 'it's very heavy.'

'I know it's very heavy,' said the other voice. 'I'm just going to let my rope down until it's level with yours and we're back on an even keel. Don't do anything.'

Slowly the package recovered its equilibrium, the two policemen staring at the swaying plank.

'All together now, Bert. Slowly does it. Slowly. On the count of three, start lowering your rope. Don't for God's sake let go.'

Bert muttered something inaudible.

'One, two, three. Slowly now, slowly.'

Inch by inch the package was lowered into the arms of the two policemen down below. They carried it on to a makeshift trestle table underneath the portico. The blanket was wrapped tightly around the package. There was a musty smell as if the blanket or its contents had been kept in a cupboard too long.

The Chief Fire Officer had lowered himself down to ground level on the same piece of rope.

'Where's that bloody doctor gone?' he said angrily. 'Never here when you want them, doctors. They always say they'll be back in a moment, then they disappear.'

He stared at Powerscourt. Then he remembered what the Inspector had told him some hours before. 'You must be Lord Powerscourt, sir,' he said, holding out a blackened hand. 'Chief Fire Officer Perkins, Oxfordshire Fire Service.'

Perkins was a giant of a man, well over six feet tall, in his early forties. Unlike the policemen he was clean-shaven. Powerscourt wondered if they worried about their beards catching fire in emergencies.

'Good day to you, Chief Officer Perkins,' said Powerscourt. 'Do I understand that you are anxious for the presence of the doctor? I believe I know where he has gone. I could fetch him if that would help?'

'That would be right handsome of you, sir, right handsome. Is he far away?'

'I believe he is just around the corner with Old Miss Harrison,' said Powerscourt. 'I shall be back directly.'

The church clock struck one as Powerscourt collected the doctor from Samuel Parker's cottage. The sun was shining on the lake now, the Pantheon of his dreams staring inscrutably at him across the water.

'How is Miss Harrison, doctor?' asked Powerscourt, as they walked back to the burnt-out remains of Blackwater House.

'It has been a terrible shock,' said Dr Compton carefully. 'I feel sure that she will recover in time. But for the moment her mind is wandering, and wandering in German, I'm afraid. I think I should like to send her away for some time to recover her strength.'

Powerscourt restrained himself from saying that all members of the Harrison family, in his view, should be sent away from Blackwater and indeed from London without delay.

Chief Officer Perkins was waiting impatiently by his trestle table. The two policemen stood on guard at either end.

'Dr Compton,' Perkins began, 'I would be most grateful for your assistance. We have recovered this body from one of the bedrooms on the upper floors. It is, I am relieved to say, the only fatality of this terrible fire. But I do not like to continue our work inside until this body is identified. Are you willing to try to identify it?'

120

Dr Compton nodded gravely. The two policemen pulled back the blanket. Both turned white. The doctor shook his head.

'Seldom have I seen such terrible burns. Most of the face seems to have been taken off by the flames. Mr Frederick Harrison was not my patient, you understand. He had his own man up in London. He only consulted me for minor aches and pains down here.'

Not again, thought Powerscourt savagely. Not another corpse that is so severely disfigured it is almost impossible to identify. He wondered if the murderer, if there was a murderer, had intended such a degree of incineration to make it impossible to identify the body.

Dr Compton was peering at a silver ring on what must have been Frederick Harrison's finger. He prodded at the teeth with a small silver instrument extracted from his bag. He sighed. He took off his glasses and folded them neatly into their case.

'I am afraid, gentlemen, that this is Mr Frederick Harrison. Or rather was Mr Frederick Harrison. You can cover him up again now.'

'How can you be sure, Dr Compton?' Chief Fire Officer Perkins was polite but firm.

'His teeth for a start. He had some very expensive dental work done a few years ago by one of London's leading dentists. He was so proud of it, he showed me the details. It was at a dinner party here in this house. Lobsters, we had, I seem to recall. I'm afraid the sight of Mr Harrison's improved molars did very little for the appetite.'

He smiled wanly at the memory of happier times.

'Then there is the ring. I would recognize that anywhere. He was given it by his great-grandfather in Germany before he died. The great-grandfather, I mean. It had a German eagle marked upon it. I would know it anywhere.'

'Thank you, Dr Compton.' Inspector Wilson was making notes in his book. His young assistant had run away from the scene. From round the corner they could hear him retching uncontrollably into the trees.

The doctor set off to care for his other patients. Powerscourt realized that the fire officer and the policeman were both unsure of who was the senior man present. In professions used to rank and hierarchy this presented something of a problem. Temporary relief was provided by the return of Wilson's colleague, the pallor of his face made more remarkable by the blackened buildings around him.

'Get yourself down to the stables and find a drink of water, Radcliffe,' said Inspector Wilson with a good officer's care for his subordinates. The young man staggered off down the path, pausing only to vomit once more into a rhododendron bush.

'Gentlemen,' said Powerscourt, temporarily seizing the initiative, 'may I take you into my confidence?'

He told them of the earlier death of Mr Frederick's uncle, the body found in the Thames. He told of the suspicions regarding the death of Mr Frederick's brother, drowned in a boating accident off the Isle of Wight. He told of his suspicion that this death too might not have been caused by natural causes.

'You mean that the fire might have been started deliberately?' Chief Officer Perkins was the first to react.

'It might have been, yes, it very well might have been.'

Chief Officer Perkins whistled quietly. Inspector Wilson stared again at the remains of the building.

'It won't be easy to prove anything, my lord,' he said, shaking his head. 'What the fire didn't destroy, the water from Mr Perkins' hosepipes may have washed away, or soaked it to the point where it's unrecognizable. Whatever it might be, that is. My God, sir, I don't think you could establish any sort of a case, any sort of a case at all, with this heap of smoking dust and rubble.'

As if to prove his point there was another loud crash from the upper floors. Dust and ashes rose from the great holes in the roof.

'That'll be the big beam in Mr Frederick's bedroom,' said Perkins. 'It's been on the point of going for some time. Made it very dangerous up there, wondering if this beam was going to knock you on the head at any moment.'

'Could I just ask you to bear what I have said in mind?' said Powerscourt apologetically. 'I know you have much to do and I do not wish to get in the way of your work in any way. I asked the Commissioner of the Metropolitan Police to send us the foremost fire investigator in London and the Home Counties. He should be here tomorrow. I'm sure you will afford him every assistance.'

Inspector Wilson had never heard of such a creature as a fire investigator. He longed to ask for more details of what they did and how they did it. He decided not to reveal his ignorance.

'Very good, sir.'

Inspector Wilson disappeared once more into the ground floor.

Chief Fire Officer Perkins began the slow ascent of a long ladder into the upper storey.

'Bert,' he shouted to his assistant, 'where are you? What have you been doing up here? Come on, we've got work to do.'

Lady Lucy Powerscourt was sitting on a small chair in the main bedroom of the Parkers' little cottage. Old Miss Harrison was still asleep, tucked firmly inside the Parkers' best blankets. Mabel Parker stood by the door, as she had done for the last three hours.

'She's not dead, is she, my lady?' she whispered for the tenth or eleventh time.

'No, she's not, Mrs Parker,' said Lady Lucy quietly, 'she's just asleep. It must have been a terrible shock to her.'

Lady Lucy had reached Blackwater just after midday, ferried to the house by Mr Parker, still waiting in vain at the railway station for Charles Harrison to appear. There was a sudden rustling among the bedclothes. Miss Harrison looked at her new surroundings with surprise and a look of astonishment on her wrinkled face.

'Hello, my dear,' she said to Lady Lucy, 'are you here too? And you so young.'

'You're looking well, Miss Harrison,' Lady Lucy smiled, 'after your ordeal.'

'I never thought it would be like this,' the old lady went on, peering around at the bedroom, the walls lined with pictures of the great mountains beloved by Mr Parker. 'It seems so peaceful. And so quiet. I thought it might be noisier than this up here. And they don't tell you about the last journey down there, do they? I'm sure somebody carried me up here. It must have been a very long way for him, a very long way.'

'I'll bring you some tea,' said Mabel Parker, departing to her kitchen for the most useful restorative known to the Parker household.

'They have tea here too,' the old lady smiled. 'I'm so glad they have tea. Tell me, my dear,' she turned to inspect Lady Lucy closely, 'how did you get here? Did somebody carry you too?'

'We're in Mr Parker's cottage, Miss Harrison.' Lady Lucy spoke quite loudly now, wondering if the old lady's hearing had been disturbed in the fire. 'There's been a terrible fire in the big house. The butler carried you to safety. You're quite safe now.'

'Fire?' said the old lady, sounding confused. 'I thought they had fire down in the other place, not up here. Oh no, surely not here. You must be mistaken, my dear. Look, there are the mountains all about. We must be quite high up.'

'You're still alive, Miss Harrison.' Lady Lucy realized that the old lady thought she had died and gone to heaven, here with Mrs Parker's best blankets and cups of tea.

'Alive?' The old lady sounded quite cross. 'I didn't like being alive much at the end, you know. No, not at all. All my relations dying and all those people coming to ask me questions about my brother. I'm quite glad to be out of it really. Especially if they have tea.'

As if on cue, Mrs Parker returned with a small tray containing a cup of tea in her best willow pattern cup and a plate of biscuits.

'They taste just like they did down below,' Miss Harrison said, happily crunching into her digestive.

'And so does the tea!'

Lady Lucy looked helplessly at Mrs Parker. Mrs Parker shook her head sadly. Lady Lucy resolved to make one last attempt.

'Miss Harrison,' she shouted, 'we are all so glad to see you looking so well. There was a fire last night in the big house. You've been brought down here to Mrs Parker's cottage. You're going to be all right. You just need to rest.'

'Fire? Fire?' said the old lady crossly. 'Why does everybody keep talking about fire all the time? Oh dear,' she looked about her surroundings again, 'they haven't made a mistake, have they? I'm not down there in the bad place, with the flames, am I?'

'You're not in hell, Miss Harrison,' Lady Lucy spoke very firmly, 'you're not in heaven either. You're in Mrs Parker's cottage!'

'Hell,' said the old lady sadly, 'I never thought I'd end up there. Oh dear, is it going to be terrible? And you,' she pointed an old accusing finger at Lady Lucy, 'what did you do to deserve to come here? What were your sins when you were on the other side?'

'Never mind, Miss Harrison.' Lady Lucy spoke very gently. 'Why don't you drink your tea? Another cup perhaps? I'm sure the doctor will be here soon.'

Lord Francis Powerscourt had walked down to the lake, where he stared moodily at the inscrutable temples. He had walked round the house time and again, angry shouts from inside escaping occasionally through the great holes in the roof. He watched a bright red fox peering carefully out from the edge of the Blackwater Park. No scarlet-jacketed riders were to be seen. No hunting horns disturbed the Oxfordshire afternoon. The fox trotted slowly off towards the woods.

He was thinking of a list of questions to send to William Burke on his return to London. Who owned the capital of Harrison's Bank? Had any share or portion passed to the female line, nieces or sisters whose lives might be in peril? And what of the chief clerk? If he had capital in the bank, then he must be warned, and soon. Powerscourt felt he could not bear another untimely death on his already troubled conscience.

He was standing in a reverie by the great castellated gateway that marked the entrance to Blackwater when he was hailed by a young man of about thirty years alighting from a cab.

'Good afternoon,' the newcomer called cheerfully. 'Would you by any chance be Lord Powerscourt?'

'I would. I mean I am. I am he,' said Powerscourt, his syntax temporarily confused as he shook the young man by the hand.

'Hardy,' said the man, 'Joseph Hardy, fire investigator, at your service, sir.' He bowed slightly. 'But everybody calls me Joe.'

Like Chief Officer Perkins Hardy was clean-shaven. He had tousled blond hair and cheerful blue eyes that looked as though he laughed a lot.

'I got your message this morning,' Hardy went on, marching purposefully up the drive. 'But the warehouses meant I couldn't get away any sooner. Damned warehouses. Forgive my language, my lord.'

'Don't worry at all,' said Powerscourt. 'But why warehouses?'

'There are far too many of the wretched things now, my lord. In the old days you sold your cotton from Alabama to a man in New South Wales, let's say. The cotton came to London, it was stored in its warehouse, then it was shipped on to Australia. Not any longer. No, sir. Nowadays the man in Alabama sends his cotton direct to New South Wales. There's no need for it to go to London. There's no need for the wretched warehouse. It's all done by telegraph these days, my lord.'

'Forgive me,' said Powerscourt, 'but why should the man in Alabama or the man in Australia delay your journey here to Blackwater? Not that I'm complaining, not for a moment. We didn't expect to see you here today at all.'

'I'm just coming to that, my lord,' said Hardy cheerfully. 'When nobody wants your warehouse, what are you to do? I'll tell you what a lot of them do, my lord. They insure it, and its contents, mostly invented, for a great deal of money. Then they burn it down. Then they claim the insurance.'

'Would I be right in thinking,' said Powerscourt, deciding he had taken a liking to the young man, 'that the insurance companies are not happy in these circumstances? And they employ you to show that the claims are fraudulent?'

'How right you are, my lord.' Joe Hardy grinned. 'It was another of those fires I was working on this morning. Those insurance companies have very suspicious minds, my lord, almost as suspicious as yours, I shouldn't wonder.' Hardy laughed.

Powerscourt told him about the fire, about the earlier deaths, about his suspicions that the inferno at Blackwater was no accident. He mentioned the policemen and the fire officials already at the scene.

'I see, Lord Powerscourt,' said Joseph Hardy. 'Could you just walk me round the outside? Show me the lie of the land?'

As they went on their melancholy journey round the charred remains of Blackwater House, Hardy pulled a notebook from his pocket and began making quick sketches of the building. The notebook, Powerscourt saw, was red. Red for danger, red for fire. 'The thing everybody always wants to know,' said Hardy, sitting down suddenly to study the west front at the back of the house, 'is how I became a fire investigator in the first place.' His right hand was working furiously. From time to time he would snatch a different coloured pencil from his jacket until a pile of them made a small pyre on the lawn.

'I've always been fascinated by fires,' he went on, glancing up at the parapet from time to time. 'I was always on at my father to make bonfires. Then I used to inspect the ashes when they went out. I used to do the same thing on bonfire night – that was always the best day of my year when I was small.'

Powerscourt could see him, a little boy with blond hair and dirty trousers trampling about in the ashes. He wondered if he had a red notebook even then.

'I made a bomb once,' Hardy laughed. 'I made it all by myself and took it down to the woods. It made a bloody great bang, it did. I hadn't got far enough away. I was blown backwards into a tree and knocked out for a couple of minutes.'

He collected his pencils and closed his book. 'Right, Lord Powerscourt, I'm going inside now. I think you should stay here. The Commissioner wouldn't be very pleased with me if you broke your neck on the remains of the stairs. I shall see you in about an hour. The photographer will be here in the morning.'

With that he disappeared into the gloom, waving happily as he went.

'Francis, how are you?'

Lady Lucy had come to seek him out, her vigil at the bedside of Miss Harrison temporarily abandoned.

'Lucy, I had almost forgotten you were here. How terrible of me.'

'You have a lot on your mind today,' said Lady Lucy. 'Who was the very blond gentleman who just went inside?'

'That, Lucy, was Mr Hardy, fire investigator,' said Powerscourt, 'and a specialist, he tells me, in bonfires in his youth and warehouses in his adult years. But tell me, how is old Miss Harrison?'

'Oh Francis, it is so sad. Her mind has gone. Dr Compton has given her a draught to make her sleep. She thought she had gone to heaven.'

'In the Parkers' cottage? That must have seemed a bit of a letdown after a life spent in there.' He nodded at the wreck of Blackwater House. 'Did she have any special news about heaven, Lucy? God and the angels well, that sort of thing?'

'You mustn't be flippant, Francis,' Lady Lucy smiled. 'There were no immediate tidings about God or the angels, I fear, but no indication either that your investigative powers were needed up there at present. She was very relieved about the tea.'

'Tea?' said Powerscourt incredulously. 'Does God drink tea? Indian? Chinese? Ceylon?'

'It was Mrs Parker's tea, silly.' Lady Lucy took her husband's arm. 'I'm pretty sure it was Indian.'

'Is she asleep now?'

'I don't know. Perhaps I should go back and sit with her again. Mrs Parker is looking pretty tired.'

'So would you be,' said Powerscourt, leading her back down the path to the Parkers', 'if your little cottage had been turned into heaven for the day. Welcome to the Kingdom of Heaven, enjoy it before Satan burns it down. The fires of hell have come to Oxfordshire, consuming all in their path.'

'Do shut up, Francis.' Lady Lucy squeezed his arm. 'Look, I think your investigator friend wants to speak to you.'

Joseph Hardy was waving cheerily to Powerscourt from the remains of the front porch.

'Lord Powerscourt, come with me. I think we have something to show you. We've rigged up a safe way of getting upstairs for you. My, what a fire this must have been.'

He sounds as though he wished he had been here himself thought Powerscourt. Maybe the normal relations of heaven and hell were reversed for Joseph Hardy – fragments of Miss Harrison's conversation with Lady Lucy flashed through his mind – so that hell, with its eternal fires, would be heaven for him. There he could tend the Devil's cauldrons, plan newer and more fiendish ways of roasting the flesh and bones of God's rejected.

'Now, there's not a great deal to see on this floor.' The Devil's latest disciple ushered Powerscourt into a room of utter devastation. 'We think the fire probably started here in what used to be the cabinet room, and then made its way up to the next floor and across to the picture gallery over there.'

He pointed to the shell of the room which had once housed the Harrison collection. Privately Powerscourt thought it was not a great loss. Many of the finest paintings, the Canalettos and the Turners, had been sold some years before.

'Up the stairs now,' said the fire investigator. 'I'm not saying there aren't a number of unusual features down here, there are, but I have to take some samples away to analyse them in my workshop.'

A ladder had been placed in what had once had been the staircase.

'Careful, my lord,' said Hardy, as Powerscourt began his ascent. 'Chief Fire Officer Perkins is waiting for us up there.'

They emerged into what had once been a corridor. The plaster had gone, the carpets had been reduced to ashes on the ground. Strands of lath hung precariously from the ceiling like stalactites in a cave.

'At the end, there, that last door, that was Old Mr Harrison's bedroom. Nobody in there, of course. There are three doors opening off this corridor on each side as you see, my lord.'

Hardy advanced half-way down the passageway. Each door except one had gone, burnt to nothing in the fire. They could hear the wind now, whistling through the open roof. It looked, thought

128

Powerscourt, as though an angry giant had stalked down the corridor, plucking the doors away and flinging them on the flames.

Chief Officer Perkins was waiting by the one door that had not completely vanished. One solitary fragment remained, running from the floor to a couple of feet above the lock.

'Did you find the key, Chief Fire Officer?' said Hardy. 'Any sign of the key?'

Perkins was crawling through the rubble on his hands and knees. The skin on his face was invisible. The dark smudges that concealed his features almost matched the black of his fireman's jacket.

'No, I have not,' said Perkins gloomily. 'I have crawled over this damned floor three times so far, and I have found nothing. I've even asked Bert to have a look. He may not be too bright, my lord, but he has younger eyes than mine.'

Bert was not to be seen. Perhaps he's crawling over some other floor, looking for a different piece of debris, thought Powerscourt.

'It was Chief Fire Officer Perkins who drew it to my attention, my lord,' said Hardy generously. 'He'd have made a good investigator, no doubt about that.'

Hardy smiled at the fireman, his teeth unnaturally white against the stains that marked his face. His blond hair, Powerscourt noticed, had turned almost black.

'Forgive me,' said Powerscourt apologetically, 'for seeming so stupid. But what is the significance of the key?' The keys of the kingdom, the keys of heaven and hell, the keys to Lady Lucy's heart, the keys to this second death perhaps.

'The point is this, my lord.' Chief Officer Perkins had risen to his feet, dust falling from his person like thin grey snow. 'This was Mr Frederick's bedroom. His door was locked. We cannot tell if it was locked from the inside or the outside. Would you lock your own bedroom door, in your own house, in the middle of your own park, miles from anywhere?'

'I would not,' said Powerscourt, 'I most certainly would not. But what you mean is that he couldn't get out. Not out of the door anyway.'

He could imagine the dead man now, coughing violently as the smoke got into his lungs and blocked his throat, scrabbling desperately at the door to his own room, trying to escape down the stairs. The smoke would have grown so thick that he would hardly be able to see anything in front of him. Then the collapse on to the floor, the last few choking breaths, the terrible constricting pains in the chest and then oblivion. God knows where he has gone now, Powerscourt said to himself, but his last moments were certainly spent in hell. Hell on earth, hell in a bedroom, hell at Blackwater with the pictures and the house he loved burning down around him.

'He couldn't get out,' said Mr Perkins finally. 'He may have tried the windows, we don't know.' Two well-proportioned holes teased them from across the room. Their secrets had gone, burnt to nothing in the conflagration.

'We'd better get out of here now,' said Hardy, still cheerful. 'The light's going.'

'Perhaps,' said Powerscourt, tiptoeing along the shattered corridor, 'we could discuss this on the lawn outside. There must be more you have to tell me.'

They found an old table and four rusting chairs in the stables. Surrounded by four handsome horses in their stalls, they held a melancholy conference, Inspector Wilson, his face cleaned except for one dark smear below his left eyelid, Chief Fire Officer Perkins, dust and fragments of ash still falling from his body every time he moved, Fire Investigator Hardy, smiling incronguously as his mind raced through calculations of the temperature and speed of burn of the fire, still taking notes in a book that had turned from red to dark grey, Powerscourt looking troubled. The only noise was the occasional rustling of the horses and the rising whisper of the wind.

'Inspector Wilson,' Powerscourt began, 'let me trespass on your province to begin with a short summary of what we know.

'Point Number One,' he rapped his forefinger lightly on the table, 'at an early stage in the evening there were four people in the house. Miss Harrison, Mr Frederick Harrison, Mr Charles Harrison and Jones the butler in his own quarters in the basement.

'Point Number Two,' the finger tapped again, 'Mr Charles Harrison leaves the house at an unknown time to return to London. Our only evidence for that, if I remember right, is the butler reporting Mr Charles as saying that he would be leaving. He did not see him go.'

'Correct, my lord,' said Inspector Wilson.

'Point Number Three,' Powerscourt went on, 'is that at about half-past one in the morning the butler becomes aware of the fire and rushes upstairs to rescue Miss Harrison who sleeps on the other side of the house.

'Point Number Four is that at some stage in the evening Mr Frederick Harrison retires to bed for the night. And then proceeds to lock himself into his own room, from which he never escapes.'

One of the horses was listening carefully, a noble head and a pair of intelligent brown eyes fixed firmly on the strange quartet. Powerscourt wondered if this was Clytemnestra or Callimachus, Catullus or Cassandra in the Harrison horse naming system. Cassandra, he decided gloomily, prophecies destined never to be taken seriously. The horse listened on.

'For what it's worth,' said Joseph Hardy, 'I think the fire was started deliberately. I cannot be sure yet,' he glanced down at his little book, pages and pages of which Powerscourt saw were covered by calculations, 'but it has all the signs of that. Would you agree with that analysis, Chief Fire Officer Perkins?'

'I think I would,' said Perkins, flakes of dust falling from his upraised hand. 'I mean, I am not an expert in these matters, but there are some very strange circumstances surrounding it.'

'Let me put some possibilities to you, gentlemen,' said Powerscourt. 'Is it possible that Miss Harrison, for reasons best known to herself, decides to start the fire, locks her brother in his room, retires to her own quarters and waits to be rescued by the butler?'

Hardy was listening intently, still making notes in his book.

'Or is it possible that the butler is the villain of the piece? He goes upstairs to check Mr Frederick has retired, starts the fire downstairs, pops back upstairs to lock Mr Frederick in and then earns his hero's reward by carrying Miss Harrison to safety.'

Inspector Wilson too had extracted his notebook from about his person. He was following Hardy's example, scribbling furiously.

'Or is it possible that a person or persons unknown enters the house after everybody has gone to bed, starts the fire, locks Mr Frederick in and flees into the night?'

Hardy looked up suddenly. 'The key. The key, my lord,' he said, looking at Powerscourt with a pleading look, 'the key is the key. Sorry. I didn't mean it like that. If we knew where that key was, then surely we would be well on our way to solving part of the mystery. We must search for it tomorrow. We must search everywhere.'

Powerscourt looked at the Inspector to his left. He had just turned a new page and had written the word KEY in large block capitals at the top.

Two of the horses neighed suddenly. A couple of wood pigeons took off from the roof of the stables and vanished into the trees above the lake.

'There is another possibility,' Powerscourt began. 'And that is as follows . . .'

He never finished the sentence. From the bottom of the drive, less than a hundred yards away, the wheels of a carriage could be heard. The little group rose from their chairs and began to move towards the main house.

'Wait, wait,' whispered Powerscourt, restraining Chief Fire Officer Perkins. Another cloud of dust fluttered off his trousers on to the ground. 'Let's just see who it is.'

He knew who it was. All day he had been waiting for this latest visitor to the House of Harrison. Rejoice more in the lost sheep who is found than in the ninety and nine who did not stray.

Above all Powerscourt wanted to see what Charles Harrison would do. He probably knew already about the fire. Heaven knew enough messages had been sent after him all day. But if he didn't know how bad it was then surely he would pause and look at the front of his house, to survey the damage. He would walk round the side to the west wing at the rear to check on the devastation there. He might just stand and stare at the terrible ruin at the front, the gaping holes where the windows had been, the blackened stone, parts of the roof open to the sky.

Charles Harrison did none of these things. He walked straight in through what had been his front door. Even in the stables they could hear him shout.

'Anybody home? Anybody home?'

13

'I called on Parker in his cottage on the way here. He told me about the fire. And I gather my uncle has perished in the blaze.'

So Charles Harrison knew about the fire before he got here, thought Powerscourt, staring keenly at the last remaining male member of the House of Harrison. That would explain why he didn't look around the outside of Blackwater before he went in. Or would it?

Melancholy introductions had been made on the portico outside the east front, Inspector Wilson and Chief Fire Officer Perkins apologizing for the grime on their hands, Fire Investigator Hardy staring fixedly at an innocent-looking bundle of ash lying on the floor inside.

'This is a sad occasion, indeed,' said Harrison, turning to look at the open windows of what had once been the picture gallery, 'my poor uncle. My poor uncle.' He took off his hat as if already at the graveside. Powerscourt thought he didn't seem very upset about his relation's death. He remembered Charles Harrison's unhappy upbringing, brought up by a family that didn't really want him.

'Could I ask you, gentlemen,' Harrison went on, 'to grant me some repose before any proper interviews and exchanges of information take place? Could we meet in the library here tomorrow morning, at, say, eleven o'clock?'

'That'll give him eighteen hours to think about his story,' Hardy said to Powerscourt later as they walked down the drive.

'Do you suspect Mr Charles Harrison of being implicated in the fire?' asked Powerscourt.

'I'm not saying I do and I'm not saying I don't,' replied Hardy enigmatically, 'but there's something about his manner that doesn't ring quite right. I've watched enough people who have started fires in my time trying to pretend that they had nothing to do with them afterwards.'

Police and fire departed in one of Perkins' fire engines. Powerscourt decided to pay a brief call on Samuel Parker to ask for a lift to the station.

'Mr Parker,' he began, ushering the head groom on to the little path in front of his house, 'Mr Charles has just called, I understand.'

'That he has, sir, that he has. He popped in to see old Miss Harrison, so he did, but she was asleep, thank God. Lady Powerscourt left after she dropped off. I took her to the station, my lord.' He rubbed his forehead as if the old lady was becoming rather a trial to the Parker household.

'Is she any better? Miss Harrison, I mean?'

'It's hard to say, sir,' said Parker, shaking his head. 'The doctor is coming again in the morning, I understand, so he is. She was talking about fire the last time I saw her.'

'Oh dear. Could I ask you a favour, Mr Parker?' Powerscourt felt a great urge to escape from Blackwater as quickly as possible. 'Could you take me to the station as well? I have to be back in London tonight. I shall return in the morning, of course.'

As they rattled along the lanes Powerscourt asked a question he knew he should have asked before. It wasn't important, just a piece of routine.

'Jones, the butler, the man who rescued Miss Harrison,' he began, 'has he been with the family long?'

'Jones isn't his real name, sir, not proper like.' Samuel Parker was driving quite slowly, his face fixed firmly on the road ahead. 'I'm just trying to remember what his real name is now.'

'Does he not come from these parts?'

'No, he does not, my lord. He's German too, like the Harrisons. Goldman, Goldstein, Goldfarb . . .'

Powerscourt wondered if the horses in front had been named after German families once known to the Harrisons in a previous life.

'Goldschmidt, that's what it is. Jones's name, I mean. Goldschmidt. I remember Mabel saying it must be the same word as our own Goldsmiths. Goldschmidt.'

Parker sounded pleased with his feat of memory.

'Why did he call himself Jones?' asked Powerscourt. 'He could have just changed his name to Goldsmith, perfectly good English name.'

'I don't rightly know, my lord,' said Parker, 'but I do know that he came here with the Harrisons when they moved up from London. So he must have worked for them before.'

'Did Old Mr Harrison ever talk about him as he was going round the lake, that sort of thing?' Strings of possibilities, all of them unpleasant, were running through Powerscourt's brain.

'No, he didn't, my lord. But the rumour about the place was that his family had been bankers in Frankfurt who'd all been ruined in some smash, my lord.' Parker didn't sound too familiar with financial smashes.

'So the two families must have known each other before,' said Powerscourt, alighting from the carriage outside the station. 'Thank you, Mr Parker, thank you very much indeed. Perhaps I shall see you tomorrow. I have to be back for eleven o'clock.'

Two hours later he was knocking on Lord Rosebery's front door in Berkeley Square. Lyons, Rosebery's imperturbable butler, a man blessed with an encyclopedic knowledge of train timetables, showed him into the library.

Rosebery and Powerscourt had known each other at school. Rosebery had been intimately involved with one of Powerscourt's cases five years before. Since then he had fulfilled one ambition. He had become Prime Minister, only to leave office after a year and a quarter. Some said his premiership was destroyed by bickering and intrigue among his Cabinet colleagues. Others said it was brought down by Rosebery's inability to make decisions. 'Just not worth the effort, my dear Francis,' had been his verdict to Powerscourt on his great office two days after leaving it. 'Dealing with horses is so much more satisfactory. They don't conspire behind your back all the time.'

Powerscourt told Rosebery of his latest case, of the succeeding tragedies that had fallen on the House of Harrison. Rosebery had married into the richest and most powerful banking family in Europe. His relations were strung out across Paris and Vienna, Berlin and London and New York in the worldwide empire of the Rothschild Banks.

'The butler at Blackwater, Rosebery, is supposed to be a man called Jones,' said Powerscourt, sitting on an ancient chair in the Berkeley Square library.

'What of it?' replied Rosebery. 'Perfectly respectable name,

Jones. Man called Jones trained some of my horses once. Damned rogue. Bloody animals never won anything at all.'

'But you see,' Powerscourt went on, 'he's not really called Jones. He's German, like the original Harrisons. They say he came from Frankfurt some years ago, that his family were bankers and that they were once involved in some terrible smash. Goldsmith is his real name.'

'Goldsmith?' said Rosebery. 'Plenty of those in Frankfurt, I shouldn't wonder. Now I see why you are here, Francis. Do you want some information about these Frankfurt Goldsmiths? From the horse's mouth, as it were? Or at least a Rothschild's mouth?'

Powerscourt smiled at his friend. Age was catching up on Rosebery rather suddenly. For years he had sported the face of a cherub. Now the lines of time were beginning to creep slowly down his face. It was a wrinkled cherub he was looking at this evening.

'Just suppose, Rosebery, that the smash of the Goldsmiths had some link with the Harrisons, then also bankers in Frankfurt. There might be some unfinished business . . .'

'My God, Francis, you've got a devious mind,' said Rosebery. 'I suppose you have to in your business. Do you think it is possible that there is some vendetta running between these two families? That the butler has followed the Harrisons to England to take his revenge twenty years after the event? Why would he wait so long?'

One of Rosebery's clocks struck the hour of eight. Outside in the hall other timepieces followed, not quite in unison, a straggled peal.

Powerscourt shrugged. 'I don't know, Rosebery. I have seldom felt so baffled by a case. I just need more information.'

Rosebery reached for some writing paper on his desk. 'The man you want,' he said, 'lives just round the corner from here in Charles Street. He's an old gentleman by the name of Bertrand de Rothschild, he must be nearly eighty by now. I don't think he ever cared very much for banking. Come to that, I don't think the family members in the business would have wanted him around anyway. He's a scholar, a collector of rare books and manuscripts like myself. He's got one or two rather fine Poussins.

'But, Francis, the old boy has been writing a history of the Rothschild family for the past twenty years. They have connections in Frankfurt, as you know. I very much doubt if he will ever finish it. Every time you ask him how it's going he says he has just discovered some more documents he has to read. But if any man in Britain knows about these Frankfurt Goldsmiths, he does. Would you like to see him, Francis?'

'I would, very much,' said Powerscourt

'And I presume,' Rosebery went on, 'from the agitation in your manner that you would like to see him tonight or tomorrow morning or even earlier? I am writing to him now. The man can wait for the reply.'

Six miles to the north the bells of St Michael and St Jude had just finished the last stroke of eight o'clock. The noise echoed round the little houses of the parish, just a short pause before the bell ringers began their weekly practice.

'Steady, Rufus, steady. For heaven's sake, steady there.'

Richard Martin was taking his neighbour's dog for a walk. The old lady had fallen down and injured her leg so every morning and every evening Richard took the red Irish setter around the local streets.

His mother had noticed how cheerful Richard became before these evening walks. She suspected that they were used for secret rendezvous with Sophie Williams.

'Don't you be taking that dog round to meet that young woman of yours, Richard. You know what I think about her. You know what your father would have thought. Don't bring your old mother in sorrow to an early grave.'

She was sewing furiously by the fire, turning the collars on Richard's shirts.

'It does me good, Mother,' Richard told her every evening now. 'It's good exercise, taking the dog for a walk. You know how I like dogs.'

His mother reflected that never once in all of his twenty-two years had Richard shown any interest in four-legged creatures, cat or dog, never once as a child had he asked for a pet of any kind.

'Richard, how are you?' Sophie had appeared out of the shadows, skipping happily along the pavement.

'I am well, Sophie. Hold on, Rufus!'

The dog was trying to escape into a little alleyway off the street.

'Can I take the lead? Please, Richard?'

Richard wondered if they would compete for the affections of their children as they competed for the affections of Rufus. If they

137

ever had any children, that is. Sophie took the lead into the hands of a teacher.

'Come, Rufus. This way. There's a good boy.'

Richard saw how fifty six-year-olds might be summoned into silence and good behaviour. To his astonishment the dog obeyed her command without a whimper.

'It's all cleared up now, Richard,' said Sophie, 'that business with the headmistress. Mrs White called me in again today. She said that what I did in my own time was my own business. And as long as she is sure I am not trying to convert the children, the matter will be forgotten. And she knows perfectly well that I would never try to convert the children.'

Rufus was suddenly tired of his good behaviour. He made a very determined attempt to climb into a dustbin. Behind them the bells of St Michael and St Jude were chasing each other up and down the mathematical intricacies of a Kent Treble Bob.

'Rufus! Rufus!'

Sophie looked very firmly at the dog. The dog looked back as if it knew it had broken the rules. It trotted obediently but sulking at her heels.

'Good boy. Good boy,' said Sophie, patting the animal firmly on the head. 'But what news of the City, Richard?'

Sophie knew Richard was worried about something at the bank.

'Well, I've got a new friend, Sophie.'

'Male or female?' asked Sophie sharply. Richard felt there might be hope for him yet.

'Male. In spite of all your efforts there still aren't many young women working in the City. He's a very clever young man called James Clarke who works for one of the joint stock banks. I met him waiting outside the Bank of England. He seems to know all there is to know about arbitrage.'

Sophie felt that she didn't want to join the male club of arbitrage experts just now.

'But what of the bank, Richard? That's what was worrying you before.'

'I'm still worried, very worried.' Richard paused to jump out of the way of Rufus who had suddenly decided to cross to the other side of the road.

'Rufus! Rufus! Really!' Sophie's voice had the normal effect. Rufus crept back into position, tail down, a sad look about his eyes.

'The thing is, Sophie . . .' Richard realized to his regret that

Sophie's nearer arm was fully occupied with the dog and therefore not available to him, even if he dared. 'The thing is, you would expect everything to be very quiet at the moment. Well, it is and it isn't. There isn't any new business coming in.'

'What's the problem then?' asked Sophie.

'It's the money, Sophie, the bank's money. In normal times, money comes in, money goes out. Now it's only going out, and it's going out very quickly in ways I don't quite understand. They've changed the accounting systems and a new man from Germany is coming to take charge of all that. But if it goes on like this, in three months' time Harrison's Bank won't have any money left. They'll have sent it all abroad. They won't have anything left to meet their obligations in the City. They'll be a bank with no money. It's unimaginable.'

Even Sophie could grasp the significance of that. 'A bank with no money, Richard? That's impossible, surely. What happens then?'

'I don't know Sophie. I have no idea.'

There was an enormous painting of W.G. Grace above the mantelpiece. The bearded batsman had been captured at the wicket, staring defiantly at the incoming bowler. Apprehensive fielders seemed to have retreated towards the boundary. A huge spire dominated the outfield, nearly as imposing as the great man at the crease. Next to this portrait was a late Poussin, a mythological scene with storms and a violent flash of lightning. Powerscourt was waiting for Bertrand de Rothschild in his great house in Charles Street at eight o'clock the following morning. Bertrand was late.

'Cricket, Lord Powerscourt, good morning to you. Finest game in the world, I always think. How do you do?'

An old man in his late seventies with a trim white beard was advancing towards him. The suit looked as if it had been made in Paris, the silk shirt might have come from Rome.

Powerscourt smiled at the old man. 'Good morning, sir. And thank you for seeing me so promptly. Yes, I am very fond of cricket. I have a little ground at my place in Northamptonshire.'

'Have you indeed,' said the old man, seating himself at a great desk by the window. 'Do you play yourself Lord Powerscourt? Or is this merely the interest of a connoisseur?'

'I bat, sir,' Powerscourt replied. 'I open the batting, not very successfully, I fear.'

'Tricky job, that, opening,' said Bertrand de Rothschild. 'The bowlers are fresh and raring to go. Now then,' he went on, 'Rosebery tells me you are a man in a hurry today. Perhaps you are like the batsman who wants to score a hundred before lunch.' He laughed slightly at his cricketing reference.

'I fear I am in a hurry, sir.' Powerscourt smiled gravely at the old man. 'I have a train to catch this very morning not long from now.'

'I have looked up my notes on the people you are interested in, Lord Powerscourt. Let me give you the main points now. If you need further information I shall be happy to conduct further inquiries.'

Powerscourt expressed his gratitude. The old man adjusted his spectacles and consulted a pile of papers on his desk. He had a gold pen in his hand which he turned over from time to time at regular intervals.

'There were a great many banks in Frankfurt in the early 1870s, Lord Powerscourt. The competition for business between them was very fierce. The Goldsmiths, or Goldschmidts, of whom you speak must have been in the firm of Goldschmidt and Hartmann. They were great rivals of the Harrisons, the ones who are now in the City of London.'

The old man peered at Powerscourt over the top of his spectacles. 'In fact, at one time there was a lot of competition between them. Both were trying to secure the accounts of the Duke of Coburg, not a great prize, you might think, but it opened many doors to other profitable opportunities. Very profitable opportunities, in fact.'

The old man paused. The gold pen was spinning ever faster in his hand.

'The competition grew very bitter. At one point it seemed as if Goldschmidt and Hartmann had triumphed. Things looked so bad for the Harrisons that the senior partner threw himself off the top of the tallest church spire in Frankfurt. He was dead before he reached the hospital. I believe . . .' The old man paused again, peering steadily at Powerscourt over the top of his spectacles, the pen flying like a tumbler in a circus. 'I believe he was related to the Old Mr Harrison whose body was found in the Thames with no head and no hands.'

His pale blue eyes stared on. Powerscourt said nothing.

'Then the tables were turned,' Bertrand de Rothschild went on, 'and the Harrisons triumphed. The firm of Goldschmidt and

140

Hartmann was broken. The Frankfurt bankers blamed them for Harrison's death. I believe he was called Charles, like the one in the bank here.'

My God, thought Powerscourt, how many dead Harrisons were there, dying not in their beds but in fires and boating accidents, committing suicide or found floating in the Thames? There must be a ledger full of them by now, lying in the vaults of their banks.

'The Goldschmidts went bankrupt, Lord Powerscourt. They lost everything. They had to leave the city. Some went to Berlin, I believe. Some went to America.'

The pen suddenly fell on to the table. Bertrand de Rothschild had lost control. It rolled unevenly across the surface and dropped to the floor.

'Have you found any Goldschmidts, Lord Powerscourt?'

The old man's face was bright, the eyes keen. He's like a blood-hound on the scent, Powerscourt said to himself, fascinated by the terrible intensity in de Rothschild's face.

'Have you found any Goldschmidts up there in Blackwater, hiding in the temples perhaps, lurking in the lake with the river gods?' He laughed an old man's laugh. 'Have the ghosts of Frankfurt come to Oxfordshire, the past replayed once more?'

Powerscourt smiled. 'You should have been an investigator, sir. You would have been a very good one.'

'I suppose I am an investigator,' the old man replied, bending in obvious pain to pick up his golden pen once more, 'except I investigate the past and you investigate the present. I imagine the present is more dangerous than the past.'

'Mr de Rothschild, I cannot thank you enough for your information,' said Powerscourt, looking at his watch and thinking of his train. 'I am most grateful.'

'You have not answered my question, young man. Have you found any Goldschmidts up there in Blackwater?'

He was leaning forward intently, the pen spinning in his fingers again, light dancing off the gold.

'I do not know, sir, I do not know.' Powerscourt looked around for his gloves.

'I think that means that you have found some link,' said de Rothschild, his eyes bright with the joy of the hunt. 'Why else would you be here? But I can see that you do not want to tell me. I do not blame you for that. Sometimes the past may be more dangerous than the present, is that not so? Have no fear, I shall tell

141

no one of our conversation here this morning. But it is interesting, very interesting. For a historian, you understand.'

The old man rose from his desk to escort Powerscourt to his front door. Another series of cricket paintings lined the passage to the entrance hall.

'Tell me, Lord Powerscourt, do you have a favourite stroke? At cricket, I mean.'

'I do,' said Powerscourt, relieved that the conversation had returned to cricket. 'I have always had a great weakness for the late cut.'

'The late cut, Lord Powerscourt!' De Rothschild was waving an imaginary cricket bat in his hands. 'Such a very risky shot, I believe. If your eye is not absolutely right, if your judgement is ever so slightly at fault, then it's the end of your innings, am I not right?'

'You are absolutely right, Mr de Rothschild.'

'And are you often out playing this shot, this late cut of yours?'

'No, I am not,' said Powerscourt happily, walking out into the cold morning, 'I have not been out cutting for years.'

'Oh, very good, Lord Powerscourt, very good. I like that. I do like that.'

The old man's cackling laughter followed him down the street.

14

The message had arrived by a strange and roundabout route. It had been sent, addressed to Powerscourt, care of William Burke in person at his bank. It came from the British Embassy in Berlin, despatched the day before.

'Germanii ad lapides nigros in Hibernia arma et pecuniam mittent. Maius XVII–XX. Iohannis.' The Germans are going to send weapons and money to the black stones in Ireland, Powerscourt translated it from the Latin for the tenth time as he sat in his solitary railway carriage on the way to Blackwater, between 17th and 20th May. Johnny. Nothing more. A week away, Powerscourt reminded himself. I've got a week to get to Ireland.

Inspector Wilson was waiting for him five minutes before the appointed hour of eleven o'clock on the portico of Blackwater House.

'Good morning, my lord. Nasty-looking day we've got here.'

Powerscourt wondered briefly if the entire population of the islands spent their time thinking and talking about the weather. The sky was overcast, dark clouds threatening to pour yet more water into the upper storeys of the house behind them.

'Perhaps you could just get the details of his movements from Mr Charles Harrison in the library, Inspector. I want to have a quick word with the butler about the events of the last two days.'

Or the last twenty years, he said to himself, smiling benevolently at the Inspector.

'Very good, sir. The fire people are crawling about the place again,' Inspector Wilson reported. 'That Mr Hardy, sir, I've never seen such a cheerful soul. Singing away to himself he was, first

143

thing this morning, crawling in and out of the floorboards. Some song about keys, my lord.'

'Perhaps he's in love, Inspector,' said Powerscourt.

'He's certainly in love with fires, I can tell you that,' replied the Inspector. 'If he weren't official, in a manner of speaking, I should say he was a pyromaniac.'

Inspector Wilson disappeared into the rubble and proceeded towards the undamaged library. Powerscourt walked slowly to the servants' entrance, contemplating his interview with Jones the butler.

He found him in a large room in the servants' quarters, polishing the silver. There was an enormous range in one corner, with copper pans hanging in orderly ranks below. There was a huge sink with a long draining board, cups and plates drying in regular rows. A portrait of Queen Victoria, listing slightly on its hook, hung above the fireplace, the monarch gazing strictly down on her subjects in the servants' hall. There were a couple of armchairs behind the table with the candlesticks.

'You must be Mr Jones, the butler here,' said Powerscourt cheerfully.

'That I am, sir. You must be Lord Powerscourt.' A greyish hand stained with silver polish was extended.

'And are you also Mr Goldschmidt, perhaps I should say, Herr Goldschmidt, formerly of Frankfurt and a member of the bank of Goldschmidt and Hartmann in that city?'

Ever since he left London Powerscourt had been wondering when to play his Ace of Trumps. Play it too soon and he would lose the hand. Play it too late and all advantage might be lost. As he shook the butler's hand he had had no idea of when to drop his bombshell. But he dropped it.

There was a long pause. Jones went on polishing his candlesticks. Powerscourt could see fantastic reflections of the room, of Queen Victoria, of himself strung out to an impossible length like an El Greco portrait.

Jones looked up at him. He was quite a short man, his hair turning grey, clean-shaven. He was almost skeletally thin. He picked up the last candlestick from the kitchen table. 'Perhaps I could just finish this one, my lord. I always believe in doing the job properly.'

What job? Powerscourt wondered desperately. The job of revenge, after a whole generation had passed by? The cloth

144

squeaked from time to time as he worked it over the surface. Jones's feet, Powerscourt noticed, were shuffling nervously from side to side, scraping on the floor.

'Perhaps you'd better come this way, my lord.' The last of the candlesticks was gleaming now, standing in a neat line with its fellows, waiting for candles, waiting for the light.

Jones led the way down a narrow passageway. Shelves lined with brushes and pans, dusters and cloths and blacking polish lined the walls. At the end of the passage they turned left. A few feet in front of them was a door, once painted black, now fading into the anonymous grey of its surroundings.

'Please come in, Lord Powerscourt.'

For a single frightening second Powerscourt wondered if Jones the butler had a gun in here, if his last moment on earth had come in the basement of Blackwater House. Then he saw the room. It was the most astonishing room he had ever seen. Directly in front of him were two windows whose tops were level with the lawn. To his left was a wall covered entirely with reproductions of the life of Christ, from the Annunciation through the feeding of the five thousand to the last supper and the agony in the garden. Most of them were cheap things but Powerscourt thought he recognized a couple of Raphael prints. Below them was a simple bed. It looked like a monk's bed, hard and unyielding. Fra Angelico comes to Blackwater, he said to himself, his mind taken over by the religious images.

But the wall opposite was the most extraordinary of all. In the centre was a huge cross, made up of gold coins set into an iron framework. As he looked at it, Powerscourt could see that the coins must have been melted ever so slightly and pressed together with a heavy object in a blacksmith's forge. The cross had a rough, unpolished air that made it more dramatic. On either side of the cross the wall was covered with shells. Identical shells. Shells that had marked out a route march across a continent, shells that had guided pilgrims to Spain for centuries to the sacred shrine of St James in Santiago de Compostela. They were the Atlantic starshell, the signposts on the great trail that led from the church of St Jacques in Paris or Ste Marie Madeleine in Burgundy or the cathedral of Notre Dame at Le Puy-en-Velay in the Auvergne, across the high pass of Roncevalles in the Pyrenees, and on across the last two hundred and fifty miles on the Camino de Santiago till the pilgrims stood in wonder and relief before the Portal de la Gloria. They were

145

signposts on the long journey to the body of St James the Apostle, brought with its severed head in a stone boat from Palestine to the north coast of Spain in the fourth century, then entombed in glory in the cathedral at Santiago. There must have been hundreds of starshells on the walls. Powerscourt knew the story. As a child he had been fascinated by the invocation to St James that gave the Spaniards a desperate victory in the last battle against the Moors a thousand years before, the battle that decided that the cross and not the crescent should rule over Western Europe.

There were no chairs in the room. Jones the butler sat quietly on the edge of his bed.

'He had no head either, had he, St James the Apostle,' said Powerscourt. 'When they sent him to Spain the severed head was carried in the boat.'

'That's what the legend says, my lord.'

'Old Mr Harrison had a severed head too, didn't he,' said Powerscourt brutally. 'Only he didn't leave in a stone boat, he was found floating by a steel one, right by London Bridge.'

Jones the butler rose from his bed and knelt before the wall with the shells and the gleaming golden crucifix. He made the sign of the cross. He prayed for a long time. Powerscourt waited, saying nothing. Outside another carriage drew up at the portico of Blackwater House. Powerscourt wondered if St James the Apostle had left Santiago on another journey, called to the salvation of another of his faithful. At last Jones began to speak. He rose slowly to his feet and went back to sit on the bed.

'I must tell you my story, Lord Powerscourt. I am Jones the butler here. I was once Immanuel Goldschmidt of the city of Frankfurt. I am also the pilgrim and the servant of these shells and of what they mean. I have never told my story before.'

15

Powerscourt sat on the floor at the end of the bed, facing Jones the butler. Overhead he could hear footsteps walking towards the library. Jones kept his eyes fixed on the cross and the shells as he began to speak.

'Twenty years ago, perhaps it was twenty-five, I was Immanuel Goldschmidt. I worked for my father's firm in the city of Frankfurt. We were bankers, my lord, like the Harrisons.'

Powerscourt was looking at the flagstones on the floor, polished over and over to a smooth finish. He wondered if it was a penance.

'There was a feud between the two banks, my lord. Terrible things were done, my lord, so terrible that I can hardly bear to remember them.'

Jones stared on at the wall, looking for a message in the shells.

'The feud was about winning a certain account. Whoever won that account would become rich, rich with all the vain trappings of this world. Certain people bore false witness against one of the Harrisons. I, my lord, was one of those that bore false witness, telling the holders of this account that the Harrisons were embezzlers, that they would cheat the account holders out of all their money. Mr Charles Harrison seemed to have lost the account. He killed himself. He jumped off the highest building in the city.'

Dead before he even reached the hospital, Powerscourt remembered, his back growing stiff against the stone wall.

'Then the truth came out,' Jones went on, 'the Goldschmidts were disgraced, ruined. He shall cast down the mighty from their seats and the rich he hath sent empty away. They that were powerful shall be cast down, and the humble exalted.'

'So what did you do? Did you come to England? To work for your old enemies?'

Powerscourt sounded incredulous. Jones the butler carried on as if there had been no interruption.

'I knew I had done wrong. I had borne false witness against Mr Harrison. Then he committed suicide. It was as if I had killed him myself.'

Perhaps you waited, thought Powerscourt. Perhaps you waited twenty-five years and then killed some more members of his family, the family that had ruined yours. He looked at Jones's hands. There was no blood on them, only the greyish discoloration of the silver polish, the blue veins standing out on the back.

'I fled from the city where I had done wrong. I had a little money. I carried it in a leather belt.' Jones looked up at Powerscourt and pointed at the cross on the wall. 'The belt is nailed to the framework of the cross. Underneath the gold coins.'

Powerscourt held his gaze. The face told him nothing.

'I went west. I don't know why. By the time I reached Lyons I was destitute. I had no money. I had nowhere to sleep. I had nothing to eat. I would lay my head underneath the bushes in some city park or huddle at the back of the great railway sheds in the darkness. They were so big that nobody could have patrolled them all. I was having hallucinations I was so weak.'

'What did you see?' asked Powerscourt.

'I cannot remember much of those times, my lord,' said Jones the butler. 'I remember seeing high buildings, higher than you ever saw in this world, and myself falling from the top. It was a very long way down.'

Jones paused again. He shifted uneasily on his bed, the springs creaking beneath him.

'That was when I met Father Paul, my lord. He was a Dominican.'

Jones stopped again, as if that explained everything.

'He found me lying on one of the station platforms. It was the platform for through trains to Cologne, Hamburg and Bremen, my lord. That's what Father Paul told me afterwards. He gave me food. He gave me shelter. He heard my story.'

Jones made the sign of the cross again.

'When I was well he told me I had to go on a pilgrimage to atone for my sins. I had to walk from Lyons to Santiago de Compostela, my lord. Father Paul said he would meet me at the other end. He said he would meet me by the west door of the cathedral in

Santiago the day before the Assumption of the Blessed Virgin Mary. That's 15th August, my lord.'

'So how long did it take you? To walk there, I mean?' Powerscourt wondered, as he had wondered ever since the start of the man's story, if Jones was telling the truth.

'It took three months, my lord. Father Paul gave me a good pair of boots. He gave me a map with the names of the Dominican abbeys on the way. Every time I stayed there I had to attend the services, even though I was not a member of his Church. He said I had to remember my sins and pray to whatever God I believed in.

'Conques, my lord. The Dominicans had a beautiful abbey there. Moissac, the abbey was full there, some of us had to sleep in the stables. San Juan de Ortega in Spain, my lord, the abbot was completely blind but he could walk unaided from the refectory to the chapel and then back to his cell. He said the Lord was guiding him. Villafranca del Bierzo, my feet had been bleeding for some time by then. The Dominicans said I must not have any treatment until I reached Santiago.'

'Did you get there in time? In time to meet Father Paul?' Powerscourt was fascinated now.

'I met him on the day we arranged, my lord. He had come in a boat from Bordeaux. Some of the pilgrims did that, my lord. They take you to a special place in the cathedral if you are a pilgrim. There must be a thousand candles lit before the high altar and there is a huge sphere, full of incense, that swings above your head. Then we attended the service for the Assumption.

'*Prospere procede, et regna. Assumpta est Maria in caelum; gaudet exercitus angelorum.*' Jones the butler's hands were folded in prayer.

'In splendour and in state, ride on in triumph,' Powerscourt translated. 'Mary has been taken up into heaven. The whole host of angels are rejoicing.'

'Exactly so, my lord. The next day Father Paul baptised me into the Roman Catholic Church.' Jones the butler crossed himself again. 'I can still remember how cold the water was. They say it came from a spring at Padron. That's where the boat was found. The boat with the body of St James the Apostle that had come all the way from Palestine.'

With a severed head in its cargo, thought Powerscourt. The severed head of a saint, not a Harrison.

The sun was breaking through the clouds now. Shafts of light fell on the gold coins of the cross, glowing in Jones's basement cell.

149

'He gave me my life's work, Father Paul. He said I had to do penance for my sins. I was to find out the Harrisons and serve them all my days. You must love your enemies, he said. Only thus can you find God.'

Powerscourt wondered if he had found God here at Blackwater, surrounded by the pagan temples by the lake. Perhaps he had.

'Why did you come to England? Why did you not go back to Germany?'

'Father Paul said I could not go back to Germany. Not ever. My homeland was to be denied me. I had to be an exile from own country. He said it was my fate to wander, like Ruth, my lord, amid the alien corn.'

Far off the bells of Blackwater church were ringing the hour of twelve. It's the Angelus, Powerscourt remembered.

Jones the butler rose from his bed once more and knelt in front of his altar and his shells.

He prayed.

Forty miles away a young woman was drawing by the side of the Thames. Marie O'Dowd came from Dublin. She was a teacher. She had a good reason for being here in London, attending an interview for a position as a teacher in a Catholic school in Hammersmith.

Marie was twenty-three years old with masses of curly brown hair. Her eyes were green, green for the countryside in the rain, her lover said, green for the Wicklow Mountains in the morning, green for Ireland.

The top page of her sketchbook showed the view from Hammersmith Bridge, the river sloping away towards Chiswick, the great bulk of Harrods' new depository on the other side. She worked fast, pausing to smile shyly at the passers-by who stopped to admire her work. When she was alone, she flicked to the page below. This showed a very detailed drawing, as accurate as her accurate eye could make it, of the ground directly below the bridge, of the distances between the ironwork, spaces where a man or a woman might hide a parcel, or a package. Or a bomb.

Marie O'Dowd had sketched three of London's bridges this morning. Each page had its shadow, the one with the details, the one with the spaces for the parcel.

This afternoon she was going to Piccadilly and Ludgate Hill to sketch what she thought was the route of the procession on Jubilee Day. Tonight she would go back to Dublin and give her sketchbook to her lover. To Michael Byrne, the man who waited by the dark waters of Glendalough, the man determined that Queen Victoria's Jubilee would be a very special day.

16

Jones the Blackwater butler rose to his feet once more. The flag-stone where he knelt had a small indentation in the centre. It was even more polished than its fellows. 'Forgive me, my lord,' he said quietly. As he rose his arm brushed on the door of the spartan wardrobe where he kept his clothes. Powerscourt caught a glimpse of neatly ironed shirts, of black trousers hanging evenly in their presses. But something glowed at the bottom. Powerscourt could not see what it was.

'Thank you for telling me your story,' said Powerscourt, still not sure whether he believed it or not. It would be frightfully difficult to check, he thought. The Dominican, if he could ever find him, if indeed he was still alive, would not tell him anything. Did the authorities at Santiago keep records of the pilgrims who passed through the shrine? Probably not, and they were not likely to be accurate with so many different nationalities trudging across Europe to stand before the Portal de la Gloria.

'Perhaps you could take me to the library, Jones. I need to speak to Mr Harrison.' The cross of golden coins remained impas-sive on its wall, Jones's belt still anchored inside. The hundreds of shells looked out at the life of Christ on the opposite wall. Jones led the way out of his little cell. As he entered the passageway Powerscourt darted back to open the door of the wardrobe. The bottom was lined with bottles, not of some sacred liquor, or Communion wine, but of whisky. There must have been over a hundred of them, lying in formation on the bottom. Was Jones going to make another cross, this time composed of the bottles he had consumed, alone with his shells in his base-ment cell? Or was he merely a hopeless drunk, his fantastic story concocted and embroidered while he lay on his little bed, staring at his cross, growing drunker and drunker on his whisky?

Powerscourt hurried back to the corridor. They passed through the basement room where he had first met Jones that morning, the polished candlesticks still standing to attention on their table. They went up the stairs. Powerscourt passed a settee with a scallop-shell crest in the inner hall. He shook his head in disbelief. More shells. Was the whole house and its mysterious lake an enormous puzzle, clues and distractions lying about in equal measure?

'Mr Harrison. Lord Powerscourt, my lord.'

Jones spoke in funereal tones. Powerscourt shook Charles Harrison warmly by the hand and stood back to look at his library. It was one of the most beautiful libraries Powerscourt had ever seen. It had a green carpet with a pattern of interlacing motifs like a Roman pavement. The books, thousands of them, were set into the walls. Two elegant Regency windows looked out over the garden. The barrelled ceiling, green like the carpet, arched across the library. At the far end, on a handsome Chippendale desk, stood a statue of Hercules, hand on hip, staring across the mahogany at the leather-bound volumes in the corner of the room.

'I was just telling the Inspector about the arrangements here, the night-time routine, all that sort of thing,' said Charles Harrison.

Inspector Wilson was looking out of place, standing awkwardly by the marble fireplace.

'Could I ask you, Mr Harrison, if you saw anything unusual on the night of the fire, when you left the house and returned to London, I mean?'

'Any sign of any intruders, Lord Powerscourt? No, I did not. I left, as I said, about half-past ten in the evening. The good Inspector tells me that the fire people think the blaze must have started in the early hours of the morning. Any intruders must have come later than that.'

Powerscourt watched Charles Harrison's red eyebrows contracting and expanding as he spoke. 'Quite so,' he said thinking in his head about railway timetables and early morning milk trains.

'Could I ask you one question before I go?' Charles Harrison sounded almost apologetic. 'I have to make arrangements with the vicar about the funeral. Then I have to go back to London. There is so much to see to at the bank. Maybe it is best that we are kept busy at a time like this, we have less time to grieve. But to my question.'

Charles Harrison looked from Inspector Wilson at the fireplace to Powerscourt glancing idly at the collected works of Voltaire, published in Paris in the year 1825.

'Do you think there is an attack being mounted on my family? First Old Mr Harrison is found floating in the Thames, now my uncle perishes in this fire. Is it all a coincidence? Or is it a conspiracy? Do you think my own life is in danger? Should I take precautions, whatever you gentlemen might advise?'

Inspector Wilson looked at Powerscourt. Powerscourt looked carefully at the cover of *Candide*. He turned to face Charles Harrison, flanked by the naked back of Hercules.

'Mr Harrison,' he began. He did not know quite what to say. 'I wish I could give you an answer to that, I really do. Until further inquiries are made here we do not know the precise cause of the fire. It was almost certainly started by natural means. Most fires are.'

He caught the Inspector giving him a very curious glance. He looked as if he might be about to speak. Powerscourt hurried on. 'Once we know more, of course we shall let you know. In the meantime, all I can say is that we know nothing of any conspiracy against your family. But it might be prudent to be careful over the coming weeks.'

Charles Harrison looked sombre. He thanked them both and set off on his melancholy business. As he left the library he turned back. 'Please feel free, gentlemen, to use this room as long as your inquiries continue. It is the most beautiful room in the house, or what remains of the house.'

Shortly afterwards they heard the sound of carriage wheels fading down the drive. Inspector Wilson lowered himself into an armchair.

'Did you mean what you said just now, sir? About the fire starting by accident and there being no danger to Mr Harrison?'

'I did not, Inspector. I most certainly did not. But it seemed the best thing to say for the moment. God help me if I am wrong again.'

From the other side of the house the shouts of the firemen and Mr Hardy's instructions to his photographer drifted through the open window.

'Inspector,' said Powerscourt, 'I know I have no official standing in this matter. I am here merely as an observer. But there are certain lines of inquiry I would wish to ask of you.'

'You're official enough for me, my lord. I have this note here from the Chief Constable himself instructing me to give you every possible assistance in your inquiries, whatever your requests may be.'

The Inspector pulled an envelope from his pocket and waved it in front of Powerscourt. 'Signed, William F. Bampfylde, Oxfordshire Constabulary.'

'That is most helpful,' said Powerscourt, joining Inspector Wilson in an armchair in front of the fire, a relief on the overmantel depicting some biblical scene he did not recognize. He hoped it had nothing to do with shells or St James the Apostle.

'Now then, Inspector, we need to find out about people who might have come in and out of the house last night. Could you check the railway station for the times of all the trains arriving and departing from the station in the night and in the early hours of the morning? Could you ask at the inn about any strangers they might have seen on the night of the fire?'

Powerscourt stopped suddenly, staring into space. A blind Milton looked down from above the entrance. Blind, like me, he thought, blind about motive, blind about the sequence of events, blind about where all this is going to end.

'How far is the river from here, Inspector?'

'The Thames, my lord? I should say it's less than a mile from the bottom of that lower lake, the one with the waterfall.'

'Could somebody have come here or left here by boat,' said Powerscourt, 'coming or going from one of those little places with railway stations up and down the river? Could you ask? Who else wanders about the place in the middle of the night? Poachers? Thieves coming to burgle houses in the small hours of the morning?'

'Plenty of both of those, my lord, especially poachers. Lots of the poorer people round here eat quite well.' Inspector Wilson nodded meaningfully at Powerscourt.

'And tell me this, if you would, Inspector. You have talked to Mr Harrison about his movements the day after the fire. Where did he say he was? Why did he not come here until the evening?'

Inspector Wilson turned back five or six pages in his notebook. 'He left here that night because he had an important meeting the next day in Norwich, my lord. Something to do with his bank. He returned from Norwich in the afternoon.'

The Inspector looked up, alarmed. He's not going to ask me to check the trains to and from Norwich, is he? he said to himself. We don't have those kind of timetables in the station.

155

'I shall take it upon myself to check the trains to East Anglia, Inspector,' said Powerscourt cheerfully. 'I know a man who could tell me inside five minutes about every known means of reaching Norwich by train.'

'My lord.' Inspector Wilson was becoming confused, his mind struggling to keep up with all the inquiries. 'Do you have a theory as to what went on? With the fire, I mean?'

Powerscourt smiled a feeble smile. 'I have many theories, Inspector. They could all be wrong. They probably are all wrong. The fire could have been caused by accident. That must remain the most likely possibility, but I should not be surprised if it was not. The fire could have been caused by somebody inside this house.'

He thought of mentioning the mysterious butler, praying in his basement cell, hiding his bottles of whisky. Did whisky burn easily? Pour a bottle down yourself in the basement. Pop upstairs to start a fire and then retire to the golden cross and the shells down below. You probably wouldn't remember a thing in the morning. He thought a further raft of suspicious information might leave the Inspector completely confused.

'The fire could have been caused by an intruder,' Powerscourt went on, 'come to steal valuables, paintings, books maybe, like these. This library must be worth a fortune with some of those shady London booksellers. Anything with an old binding is gratefully received, then sold on to America where no questions are asked about where they come from.

'Or the fire could have been caused by somebody who left the house early in the evening and then came back and let himself in again. And after he completed his business he let himself out again.'

Inspector Wilson whistled quietly to himself.

'When we know the results of your inquiries, Inspector, and when the fire gentlemen let us know their findings, we shall be in a better position to form a judgement.' Or, he thought bitterly to himself, I may be more confused then ever.

Lady Lucy was sitting on a sofa in the upstairs drawing room staring sadly at a portrait of her grandfather when her husband dashed into Markham Square. 'Oh, Francis,' she said, 'it's so sad, so terribly sad.'

'What's so sad, Lucy?' said Powerscourt, dreading yet more bad news. 'I can't stop. I have to see William straight away. I've got to go to the City. I should be in Blackwater, but William can't wait.' He sounded distracted.

'It's that poor family, the Farrells, Francis, the ones I told you about. Do you have to rush off straight away?'

'I can wait a while, Lucy,' said Powerscourt. He was concerned about the terrible sadness in his wife's face. 'What's happened?'

'Oh, Francis . . .' Powerscourt sensed his wife was close to tears. 'You remember the baby was ill, with the terrible fever?'

Powerscourt nodded.

'Well, little Peter died. The doctors couldn't save him. The funeral was this morning.' Lucy was fighting back the tears. 'Now the oldest child, a very skinny girl called Bertha, is ill with the same thing. So is the father. He is so ill he can't go to work. If they haven't any money coming in they won't be able to pay the rent and they'll get thrown out.'

'We can help with the rent, surely,' said Powerscourt gently, taking hold of Lucy's hands. 'Of course we can.'

'There's a very curious thing, too, Francis.' Lady Lucy looked across at her husband. 'I only discovered it today when I was talking to the vicar. The flats where they live are run by a charity, but they are held in the name of Harrison's Bank, the private one. Isn't that a coincidence?'

Powerscourt remembered William Burke telling him that the private Harrisons did a lot of business with charities. Then Lady Lucy remembered she had more news to tell her husband.

'There's something else, Francis,' she said. 'Somebody came here earlier today when I was out asking about Johnny Fitzgerald, wanting to know where he was.'

'What sort of person, Lucy? Was he official, a postman or somebody like that?'

'No, he wasn't. Rhys said he was just a young man who said he was a friend of Johnny's.'

Garel Rhys, the Powerscourt butler, had been a sergeant with him in India.

'But why did he come here?' Powerscourt was looking concerned now. 'Did he know Johnny was a friend of ours?'

'The first thing he said, I think, was, "Is your husband at home?" Then he said, "Is he a friend of Lord Fitzgerald?" When Rhys said he was, then he started asking where Johnny was. He said he was an old friend from before.'

'So what did Rhys tell him, Lucy? Did he say where Johnny is?'

'Well, yes, I think he did,' said Lady Lucy, looking anxiously at her husband. 'Rhys said Johnny was in Berlin, that he should be back soon. He didn't say anything about investigations or anything like that, Francis.'

'Where was this fellow from, Lucy?' Powerscourt was worried now, worried for his friend far away in Berlin. 'Was he English? Irish perhaps if he's an old friend from before?'

Powerscourt hoped he was Irish.

'Rhys didn't think he was Irish or English, Francis,' said Lady Lucy, alarmed at the look on her husband's face, 'He said the young man was very well-spoken but he did have an accent. Rhys thought he was German.'

'German? Oh, my God!' said Powerscourt, and fled into the afternoon towards the City of London.

There's one mystery down by the lake at Blackwater, Powerscourt said to himself as his cab laboured up Ludgate Hill. There's another mystery about the unknown woman behind the feud in Harrison's Bank. There's a third mystery surrounding Jones the butler. Even now he couldn't make up his mind whether Jones was telling him the truth. Twenty years would be time enough to concoct a story like that, the shells purchased block by block in the fish markets of London, the pictures on the walls picked up in clandestine visits to junk shops. A visit to one of the larger lending libraries would provide enough information about the legend of St James without going any further than Oxford or Maidenhead, or maybe even the nearest Catholic seminary where Jones would have been welcomed with enthusiasm, fresh pilgrims always welcome into the fold.

A group of policemen and soldiers, they might have been Royal Engineers, had closed off the front of St Paul's, taking measurements, carrying things up and down the steps. They must be preparing for the Jubilee Day, Powerscourt thought, now just six weeks away, its high point the arrival of the aged Queen at these very steps for a Service of Thanksgiving.

William Burke was waiting for him in his office, a small room with high windows looking out over Cheapside.

'Francis,' the financier said, 'you look worried. I got your wire. I think I have the answers you required about the capital and shareholding of Harrison's Bank.'

'Thank you so much,' said Powerscourt, sipping a cup of tea. 'What is the position?'

'It is difficult to be certain,' said Burke the banker. 'These private banks are extremely secretive about their financial arrangements.'

'They're bloody secretive about all their bloody arrangements, William,' Powerscourt butted in. 'I only wish they weren't.'

Burke looked closely at his brother-in-law. His normal irony and detachment seemed to have deserted him this afternoon.

'The Harrisons all had identical arrangements about their share of the bank's capital,' Burke went on. 'I have inspected the wills of the earlier ones who have passed away. Each time the entire capital of the deceased passes directly to the next family member. That way the capital of the bank remains intact.'

'Do you mean, William, that Old Mr Harrison's share went straight to Mr Frederick and his share goes direct to Mr Charles? So is he now in sole charge of the bank and its monies?'

'He is certainly the biggest shareholder by far,' said Burke, 'but he is not the only one. There are, you will be relieved to hear, no female relatives with any holdings. There is only one other person with a share in the bank and that is the chief clerk, a man called Williamson, who is now a partner. If my guess is accurate, he controls less than a tenth of the bank's capital.'

'So can Mr Charles now do what he wants with the bank?' asked Powerscourt.

'No, he cannot,' said Burke firmly. 'There is a clause in the original agreements, drawn up by the lawyers, which says that all the partners must be in agreement before any important decisions are taken.'

'What would happen if Williamson died, William?' Powerscourt spoke very softly, anxious about being overheard. 'Suppose he fell into the river, or his yacht capsized, or his house burnt down?'

'Then, Francis,' William Burke also lowered his voice, 'I understand his share would pass to the surviving member of the family. And then Mr Charles could do exactly as he wanted with the bank. Exactly what he wanted.'

William Burke rose from his seat and opened the window on his left.

'Look down there, Francis.' Five floors down the great exodus was beginning. The dark coats of the City were hastening to the buses and the train stations and the underground railway. There was a faint but regular tapping sound, the result, Powerscourt real-

159

ized, of so many umbrella tips hitting the ground at the same time.

'These people work with money every day of their lives. They buy it. They sell it. They trade with it. They sells shares of it to each other. They dream, almost every one of them, of being richer this evening than they were this morning. That dream sustains them as they go home to Muswell Hill or Putney or they ride the trains to Staines and Epsom. No doubt Charles Harrison has had that dream too. It is only a guess, Francis, but he must be worth well over a million pounds sterling.'

Even Burke hasn't got that much, Powerscourt knew, looking at his friend. He could tell by the faint note of envy that crept into his voice.

'Let me introduce you to one of my young men, one of my brightest young men, Francis.'

Burke disappeared briefly and could be heard issuing his instructions outside.

'You remember you asked me if I could place somebody inside Harrison's Bank, Francis? And I said I could not do that? Well, I thought about it and I asked Mr Clarke, Mr James Clarke, from our offices here, to befriend a young man of his own age in Harrison's Bank. I believe he has done that.'

There was a knock at the door, a firm knock as if Mr James Clarke was not intimidated by what he might find on the other side.

'Let me introduce Lord Francis Powerscourt, James.' Burke ushered the young man to a chair. 'Lord Powerscourt may shortly be joining as us a non-executive director. He has particular interests in Harrison's Bank.'

Powerscourt smiled to himself at the prospect of joining his brother-in-law's bank. Maybe he would become really rich through this new association. He could buy himself a yacht, or the Blackwater library.

'I have made friends with a young man called Richard Martin,' said Clarke. 'He has worked as a clerk at Harrison's Bank for some time. His father died three or four years ago. I believe he supports his mother. And he has a sweetheart called Sophie, though I think he has few hopes of her.'

'Why is that, Mr Clarke?' asked Powerscourt.

'She's a suffragist, Lord Powerscourt. She campaigns for votes for women, all that sort of thing.'

'I see,' said Burke, who thought it would be a disaster if women were given the vote. He would trust his own wife, he knew, with any question of domestic comfort or the education of his children but he did not want her deciding the Government of the country. It would be chaos, administration by whim and instinct rather than sober judgement.

'What does he say about his bank?' asked Powerscourt.

'Well, he is very discreet, as all young bankers should be, isn't that right, Mr Burke?' Clarke appealed to his superior.

'Absolutely, James, absolutely. It is one of the first things you all learn here.'

'But he is worried, sir,' Clarke went on, 'I know he is worried. I think he fears that something terrible may happen to the bank and that he may lose his position and not be able to support his mother.'

'Could I make a suggestion, William?' Powerscourt was appealing to his brother-in-law. Clarke had never heard his director referred to as William before. All the young clerks were convinced that Burke's Christian name was Ezekiel. 'In my capacity as a prospective non-executive director, you understand,' Burke and Powerscourt smiled at each other, 'I think you should tell this young man that there may be openings for him here with Mr Burke in this bank. In case anything should go wrong at Harrison's, you understand. Maybe he could come here for a possible interview so Mr Burke could form a view as to his potential. But for the moment, it is desperately important that he stays where he is. There have been strange goings on there as you know. I could produce you a letter from very high authorities asking for your co-operation in this matter. I cannot tell you how important it is that he stays in position at Harrison's Bank. Maybe he can perform some service in the future.'

James Clarke looked sombre at the mention of higher authority. Surely the word of William, not Ezekiel, Burke was word enough?

'Could I ask one thing, sir?' he said, looking solemnly at Powerscourt. 'Are you anxious that things should happen quickly? Richard Martin's interview with Mr Burke here, I mean. I do not wish to be seen to put pressure on him.'

'You must form your own judgement on that,' Powerscourt replied. 'Speed is important, yes. But I would not want to lose this young man, as it were. You must decide when the best moment is.'

'Very good, sir.' James Clarke left them, heavy with new responsibilities.

Powerscourt too took his farewells, saying he had to call on the Commissioner of the Metropolitan Police. He thought as he went of Johnny Fitzgerald's message in its Latin code about the arms and money being sent to Ireland. How had he heard it? Where had he heard it? Was it accurate? And he remembered checking a map of Ireland the night before. He could find no place called Blackstones, as mentioned in the message. But there was a place called Greystones, south of Dublin. It was a just a few miles from his old home.

17

British agents used to meet their informants in Dublin in a strange variety of places, walking by the docks on Sunday afternoons, in empty train compartments, in the side chapels of the empty Protestant churches, even in cemeteries where the British would appear with bunches of improbable flowers to mourn the deaths of their adversaries. Fergus Finn was going to meet his contact in the wide open spaces of the Phoenix Park. It was quiet on weekday mornings and they could talk beneath the trees without being seen.

'I have some news for you now,' said Finn, drawing his thin coat around him against the rain that flew into their faces and dripped from the branches above. 'And I think it's worth a lot of money.'

'What makes you say that?' asked the agent wearily. He carried in his jacket pocket enough for Finn's latest subvention. Long experience had taught him to carry at least twice as much money as seemed necessary.

'Michael Byrne now, you've heard tell of Michael Byrne?'

The agent nodded, his eyes sweeping the park to make sure they were not being watched.

'He's got a sweetheart,' Finn was talking very quietly,' a pretty wee thing called Marie O'Dowd. He's been sending her over to London.'

'Do you know why?' asked the agent.

'It'll be some sort of reconnaissance mission, don't you see. She's a teacher, that Marie. She goes for interviews for jobs at the schools in London. That's what her auntie told my ma's cousin when they met at Mass the other morning.'

'She could just be intending to go and live in London, couldn't she?' said the agent, who had moved to Ireland from England's capital. 'Lots of people like London better than Dublin, you know.'

As he thought of the squalor and the poverty, the lies and the treacheries and the betrayals, the sheer elusiveness of Dublin's inhabitants, the agent knew where home would be for him.

'You don't understand, man,' said Finn, 'she's besotted with Michael Byrne, totally besotted with him. She'd do anything for him. It's as if Michael Byrne himself has been walking the streets of London.'

A troop of horse, part of the detachment guarding the Viceroy's residence, trotted past the clump of trees, the horses' coats shining in the rain.

'Do you know if she did anything particular for him when she was in London?' said the agent.

'That I do not. She was always drawing things, that one. She's got one of the best eyes in Dublin, you know. She could do you a perfect picture of the front of Buckingham Palace in about five minutes.'

The agent looked thoughtful, even alarmed. All agents were trained to show no emotion at all, not even anger, when dealing with their informants.

'Very well,' he said. 'We have been here long enough. Here is your money, and a little bit more besides. That's all there is today.' Nothing upset this agent more than arguing with the treacherous Irish, bartering information for scraps of gold as if they were in some oriental market.

Fergus Finn took his forty pieces of silver and went back to his office. The agent waited under the trees for a full fifteen minutes before he walked back across the city to his quarters in Dublin Castle.

News of the meeting reached Dominic Knox, senior officer in the British service responsible for intelligence gathering in Ireland, the following day. He swore as he looked out on the cobblestones of Dublin Castle at the little chapel built to commemorate British rule in Ireland. The names of the English rulers were written round its walls. It was one of the very few places in Dublin where the name of Cromwell could be found. The sentries stood to rigid attention in their dark blue boxes. The Viceroy's carriage was waiting haughtily at the main entrance. Inside the castle walls was all the authority and certainty of the British Empire. Outside in the smoke and grime of the filthy city a handful of badly organized fanatics were trying to plot the end of English rule in Ireland.

Knox sent a message to his counterpart in London. They were to circulate all the elementary schools in London – he corrected himself as he struggled with his codes, all the Catholic elementary schools in London – asking for details of all applicants for positions. All applicants from Ireland. It was to be part of an administrative survey into the provision of teaching staff in the capital. The circular should be sent out immediately.

The Commissioner sent his apologies. He was delayed at a meeting. Powerscourt drank cup after cup of Metropolitan Police tea, strong and sweet. He chatted briefly with Arthur Stone, the assistant who had told him about the fire at Blackwater. There was a further message from the Commissioner. His meeting was taking much longer than expected. Powerscourt drank more tea, wondering why even these offices had to be so drab.

'My dear Lord Powerscourt.' The Commissioner was effusive in his apologies. 'It's the Jubilee, the wretched Jubilee. The nearer it gets the more anxious the organizers become. You'd think they were orchestrating the Second Coming.'

Powerscourt told the Commissioner about the fire, about his suspicions that it had not started accidentally, about the whisky butler in the basement, about the mystery of the missing key.

'If the fire was started deliberately, do you think the purpose was to kill Frederick Harrison?' The Commissioner was putting some papers in a folder labelled 'Jubilee 1897'. Powerscourt felt sure that somewhere in the building was a folder labelled 'Jubilee 1887'. He wondered if they had one ready yet for Victoria's funeral.

'That is the only conclusion I can draw,' said Powerscourt wearily. 'But I cannot find any clear motive unless it is to obtain for Mr Charles Harrison the complete control over the bank's affairs.'

'Does he have that now – that control, I mean?' The Commissioner looked keenly at Powerscourt.

'Not quite yet. Almost, but not quite. There is a senior clerk by the name of Williamson who has to approve all major decisions, according to the rules of the partnership. But he could just ignore that. As to why he wants control of the bank now, if that is his purpose, when it would pass to him naturally in a couple of years, I have no idea at all. But I feel Williamson's life may be in danger.'

'Would you like us to watch him,' said the Commissioner, 'to make sure he is safe?'

'I would be most grateful,' said Powerscourt. 'I have all the necessary details with me here.'

'Is there anybody else you would like us to watch, Lord Powerscourt? Anything that might help you in your inquiries?'

Powerscourt thought about this generous offer. This might just shorten the odds against him. 'There is, sir, if you can afford the necessary manpower. I should like you to watch Mr Charles Harrison.'

Powerscourt spent some time reading the back copies of the financial papers in the London Library. He spent some time in trains, always enjoyable for him. He travelled to Blackwater where, officially, he was keeping an eye on things, maintaining contact with Inspector Wilson, wandering about the ruined house, having desultory conversations with Jones the butler. He walked round the lake alone, stopping to peer into the temples, pausing to read the epitaphs in the churchyard. He walked to the river, mentally timing how long it would take a man on a fast horse to get there from the house, admiring the boathouse with the well-kept rowing boats by the side of the Thames.

But, if he was honest with himself, he knew the real reason he was there. He had fallen in love. Perhaps it's more of an infatuation, perhaps it will pass, he said to himself.

He had fallen in love with the library, its green surroundings, the promise of the books that lined its walls, the air of serenity that pervaded the long room. Here he would sit, sometimes making notes of things to do, sometimes wandering around and pausing to bring down a Thucydides or a Clarendon, a Plutarch or a de Tocqueville from the tall cases that reached up to the vaulted ceiling. He thought of his other recent train journey, a visit to the seaside to another Harrison, Lothar of Harrison's Private Bank, in his grand house in Eastbourne a few days before.

A row of goat carts had been waiting patiently for their little passengers outside the front door of the Harrison house, right on the front near the pier. Behind them on the beach the bathing machines were unlikely to have much custom on this day for the rain was pouring down, the wind strong from the sea. Through the windows of Lothar Harrison's drawing room on the first floor a couple of fishing boats could be seen, beating slowly back towards the shore.

'I gather you have been to see my brother Leopold in Cornwall, Lord Powerscourt,' said Lothar with a smile. 'And that you are interested in our family history.'

'I must confess,' said Powerscourt, 'that I found your brother crystal clear on the subject of money and banking, but somewhat, how should I put it, hesitant, on the subject of women.'

Lothar Harrison roared with laughter. 'Hesitant,' he said, 'I like that, Lord Powerscourt. How can I assist you in your inquiries?'

'I am also hesitant,' Powerscourt went on with a smile, 'because of the impact it had on your brother, to mention the words family feud, but I would be most interested to know the full story. If only,' he went on quickly, 'so that I could eliminate any suspicions of it having a bearing on the recent murder.'

Lothar Harrison walked to his windows and gazed out at the grey sea. 'I will tell you all I know,' he said at last, 'because I do not think it could have any bearing on what has just happened in London. The people concerned are too far away.'

He turned and walked back to his armchair. Powerscourt noticed that Lothar had an enormous collection of paintings of railway engines from all over the world on his walls. Thomas would be happy here, he felt. Thomas would be happy here for hours, if not days.

'I'm afraid you're going to have to listen to some more Harrison family history,' said Lothar. 'I'll make it as simple as I can.' He paused and looked in the large mirror over the fireplace. Powerscourt thought he must have been looking at the reflections of some mighty trains built to cross the Rocky Mountains.

'My uncle, my late uncle, Carl Harrison was the youngest of three brothers. The sister, as you know, still lives in Blackwater. My father, the middle brother, died in Frankfurt before we moved to England. The eldest brother, Wolfgang, had nothing to do with the bank at all. He was a soldier. The trouble came with his son, also called Wolfgang, who made a most imprudent marriage to a woman called Leonora. Everything went fine in the early years. She produced a son called Charles who now works in the City Bank. Then she ran off with this impoverished Polish count. He was a perfectly charming fellow but he seemed to think that the world owed him a living. I don't think he ever did a day's work in his life. Two years after she left, Wolfgang drank himself to death with a broken heart. Before she departed, Leonora stole all the family jewels. When they had all been sold and the proceeds spent, she came back and asked for more money. That's when the family fell out. My brother Leopold was adamant that we should give her more money. By this time other members of the family

167

were bringing up Charles who seemed to hate everybody because his mother had run away. I think he blamed her for his father's death as well.'

Now it was Powerscourt's turn to look in the mirror. He found himself looking at an enormous empty landscape somewhere in the vast spaces of the American Mid-West. The train lines were like pencil marks drawn by a ruler across the earth. Just visible towards the horizon a train was marking its passage with a cloud of smoke. Wild birds were circling overhead. He was wondering about Charles Harrison. Had the events of his past made him so disturbed that he could set about cutting off his relatives' heads? And their hands?

'Did you give Leonora the money?' asked Powerscourt.

'That's when the row started. My brother and I wanted to make her an allowance. We said we couldn't have her starving somewhere. My uncle Carl refused to give her another penny. He said he didn't care what happened to her. Willi and Frederick supported their father.'

Lothar Harrison paused, memories of the family arguments of long ago filling his thoughts.

'What happened to Leonora?' said Powerscourt gently. 'Did you give her the money?'

Harrison shook his head. 'Uncle Carl prevailed. She didn't receive another penny, however many begging letters she wrote. I think she was last heard of living in a garret in Vienna with her impoverished Pole. I believe she's still alive.'

'Do you think,' Powerscourt asked, 'that the family row could have anything to do with the murder?' He realized to his horror that those who opposed giving Charles Harrison's mother the money were all dead, drowned, burnt to death, head and hands cut off, floating by London Bridge.

'I don't believe it could for a moment,' said Harrison firmly. 'It's all so long ago.'

'And do you know of anything else in the family past which might have a bearing on the death?' Powerscourt thought he knew the answer. He wondered how much of the truth he had been told. As little as possible? Enough to put him off this particular line of inquiry? Was any of it true? It would, after all, be very difficult to track down a couple of elderly persons of German and Polish extraction, living in penury in Vienna.

'I don't think there is, Lord Powerscourt.' Lothar Harrison had been very definite. Had he been too quick with that last answer?

168

Powerscourt wondered, as he left for the station. Were there more dark secrets hidden in there behind the railway engines?

As he made his way along the sea front, the voice of an old crone, seated on the top step of a gypsy caravan across the street, followed him towards the centre of the town.

'Cross my palm with silver,' the old gypsy woman with a rumpled bonnet on her head proclaimed. 'Learn your future. Hear all your tomorrows. Cross my palm with silver.'

Powerscourt wondered if she was any good at solving murders.

Inspector Wilson found him in the library one sunny morning, with news about trains and travellers on the night of the fire.

'Let me tell you about the trains first, my lord. There are trains here that go to London or connect to trains that go to London at 10.47, 11.17, and 11.47 every evening. Three miles down the road there's another station at Marlow that links in with Maidenhead. That's got trains at 11.25, 12.05 and 12.50, arriving in London a couple of hours later. If you want a later train, then you've got to get yourself further down the river again, to Henley. There's some funny train that stops there at 1.30 in the morning.'

'What happens if you go as far as Reading, Inspector?' Powerscourt widened the net.

'Reading, my lord, that's a place where you could catch a train to almost anywhere. You could connect yourself to all sorts of lines there. But it's a long way from here, even with a fast carriage, and there were no carriages seen on the roads round here that night.'

Inspector Wilson looked at Powerscourt for enlightenment.

'Suppose you took a boat, Inspector, and rowed yourself down the river. For a strong man, it shouldn't take more than a couple of hours. Nobody would see you, and if they did, they would think you were out fishing.'

'I suppose you could do that,' said the Inspector doubtfully.

'I have no doubt at all,' Powerscourt went on, 'that from Reading you could go cross country, or go into London and change stations, and be in, let us say, Norwich, in time for a meeting the next day.'

Mr Charles Harrison had been going to Norwich.

'What about the people who were seen about the place, Inspector?' Powerscourt went on. 'You said you were going to deal with the trains first.'

'Not much luck with the people at all, my lord. There are no reports

169

of anybody who might have been an intruder. There are no reports of anybody who might have been recognized as a resident of Blackwater House either, my lord.'

'I didn't think we'd have much luck there,' said Powerscourt, staring once more at the busts of the blind Milton on either side of the door.

There was a knock at the door. Jones the butler appeared.

'Mr Hardy, my lord, Inspector.'

The blond-haired fire expert bounded into the room.

'Good morning, Lord Powerscourt, Good morning, Inspector, good morning everybody! What a beautiful morning!'

He sat down by the fireplace. Of course, thought Powerscourt, Joe Hardy would always sit by the fireplace.

'My investigations are almost completed, gentlemen. And what fun they have been. Oh, yes, a most enjoyable little problem. Most enjoyable!'

His exuberance was infectious. Inspector Wilson smiled at him benignly, as if he were a newly trained puppy come for its master's approval.

'And what have you found out, Mr Hardy? What are the fruits of your investigations?'

'That's why I'm here. You see, I am not going to tell you now. But I am arranging a little demonstration for you both tomorrow morning. Just a little demonstration.' Hardy rubbed his hands together at the prospect. 'There's a big empty barn just behind the stables. Mr Parker tells me I may borrow it. Mr Harrison will not be here.'

'Are you going to make a special fire for us?' asked the Inspector incredulously.

'I am. I shall have the bits and pieces ready for you tomorrow. It's going to be tremendous fun. I haven't enjoyed myself so much since I was little. And Chief Fire Officer Perkins is coming too. He's going to bring his best fire engine, just in case anything goes wrong.'

He smiled happily at them both.

'But I don't think it will.'

18

'Dear Lord Powerscourt,' the letter read. It was breakfast time in Markham Square. Master Thomas Powerscourt was inspecting a book full of photographs of railway engines, recently purchased by his father. Miss Olivia Powerscourt was smearing her face happily with jam and fragments of toast. Lady Lucy was reading a letter from her brother.

'I am writing,' Powerscourt's correspondent wrote, 'to invite you to be a member of my team in a forthcoming cricket match. Every year I organize a game near the beginning of the season at my country place in Buckinghamshire.'

'Big green engine!' shouted Thomas Powerscourt, pointing to a smoking monster in front of him.

'Splendid,' said his father.

'There is a team from the City and a Visitors Eleven. As you no doubt know, being a keen follower of cricket, there is a touring party of Americans called the Philadelphians coming to our shores this summer. They are the Visitors this year.'

'Big black engine! Big black one!' Thomas Powerscourt began making train noises. 'Chuff,' he went, 'chuff, chuff, chuff, chuff, chuff.'

'I should like you to play for the City Eleven. Their ranks are drawn from banks of all sizes, the discount houses, the insurance people. The wicket-keeper, appropriately enough, comes from the Bank of England.'

'My brother is going to France for the summer, Francis,' said Lady Lucy, 'somewhere near Biarritz. He wants to know if we would like to join him.'

'Blue engine! Blue engine!'

'Naturally enough, I am proposing that you should open the

batting for the City. A special train will be departing from Marylebone station at ten o'clock. Play commences at twelve.'

'Thomas, Olivia.' Lady Lucy moved swiftly to restore order. 'Time to get cleaned up. Nurse Mary Muriel is waiting for you. Francis, my love, haven't you a train to catch?'

'Red engine! Big red one. Chuff, chuff.'

Thomas moved slowly out of the dining room station on to the main line upstairs. His sister trotted happily behind him.

'Please feel free to bring as many members of your family as you would like. Then they can join me in applauding your late cuts. Bertrand de Rothschild.'

There was a small fire going in the centre of the barn. Joseph Hardy had arranged a trestle table at some distance away, covered with two rows of photographs.

'My little demonstration begins here, gentlemen,' he announced. The top row were photographs and drawings of the house as it had been before the blaze. Below it were the photographs taken by Hardy's man the day after the fire. They had been arranged in such a way that the room below corresponded with the one above.

'Before on the top, gentlemen, after on the bottom. Are you with me so far? Now,' Hardy went on, 'I would like you to look closely at the furniture in the picture gallery prior to the blaze. Then would you please cast your eyes on the furniture and the curtains and so forth in Mr Frederick Harrison's bedroom above.'

Hardy was walking along the side of the table, facing his little audience of Powerscourt, Inspector Wilson and Chief Fire Officer Perkins, pointing now at a painting, now at the wood panelling on either side of the fireplace.

'Look, if you would, very carefully at the photographs taken after the fire.'

Powerscourt peered closely at the photographs. At first he could see nothing remarkable, only dust and rubble.

'You will notice, I am sure,' said Hardy, flattering his audience as he went on, 'that the fire has taken much more serious hold in some places than it has in others.' He pointed to a jagged line leading up the wall of the picture gallery. 'Look here. In all this area the plaster has been burnt completely away. We are right down to the bare brick. But,' he drew a small ruler from his pocket, 'along all the rest of the wall, the fire has taken hold, certainly, but the plaster has not been burnt away. What do you deduce from that, gentlemen?'

Hardy put his ruler away and looked directly at Powerscourt.

'I would deduce that the fire must have been much hotter in that part of the room where the plaster has all gone. Much hotter.'

'You are absolutely right, of course,' said Hardy with a smile. 'Fires never burn evenly but you would not expect to find such a disparity as this.

'Now look here!' He sprang round the table and pointed dramatically to the bedroom. 'This is not a photograph of the room as it was, but a drawing made up of the recollections of the servants and Jones the butler. Jones had a remarkable memory for every detail in the room, I'm glad to say.'

Did he indeed? said Powerscourt to himself. He found it upsetting that the whisky-loving butler should have such an accurate memory. Maybe he had stopped drinking years ago.

'Look at the fireplace here. There was wood panelling on either side of it, going all the way up to the ceiling, right round the room. To the left of the fire, going away from the door,' out came Hardy's ruler again, 'the wood panelling is severely burnt, but it has not completely disappeared. But to the right of the fireplace it has vanished altogether, totally burnt away. You can see the same with the floorboards. Away from the door, they are severely damaged. Towards the door, the damage is much more severe.

'In fact, gentlemen, the most dramatic way of looking at this is as follows.' Hardy brought out a piece of chalk and drew a ragged line from the fireplace to the door. Then he drew another ragged line towards the door, following the area of maximum impact of the fire. It looked like a straggly corridor.

'If you would like to move over here just a moment.' Hardy led them over to a piece of carpet lying all on its own on the stone floor. There was a label saying, 'Door' and another one saying 'Fireplace' attached. Powerscourt felt sure that the distance corresponded to the same gap in Frederick Harrison's bedroom. Hardy took a bottle from his pocket. He walked backwards, quite slowly, from the fireplace, pouring the liquid as he went. When he reached the door he stopped.

'The pattern is not identical, of course. But you can see the remarkable similarities in the shape between the carpet and the chalk lines on the photograph.'

Outside a couple of horses whinnied. Mr Samuel Parker could be heard talking to them in a low voice.

'God bless my soul. God bless my soul,' said Inspector Wilson as the meaning of the chalk lines became apparent to him. 'Do you mean to say . . .'

Joseph Hardy held up his hand. 'I haven't finished yet, Inspector,' he said, smiling again at his handiwork. 'Nearly but not quite. Could I ask you to look at the fire for me now, gentlemen? At present it is a perfectly normal blaze. I am going to put on two different sets of wood.'

He bent down to a wooden basket several feet away from his fire. 'The first is wood panelling of the same type as that found in Mr Harrison's bedroom. It is about the same age. It was originally painted in the same colours. It is about the same temperature as the wood in the fireplace would have been before the fire took hold.'

'How did you get the piece of wood? How can you be so sure it is of the same age and so on?' asked Powerscourt.

Joseph Hardy frowned at the interruption. 'In my line of work, my lord, you have to take great care.' Hardy threw two pieces of wood on to the fire. 'Some of the firemen down in London, my lord, let me keep all kinds of pieces of stuff from all sorts of different fires. I keep them all carefully labelled in my store room.'

They stared at the two pieces of wood. At first nothing happened. Gradually, but quite slowly they began to burn.

'Now look at these two, gentlemen.' Hardy tossed another two pieces of wood on to the fire. They burst into flame immediately. They blazed much more fiercely than the others. Powerscourt drew back from the heat.

'These two have been soaked in inflammable liquid. That is what I believe happened on the night of this fire. The arsonist poured his petrol or his oil down one section of the picture gallery wall. He also poured a whole lot more in Mr Harrison's bedroom in the area between the door and the fireplace. You will remember, gentlemen, that we never found the key that locked Mr Harrison into his room.'

Inspector Wilson, Chief Fire Officer Perkins and Powerscourt stared at Hardy. Even he had gone serious as he looked at the flames leaping up in his fire.

'Do I need to say anything more, gentlemen? I am anxious to put this fire out if you have seen enough. We have some buckets of sand prepared for the purpose.'

'I think we have seen enough, Mr Hardy,' said Powerscourt.

'There's only one thing that has to be said, my lord,' said Hardy as he and Perkins hurled the sand over the blaze. Thick smoke was pouring up to the roof of the barn now. 'I think Mr Harrison was murdered. I'm certain of it, in fact. The murderer soaked the key parts of the house in some inflammable liquid and then put a match to it. Mr Harrison must have gone to sleep before the fire began. The murderer then locked him in and disposed of the key. Poor man.'

Hardy paused as he thought of the horrible end, a man burnt to death in his own house, smoke finishing him off, his own bedroom door locked from the other side.

'But I couldn't say who did it. That is outside my province altogether.'

Hardy looked at Inspector Wilson and Powerscourt, the Inspector looking sombre after his demonstration, Powerscourt now pacing up and down the barn.

'That's up to you gentlemen. That's up to you now.'

Lord Francis Powerscourt was sitting in total darkness, staring helplessly out to sea. Night had fallen over the east coast of Ireland and the little town showed no signs of movement. This was Greystones, the place Johnny Fitzgerald had identified as the site for the German arms shipments to the Irish revolutionaries. At least Powerscourt thought it was the place. He wondered yet again if he had decoded the message correctly or if Fitzgerald had misheard the information in Berlin. Four days, or four nights, Fitzgerald had said, on which the Germans might land guns and money for the Irish.

Powerscourt had checked into the Imperial Hotel, Greystones, as James Hamilton, the name of Lucy's father. He smiled to himself as he thought of it. He couldn't have brought Lucy with him, not on an assignment as potentially dangerous as this, but she was with him in spirit. He wondered if she had gone to bed yet, back in Markham Square, trying yet again to get to grips with the latest Joseph Conrad.

To Powerscourt's left, from his windows on the top storey, a miscellaneous collection of cottages curved around one side of the little bay. In front of them was a stony beach, the fishermen's boats drawn up in random order. To his right a long passage of rocks and gullies marked the way to the other, longer beach that stretched way down the coast towards Wicklow. But the beauty of

Greystones, if this indeed was the right place, was a tiny harbour just two hundred yards from Powerscourt's hotel. Nothing very big could have put in there, but a small boat could easily come in from a mother ship further out to sea. The place was completely deserted. There were no coastguards, no lighthouses, nothing at all, only the water lapping monotonously against the green-covered stone of the quays and the pebbles on the tiny beach.

The moon was almost full, turning the sea into a mass of shimmering grey and silver. Powerscourt had his best field glasses with him, temporarily borrowed from Johnny Fitzgerald. For the tenth time that evening he scanned the wide expanse of the Irish Sea. There was nothing to be seen, not even the dark smudge of a coal steamer heading north towards Dublin. He wondered yet again if he had come to the right place. He thought of Lady Lucy and his children. He wondered if Thomas would like climbing across the rocks. He thought of Lady Lucy's adopted family, the Farrells, and wondered sadly if any more of them had died. He thought of his investigation, of the headless man found floating by London Bridge, of the strange history of the Harrison family that might yet consume them all. He wondered about Jones the butler and whether he was telling the truth. He thought of Charles Harrison, a sad and embittered little boy, one parent dead, the other fled with her Polish lover, brought up by dutiful but unloving relations. He wondered about the link, if there was one, between the Germans in Berlin and the Harrisons in London and the Irish insurgents in Dublin.

Suddenly he realized that they too must be staring out to sea on this moonlit night, watching for their ship, praying for copious supplies of money and guns and explosives. He turned his glasses on to the streets of Greystones. Was there somebody down there, watching like him for the sign, for the sails? He thought of Theseus' father, warned that his son's boat was coming home to Athens, watching desperately from the rocky citadel for the ship to come in. White sails meant he was alive, black that he was dead. Legend said Theseus had forgotten to change the sails so his father hurled himself off the rock to his death, leaving the throne of Athens to the slayer of the Minotaur. Powerscourt thought Theseus had enjoyed power too much on his travels to want to play second fiddle ever again. The failure to change the sails was deliberate. A patricide ruled in Athens, but only the immortal gods would ever know and they came for Theseus in the end. Powerscourt wondered if a returning Harrison would have changed the sails. He thought of more black sails in Turner's painting of a burial at sea, the great ships riding very still, the body lowered reverently into the water, black sails marking the passage of another English hero.

Every five minutes Powerscourt would scan the horizon from north to south. He checked in the doorways of the cottages to see if his counterpart was lurking there in the shadows, hoping for the weapons that might help bring freedom to the troubled island. He remembered other night watches, on the side of a mountain in India where he and Johnny Fitzgerald had waited for five days and nights for a meeting between rebel tribesmen that must have happened somewhere else. Johnny had discovered another way to make his fortune. Luminous playing cards, playing cards you could see properly in the dark, he had declared, would earn some lucky man his fortune. Nights on duty for soldiers, sailors and sentries would never be the same again. Think of the joy, Johnny said, when you produced the Ace of Spades at three o'clock in the morning when you could hardly see your own hand in front of your face.

From time to time Powerscourt would walk up and down his room, stretching his legs, rubbing his eyes. By four o'clock he had decided that nothing would happen this night. There was no boat or pleasure boat to be seen out to sea. No vessel from Hamburg or Bremen had come to disturb the peace of the waters off Greystones. Powerscourt wondered if they had got it wrong, if he should be in some other desolate cove in Kerry or Connemara, or somewhere on the wild and rugged coast of Donegal, all easier to reach from Germany. He made a final tour with the field glasses. There was nothing there. As dawn began to climb out of the eastern sky, grey-fingered, Powerscourt thought, he went to bed and slept fitfully as a new day dawned over the Irish Sea.

19

'Will you go and see your old home, Francis?' Lady Lucy's voice came back to him as he stirred from an uneasy sleep at half-past eleven in the morning. Even in Ireland, he reflected bitterly, they wouldn't serve breakfast at this hour. Lucy and Powerscourt had been drinking tea at home when he told her of this expedition to his native country. He had smiled at her. He had always meant to bring Lucy to Ireland on one of those Journeys to the Unknown as he referred to them. Once he had gone as far as to book the tickets. But he never had. Perhaps he was superstitious about taking a second wife on the same journey that led to the drowning of the first.

'I don't know if I will or not, Lucy. Maybe I'll be too busy. Do you think I should?'

Lady Lucy cast a protective glance towards the small figure of Olivia who had fallen asleep on the sofa, her left arm wrapped round her face as if to protect her from evil.

'Yes, I think you should, Francis. It might do you good to look at it all again. And the gardens should be very beautiful at this time of year.'

'I just wonder about the ghosts, Lucy. I should think they're very strong too, in the springtime with the soft light lying across those mountains.'

Yet here he was, in the early afternoon, the Wicklow countryside drowned in sunshine, outside the driveway to Powerscourt House, Enniskerry, where he and his sisters had lived until he was a young man. An old gardener called Michael O'Connell recognized him on his way up through the rhododendrons. Powerscourt wondered if he was the first ghost.

'Lord Francis, how very nice to see you again. I'd have recognized you anywhere. The family are away just now if you want to have a look around. Nothing much has changed, you'll be glad to hear.'

Powerscourt remembered the old man teaching him how to string conkers, how to make bows and arrows, how to ride a horse. He had fought at Crécy on these well-kept lawns. He had hidden inside the Wooden Horse and sacked Troy, better known as the stables, under the old man's watchful eye. A small shed behind the house had done service as the Black Hole of Calcutta. He had lain low on the hills around the house, one of Wellington's riflemen at Waterloo, while the French artillery pounded their positions, waiting for the final, doomed, onslaught by Marshal Ney and the Imperial Guard.

Then he was at the side of Powerscourt House. It stood on the top of a hill, looking out over the mountains. In front of it was the most remarkable ornamental garden in Ireland, a copy of some ornate Italian extravaganza outside Rome. A long long flight of steps led down to a spectacular fountain in a little lake at the bottom. Bronze putti holding bronze urns marked the passage at the sides of the steps. Powerscourt remembered two of his father's friends racing their horses up the steps for a bet, the winner making off with fifty pounds. He remembered trying to slide down them in the winter when they had frozen solid and he had nearly broken his neck half-way down.

He looked up at the house. That window there, third from the left on the second floor, had been his bedroom. He had looked out across the steps and the waterfall to the blue hills beyond. He remembered his mother coming to see him one day, so excited because she was going hunting on a cold clear winter's day. He had asked her why she liked it so much. She ruffled his hair with a laugh, he must have been about ten at the time.

'Quite simply, my darling, it is the most exciting thing in the world. When you're riding fast across the countryside, the horse firm and strong beneath you, jumping over hedges and all that sort of thing, it's exhilarating, it's wonderful. It makes me feel so alive.'

Powerscourt had smiled, he remembered. He never liked hunting. The nearest he had ever come to the same feelings was one hot and dusty day in India when he and Fitzgerald had ridden with the cavalry against a rebel army. He recalled thinking that you were bound to feel very intensely alive because any second you could be equally intensely dead.

He looked down to the windows of the great drawing room on

the ground floor. He had tried to hide in there once before a ball. His father loved dancing, especially with his mother, and once a year the Powerscourt Ball attracted the cream of local and Dublin society. He saw him now, looking very dashing in his white tie and tails, entertaining a group of ladies before the fire, the laughter rising right through the house and the band playing over and over again the waltzes his parents loved so much.

Then he turned on his heel. The memories were coming too fast. The ghosts were winning the battle. He felt the tears coming and he wasn't sure he could stop them. He saw his mother in the soft evening light brushing his sisters' hair. She always used to do it before they went to sleep, the hypnotic rhythm of the brush, mother and daughters mesmerized by the sheen on the hair. He could see his father in his study, staring sadly at the account books, telling his only son that it hadn't been a good year, but that things would look up after Christmas. Powerscourt thought now that he had been putting a brave face on it for the little boy. Things never looked up at all, not after Christmas, not after Easter, not after the summer holidays.

Powerscourt was fleeing the ancestral home as fast as he could now. The influenza had come back, the terrible influenza that had carried off both his parents, the unbearable funerals, the torrents of tears by the gravesides, the desolation that seemed to be with them all for ever. He had thought of going to look at the headstone in the church by the side of the front drive. He couldn't do it. He set off back to Greystones, his face wet with tears, as the wind rose among the trees and his sodden handkerchief began to drip on to the grass beneath.

He thought suddenly of Lady Lucy. Had she known how terrible it might be for him? Did she realize how powerful the memories would be? Probably she did, he thought. He thought of her, holding Thomas solemnly by the hand, Olivia clutched to her shoulder, all waving him goodbye to him at the front door in Markham Square before he left for Ireland. 'Come back safely, my love,' she had whispered as she kissed him goodbye. I must be strong for Lucy, he said to himself as the sobbing began to subside. I must be strong for Thomas and Olivia. As he thought of his wife and children, his tears dried and by the time he returned to Greystones he was composed.

There was a storm that night. The afternoon sun had disappeared by tea-time. A strong wind began to blow in from off the sea. By nightfall the waves were crashing against the walls of the little harbour, cascades of spray shooting up from the rocks beneath the Imperial Hotel. Powerscourt went for a walk along the sea front. The words of a hymn floated out from a tiny church behind the beach.

> Abide with me;
> Fast falls the eventide:
> The darkness deepens;
> Lord with me abide!

He thought suddenly of the sailors on their mission from Germany. Were they somewhere out to sea praying to their German gods that the storm would abate, making everything fast, taking in sail as quickly as they could? 'God help sailors,' an old gentleman with two mufflers said to Powerscourt as they passed each other by the little railway station, 'on a night like this.'

He went and sat on the rocks as far out as he dared. The spray rose in front of him. The noise of the wind was matched by the dark waters hurling themselves in vain against the rocks. It's like a siege, Powerscourt thought. The sea is laying siege to this little patch of Ireland. The waves are the artillery, pounding relentlessly, night and day, against the enemy ramparts. The defenders try to close their ears to the onslaught. The defenders are going to win. The rocks are refusing to give way.

Nobody could come into the little harbour on a night like this, he felt sure. However big the mother ship, no little boat with its deadly cargo could make the journey from those great seas into Greystones.

But he didn't sleep. All through the night he kept watch from his windows on the empty grey sea, flecks of white on top of the waves. On the beaches the sea pounded in, crashing up the shore, leaving a trail of dirty foam in its wake. Nothing moved in the streets of Greystones. Even if you had wanted to give or receive a signal, it would have been lost in the fury of the night. Powerscourt was thinking of where he could take Lady Lucy when this case was over. Verona perhaps, city of doomed lovers, Vicenza with all those buildings by Palladio. He felt sure Lucy would like Verona. He could buy her a copy of *Romeo and Juliet* to read on the train. Or would she have read it already? She might have forgotten it.

As dawn broke the rain had come. It was now sweeping in from the mountains, lashing the little town, rattling off the roof of Powerscourt's hotel like gunshot. Powerscourt dreamed of battles at sea as he fell asleep, the terrible carnage of Trafalgar where the smoke of the carronades hung in thick curtains across the sea, and a sniper high up in the rigging of a French ship took careful aim at the one-armed Admiral in his gold braid on the deck of the *Victory*. Snipers. Something told Powerscourt that snipers were terribly important and he should remember them when he woke up.

By then he was in another country. The rain had stopped. The wind had died down. The little town, its grey buildings, its grey beach with the hills behind, were bathed in sunshine. The hotel gardeners were busy under Powerscourt's windows, clearing away fallen branches, tending to the roses that threatened to fill one whole wall with red. Along the sea front the more adventurous citizens were promenading round the bay, commenting excitedly to each other about the change in the weather. 'Isn't it grand, just grand,' floated regularly up to his room.

Powerscourt reached for the binoculars. Johnny Fitzgerald's timetable for the German invasion was nearly finished. Surely they must come today, or tonight. He had no doubt that they would have to land under cover of darkness, sending their deadly packages into the tiny harbour while Greystones and County Wicklow slept. He scanned the horizon. A couple of cargo ships could be seen far out to sea, trudging steadily towards Howth or Dublin. The seagulls were flying regular sorties across the rocks in front of the hotel. A pair of small yachts seemed to have set out from Bray or Killiney further up the coast for a day's sailing. They looked too small to have made the journey across the North Sea.

At two o'clock he went for a walk. He patrolled the streets of Greystones, his binoculars round his neck, pausing from time to time to fix his glasses on the birds. He made polite conversation with some of the local people. Yes, the weather was much better today. Hadn't it been terrible the last few days. Did they get many big yachts coming into Greystones, putting in for supplies or to visit the local attractions? No, sir, they did not. Birdwatchers, he decided, were almost as innocent as fishermen in the eye of the beholder. But all the time he knew that his counterpart must also be watching the seas beyond the town, hiding behind some

182

curtains in an upstairs room, lurking in the heather on the coastal path to Bray, rebellious binoculars scanning the horizon.

It was five o'clock when he saw it. Far out to sea, moving gracefully south towards Wicklow, was a large yacht. It was so much bigger than the ones he had seen earlier in the day. Tiny dots of sailors could be seen through the glasses moving about their business. He couldn't see a name. Maybe it had been removed. The visitor did not even move in towards the shore as it passed. It sailed serenely on as if it had a rendezvous in some other harbour far far away. But Powerscourt was sure. He was certain. This yacht would turn round when it was dark. It would come back to anchor some way from the harbour. A small boat would be lowered from the side. Packages and people would follow. The rendezvous between the German paymasters and quartermasters and their Irish clients was about to begin.

He ate a hearty supper. He ordered with some amusement a main course described as Powerscourt lamb. His father, he remembered, incarcerated with his account books in the corner of the great house, would often remark that at least the lamb sold well. He checked the horse he had rented from the hotel stables, thick sacking wrapped round its hooves to ease the noise it might make on the roads or tracks of Wicklow. As the sun set behind the mountains in a mass of pinks and reds that promised a fine tomorrow, he settled in his observation post on the top floor.

He made a regular orbit with the binoculars. Harbour. Nothing there. North towards Dublin, nothing moved. South towards Wicklow and the mountains inland. Nothing there. The streets of Greystones itself, hosts already perhaps to Irish insurrectionaries who could have come south from the capital to collect their booty. Nothing moved. The moon was full now, weak at first but growing stronger as night settled over Ireland. There were a few clouds that caused a deeper darkness. Moonlight was a mixed blessing. It could show you where your unknown adversaries were going. It could show them they were being followed, a lone agent perhaps of the intelligence networks directed with such deadly precision from Dublin Castle on their trail. A couple of dogs were on manoeuvres, sniffing hopefully around the rocks and the cottages. Far out to sea nothing stirred. There was a slight wind, enough to fill a sail. The waters, sometimes grey, sometimes black, seemed to mock Powerscourt at his lookout post on the top floor of the Imperial Hotel.

It was a dog that gave the first clue. Far off in the distance, probably on the road from Bray, came sounds of barking. Ten minutes later a horse and cart trotted carelessly into the village and stopped outside a shop just fifty yards from the harbour. There was a quantity of hay and what looked like tarpaulin sheets in the back. Nobody stirred. No inhabitants of Greystones peered sleepily from their windows at this strange apparition of the night. Turn your faces to the wall, While the gentlemen go by. There were two men with the cart. Both were wearing dark clothes. Powerscourt checked his watch. It was a quarter to two. He wondered if even on secret and dangerous missions the Germans had a timetable. The boat will come at two o'clock in the morning. Loading will be complete by two fifteen. The mother ship will depart at two thirty. Thank you, gentlemen.

He swung his binoculars out to sea again. He could see nothing at all. The clouds had obscured the moon. Perhaps the timetable even extends to periods of cloud cover. Wait. Check the focus again. What was that, out there on the right? There was a smudge, a blob on the sea. The blob appeared to be moving. Moving towards Greystones. At five to two the weather turned against the invaders. The clouds passed on. In the moonlight Powerscourt saw the yacht, moving gracefully towards him, a couple of miles out to sea. Shortly after two it veered sharply in towards the coast and stopped about eight hundred yards from the harbour.

Powerscourt checked the reception committee by the shop. Nothing stirred. Perhaps the timetable said two thirty or even three. He could see the yacht more clearly now. A boat was being lowered from the deck. Three men in dark jerseys settled into it. Then followed a series of heavy-looking packages. Powerscourt couldn't see what they were. He thought suddenly of British sailors on cutting-out expeditions in naval wars of the past, dangerous nocturnal missions to capture a fort or blow up some enemy vessels while the soldiers or the sailors slept. But this was no friendly mission. Her Majesty's enemies from overseas had come to give aid and assistance to some more of Her Majesty's enemies at home. The boat set off. Powerscourt thought they must have muffled oars. He could catch no noise at all as two men rowed steadily towards the quays.

At twenty past two the cart trotted slowly forward towards the harbour. There was just room to turn it round to face back towards the shore. The two men got out and waited by the steps that led

184

down to the water. One of them was smoking a pipe as if he spent every evening like this, waiting for guns to come out of the sea.

As the boat drew up there was a brief greeting. Then the dark jerseys unloaded the packages from their little boat. One thick oilskin packet went into the inside pocket of the man with the pipe. Powerscourt thought that was probably money. Then came the heavy ones. Powerscourt saw to his astonishment that two wooden coffins with brass handles were being placed in the back of the cart. Two more followed. Hay and the tarpaulins were quickly strewn on top of them. Coffins. What on earth were they doing with coffins? Surely the Germans weren't exporting dead bodies to Ireland for some final Celtic cremation up in the black hills of Wicklow? The Irish might want to put their enemies into wooden boxes but they were perfectly capable of making their own. Then it struck him. As the rowing boat set off back to the yacht, the Germans pausing only to give a solemn salute when they left the steps, Powerscourt thought he had the answer. He swore violently to himself as the cart trotted gently along the bay and passed the Imperial Hotel, unaware of the tall figure hiding behind his curtains to watch their passing.

20

Powerscourt couldn't decide about the horse. Should a mounted Powerscourt set off in pursuit of the coffin-laden cart? Or should it be a single infantryman running along the country roads? He had a very thick coat for the night was cold. He had stout boots in case the going got rough. He had heavy leather gloves. He took another look at his quarry. The cart, little clouds of pipe smoke drifting up into the moonlight, had reached the end of the village and was heading south on the coast road. He sped down the stairs and led his horse in pursuit. The binoculars were his only weapon. He didn't like to think what might happen if the enemy found out they were being pursued. He smiled grimly to himself as he remembered that they had the coffins ready for him, an unknown body to be buried in an unknown grave. He wondered for the tenth time since he first saw them what was inside the coffins that arrived from the sea so secretly, now trotting serenely along the lanes of Wicklow.

The hearse was going quite slowly, no more than five or six miles per hour. Occasional bursts of conversation or laughter drifted back towards Powerscourt trotting very slowly on his horse. It was called Paddy, not a name that would have found favour with Old Mr Harrison and his collection of classical heroes. Hercules, Powerscourt thought, that's what you would want your horse to be called on a night like this.

The road was still skirting the coast, the moonlight bright on a silver sea. Owls were calling from the woods ahead. They were passing the walls that surrounded a great estate. Powerscourt remembered playing there as a child. Just beyond the main entrance, a proud and elaborate pair of gates topped by a couple of stone lions, there was a church, flanked by a handsome vicarage and a row of empty houses. My God, that's clever, Powerscourt thought to himself. They're going to bury the coffins in a Protestant cemetery. Nobody in authority would think of looking there. Catholic ones, of course, but the dead of the Church of Ireland would never be suspected of harbouring German coffins with their unknown cargo.

He left Paddy tied to a tree some hundred yards from the church and tiptoed forward to get a better view. These were grave robbers in reverse, he said to himself, come to leave rather than take, their mission unknown, the coffins to stay with their dead companions until Judgement Day was closer. The Irishmen had their spades out and were digging fast but quietly. The first layer of turf was carefully removed and laid in neat piles beside the headstone. Then the dark Wicklow earth was thrown as quickly as they could into a mound. Powerscourt could hear the dull thud as the spade hit the coffin.

Like figures in a dance the men moved automatically towards the two ends. Powerscourt wondered if they were undertakers by profession. After a couple of grunts the old coffin was hauled out of the hole. A further period of digging followed. The hole was being made deeper. They're superstitious, Powerscourt thought. They're going to leave the body in its grave. They're just going to put a couple of German coffins in underneath. Neither man spoke. Some bird or animal howled in the distance, a protest at the desecration of the dead. They stopped digging. Two of the coffins were lowered into the open grave. The original coffin was put in on top. The earth was replaced. Powerscourt was getting pins and needles in his leg. He hoped the horse was all right, waiting by its tree. Only two of the seaborne coffins were interred. There must be two left. Powerscourt wondered if another grave was going to be opened up, or if they were destined for a different resting place.

Powerscourt had to know what was inside those dark boxes. He searched desperately in his pockets. He didn't have a penknife. He didn't even have a screwdriver. He doubted if he could open one of those coffins with his bare hands and the stones that lay around the paths. He swore to himself. If only Johnny Fitzgerald was here. He always carried a strange miscellany around in his pockets.

It seemed the burial party was about to move on. Powerscourt drew back into the shadows as the two men mounted the cart once more. There was a certain amount of business with matches being struck to relight the pipe. No smoking in church or cemetery, he thought. Take off your hats when you go in and make the sign the of the cross.

As he strained forward from his tree, Powerscourt's prayers were answered. The gravediggers were having a conversation. The words floated back to Powerscourt across the cemetery.

'Do you think those rifles will be safe in there, Michael?' asked the first gravedigger. The man called Michael laughed. 'Oh yes, they will. But not as safe as where we're going to take the others.'

So that was it. Rifles, German rifles, the latest German rifles were in the coffins. Deadly rifles, Mausers or Schneiders, with the very newest sights, no doubt, capable of killing a man at eight hundred yards or more. Snipers' rifles. He remembered his dream. With one of these an accurate marksman, perched on top of Admiralty Arch, could pick off somebody in a carriage leaving Buckingham Palace before they were half-way down the Mall.

The deadly cortege moved off away from Greystones towards the mountains. Powerscourt crept quietly into the churchyard. The grass on the top had been perfectly replaced. Two bunches of withered flowers had also been left to conceal the disturbance. They must have brought those with them, he thought, hidden on the back of the cart. He felt renewed respect for his adversaries. George Thomas Carew, the tombstone said, of Ballygoran, 1830–1887. Powerscourt had eaten his strawberries as a child. The Carews said they were the finest strawberries in Ireland, eaten with lashings of home-grown cream on the Carews' immaculate lawn, Carew children playing happily on the grass, George Thomas Carew presiding happily at the head of his table. Powerscourt remembered the smell that followed Mr Carew wherever he went. He smoked a pipe. His children used to joke that he smoked it in his sleep. May he rest in peace, he said to himself, tiptoeing back towards his horse. One of the Carew daughters had been very pretty, he remembered. She must be married now with a family of her own. Pray to God she never hears what has been done to her father's grave.

Distant smoke signals told him the way to go. The road was rising now, going away from the sea into the dark of the mountains. Clouds had obscured the moon once more, Paddy's muffled feet sounding very soft on the grass verge. He remembered McKenzie, the tracker he had worked with in India who could follow anybody anywhere, telling him about the American Indians and the smoke signals they could send hundreds of miles across the plains. Much more efficient than that bloody telegraph, McKenzie had said.

Quite soon there was a crossroads, he recalled. The left-hand fork led down into a valley and a little village at the bottom. The right-hand turn took you up into the heart of the mountains through a bare and bleak landscape where the wind howled across the empty scrub. The cart was about two hundred yards ahead of him, he thought. He paused regularly in case he got too close. Suddenly he remembered the date. This was 1897. In one year's time it would be the hundredth anniversary of the rebellion of 1798, a terrible, doomed uprising that left thousands of Irish dead, slaughtered on the battlefield or hanged in reprisal for revolt. Powerscourt shuddered as he remembered the atrocities done to innocent Catholics, the punishment triangles set up in the squares of the little towns of Wexford forty miles south of here, fathers forced to kneel while their sons were lashed until the blood dripped down on to their parent beneath them. Then the roles were reversed, the bleeding sons forced to kneel while the fathers were lashed until a father's blood ran down to mix with the son's. This is my blood. He recalled the flights of oratory as the Irish protested in vain at the reign of terror imposed on them: 'Merciful God what is the state of Ireland, and where shall you find the wretched inhabitants of this land? You may find him, perhaps, in jail, the only place of security – I had almost said of ordinary habitation! If you do not find him there, you may see him flying with his family from the flames of his own dwelling – lighted to his dungeon by the conflagration of his hovel; or you may find his bones bleaching on the green fields of his country; or you may find him tossing on the surface of the ocean, and mingling his groans with those tempests, less savage than his persecutors, that drift him to a returnless distance from his family and his home without charge, or trial or sentence.'

A sixteen-year-old Powerscourt had once declaimed the whole speech from the rooftop of Powerscourt House when his parents were away, his sisters a captive audience on the steps beneath. Two of them had fallen asleep, he remembered bitterly. One of the men in the cart was whistling softly as they headed into the mountains at the crossroads. The road had turned into little more than a track now. Puddles left from the recent rain glistened in the moonlight. Powerscourt wondered if the muffled feet would slip more easily. He checked his watch. It was a quarter to four. Not much time left for the second burial of the night. The cart was moving slowly now as the path wound its way ever higher into the mountains. On Powerscourt's left the hill sloped precipitously down to a stream below. Then disaster struck.

A dog barked from up ahead. It seemed to come from the cart. Powerscourt hadn't noticed any animals at all in the vehicle, only the straw and the tarpaulins and then the coffins beneath them. He stopped. The cart stopped. The barking did not. He heard one of the men get out. He could hear whispering up ahead. Did they suspect they were being followed? You could suspect anything in the shadows of this night, carrying cases of German rifles across a darkened landscape to be interred with the already buried dead. Powerscourt swore. If they thought they were being followed they would come back another night and dig up the grave of George Thomas Carew and move his companion coffins somewhere else. They might not bury the other two at all tonight, merely returning the cart to the remote farm it had come from and turning gravediggers again another time. The knowledge he had was priceless. Once the authorities in Dublin Castle knew where the rifles were buried they had the manpower to watch them right round the clock. But even the suspicion of a follower, the fear that they had not been alone, and the guns would be moved. The dog kept barking. Powerscourt thought it could bark all night. Maybe it had enjoyed a long sleep and its lungs were fit to bark until dawn.

He heard somebody coming down the path towards him, very quietly. He retreated towards the trees behind. The man held something in his hand. Still the dog barked. It was enough to wake the dead, even though they had been disturbed once already this evening.

The pistol shot was louder than the dog. It echoed around the mountains. Powerscourt knew nobody would take any notice. Turn your faces to the wall, While the gentlemen go by. One hundred yards was too far for a pistol. Powerscourt thanked God they hadn't taken out any of those German rifles from their coffins. But then, he smiled incongruously, they would come with pages and pages of instructions, impossible to read in the dark, probably impossible to understand in the daylight.

The man fired again. Powerscourt felt the bullet pass a few yards away from him and land with an ominous plop in a pine tree further down the hill. He could run. His horse would be faster than man or dog. He didn't like the thought of running away.

A third pistol shot. The dog was barking non-stop now, engaged in a trial of noise with its master.

Powerscourt looked down at the terribly steep slope to his left. The man fired again, twice in quick succession. Powerscourt screamed. He fell to the ground. His body rolled down the slope, slowly at first, then with increasing speed, bumping into rocks, bouncing off trees, until it came to a stop two hundred and fifty yards beneath, the head dangling forward into the stream. The other man came from the cart to peer down below.

'Who the divil was that, do you suppose?' said the first gravedigger.

'God knows. He's dead now. If the bullet didn't get him, the fall will have done,' replied his friend with the pipe.

'Do you want me to go down and make sure he's dead? Finish him off if he's not?'

'I'm sure the bullets got him. He'll have been dead before he reached the bottom.'

The man with the pipe was a regular winner at shooting competitions all round the county. He was certain. The two men made their way back to the cart. At the bottom of the slope, his curly hair floating in the stream, the body of Lord Francis Powerscourt lay very still. By the side of the path above, the horse waited for its master.

21

The cart moved off up the hill deeper into the impenetrable mountains. The dog was quiet now, its duty done. A mile and a half further up, the cart stopped by a tiny chapel on the hillside. Stunted trees, their branches bent into weird positions by the wind, guarded a desolate graveyard. The headstones were poor up here, not the marble slabs that graced the tombs of the Protestants in the lush valleys below. The gravediggers resumed their routine in silence, the pipe once again left burning fitfully by the side of the road. The earth was rockier here and it took longer to dig down the extra depth to hide the German visitors. Faint streaks of dawn were appearing in the Irish Sea behind them as the two men mounted their cart once more, their mission accomplished, the weapons hidden where no one would know their burial place.

'Are you going back to Dublin this morning?' said the first gravedigger.

'I am that,' replied the man with the pipe. 'I've a class to teach at nine o'clock this morning. I'll get the train from Greystones if you can drop me off.'

At the bottom of the hill Lord Francis Powerscourt was examining every bone in his body, very slowly and very carefully. Christ, he was sore. He remembered the training McKenzie had given them in falling down hills without being hurt. He thanked God he had paid attention. He thought he would try standing up. It was extremely painful. His left ankle didn't feel too good. It was a sprain, a bad sprain, he told himself. He could feel bruises, nasty bruises, all over his arms and his legs. Blood was running from a deep cut on his temple, dripping on to his coat. His head felt as if it had been battered by a hundred rocks. But he wasn't dead. Not yet anyway.

Powerscourt looked up the slope. He could just see the horse, still waiting by its tree. With the horse he could go back to his hotel or he could try to complete his mission. He had heard the cart going on up the path. Then the sound had been blown away by the wind. If he waited an hour or so he could ride after them in the hope of discovering where the other rifles were buried. Then he would know all there was to know, all except, he reflected wearily, the names of the two men, the dates of their proposed assassinations, the destinations of any bombs.

Afterwards he told Lady Lucy that he hadn't thought he would ever make it back to the path on the hill. Every step was painful with his bad ankle. His head throbbed. The blood was still flowing on to his coat. The various bruises around his body ached with a throbbing pain.

He crawled the last hundred yards to the horse, inching his way up the slope, digging his bruised elbows into the hard ground, stray rocks doing him fresh injury on his via dolorosa. He thought of his children to ease the pain. He thought of sitting in some quiet English garden with Lady Lucy, green lawns spread in front of them, a river or a lake at the bottom. Sometimes he thought he was hallucinating and Lucy was actually beside him, helping him up the slope.

'Don't worry, Francis, not much further to go. Just a few more steps, my darling.' Lady Lucy was mopping the blood from his face, stroking a soothing salve on to the bruises that pulsated all over him.

At last he reached the horse. He leaned against Paddy's side for a full five minutes, thanking the horse for waiting for him. He knew it would be painful getting up into the saddle. It was excruciating, the pain shooting up his left ankle in blinding flashes. Then he began to ride very slowly up the hill in pursuit of the cart. He hoped he would find another church. He thought he might collapse inside it, sanctuary for the wounded man, respite from his enemies.

Our Lady of Sorrows, the name perfectly matching his mood, held no secrets for him. The gravediggers must have run out of flowers by now, he thought. But then maybe any flowers would have looked out of place in this desolate spot. The eternal rest of Martha O'Driscoll, 1850–1880 had been disturbed. Poor woman,

Powerscourt thought, she had only lived for thirty years before having to wait for the Second Coming up here with the mountains glowering down on her and the wind whistling through the damaged trees. And then she got company, German rifles come to disturb the long sleep of the dead.

Powerscourt set out to ride back to the hotel. The horse seemed to know the way. Once or twice he nearly passed out on the road down the mountain. At a quarter to seven in the morning Paddy trotted slowly into the stables of the Imperial Hotel. Powerscourt noticed that the wind had caused some damage to the roses in the night. Red petals lay strewn across the lawn like patches of dried blood.

As he staggered upstairs and fell asleep the first train of the morning was pulling out of Greystones station on its journey up the coast towards Dublin. Sitting very quietly, looking out to sea, a man lit a fresh pipe.

22

'Gentlemen, gentlemen. Could I have your attention, please.'

A portly man with a huge handlebar moustache had climbed on to a bench in the home side's dressing room. The creases on his cricket flannels were razor sharp, his white sweater was immaculate.

'Hopwood's the name, Aston Hopwood. I'm your captain for the day.'

He surveyed his companions, some still lacing up their boots, others rehearsing imaginary strokes with great concentration.

'I've got to do the batting order before the toss,' Hopwood said. 'Someone here called Powerscourt? Opening batsman?'

Lord Francis Powerscourt raised a nervous hand in acknowledgement. Nearly a fortnight had passed since his ordeal in Ireland and his aches had almost gone. He had passed on all he knew about the German rifles lying in Irish graves to Dominic Knox of the Irish Office. Knox had been effusive in his thanks.

'Welcome to the team, Powerscourt.' Hopwood boomed. 'Smythe? You happy to be the other opening man?'

An elderly gentleman who looked as though his cricketing days should have been over long ago nodded his consent.

'Where's the Bank of England?' Hopwood demanded of the changing room. The Bank was nowhere to be seen.

'Bloody Bank,' said Hopwood bitterly. 'He's always late. Anyway, I'll put him in at Number Three.'

Gradually Hopwood worked his way down the batting order. Powerscourt noticed that James Clarke, William Burke's bright young man, was down to bat at Number Nine. Clarke's whites had not received as much attention as those of his colleagues. The trousers were too short and his sweater too small.

195

'What do you know about the opposition, Hopwood?' asked a slim young man who was a fast bowler. Powerscourt was to learn later that he was known as Ivan the Terrible because of the speed and ferocity of his deliveries.

'They're a party of Americans come to tour here this summer called the Philadelphians. Bloody Americans.' Hopwood shook his head, remembering a recent coup where an American firm from New York had removed a valuable contract from right under his nose. 'I don't know much about them as cricketers. Expect they'll run about a lot and make a great deal of noise. I don't know what they all do for a living. There's a couple of money people, an academic from somewhere called Princeton, maybe a preacher or two.'

Aston Hopwood departed to the cricket square for the toss. The pavilion was new, built in the mock Tudor style, and it nestled among the tall trees that surrounded the little ground. Rows of chairs had been placed on either side of it and further chairs or benches were dotted about the outfield. To one side was a huge marquee with rows of servants hurrying to and from the great house bearing trays of food and consignments of glasses.

Powerscourt felt acutely nervous. He hadn't expected such a large crowd to witness his humiliation. Lady Lucy was talking to William Burke, taking a tour of the little ground.

'It's so pretty, this cricket ground, isn't it,' said Lady Lucy. 'Look, here are the umpires coming out with the two captains. Do you know who the umpires are, William?'

Burke inspected the two men in the white coats. 'The one on the left is a Bishop, Lady Lucy, Bishop of Oxford, I believe. They say he's a coming man. And the other one is a policeman, Chief Constable of Oxfordshire, name of Bampfylde.'

'Mr de Rothschild isn't expecting any trouble, is he? I mean, they seem very grand personages to be the umpires, William.'

'There was a terrible fight here some years ago, Lucy.' William Burke laughed. 'A man from one of the tea importers had a very good lunch. He'd not been drinking his own produce at lunchtime, he had rather a lot of Rothschild's vicious punch. The stuff tastes perfectly innocuous but it's lethal, Lucy, absolutely lethal. In the third or fourth over after lunch, there's a huge appeal and the umpire says the tea importer has been caught behind. Finger goes up, normal sort of business. Not Out! shouts the tea man. Yes you are, says the umpire. No I'm bloody not, says the tea man. Then the tea man advances down the wicket and knocks the umpire out cold. There was a general scrimmage all round. The match had to be called off. Ever since then old Rothschild has tried for very important men as his umpires. He even got the Governor of the Bank of England to do it one year. Only trouble was, he was half blind and had to be replaced after lunch. The poor man could hardly see a thing.'

'So with the Bishop at one end and the Chief Constable at the other, it should be a peaceful day.' Lady Lucy smiled at her brother-in-law, glancing round the ground to see if either umpire had brought any reinforcements, members of the heavenly host hiding in the long grass, plain-clothes policemen lurking in the woods.

'Let's hope it'll be peaceful, Lucy. Ah, I see the visitors have won the toss. The Americans are going to bat.'

Richard Martin and Sophie Williams had come to watch Richard's friend James Clarke play for the City Eleven. They were lying in the grass as far away from the pavilion as they could get.

'I've never seen a place as grand as this, Sophie,' said Richard, thinking they had indeed arrived at a different world.

'Neither have I, Richard,' said Sophie, stretching out her long legs. 'Isn't this grand. I hope your friend James does well.'

Richard was worrying about lunch. His mother had made a picnic for two, thinking she only had to provide for Richard and James.

'I think you'd better make some more sandwiches, Mother,' Richard had said. 'You get very hungry playing cricket.'

His mother had looked at him suspiciously, but, for once, she said nothing. Now they could see an incredible meal being laid out, probably full of foods they had never seen in their lives and wouldn't know how to eat. They could hardly sit under the trees and eat their sandwiches. They would look out of place.

'Who's this man bowling?' said Powerscourt to Aston Hopwood as they settled in the slips for the opening over.

'Man by the name of Harcourt. Stockbroker. Quick but a bit erratic,' said Hopwood, crouching to his work.

The American who opened the batting was a broad-shouldered fellow from Philadelphia. The first two balls he ignored. The third was so wide that the Bank of England had to dive dramatically to his left to stop it. The fourth and fifth balls were hit to the square leg boundary with tremendous force. The last ball was played defensively back to the bowler.

'Bet you a pint of beer,' said one of Rothschild's elderly gardeners to his colleague, watching from the side of the pavilion, 'this bloke makes fifty.'

'You're on,' said his colleague, pausing to remove his pipe from his mouth. 'Bet you he bloody doesn't.'

William Burke had steered Lady Lucy towards a little group of spectators from Harrison's Bank.

'Mr Harrison,' said Lady Lucy. 'I hope your aunt is well.'

'She is much better, thank you, Lady Powerscourt,' said Charles Harrison. 'The doctors are pleased with her. They are thinking of sending her to the Italian Lakes to recuperate.'

'Watch out!' said Burke suddenly. The broad-shouldered American had struck a mighty blow. The ball sailed happily over Lady Lucy's head and came to earth in the long grass. A trio of small boys raced to recover it.

'My goodness,' said Lady Lucy. 'This American seems to be a very fierce fellow. Do you play cricket, Mr Harrison?'

'Alas, no, I do not.' Charles Harrison smiled a self-deprecating smile, stroking his red beard.

'You never played it at school or university, Mr Harrison?'

Charles Harrison paused to applaud another massive blow which despatched the ball right over the pavilion. It landed on one of the great rollers used to treat the pitch and bounced on again to land in the ornamental topiary at the back of the house.

'I regret, Lady Powerscourt, I regret it very much,' replied Charles Harrison, rubbing his hands together apologetically. Lady Lucy noticed that even the hairs on the back of his hands were red. 'At the Friedrich Wilhelm University in Berlin, we had little time for cricket.'

Privately Charles Harrison was annoyed with himself. I didn't have to say that, he said to himself. I could just have said I went to university in Germany. He pressed on. 'But still, Lady Powers-court, it isn't too late to start.' He began practising imaginary cricket shots.

After eight overs the Americans had made seventy-five runs without losing a wicket. Aston Hopwood, Powerscourt and the Bank of England were having a conference in the slips.

'Only one thing for it, dammit,' said Hopwood.

'What's that?' asked the Bank of England.

'Didn't like to take either of these two off too quickly. I do a lot of business with them, don't you know. But now, there's only one thing for it. Thank you, Hudson, thank you. We're going to change the bowling now.'

Aston Hopwood summoned Ivan the Terrible from his position in the deep. He and the Bank of England retreated further back from the wicket.

'Bit erratic sometimes, the Terrible,' he said to his colleagues. 'I mean, he's quick, but I'm not sure he knows where the damn thing is going.'

Powerscourt moved back to join his fellow fielders. Ivan had retreated to a position not far from the pavilion to begin his run-up. A look of dislike, almost of hatred for the batsmen, passed across his normally placid features. He approached the wicket at ever-increasing speed and sent his first ball down at remarkable pace, but well wide of the stumps. The American blinked, stared back at Ivan the Terrible and waited for the next ball. There was a hush around the ground, the little patches of conversation dying away as Ivan went to war.

His second ball pitched short, rose steeply and flew over the outstretched hands of the Bank of England for four byes.

'Bloody hell!' said Powerscourt.

'Ranging shots. Ranging shots,' said Hopwood, 'let's hope the next few are on target.'

The next ball flew at great speed towards the American's off stump. There was a faint click. Powerscourt sensed a red blur hurtling to his left. He stuck out his hand. He found, to his amazement, that the ball had lodged in his palm, a great sting spreading up his arm.

'How was that!' shouted Aston Hopwood and the Bank of England in unison.

The Bishop's finger rose. The American departed. Powerscourt found himself the subject of congratulations from all sides.

'That's one pint of beer you owe me now,' said Rothschild's gardener with the pipe to his friend. 'Bugger only made forty-two.'

'I tell you what,' said his friend. 'Double or quits. This Terrible fellow to take five wickets.'

'I'm not taking you up on that. Bugger might bowl them all out at this speed.'

The next American showed no signs of being intimidated by Ivan the Terrible. He took a mighty swipe at his first ball and missed completely. He took a mighty swipe at the next ball and crashed it back down the pitch for four runs.

'They don't seem to believe in defence or playing themselves in at all,' said the Bank of England to his colleagues.

Ivan the Terrible paused at the far end of his run up to stare at the American. The American stared back, drawing his bat back to strike another blow.

'For what we are about to receive,' muttered Hopwood.

The next ball was slower than its predecessors. The American misjudged his shot completely. He paused to look briefly at the ruin that had been his wicket and set off back to the pavilion, pausing to clap Ivan the Terrible on the shoulder on his way.

'That was a pretty eventful over,' said Burke to Lady Lucy. 'He's very fast, that chap.'

'Didn't Francis do well, William. I'm so proud of him.' Lady Lucy gazed proprietorially at her husband, deep in conversation with his colleagues in the slips.

'He did very well, Lucy, that was a difficult catch. I wonder when Hopwood's going to put my young man on to bowl.'

James Clarke, however, remained in the outfield. Ivan the Terrible bowled a further three overs and sent a further three Americans back to the pavilion. Then Hopwood took him off.

'Can't have the bloody game finishing before tea,' he said to Powerscourt. 'I'll bring him back later on if we have to. He's pretty puffed already.'

A small wiry American had come in to bat at Number Three and hung on to his wicket like a limpet. Not for him the mighty blows of the first batsman. He proceeded with nudges and glances, a lot of quick singles and a general process of accumulation that aroused the wrath of the Bank of England behind the stumps.

'Why don't you hit the bloody thing?' he asked the batsman sarcastically after a well-placed prod had brought him another two runs.

'Temper, temper,' said the American. 'Every run counts.'

By lunch the Americans had advanced to one hundred and twenty-five for four, a respectable total but considerably less than might have been expected from their lightning start.

'Mind the punch,' said Hopwood to his team as they returned to the pavilion. He too had been involved in the fracas several years before. 'That stuff's bloody lethal.'

James Clarke had raced off the field to find his friends.

'Richard, Miss Williams,' he said, 'come and meet my governor. He's just over there."

William Burke was happy to escort the young people to lunch and to guide them through the culinary delights on offer. Somebody needs to look after such a pretty girl as this Miss Williams, he said to himself. Some of these wolves from the City wouldn't do her any good at all.

'Ham, Mr Martin? Miss Williams? Some lobster? Some ptarmigan pie?'

Lunch was taken at tables in the marquee or sitting on the grass. Powerscourt sat with Lady Lucy under a large tree. William Burke had taken Richard Martin and Sophie Williams and James Clarke on a tour of the gardens. Out of the corner of his eye Powerscourt saw Charles Harrison watch them go, a look of extreme disquiet on his face. The Bank of England had given very definite instructions to one of the waiters. Some of the Americans were receiving regular refills of the Rothschild punch. The two old retired gardeners had fallen asleep under their oak, snores drifting out across the cricket field.

'I don't think the wiry one will last much longer,' the Bank of England said happily to Powerscourt and Hopwood as play resumed.

'Why not?' said Hopwood. 'He looked pretty well set to me before lunch.'

'That was before he met the punch.' The Bank of England grinned.

Initially the wiry American showed no signs of having been affected by the punch or anything else. He attacked the bowling with great vigour for a couple of overs. Then he went into a slow decline. His running between the wickets became erratic. He missed perfectly simple balls. Eventually he fell over on to his own wicket when confronted by James Clarke's off spinners.

'Bad luck. What rotten luck!' The Bank of England waved him happily off the field.

'That were that punch, that were,' said the retired gardener with the pipe. 'He was quite all right before lunch, that thin bloke.'

'Hit wicket bowled punch,' cackled his friend. 'Do you think there's any of the stuff left?'

Shortly before three o'clock the American innings closed with the score at one hundred and seventy-six.

'Respectable score,' said Hopwood to Powerscourt as he buckled on his pads, 'but we should be able to knock that off fairly easily.'

Powerscourt felt his knees go weak as he walked to the wicket.

201

True, he had put in some practice with his local team in Northamptonshire in the weeks leading up to the match. But here he was in front of this large crowd against bowlers he had never seen before.

A tall thin American with a black moustache was preparing to open the bowling. He advanced off a run up of only a few paces and sent down a ball that was quite fast but well wide of the off stump. Steady, Powerscourt said to himself, steady. The next two balls he played defensively. The fourth he tucked away on the on side for a single. He was off the mark. He breathed again.

William Burke seemed to have taken Richard Martin and Sophie Williams under his wing. They were chatting happily with James Clarke under a tree just behind the bowler's arm. Lady Lucy was sitting by Bernard de Rothschild who kept up a running commentary on the proceedings. Oliver Smythe, the other opener, was now facing the bowling.

'Well played there, Smythe, splendid cover drive. Don't think much of the American bowling, my dear, well hit, sir, well hit, oh dear, that fielder is going to catch it, he's running for it very fast, he's not going to get there before it drops, he is, he dives, he's got it! Eighteen for one!'

The next over proved a disaster for the City. Three of them were out to a slow American spinner who seemed to turn the ball to a diabolical degree. Hopwood was the last to go with the score at twenty-two for four.

'Hang in there, Powerscourt. For God's sake hang in there. One or two of these fellows coming up can hit a ball but they won't last long. We need an anchor at the other end.'

Powerscourt dug himself in. Whatever happens at the other end, I've got to stay here, he said to himself. Captain's orders. He remembered an innings he had played once for his college at Cambridge where he had batted right through against the superior forces of St John's until the last over of the day, only to run out of partners with three balls left.

Lady Lucy was watching him anxiously, staring out at the pitch beneath her parasol. Powerscourt nudged away a couple of singles. A short ball on the leg side he pulled imperiously to the square leg boundary for four. The Bank of England was with him now.

'You close off your end, Powerscourt. Don't believe in pussyfooting around myself. Smite the Philistines, that's what I say. Smite them.'

202

His superiors at the Old Lady of Threadneedle Street would not have been happy with the rashness of his play. He charged down the wicket. He aimed to hit every ball, good or bad. For a while he smote the Philistines most effectively and the City score advanced to the more comfortable total of sixty. Then the Philistines laid a trap for him. Two fielders were sent to the boundary in the part of the field where he most often hit the ball. A slow innocuous delivery was hit for six. The next ball was slightly faster. The Bank of England mishit his shot. The ball rose high in the air into the welcome arms of an American. Sixty-six for five and the City were running out of batsmen.

A broker friend of Hopwood's and a discount man followed him rapidly back to the pavilion. With half an hour to go before tea the youthful figure of James Clarke strode to the wicket, the score board showing seventy-four for seven.

'Good luck, James! Good luck!' Sophie Williams thought she must be more nervous than her new friend.

'Fifty at least!' said Richard.

Powerscourt could see after just one over that James Clarke was a very fine cricketer indeed. He faced the bowlers with great assurance and drove them effortlessly round the field. The score advanced rapidly. Powerscourt saw that his own total had reached twenty-five and that if James continued to score at the same rate he would soon be overtaken.

'Just hang in there, sir. We'll beat the bastards yet,' Clarke advised him on one of their midwicket conferences as the score rose towards one hundred.

'Bet you that pint of beer,' said the old gardener with his pipe, 'bet you this left-handed one, Powerscourt do they call him, bet you he won't get out at all. He'll carry his bat.'

'Bet you he won't,' said his friend, 'they get worn out, those people. He'll try some fancy shot and get himself out. You mark my words.'

With one over left before tea Powerscourt received the ball he had been waiting for all day. It was short. It was outside the off stump. It was perfect for a late cut. He caressed it to the boundary.

'Capital! Capital!' croaked Bertrand de Rothschild, seizing Lady Lucy by the arm. 'That's his late cut! He's played it at last! And what a fine stroke it was!'

Lady Lucy wondered if there were early cuts as well but felt she should not inquire. A prolonged burst of applause ran around the

203

crowd. The City had passed one hundred. Perhaps they could win it after all.

'Do you think we can do it, Mr Burke? Do you think we can win?' Richard Martin was growing rather fond of his new friend.

'Let us hope so, Richard. If these two can take us to a hundred and fifty or so, we should have a good chance.'

Aston Hopwood held a council of war with his batsmen behind the pavilion at the tea interval. 'Well played, both of you, well played. You've got to stick at it. Thing is,' he said a little defensively, 'I got odds of eight to one against us winning when the score was twenty-two for four. Eight to one. So I put twenty pounds on. The odds looked too good to miss.'

James Clarke grinned at the stockbroker. 'Do we get a bonus if we win it for you, sir?' he asked.

'Cheeky young monkey! That's what you are!' Aston Hopwood roared with laughter. 'Now then,' he went on, 'I've got the last two batsmen practising non-stop until they go in. Supervising them myself, getting them ready for the fray. Wish I'd done the same for some of the others.'

Powerscourt managed a quick word with Lady Lucy.

'Are you all right, Francis? You look quite done in to me,' she smiled.

'Nonsense, Lucy, I'm just getting warmed up. I do hope we can pull it off, that's all.'

Bertrand de Rothschild came up, munching happily on an enormous slice of fruit cake.

'Exquisite late cut, sir, exquisite. Are we going to see any more?'

'I hope so,' said Powerscourt, smiling.

James Clarke was pulling at his sweater. The two umpires, God and Law and Order, were marching steadily towards the wicket. Some of the Americans were doing physical jerks, one of them performing a dramatic series of cartwheels to the amazement of a group of children.

James Clarke carried on after tea just as he had before. Powerscourt continued to collect his ones and twos as the score mounted steadily towards one hundred and fifty. Clarke saw that in with a massive six straight down the ground. Then he made his only mistake. With twenty runs more needed for victory he mistimed his stroke. The ball went straight up into the air.

'Mine!' shouted the wicketkeeper as three fielders converged on the ball. And it was. The Americans clapped him off the field. The crowd rose to their feet. The City were one hundred and fifty-seven for eight.

Aston Hopwood put his arm round James Clarke as he walked back up the pavilion steps to take his pads off.

'Sorry, sir,' said Clarke. 'And I'm sorry about the bet.'

Aston Hopwood roared with laughter.

'Don't worry about the bet. I managed to place another one, you see. I don't think I'll be out of pocket today!'

'What was your other bet, sir?'

'Bet some fool from Burke's Bank that you'd make fifty. The fellow said if you were any good why were you batting so low down the order. I didn't tell him I'd seen you play before so I got odds of ten to one off him. And you made fifty-eight!'

Hopwood clapped him on the shoulder.

'How much did you put on, sir?'

'How much? Twenty pounds. Hardly worth putting on any less, was it!'

Clarke hurried off to join his friends and William Burke. Ivan the Terrible had reached the crease. He hit his first two balls for four. Thirteen to go. The last ball of the over was despatched for two more. One hundred and sixty-seven, ten runs away from victory.

Powerscourt was now facing the bowling. The first ball was just where he liked it, short and outside the off stump. He leaned back into his stroke. Another late cut would leave the City six runs short of victory. But the ball bounced higher than he expected. It must have hit a bump in the pitch. He heard the snick as the ball clipped the top of his bat. He heard the smack as it disappeared into the wicketkeeper's gloves. He heard the appeal, shouted in triumph by the Americans.

He saw the Bishop's finger. After batting all through the innings, with victory a couple of blows away, he had thrown it all away.

'Hard luck, oh hard luck!'

The Americans applauded him off the field. Sixty-two runs he had made, he saw from the scoreboard.

'That late cut!' Bertrand de Rothschild croaked to Lady Lucy. 'I warned him about it, you know. I told him what a dangerous shot it was. What a time to play it! What a time!'

'If my husband hadn't played so well, sir, the match would have been over long ago.' Lady Lucy rose in search of her husband. Powerscourt didn't return to the pavilion. He went to share the last moments with Burke and his little party, above all with James Clarke. They had nearly won the match together. Now they could watch until the end. As he flopped down on the grass he saw Charles Harrison lurking behind William Burke. He was partly hidden in the trees. Did he mean to be hidden from view? He was straining forward as if trying to hear what was being said.

'Well done, Francis! Well done!'

'Jolly well played, sir. What rotten luck!'

The last man made his way slowly to the crease. Aston Hopwood had followed him so far on his way that the Oxfordshire Police umpire had to order him back. He stopped for a brief conference with Ivan the Terrible.

'Man from accounts,' Aston Hopwood was telling anybody who would listen in the pavilion. 'One of the big insurance companies. Spends his whole bloody life working with figures. Hope to God he's grasped the significance of these.' Hopwood nodded vehemently at the scoreboard. One hundred and sixty-seven for nine. The scorers were leaning forward out of their window to catch the last overs of the match. The small boys had given up their own games in the long grass and were watching intently. A couple of cows from the Rothschild farm had ambled up to the fence at the edge, chewing ruminatively. Sophie Williams was clutching Richard's arm in her excitement.

Accounts faced his first ball. It was well wide of the wicket. He missed the next one altogether. The last two balls of the over he blocked defiantly, wiping at his glasses after each one.

'Anyone take ten pounds on a tie?'

Aston Hopwood found no takers.

Ivan the Terrible was now facing the American spinner. His balls were slow but liable to turn quite alarmingly. The first ball Ivan left alone. The second he smote for six into the field with the cows.

'Well done, Ivan, well done!'

The cows moved slowly off back to more peaceful pastures.

'One four would do it,' James Clarke whispered to Powerscourt. He crossed his fingers. The next ball was well wide. Perhaps the Americans are as nervous as we are, thought Powerscourt.

'Come on, Philadelphians!' A huge shout rose from the rest of the American party. The bowler took heart. His next ball seemed to land well outside the stumps. Ivan the Terrible gathered himself for one last match-winning blow. But he missed. The ball turned. It removed Ivan the Terrible's middle stump. The match was over. The Americans had won.

William Burke rose to return to the pavilion. 'Remember,

Richard, remember,' he shouted back to the little group as he departed. 'Come and see me in my office on Monday. We have a lot to talk about.' He waved cheerfully.

Powerscourt stared at the trees. Was Charles Harrison still there? Would he have overheard?

'Come on, Lord Powerscourt. I think we should get a glass of beer now!' James Clarke looked at his batting partner. He had turned white.

Hurrying away to the other side of the ground, his face as black as thunder, was Charles Harrison. Powerscourt felt sure he had heard Burke's parting words. If only he had said something, if only he had warned his brother-in-law, this could have been avoided.

A huge shout now came across the pitch. Somebody was hurrying across to join them.

'Francis!' said the voice, 'I hear there's been a bloody miracle. I hear you actually made some runs today!'

Powerscourt felt that there had indeed been a miracle at this cricket ground. For there, advancing towards them with an enormous grin, was a face he had not seen for some time, a face he had missed more than he cared to admit. He might have come too late for the match, but Johnny Fitzgerald was in time for the beer.

Part Three

Jubilee

23

'I've brought back two new pieces of information from Berlin.' Johnny Fitzgerald was back in the Powerscourt house in Markham Square later that evening, Lady Lucy pouring tea. Powerscourt felt stiff, his limbs aching from all that running between the wickets. Secretly he felt very proud of himself, over sixty runs to his name and a good slip catch. Maybe now at last, with Johnny Fitzgerald back home again, his luck would turn for the better.

'God knows what they mean, mind you. The secret society people are obsessed with Jubilee Day. I overheard them talking about it more than once. One of them said he was going for a holiday, but only after Jubilee Day. They all laughed at that. And they talked a lot about the hotel room. No idea which city or which hotel or which room. But one of them was checking with another that he had booked it last October. That's eight months ago now. What do you make of that, Francis?'

Powerscourt laughed. 'I have absolutely no idea. Maybe its importance will become clearer later.'

Powerscourt told Fitzgerald about the rifles in the coffins that had made the journey to Ireland. Fitzgerald explained there was a bar in Berlin divided into little sections where the people he suspected of belonging to the secret society went to drink.

'I heard this very strange conversation in the next booth in there one day, Francis. The fellows were whispering. I had to press my ear against a crack in the panelling to catch what they were saying.

'I am absolutely certain there are secret societies in Berlin,' Fitzgerald went on. 'They're based round the university. And I'm pretty sure I got very close to them. I'd been trailing my coat pretty hard with all my rhetoric about being an Irish revolutionary and hating the English. I think I was getting fairly close to an exploratory conversation with one or two people. We'd skirted round things a bit already, how would I feel about working for the Fatherland against England, that sort of question. Then all the wires were cut. My contacts disappeared. The people I knew treated me as though I had the plague.'

'How long ago was that, Johnny?'

'It must have been over a fortnight ago.'

'Lucy,' said Powerscourt, 'how long ago since that German character came to our front door asking for Johnny?'

'Oh, it was just after the fire,' said Lucy.

'What was that, Lucy?' Johnny Fitzgerald leant forward in his chair. 'Some fellow came to the door and asked for me? How did he put it? What did he say?'

Lady Lucy thought carefully. 'He came to the door and said he was trying to get in touch with you. He asked if you were a friend of Francis's. He was polite but very insistent. Rhys told him you were in Berlin.'

'And that I was a friend of Francis'?' Fitzgerald said. 'Rhys confirmed that?'

Lady Lucy nodded.

'What do you think was going on, Francis?' asked Fitzgerald. 'I mean it's always nice to be popular, but this might be going a bit too far.'

Powerscourt was rubbing carefully at the inside of his thigh. He thought he might be getting cramp.

'It all depends which way the link goes,' he said finally, his mind racing from Blackwater to the City to the German capital. 'Is it Berlin to London or London to Berlin?'

'Do you remember, Francis?' Lady Lucy interrupted the riddle, suddenly remembering a titbit of gossip from the cricket match. 'Mr Charles Harrison went to university in Berlin. He didn't go to one here in England or anything. The Friedrich Wilhelm University, he said. Maybe he belongs to this secret society. They don't play cricket there, he told me. And then he looked cross with himself as if he hadn't meant to tell me.'

Powerscourt stared at his wife. He already knew that, but the significance might have escaped him.

'They don't play cricket there, he said,' Lady Lucy went on. 'I wonder what sort of games they do play.'

'What does the riddle mean, Francis?' said Fitzgerald. 'The link you were talking about just now. Berlin London, London Berlin. Do we change at Paris or Frankfurt?'

Powerscourt smiled. 'It could work two ways. Let's assume that there is a connection between recent events at Harrison's Bank and a person or persons in Berlin. Suppose Charles Harrison is a member of this secret society from his time at the university. He knows that I am investigating the death of his uncle. He knows that you are a colleague of mine and that you are not in London. Perhaps you are in Berlin. He decides to find out. So he sends his young man round to knock on our front door where he learns that you are not here but in Berlin. He wires this news to Berlin. Fitzgerald is in town. He must be doing Powerscourt's business. So they stop talking to you. You are frozen out, as you say. Probably just as well that's all they did.'

Powerscourt wondered if they had thought of more offensive measures against Johnny Fitzgerald.

'Or,' he went on, 'it could work the other way round. The messages begin in Berlin. They go to Charles Harrison in London. We have this curious customer here, Fitzgerald. He seems to want to know all about our secret society. Do we trust him or not? Is he friend or foe? Supporter or spy?'

Lady Lucy poured some more tea. Fitzgerald was thinking back to his last contact with the man from the secret society.

'The chap did go very frosty at the end,' he said, 'man by the name of Munster. Creepy sort of character. I didn't quite trust him. Mind you, it sounds as if he would have trusted me even less.'

Powerscourt's leg was going numb. If he sat still any longer he would be locked into his chair. He rose and began to hobble stiffly around the room. 'The question is this,' he said with a grimace as the cramp shot up his leg. 'Who's in charge of whatever is going on? London or Berlin? Who is calling the shots?'

He came back to his chair and sank slowly down. He continued rubbing his thigh. 'If we knew the answer to that, we might, we might just know the answer to everything.'

There was a firm knock at the drawing room door. Rhys the butler came in with a letter on a tray.

'This has just come for you, my lord,' he said. 'The man said it was very urgent.'

Lady Lucy watched her husband's face as his eyes flickered down the letter. She watched them go back to the top and read it again. She watched him turn pale, very pale.

'Bad news, Francis?' said Lady Lucy.

'Tell us what it says,' said Johnny Fitzgerald.

'Williamson is dead,' said Powerscourt very quietly. He paused and looked down again at his letter. 'The clerk at Harrison's Bank who still had some shares in the business. The one man who stood between Charles Harrison and total control of the bank. Run over by an underground train at Bank station this evening. It's not clear at all if he fell, or if he was pushed. The Commissioner says their man meant to be looking after Williamson lost him in the crush. Death would have been instantaneous.'

Powerscourt remembered the only time he had met Williamson, a careful, rather worried old gentleman anxious to secure the best for his bank and its clients. He need worry no more.

'How terrible,' said Lady Lucy.

'That makes a quartet of death now,' said Powerscourt. 'One in the yacht, one in the Thames, one in the inferno at Blackwater, one under the wheels of a train. There's only one person left in charge of Harrison's Bank. Nobody else can stop him now. He's on his own.'

London was filling up for the Jubilee. Many of the fifty thousand troops from all corners of Victoria's Empire had arrived. They walked open-mouthed around the great shopping streets, dazzled by the wealth on show. Some of them went to the Victorian era exhibition at Earl's Court displaying sixty years of British art and music, women's work and sport. Stands were being erected all along the route with the newspapers complaining that large sections of the West End had been turned into a timber yard.

At the War Office General Arbuthnot was holding a final meeting with the Metropolitan Police and Dominic Knox of the Intelligence Department of the Irish Office.

'What do you think, Knox? Are we to expect a terrorist attack or not?'

'You are always asking me for a definite answer,' said Knox, irritated with this need for simple certainties in the battle against a devious and invisible enemy. 'On balance, I should say that there will be an attempt at some kind of outrage. It may be that we will be able to prevent it. But I do not believe it will take place on the main route of the procession.'

'Why not?' said the General.

'Think of it, man, think of it.' Knox addressed the General as though he was talking to a rather stupid child. 'This isn't like a football match with supporters of two different teams attending. There is only one team, Victoria's team. Fifty thousand soldiers are going to march along the route. All of them are to be told to keep their eyes open for anything unusual in the crowds. There will be policemen everywhere charged with the same mission. Plain-clothes men will be placed among the crowd at certain points – one entire stand near Fleet Street will be filled with them. Nobody could attempt to fire a shot or place a bomb with that amount of surveillance, not unless they are on a suicide mission. And however much the Irish profess their love for their country and its freedom, none of them has so far been prepared to blow himself up in the process.' General Arbuthnot always found it difficult talking to Knox. The man was so elusive, so quick to qualify whatever decisions he might have made.

'So where might we expect something, do you suppose, Mr Knox?'

'I don't know, General.' He's off again, thought the General, longing for the ordered certainties of the parade ground. 'I'm afraid I just don't know.'

Lord Francis Powerscourt had gone back to Blackwater. He had forbidden himself the library in case of distractions. He knocked once more at the door of Samuel Parker's cottage.

'Good morning, my lord,' said Parker. 'Good to see you again.'

'I trust Mrs Parker is well? And you must be relieved to have Miss Harrison off your hands?'

Powerscourt smiled. From what Lady Lucy had told him, old Miss Harrison would not have been an easy visitor, residing in her mind somewhere between heaven and hell.

'She's gone to those Italian Lakes, my lord. Mabel was right glad to see her go. Old Miss Harrison began talking to her one day as if she was an angel.' Samuel Parker shook his head sadly. 'I'm not saying that Mabel mightn't have looked a bit like an angel when she was young. But you'd have to be off your head to think she was one now.'

'Mr Parker,' Powerscourt was moving on from the civilities, 'I wonder if I could borrow your keys, the ones to the temples round the lakes you had with you before. I'd just like to have another look

215

around. And is there a boat anywhere I could borrow – a rowing boat, I mean? I thought I might have a poke about on that little island.'

'The island, my lord? I've just remembered. I don't think I mentioned it last time, it quite slipped my mind. But sometimes Old Mr Harrison used to row himself over there, all on his own, my lord. He wasn't a very good rower, mind you, it used to take him about ten minutes. He went round in circles sometimes.'

Parker disappeared behind his front door and came back with one of the largest bunches of keys Powerscourt had ever seen.

'The temples are all marked, my lord. And you'll find a boat underneath the Temple of Flora.'

Parker watched him go, the sunshine dancing on the lake. I'll say one thing for Lord Francis Powerscourt, he said to himself as he went inside to tell Mabel the latest news, he doesn't give up easily.

Powerscourt wandered slowly round the lake. Somewhere there must be a key or a clue to the terrible events that had engulfed the House of Harrison. Round these paths the old man had wandered on his pony, the faithful Parker accompanying him. By these temples he had stopped and taken out his writing desk, already trying to solve the mystery that brought Powerscourt to this water's edge. Inside these temples, perhaps, he had conducted his correspondence with his contacts in Germany, sending Parker to post them on his own to avoid the postal system in the main house. Inside them too, he had read his replies, returning to Blackwater to mutter to his sister after dinner about conspiracies and secret societies. Old Mr Harrison had made some connection between events in Germany, perhaps in Berlin, and the deaths that struck his family and weakened his bank.

Powerscourt walked into the echoing dome of the Pantheon. The statues mocked him. We know, we are gods, they seemed to say. You are merely an ignorant mortal doomed to wander in the shadows of ignorance for the rest of your days. The cupboards and the window seats in The Cottage had no secrets for him. The sun was flooding the Temple of Apollo, the lead statue of the hero glowing in the light. Once again Powerscourt tapped on the lead as he had tapped on the marble of the other statues. No hollow sound, no promise of a secret cache here. The whole lake seemed to be laughing at him, mocking his ignorance and rejoicing in its older, superior knowledge.

By the Temple of Flora, where yet more statues failed to yield up any secrets, he found the boathouse. He was looking out at the Pantheon and the little island that lay half-way between it and The Cottage. Powerscourt rowed slowly, remembering the flat fens he had rowed past in his days at Cambridge, the thrill of the chase, the wonderful excitement of making a bump on the boat ahead. No other boats followed him here, only the ripples on the water. He tied his boat to the nearest tree and went to explore.

The island was very small, some seventy yards long and fifty yards wide. It was ringed by trees so the little clearing at the centre was almost invisible from the shore. Powerscourt suddenly heard the voice of the Sibyl in Book Six of the *Aeneid* sounding in his brain.

'In a dark tree there hides a golden bough and it is sacred to the Juno of Hell: It is not given to anybody to approach earth's hidden places except he first plucked from that tree its golden foliage.'

Golden boughs and golden foliage seemed appropriate to a banking family, thought Powerscourt, looking round for dark trees with golden foliage. There was a dark tree, but it was old and withered. It had a hollow centre reaching up to his shoulder. Feeling slightly self-conscious he put his hand inside. There were leaves and clods of earth lying on the top. There was something hard beneath them. When he had brushed the mould away Powerscourt saw there was an ill-fitting piece of wood lying across the hollow, like a badly made trapdoor. He tried to move it with his hands. It didn't move. He tried levering it up with Mr Parker's largest key, a formidable instrument over two feet long. There was a crack, then a harsh creaking noise as the wood came away. Powerscourt peered inside. The top of the tiny chamber was covered with towels. There must have been half a dozen of them. He thought of the housekeeper at Blackwater, checking her stores, looking in her books, complaining to anyone who would listen that her towels kept on disappearing.

At the bottom of the towels was a small black document box, made of iron and sealed with a formidable lock. As he lifted it out of its hiding place he could see the legend 'C.F. Harrison' written on the side.

Powerscourt peered through the trees. For some time he had wondered if he was being watched. There was nothing definite, just the sense of hidden eyes following him round the lake. Perhaps it was the statues.

He looked at the lock. He wondered if any of Mr Parker's keys would open the box. He wondered about Mr Parker. Surely he must have known about the cache on the island on the lake? Surely he must have known that his master sometimes took things to and from his box? Was Mr Parker to be trusted, or was he yet another mystery in the labyrinth that was Blackwater?

Powerscourt sat on the ground and began working through Mr Parker's keys. There must have been over fifty on the ring. Beyond the island a cormorant beat its way across the lake, making guttural calls to its fellows. Blackwater foresters could be heard way in the distance sawing at a rotten tree. He wondered if the key had been kept by Old Mr Harrison himself on his own key ring. Perhaps it had been removed, like his head, before his last macabre voyage down the Thames to London Bridge. Then he found it. The key was stiff, maybe the lock was stiff after all that time in the tree. Powerscourt turned it and found a very small pile of papers at the bottom of the box. Damp had got to some of them, the ink fading before its time. There was a musty smell as if the papers themselves were going bad.

He pulled out four letters, all written in German. There were also two newspaper articles, going yellow with age. Both related to the fall of Barings Bank some seven years before. The old man had made marks on the articles in a red pen, circling some passages and underlining others. Maybe Harrison's had been involved in the rescue, Powerscourt thought.

Should he put the letters back in the box? Should he take the box away with him? Should he take the box back to Mr Parker and tell him he was taking it and its contents back to London? He looked at the key, sitting comfortably on Mr Parker's key ring. It looked as though it had been there for years. He wondered once more about Samuel Parker, sitting on the ground, looking out over the water. He could see his little rowing boat bobbing gently up and down. The classical façade of the Pantheon was on his other side, the statues within guarding their ancient mysteries. Was Samuel Parker secretly in league with Charles Harrison, reporting Powerscourt's every move and repeating every word he said? He couldn't be sure. He even wondered about an unlikely alliance between Parker and Jones the butler, praying together perhaps on the stone floor, whisky bottles drained beside the shells and the golden cross as they planned a campaign of fire and murder.

Whatever he did he must act fast. Powerscourt thought he had been on the island for about ten minutes. That he could describe satisfactorily. Anything longer might be a problem. He took the letters and the newspaper articles out of the box. He folded them carefully and put them in his pocket. Please God I don't have an accident on the way back to the shore, he said to himself, the papers would become so sodden you couldn't read anything at all. He locked the box and put it back in the tree. He covered it with the towels and its trapdoor. Then he gathered some leaves and moss from the bottom of the tree and placed them on top. He found a branch lying on the ground and brushed the area around it, trying to remove any footprints that might reveal his presence.

Then he went back. Mr Parker was waiting for him at the boathouse. Powerscourt wondered if Parker had watched his every move. He looked back to the island, reassured that you could not have seen a man removing boxes from the hollow tree. 'Did your mission meet with success, my lord?'

'In a way it did,' said Powerscourt, handing over the keys. 'I'd completely forgotten how much I enjoyed rowing. Maybe I shall get back on the river.'

Powerscourt was lost in thought about possible links between Blackwater, Berlin and Harrison's Bank when he returned to Markham Square. The noise hit him as soon as he opened the door. There seemed to have been an insurrection on the upper floors. Doors were banging. Fists were beating on the walls. Occasional screams broke through the high-pitched racket. Punctuating the sound effects came the repeated cry 'I don't want to go to bed! I don't want to go to bed!' Thomas Powerscourt was not on his best behaviour.

His father took the stairs two at a time and confronted his wayward son. He was wrestling with the nurse in the corridor outside the bathroom over a pyjama top which she seemed to think he should be wearing. Thomas, for his part, had correctly identified the donning of the pyjama top as a form of surrender to the demands of bedtime. 'I don't want to go to bed, Papa. I don't want to go to bed.' He stamped a small foot defiantly on the floor.

Powerscourt couldn't help smiling at the intensity of his son's passion. Men had presented Bills or Budgets in the House of Commons with less feeling than this.

'Now then, Thomas, let me tell you something.' He picked up the angry bundle and pressed him tight against his shoulder.

'Everybody goes to bed. I go to bed. Mama goes to bed. Your grandparents go to bed. The Prime Minister goes to bed. Queen Victoria goes to bed. I expect God goes to bed.'

He suddenly realized he might have made a mistake. He could be involved for hours in discussion about what kind of bed the Almighty slept in, whether God wore pyjamas, what time he retired, who read him a bedtime story. He took a quick look at Thomas. The waves of wrath seemed to be subsiding. Thomas looked as if he was about to ask a question.

Powerscourt thought rapidly about a diversion. He searched desperately in his pockets. Help was at hand.

'Look, I've got you some more coins. For your collection. French ones. I don't think you've got any of those, have you?'

He produced two gold French coins from his pocket. The little boy was fascinated by coins and had amassed a large collection, kept in remarkably tidy piles on a shelf in his room. Lady Lucy was already convinced he was going to be the foremost banker in London when he grew up. Powerscourt would tell her gloomily that the coin obsession could just as easily lead to an alternative career as London's most successful burglar.

Thomas inspected them carefully. The crisis seemed to have passed.

'Can I go and look at them in my room, Papa?'

'Of course you can. Nurse Mary Muriel will see you into bed,' said Powerscourt in what he hoped was his most authoritative voice. It worked.

'I'd better see to Olivia,' said Mary Muriel, looking anxiously at her employer. 'I think she's still in the bath.'

'Don't worry about her,' said Powerscourt with a smile. 'I'll look in on her now.'

Olivia Eleanor Hamilton Powerscourt was sitting happily in a few inches of water. Even at the age of two and a half she seemed to have the smile of satisfaction children sometimes wear when their elder brothers or sisters are in trouble with the authorities.

'Hello, Olivia,' said Powerscourt, sitting on a wet chair at the side of the bath.

'Thomas naughty,' said his daughter, pointing out of the door. 'Thomas naughty boy.'

'Never mind about Thomas,' replied her father, anxious to change the subject. 'We'd better get you out of the bath.'

He reached down and let the plug out. 'Watch the way the water goes out. It'll go round and round in circles in a minute.'

The little girl looked at him with disapproval. Then she watched, fascinated, as the water did indeed go round in circles.

'Olivia,' said her father, 'I'm going to turn you into a parcel.'

Little Olivia's favourite person in the whole world was her grandmother. Powerscourt's parents were dead, but Lady Lucy's had two houses, an eighteenth-century mansion in Oxfordshire and a huge castle in Scotland, full of dark corridors and Jacobite ghosts.

'I simply don't understand it, Francis,' Lucy had often said of her mother. 'When we were little, there was no affection at all. If you were lucky you got an occasional peck on the cheek, that was it. The horses and the dogs seemed to get much more love than the children. Just look at the difference now.'

Maybe it was because Olivia Eleanor Hamilton Powerscourt was Lady Macleod's first granddaughter after a large collection of boys. The old lady would take Olivia round the garden, showing her the flowers. She would take her to the stables and promise her a pony of her own when she was a little bit bigger. Biscuits would appear at regular intervals. At bedtime she would read stories to the little girl as if she wanted to do nothing else for the rest of the evening. Perhaps she didn't. But the last time the family had been there Powerscourt had seen a very special event. The butler had walked into the room in the middle of the morning with a very large parcel for Olivia's grandmother. Her name was written on it in large letters. There was an impressive collection of stamps. It was wrapped in thick brown paper with copious amounts of string. Olivia had been fascinated. She had been enrolled as her grand-mother's principal assistant in the unwrapping of the parcel. This, Powerscourt remembered, had taken almost an hour. Knots had to be undone. The string had to be carefully rolled up in little bundles. The brown paper had to be taken off very carefully. It too had to be folded. There was another layer of paper inside which required similar treatment. The final contents, a jumper of a sensible brown colour, had proved of little interest after all the previous excitement.

Powerscourt had an enormous white towel in his arms. He picked Olivia up. A pair of blue eyes, rather like her mother's, peered up at him, trusting, clear, unfathomable. Powerscourt often thought she had been here before. He wrapped her very tightly in the towel.

'First of all,' he said to Olivia, 'we have to make sure the parcel is wrapped up very tight.' He made a number of folds in the towel and tucked the ends very firmly in position. Olivia had disappeared completely. She looked like a small white mummy, awaiting final incarceration in some dead Pharaoh's tomb.

'All right in there, parcel?' asked Powerscourt, suddenly worried that she might suffocate.

'Parcel all right,' reported the small package.

'Now we've got to put some string round it.' Powerscourt's fingers made a series of loops round the package, pausing occasionally to fasten imaginary knots.

'Address now,' he said. He began to write heavily with his finger on Olivia's back. 'Lady Cynthia Macleod, Beauclerc House, Thame, Oxfordshire. I think we'd better write it on the front of the parcel as well.' He turned the towel over. There was a yelp from within.

'Tickles,' said Olivia Powerscourt with great delight, 'tickles.'

'Now we have to put the stamps on,' said her father. He stamped his fist all around the package, finishing with a final triumphant flourish on the top of her head. 'Now you have to be handed over to the postman. Please Mr Postman, could you take this parcel for Oxfordshire. It's got all the stamps on. "Yes, sir," says the postal gentleman, "we'll take care of it for you." '

Powerscourt now threw Olivia around, explaining that she had joined all the other parcels in London at a great sorting office.

'Warwickshire, Devon, Dorset, Norfolk.' He threw various imaginary missives round the bathroom. 'Ah,' he put on another voice, 'this one's for Oxfordshire. Put it in the train up there.'

'Twain, twain, am I on a twain, Papa?' said the little girl. Like her brother she was very excited by railway travel.

'Chuff . . . Chuff . . . Chuff . . . Chuff.Chuff.Chuff.' Powerscourt did his best to reproduce the noise of the mail train on the London to Warwick line. He made screeching sounds.

'The parcel's reached the station now, Olivia.' He threw her on to an imaginary platform. 'Now Grandmother's postman gets the parcel. Clip-clop. Clip-clop.' Those horse noises again. Powerscourt was glad he didn't have Thomas on his back this time. 'Knock knock.' Powerscourt beat his fist hard on the panels of the bath. 'The postman is knocking at Grandmother's front door. There's no answer. Knock knock. Where can the butler be? Ah, here he comes. "Parcel for Lady Macleod," says the postman. "Thank you so much," says the butler. But where is Grandmother? The butler cannot find her.'

Powerscourt walked up and down the bathroom searching for an imaginary Lady Macleod.

'"Did I hear someone at the door?" says Grandmother. "Parcel for you, Lady Macleod," says the butler.'

Powerscourt handed the package over. He sat down again with his little daughter on his lap.

'"Who could be sending me a parcel like this?" says Grandmother. "I suppose I'd better open it. What a pity Olivia isn't here to help me – she does like parcels so."'

Powerscourt began to unwrap the towel.

'It's so well wrapped,' he said, in his best grandmother voice, 'whatever can it be? Not another jumper surely.' There was a squeal of delight from inside. 'What was that noise? I must unwrap the rest of this quickly. My goodness me, I think it might be a person in here. I hope they're all right after all that journey in the trains and things.'

With a final flourish and a roll of imaginary drums on the side of the bath, Powerscourt opened up the towel.

'What a nice surprise! It's Olivia! How wonderful to see you!'

All that travelling had left the little girl completely dry. Her father looked around for a nightdress. She was still snuggling up to him very tight. Olivia looked at him with her most entrancing look. She's practising on me, thought Powerscourt. She's been practising on me since she was four days old. Olivia, he felt absolutely sure, wanted something, something she felt sure a devoted father would provide.

'Papa,' she said, 'again. Again. Do it again.'

24

By half-past six on the Monday evening after the cricket match Richard Martin had still not come home. His tea was on the table. Richard always liked to have his tea once he came in, hungry from a long day in the City. Sometimes they had to work late at the bank, but Richard always knew well in advance. Only that morning he had said he would be home at the usual time.

His mother made another pot. He's gone too far this time, she said to herself he really has. If he thinks that Sophie Williams is more important than his own mother, then he'd better think again. Rufus, the dog next door that Richard used to take for walks, was barking loudly. You could hear it through the walls. Mrs Martin tried to think of who could help her in the chastising of her wayward son. His grandfather would never do it, he had always been soft on the boy, especially since he lost his father. One of her sisters might be pretty fierce but she didn't think Richard would take any notice.

Sophie Williams was worried too. Richard usually met her at seven o'clock by St Michael's church with the dog. Tonight he was not there. Always in the past he had kept his word, always he had been reliable. By eight o'clock she knew he was not coming. She wondered if she should call on his mother. Perhaps Richard was ill. Sophie knew what Richard's mother thought of her. She knew she might not receive a warm welcome at Number 67 if she rang the bell. Suffragists must have courage above everything else, she said to herself, courage in the rightness of their cause, courage in the prosecution of the battle against the monstrous regiment of men. Richard's mother was just another poor woman, brainwashed by male propaganda.

At half-past eight she rang Richard's doorbell. Mrs Martin was wondering if Richard had lost his key.

'Miss Williams!' said Richard's mother. 'What on earth are you doing here?'

'I was worried about Richard,' said Sophie, still standing on the doorstep.

'He's not come home for his tea,' Mrs Martin explained. 'I thought he was with you.'

'I sometimes see him when he goes to walk the dog, Mrs Martin. But I didn't see him tonight. I was worried.'

Mrs Martin wondered if she should pursue these evening meetings with the dog. But it was obvious that the girl was as worried as she was.

'Come in, Miss Williams. Come in. We'd better have a cup of tea.'

Lord Francis Powerscourt was pacing up and down his drawing room. Lucy was sitting by the fire with the letters from the Blackwater strong box beside her. She was making notes in a little book, a German dictionary by her side.

'Can you do them all at once, Lucy, and then tell me what they say? I don't think I could bear hearing them one by one and then waiting for the next translation.'

He paced on, hoping that at last he might have the key to the mystery, the riddle that linked a death by drowning, a death by fire, death under a tube train and a headless corpse in the Thames.

'Do sit down, Francis,' said Lady Lucy, smiling at her husband. 'All this walking up and down is making me nervous.'

Powerscourt sat down. He got up again. He walked rapidly to the other end of the room, his hand running through his hair. Then he sat down again.

'Right, Francis. I'm going to take them two at a time – you're so impatient. I shouldn't get over-excited about the first couple if I were you.

'This one here,' she held up a letter written on plain white paper, 'comes from an old friend in Frankfurt. It says that some distant cousin has just died at the age of ninety-three. She must have been older than Queen Victoria.'

'That's all it says?' asked Powerscourt.

'It is,' replied Lady Lucy, 'unless there's a message written in invisible ink. This one,' she held out another letter, written on pale blue writing paper, 'comes from Berlin. I think the writer must

225

have known the Harrisons when they were in Frankfurt. He says that there are a number of secret societies in Berlin, mostly centred on the university. Everyone is joining secret societies these days, he says, societies to do with the Navy, societies to do with the Army. But the writer doesn't know very much about them.'

Lady Lucy's clock struck the hour of ten. Powerscourt began walking up and down again.

'If you give me a couple of minutes, Francis, I can tell you what the other two say. They're both from Berlin. But please, stop walking up and down.'

Mrs Martin and Sophie Williams had drunk three cups of tea. They had talked about Sophie's work at the school, about Richard and his work at the bank.

'I must go home now, Mrs Martin. Perhaps he has had to work late at the bank after all.'

'Do you think so, Miss Williams, do you really think so? I would be so relieved if he has.'

Privately Sophie did not believe Richard was working late. He would have told her if he was. She suspected there had been some terrible catastrophe at the bank.

'I'm sure he'll be home soon,' she said. 'I'll look in on the way to school in the morning, just to make sure he got back safely.'

'That would be very kind, Miss Williams.'

'These two are both from the same man, Francis.' Lucy was holding up the last two letters, written on more expensive paper. 'I think he too was someone Old Mr Harrison knew before. He also says there are secret societies all over Berlin. The most secretive, and the one thought to be the most influential, is centred on the Friedrich Wilhelm University.'

Lady Lucy let the letter drop into her lap. 'Oh, Francis, that's where Charles Harrison went, the Friedrich Wilhelm.' Powerscourt was staring at the letter. 'Go on, Lucy, please go on.'

'The society is devoted to the work and teachings of a history professor called von Treitschke. Have you heard of this historian, Francis?'

'No, I have not. Is that all the letter says?'

'The rest is all about mutual friends. Most of them seem to be dying off. The last one,' Lady Lucy picked up the final letter in her little pile, 'is from the same man. "I have tried on your behalf," he says, "I have tried very hard to find out if the person of whom you speak is a member of the society or not. I have not been able to find out a definite answer. Secret societies after all are meant to be secret".'

'Do you think that's some heavy German joke, Lucy?'

'Probably,' said Lady Lucy. 'There's more. "I would guess from the response to my question from one of my informants that the person of whom you speak is a member. Membership is not just for the length of the university career, it goes on until you die." That's it, Francis.'

'No mention of who the person of whom you speak actually is, is there?' Powerscourt was running his hands through his hair again.

'No, there is not. Not a clue.'

'I suppose, Lucy,' said Powerscourt, 'that if some of this information was so important that it killed somebody, then you wouldn't want to put too much of it down on paper. Particularly if your correspondent felt it wasn't safe to read his letters in his own house.'

'So it could be anybody.' Lady Lucy wondered if she had guessed right.

'For all I know,' her husband said, 'it could be Jones the butler, recruited way back, plotting away all these years. Talking of Jones, just for now I'm going to follow his example. I'm going to have a very large whisky.'

Mrs Martin did not sleep that night. All through the early hours of the morning she waited for a door key that never turned in the lock. As dawn broke over North London she was sure her Richard was dead, run over by a carriage perhaps, or fallen under a train.

Sophie Williams did not sleep either. All night she tormented herself with the way she had treated Richard. Had she been too brusque with him? Had she talked too much about her work with the suffragists or her problems at the school?

At half-past seven she presented herself at Richard's front door. But it was his mother who opened it, looking terrible, her face lined with grief, her eyes red with the tears of darkness.

'Please come in, Miss Williams. Richard's still not back yet.'

With that she broke down, sinking into a chair and weeping uncontrollably.

'Maybe he's left home because I didn't treat him properly,' she sobbed. The words came very slowly, punctuated by shaking. 'Maybe he's dead and the next thing we'll hear is the policeman knocking at the door. Thank God his father's not here to see all this.'

'Don't worry, Mrs Martin.' Sophie Williams put her arm round Richard's mother. 'I'll get you a cup of tea. I'm sure he'll be back today. Maybe they had to work all night at the bank. Some banks do, you know.' Sophie spoke as though she had an encyclopedic knowledge of contemporary banking behaviour in the City of London.

'I tell you what,' said Sophie, returning with a cup of tea and a plate of biscuits, 'I'll go down to the bank after school today and ask after him there.'

'Could you do that? Could you really? That would be so kind. And then you'll come back and tell me what happened? If I hear anything this morning, Miss Williams, I'll drop a message into your school.'

Lord Francis Powerscourt felt he was in a time warp. He was back in his tutor's room at Cambridge where he had sat so often over twenty-five years before. Outside the elegant windows the front court was bathed in sunshine. The grass was immaculate, divided into quarters by the paths that led off to other parts of the college and down to the river.

The porter at the front gate had recognized him after all those years.

'Lord Powerscourt, how nice to see you again, sir. Welcome back to the college. Mr Brooke is expecting you, sir.'

Gavin Brooke, Senior Tutor in history at this establishment for over forty years, was waiting for him, showing him to a chair, leaning heavily on a stick.

'Good to see you, Powerscourt. I'm not so mobile as I once was, as you can see. College is going to the dogs, you know, going to the dogs.'

Powerscourt remembered this as a familiar refrain. Change in any form had never pleased Gavin Brooke. His hair had turned white now, his handlebar moustache a shadow of its former self.

'They can't row, they can't think, they can't write essays any more, these undergraduates nowadays. And have you seen their clothes? Those waistcoats? The neckties? Do you know, one of these aesthetes as they call themselves asked the Master the other day if they could have an Aubrey Beardsley society. An Aubrey Beardsley society!'

'What did the Master say, Mr Brooke?' asked Powerscourt. Time never seemed to matter very much in Cambridge, he recalled, there was so much of it to squander until you realized it had all gone and your three years were over.

'The Master – never did like the man, the Fellows should never have elected him, never – he refused. Refused point blank. Oh yes.'

The old man peered at Powerscourt as if he'd forgotten his name. Outside bells were ringing. Bells never stopped ringing, Powerscourt remembered, bells for meals, bells for chapel, bells built to announce the glory of God that now just marked the passage of the days.

'You sent me a telegram.' Brooke said it like an accusation.

'I did, sir.'

The old man looked at his piece of paper.

'You made it sound very urgent, Powerscourt, very urgent.'

The old man picked up a pair of spectacles, lying on the floor on top of a great heap of recent copies of *The Times*.

'"Request most urgent audience with you on matter of great importance. Must come Tuesday morning. Please advise if impossible." Audience, he grinned, 'audience. I like that. As if I were the Pope or Cardinal Richelieu himself. How can I be of assistance to you?'

'I want to know,' Powerscourt said, 'about a German historian called Heinrich von Treitschke.'

Sophie Williams' class was very excited that morning. They were making decorations for the Jubilee. Some of the children were drawing pictures of Queen Victoria, with the black pencils in heavy demand. Some were colouring in a huge map of Victoria's Empire, the red of her domains running right round the world. Some were cutting coloured paper into streamers to hang on the walls.

'What's a Jubilee, Miss?'

'A Jubilee is a celebration, Betty, rather like a birthday party. This Jubilee is for the Queen's sixty years on the throne.'

'Will she wear lots of diamonds when she goes on the big parade?'

Sophie had heard that William Jones' father was believed to be a burglar. Perhaps he hoped to collect some useful intelligence to improve the family fortunes.

'I'm sure she will, William. Just a few diamonds as it's her Diamond Jubilee.'

'Why are our bits red on the map, miss?' demanded a very small but rather clever little boy.

'Red, Peter, has always been the colour for the British Empire,' said Sophie loyally, improvising some sort of reply when she didn't know the answer.

'Why haven't we got all of it, miss? All of the map. Why are there some bits of the world that are not in our Empire?'

Sophie smiled at her little imperialist who was called Tommy and always had a dirty face. 'Some countries just like to do things their own way, Tommy.'

'Will Queen Victoria live for ever, miss? My father says she looks as though she's lived for ever already.'

Sophie looked at the little girl. Then she looked at the Queen Empress, remote and aloof in her black dress in the portrait on the wall above her desk.

'I don't think she'll live for ever. One day she'll die, just like everybody else. But not for a while.'

'Heinrich von Treitschke? Heinrich von Treitschke?' The old man made him sound like a pheasant that had gone off or a bottle of corked wine.

'Yes,' said Powerscourt, 'that's the man I want information about.'

'I shall ask you why later, Powerscourt. Let me give you the bare facts. Professor of Modern German History at the Friedrich Wilhelm University in Berlin. Believed to have been a supporter of Bismarck in his youth, God help him. Used to give very popular lectures.' Powerscourt remembered that Gavin Brooke's lectures on modern European history had never been oversubscribed. 'The fellow died last year. Thousands of people turned out for his funeral. Von Treitschke was buried like a hero of the nation.'

'Was he a good historian, Mr Brooke? Was he controversial?' Powerscourt remembered that there was nothing dons enjoyed more than attacking the reputations of their colleagues.

'Depends what you mean by good and what you mean by historian, Powerscourt.' Gavin Brooke didn't disappoint him. 'If you mean good in the moral sense, of striving towards some kind of virtue, then I should say the answer is No. If you mean good in the sense of being an original scholar, then the answer is No. If by historian you mean an accurate interpreter of the past, somebody who tried to describe what happened centuries or fifty years ago, then the answer is No. If by historian you mean someone who tells the story of the past without any theories or hobby horses of their own, then the answer is No.'

Powerscourt felt that von Treitschke, however distinguished in Berlin, was about to fail the Historical Tripos of the University of Cambridge.

'I can see you thought he was a bad historian. What sort of bad historian was he?' Gavin Brooke looked up at the bookshelves that dominated his room.

'Treitschke wrote a History of Germany,' he said. 'It's in five volumes. I've got them all up there.' Brooke peered up at his bookshelves, stretching to the ceiling. 'He was a bad historian because he was a preacher, not a historian. If there's one thing I've tried to teach everybody here it's that history doesn't move in straight lines. Nations or peoples are not marked out by God or fate for supremacy over other nations. God knows there's enough nonsense produced here about how the history of these islands has made us fit to rule the world.'

Powerscourt remembered Brooke's onslaught on imperialist historians, the ones who said it was Britannia's fate to rule the waves. They were his contemporaries. People said they had denied Brooke the chair he deserved.

'Treitschke preached a German version of the same rubbish,' Brooke continued his character assassination. 'Germany's destiny is to be the most important power in the world. That's what German history teaches, according to the late Heinrich. Of course he was too stupid to see that he's got it the wrong way round. He wants Germany to rule the world. Therefore he says that's what history teaches.'

History, Powerscourt remembered him saying, is never a straight line between two points, more a series of accidental curves along a winding road filled with crossroads signposted to different destinations. Sometimes, he remembered, Brooke said the signposts had no destinations on them at all.

'Perhaps I could ask you now, Lord Powerscourt, why you are interested in this man?'

Gavin Brooke inspected Powerscourt sharply. They never realize we grow up, we grow older, Powerscourt thought. To him I'm still twenty years old, sometimes producing essays that he liked, only yesterday or the day before.

Powerscourt explained that he was an investigator, currently looking into a strange series of deaths in a London bank that seemed to have links with secret societies in Berlin.

'Secret societies?' The old man was scornful. 'Of course there's a secret society in von Treitschke's honour. I think it was founded over twenty years ago. Why didn't you ask me in the first place?'

'How do you know about that, Mr Brooke?' Powerscourt had come to Cambridge to learn about von Treitschke the man. He would never have expected an ageing history don, who rarely left Cambridge and then only to venture as far as Oxford or the London Library, to know about secret societies at the University of Berlin.

'Lots of historians knew about it.' Gavin Brooke looked pleased with his knowledge. 'The old boy himself used to boast about it in his later years. Treitschke said he hoped the society founded in his name would do more to restore Germany to her rightful place in the world than all his lectures and all his history books. We had a German historian here, ten years ago it must have been. They'd asked him if he wanted to join. He did, just to see what it was like. He said they were all fanatical German nationalists. Whatever profession they went into, the law, diplomacy, finance, the military, they had to do whatever they could and whatever the leaders asked them to advance the German cause.'

'Did it have a name, this society, Mr Brooke?'

'It did, Powerscourt, it did. But I'm damned if I can remember it. It'll come to me.' The bells were ringing twelve, echoing round the courts and the cloisters, fading away across the meandering river and the flat lands of the Fens. The old man shuffled towards a large glass-fronted cabinet to the side of his bookshelves.

'Sherry, Powerscourt? A glass of the college's finest? Wine's gone off, of course, bloody Master has reduced the money going to the cellars.'

Powerscourt accepted a glass of the driest sherry he had ever tasted. He remembered it was always dry, the stuff the dons gave you, so dry the taste almost stripped the roof of your mouth.

'Staying for lunch, are you?' Brooke asked, 'You'd be welcome at High Table, of course. The food's gone to the dogs too, the Master said it cost too much. It's not much better than some bloody boarding school now.'

Powerscourt felt he had to move the conversation back to Berlin. 'What sort of German nationalist was von Treitschke, Mr Brooke? Did he want to conquer Russia or swallow the Austro-Hungarian Empire?'

'Sorry,' said the old man, pouring them both a second glass of sherry. His hand was shaking slightly, drops of sherry falling on the old copies of *The Times*. 'I should have told you that at the beginning. He didn't want to conquer Russia, he wanted to be friends with Russia. He wanted to be friends with Vienna too, he thought it was easier to leave the Austrians with all those nationalities in the Balkans than for Germany to have to deal with them.'

Gavin Brooke leant forward in his chair, peering at Powerscourt like some wizened old bird.

'For von Treitschke there was only one enemy. England, England with all her colonies and her trade and her fleet and her arrogance. He said, he preached, that only when Germany had a navy to beat the English would she come into her own. I think he really hated the English, you know, Heinrich von Treitschke.'

Powerscourt finished his sherry and announced that he had to return to London. Gavin Brooke saw him down the stairs, leaning on his stick, tapping his way towards the porter's lodge.

'Hope I've been some use to you, Powerscourt. Let me know how it all goes, won't you?'

Powerscourt shook him warmly by the hand. 'I am most grateful to you, Mr Brooke, your information has been invaluable.'

As he set off up the cobbled street of the Senate House Passage, young men wandering about arm in arm, he heard a shout behind him.

'Powerscourt! Powerscourt!' The old man was hobbling up the street as fast as he could, shouting as he came. 'I've just remembered.'

Powerscourt stopped by the side entrance into Gonville and Caius.

'The secret society's name,' Brooke panted, 'they named it after some bloody marching song that von Treitschke wrote years ago. "The Song of the Black Eagle". And the man in charge is called Scholl, Helmut Scholl. He's on the staff of Admiral Tirpitz.'

The old man was now completely out of breath.

'Tirpitz?' said Powerscourt. 'Isn't he the chap who wants to build up the German Navy?'

'You've got it in one, Powerscourt.' Gavin Brooke nodded furiously at him. 'I always thought you were a promising student of history.'

Powerscourt found himself thinking about Charles Harrison as the train took him back to London. During his military career he had known men who had lost their parents for whom the Army and the regiment had become the centre of their professional and emotional lives, a substitute family round the mess table and the camaraderie of regimental dinners. For Charles Harrison, educated at von Treitschke's own university, attending von Treitschke's lectures no doubt, had the German secret society replaced the family he never had in his affections? A society devoted to the greater glory of Germany and bitter hatred of England?

Then, as the train reached the outskirts of London, he thought about the cache of letters on the island at Blackwater. And about the articles on the fall of Barings Bank, seven years before.

25

It was almost four o'clock by the time Sophie Williams reached the City. She had called again on Richard's mother. No, he still had not come back. He's probably dead by now, Mrs Martin assured Sophie, wiping her eyes.

Cheapside, that's where the bank was. Richard had brought her for a walk round the City one Sunday afternoon when the place was deserted, the streets quiet, the coffee houses closed. Sophie summoned up her courage in this alien world and spoke to the commissionaire on duty at the entrance to Harrison's Bank.

'I'm so sorry to disturb you. Could I have a quick word with Mr Richard Martin, please?'

The commissionaire looked at her gravely. She makes a change from all those rude young men delivering messages and skylarking about in the streets, he thought.

'He works here,' Sophie added, looking up at the sentinel of the banking hall within.

'He did work here, miss. Until yesterday that is. We haven't seen him at all this week, not yesterday, not today. We thought he must be ill. He is ill, isn't he?'

The commissionaire looked worried suddenly. Richard Martin was a well-respected young man. He was always polite to commissionaires, he didn't give himself airs like so many of these arrogant young pups they got nowadays from the public schools.

'I don't know if he is ill or not,' said Sophie. 'We thought he might have been working late at the bank and had to stay over.'

'Bless you, miss,' said the commissionaire kindly, 'there's no likelihood of anyone working late here at the moment. The place is as quiet as the grave. Sorry I can't help you, miss. I expect he'll turn up. Maybe he went out with some of his friends and fell ill that way.'

Sophie looked at him coldly. Richard was not likely to go out on the town with friends and get so drunk he couldn't go to work the next day. That was not Richard's style at all.

'Thank you so much for your help,' said Sophie firmly. 'I shall continue my inquiries elsewhere.'

Quite where elsewhere was going to be Sophie had no idea. She moved away down Poultry towards the Royal Exchange. What was the name of Richard's friend, the one who took them to the cricket match? James Clarke, that was it. And what was the name of his governor, the nice middle-aged gentleman who had looked after them at lunch? Broad? Bucknall? Broughton? Was it Broughton? No, it wasn't, she said to herself triumphantly, it was Burke, Mr Burke of the London and Provincial Bank. She looked around at the nameplates that surrounded her. There were so many banks here, foreign ones, American ones, German ones, British ones. How was she to find the London and Provincial?

She decided to ask one of the doorkeepers at the Bank of England, resplendent in their top hats and frock coats, guardians of the guardian of the City's wealth.

'London and Provincial?' said the man. 'I'm afraid there are three or four of those around here, miss. Do you happen to know which one, or does that not matter? The nearest is just round the corner. Or is there a particular person you wish to see?'

'Mr Burke,' said Sophie firmly.

'Mr Burke, Mr William Burke?' said the man.

'Yes, that's him,' Sophie nodded.

'Why didn't you say, miss? Mr Burke is to be found at the Head Office in Lombard Street, just over there.'

Powerscourt had just sat down in Burke's office when the porter knocked on the door.

'There's a young lady here asking to see you, sir. She says she's a friend of Mr Clarke and that she met you at a cricket match last Saturday, sir.'

Very faintly, behind the deference, Powerscourt thought the porter detected a whiff of scandal. A pretty girl meets Mr Burke on Saturday, then she turns up at the office on the Tuesday. Who could tell what might have been going on, what demands for money might now be forthcoming.

'What's her name, man? What's her name?' said Burke testily. He too had sensed the suspicion in the porter's eyes.

'Miss Williams, sir. Miss Sophie Williams. A very pretty young woman, sir.' The porter sounded as if he was congratulating William Burke on his choice.

'Show her up. And ask Mr James Clarke to step this way if you would. At once. The porter left. Bloody man thinks I've been up to no good with young Miss Williams,' said Burke angrily.

'Why has she come here, William?' said Powerscourt softly. 'She works as a schoolteacher, doesn't she? What business has she got in the City? Unless, unless . . .' A terrible thought struck Powerscourt. He remembered Burke's shouted instructions to Sophie Williams' friend to come and see him on Monday morning, a scowling Charles Harrison listening among the trees. What had happened to Richard Martin? Visions of another body flashed across his mind, this one only twenty-two years old.

'William,' he said quickly, 'that young man, the one at the cricket match. Did he come to see you yesterday morning?'

'He did not,' said Burke, looking uneasy. There was a knock at the door.

'Miss Williams, Mr Clarke, do come in. Please sit down. How can I help you?' Burke smiled a cheerful smile.

Sophie Williams didn't quite know how to put it. She stumbled into her story.

'It's Richard, sir, Richard Martin. He works at Harrison's Bank. You met him at the cricket match.' She stopped, gazing helplessly at the two older men in the room. 'Last night he didn't come home. He lives very close to me. Usually we see each other when he takes the neighbour's dog for a walk. I checked again with his mother this morning. He still hadn't come home. And when I checked at Harrison's Bank just now, they said they hadn't seen him yesterday or today. He's disappeared.'

She began to cry, very quietly, tears dropping on to her dress.

'Here,' said Burke quickly, offering her an enormous hand-kerchief. 'Try to compose yourself, Miss Williams. I'll order some tea. This is terrible news.'

Powerscourt waited. James Clarke made consoling noises. Burke poured the tea.

'Forgive me, Miss Williams,' said Powerscourt, 'please forgive me if I ask you some questions. I am an investigator. I am currently looking into the strange death of Old Mr Harrison, the man found floating in the Thames by London Bridge.'

Sophie looked terrified. Was her Richard also going to be killed and floated down the Thames? She looked as though the tears were about to start again.

'Do not be alarmed, Miss Williams. I am sure nothing untoward has happened to Richard.' William Burke was using his most emollient voice, the one he used for angry shareholders. 'Lord Powerscourt is one of the finest investigators in the land. He is also my brother-in-law. I am sure he has no wish to frighten you.'

Burke looked meaningfully at Powerscourt. He hoped the domestic detail might help reassure the girl.

'Could I ask you, Miss Williams,' said Powerscourt, 'if Richard talked to you at all about Harrison's Bank? Friends often talk to each other about the details of their daily lives.'

'Well, he did. He did, a little. He was always very circumspect.' Sophie looked defensively at the two bankers who surrounded her.

'Goodness me, Miss Williams,' said James Clarke, 'we're all meant to keep things in confidence, but that doesn't really apply to close friends and family.'

'When he told you a little, Miss Williams,' Powerscourt smiled at the girl, 'can you remember what it was? A little can go a long way sometimes.'

There was a pause. James Clarke was admiring Sophie's eyes. He had been very taken with them at the cricket match. Burke was pouring more tea. Powerscourt dropped a biscuit on the floor.

'Richard's been worried about what was happening at the bank for quite a long time,' Sophie began.

'How long a time would that be?' said Powerscourt. 'Weeks, or months?'

'Months, I think. At first he wouldn't give any details, he had to keep things confidential. Then, fairly recently, he said something quite important. I mean, I think now it may be important, but I didn't then.'

She stopped and drank some tea.

'We'd been out walking the next-door neighbour's dog. Rufus, it's called. Richard said it was the money. He said that most of the time in a bank money goes in and money goes out. But that at Harrison's it was only going out. Richard said that in a couple of months' time the bank wouldn't have any money left. He seemed to think that you couldn't have a bank with no money.'

Sophie looked at William Burke. 'Can you have a bank with no money, Mr Burke? Can you? Or was Richard right?'

'I fear Richard was right, Miss Williams,' said Burke, frowning at such irregularities in banking custom. 'You can't have a bank with no money. It wouldn't be a bank any more. It's a contradiction in terms.'

'Did Richard mention any changes that had taken place?' Powerscourt spoke very gently. He thought he knew the answer. And if the answer was what he expected, then, at last, he might have the whole mystery in his hands. But he knew that almost everybody would say he was mad.

'He did, Lord Powerscourt. How clever of you to know about it. He said that new people had come in and changed all the counting systems, the accounting systems, I'm not sure which.'

'Did he say where they were from? From another bank in the City perhaps?'

Sophie Williams frowned. 'I'm sure he said something about that. But for the moment I can't just remember what it was.'

She closed her eyes, recreating the walk with Richard and Rufus the dog. Burke saw that Powerscourt was on tenterhooks for the reply. Nobody spoke.

'That's it,' she said finally. 'He said a new man had come in from Germany to change the counting or the accounting systems.'

'You're sure it was from Germany?' Powerscourt was almost whispering.

'I'm certain of it,' said Sophie Williams, 'absolutely certain.'

William Burke was watching Powerscourt very carefully. A very slight smile crossed his features.

'Is that all you can remember of what Richard said, Miss Williams? Nothing more?'

'That's all I can remember for now,' said Sophie sadly. 'I know it isn't very much. I can't see how it's going to help in finding him. You don't think, Lord Powerscourt,' she looked him full in the face, her bright blue eyes fearful of the future, 'you don't think he's dead, do you?'

'No, I don't think so. Certainly not.' Powerscourt wished he was as sure as he sounded. 'Now then, there is something you can do to help us find him. As it happens I am on my way to see the Commissioner of the Metropolitan Police on other business. It's not every day, I assure you, that I travel between Mr Burke's bank and the police headquarters, but this is such a day. If you would like to write a description of Richard, height, colour of hair, colour of eyes, what he might have been wearing going to work on Monday morning, I shall take it directly to the police.' Powerscourt handed her a sheet of the bank's best writing paper. He took a further three sheets himself and began writing furiously.

'William, perhaps you could ask one of your people to take this one to Johnny Fitzgerald. This one is for Lady Lucy. Ah, Miss Williams, you have finished your description, I see. Thank you so much.'

'Miss Williams,' Burke was organizing the despatch of Powerscourt's mail, 'could I make a suggestion? Perhaps our Mr Clarke here could take you home. You must be exhausted after such a day. And thank you so much for coming to see us. Please tell Richard's mother if you should see her that everything possible is being done to find him.'

James Clarke looked pleased with his late afternoon assignment. They heard him asking Sophie if she would like to see round the bank while she was there, if she had time, of course.

'What about your third letter there, Francis? Where do you want that to go?' Powerscourt looked grave. 'This one is for you, William. If I am right, when we have the answers, we may have solved the entire mystery. God knows where you will have to go to find the information, but we must have it by tomorrow morning.'

Burke read the letter. Then he read it again. He stared at Powerscourt as if he had just arrived from another planet.

'Francis,' he spluttered, 'you can't be serious. This is monstrous, monstrous. I've never heard anything so terrible in my life. It can't be true. Here in the City of London.'

'I'm sure that stranger things have happened here before now, William. And it is possible, isn't it?'

'I suppose it's possible,' said Burke, reading his letter once more. 'But it's monstrous. Quite monstrous.'

'Lord Powerscourt, I owe you an apology. I am so very sorry.'

The Commissioner of the Metropolitan Police had removed the four maps of London from his walls. Powerscourt wondered if crime had temporarily ceased and the righteous had finally inherited the earth. In their place was an enormous map of the route of Queen Victoria's procession from Buckingham Palace to St Paul's, crosses and circles marking the disposition of his forces.

240

'I'm sure you don't owe me an apology at all, Commissioner,' said Powerscourt politely.

'Oh, but I do. First of all we failed to prevent the death of that man Williamson. Now this. It's this wretched Jubilee, you see.' He nodded at his great map. 'We're very hard pressed for staff. We're bringing officers in from all over the Home Counties. If you want to commit a crime on Jubilee Day, Lord Powerscourt, don't come to London. Go to Weybridge or Reading or Bedford, there won't be any police left there at all.

'The reason for my apology is that one of my assistants took away the men watching one of your suspects, a Mr Charles Harrison. I only found out an hour ago. I am terribly sorry.'

'You mean,' said Powerscourt anxiously, 'you mean that there's nobody watching him at all?'

'I'm afraid so,' said the Commissioner. 'Is that serious?'

'I'm afraid it is very serious. Very serious indeed.'

Powerscourt looked back at the map. He noticed that there were times of arrival marked on all the key points of the journey, very precisely, as if it were a railway timetable. The military must have gone over the route over and over again, each detachment knowing it had exactly seven minutes to get to Piccadilly or Temple Bar.

'How can I make amends, Lord Powerscourt?' said the Commissioner. Powerscourt still stared at the map.

'I cannot be sure, but I believe Mr Charles Harrison may be about to leave the country. Indeed he may have already gone, but I do not think so. He will probably try to leave four or five days before the Jubilee Day itself. Could you keep an eye out for him and detain him if you find him?'

'Of course we could,' said the Commissioner. 'Do you know where he will be travelling to? And what should we charge him with?'

Powerscourt laughed. The Commissioner wondered if he was beginning to crack under the strain.

'Forgive me, Commissioner. I think you will find he is travelling to Germany. By rail, probably, maybe by boat. Officially you could say that the police wish to question him further about the fire at Blackwater. Unofficially – let me ask you this, Commissioner. Do you have many officers working on possible terrorist threats during the Jubilee?'

'We most certainly do, Lord Powerscourt.'

'Well, if I am right,' said Powerscourt grimly, 'and I will only know the answer in the morning, Mr Charles Harrison has placed a time bomb under the City of London. It's been in preparation for a very long time. We've got less than a week to find it. Only it's not a real bomb, Commissioner. It's a bomb made of money and it could blow the City to smithereens.'

Powerscourt and Johnny Fitzgerald were alone in their compartment as the train drew out of Paddington. The light was fading fast when they reached Wallingford station. Powerscourt explained to Johnny on the final stages of their journey what he thought was going on.

'It's as if this German secret society, or Charles Harrison and the secret society, is launching two series of attacks on the Jubilee,' he said, staring out at the colours draining from the passing landscape. 'They provide money and weapons for the Irish to take a shot at somebody on the day of the great parade. Maybe somebody in Dublin, maybe even the Queen Empress herself. And then there's the other half.'

He told Fitzgerald what he had written in his note to William Burke that afternoon.

'Is that possible, Francis? Are you sure?' Johnny Fitzgerald sounded doubtful.

'We should know the answer in the morning, Johnny,' said Powerscourt. 'I'm glad to see you've brought your burglar's kit along. You don't need a gun. I've got one.' Powerscourt patted his coat pocket. He had borrowed the gun from the Commissioner's people before he left the office.

Now they were walking the mile and a half from Wallingford station to Blackwater House. Powerscourt had hurried Fitzgerald out of the side entrance to the station, avoiding the couple of cabs left on duty. Soon they were deep in the country, trees lining the little road. There were thin clouds overhead, parting from time to time to reveal a very bright moon.

'Let me just give you the key features of the people who live in Blackwater House where we are going, Johnny. Life expectancy in the House of Harrison has not been good recently. Old Mr Harrison, as you know, found floating by London Bridge with his head cut off. Before that, his son, Wilhelm or Willi Harrison, drowned in a boating accident. The other son, Frederick, Friedrich if you prefer, burnt to a cinder in the blaze at Blackwater House. Man now in charge of the show, Charles Harrison, nephew of Wilhelm. Are you with me so far, Johnny?'

'Just about keeping up, Francis,' said Fitzgerald, 'trying my best, you know. But what are we doing here now?'

'I'm just coming to that.' There was a rustling noise in the wood to their left. A couple of guilty lovers peered out at them, fumbling with their clothes, and then retreated back to the ground.

'Christ, that made me jump, Johnny. I'm getting old. Where was I?'

'Why are we here, Francis?'

'Very important philosophical question that, Johnny. I'm sure the meaning of life, the purpose of our short stay here on earth can often be discerned in the quiet of the evening when the day's work is done – '

Fitzgerald punched him quite hard on the shoulder.

'Right, right,' said Powerscourt, 'this Charles Harrison is up to no good in his bank. A young man you saw at the cricket match called Richard Martin works for Harrison's Bank. On Saturday evening Harrison hears William Burke inviting Martin to come and see him on Monday morning. Martin doesn't make it. Martin disappears, last seen by the widow Martin on Monday morning. Martin's friend Miss Williams raises the hue and cry. That is why we are here.'

'I'm getting slow, Francis,' Fitzgerald said. 'Martin disappears in the City. I presume he lives in London somewhere with the widowed mother, as you say. I do not imagine for one moment that the Martin household is to be found round here, is it?' Fitzgerald waved at what could be seen of the countryside.

'Let me try again, Johnny. Charles Harrison is up to no good in his bank. He thinks young Richard Martin may have some inkling of what is going on. When he hears Martin arranging to go and see Burke he thinks Martin is going to spill the beans. So he makes sure Martin doesn't get to Burke in the first place. He or his associates spirit him away. And I think they may have spirited him away here. Not just here, but at Blackwater.'

'So do we walk up to the front door and ask if we can see Mr Richard Martin?' said Fitzgerald happily.

'We do not, Johnny. I don't think they would have taken him to the big house – the butler is still there in his basement, I expect, but at least half the house is a ruin.'

'So where is he?'

Powerscourt tapped Fitzgerald on the shoulder and beckoned him into a clump of trees. About one hundred yards ahead they could see Blackwater church and the row of cottages where the Parkers lived. An owl was hooting in the distance. Shimmering in the moonlight less than a quarter of a mile away the Blackwater lake was keeping its secrets in the dark.

'All around this lake there are temples and things, Johnny, perfect places for hiding somebody you wanted kept out of the way.' Powerscourt was whispering now.

'Do they have doorbells, Francis? Each one with its own High Priest to admit you to the presence?'

'Alas, they do not,' said Powerscourt. 'I think we'd better knock at the windows if we can find any. What would you do if you were Charles Harrison, Johnny? I'm sure he wants to find out what Martin knows about what's going on in the bank. Whatever he knows, they don't want him wandering about the place and talking to William Burke.'

Powerscourt and Fitzgerald tiptoed their way through the trees. The moon had gone behind a cloud, the only light coming from a few stars in the east.

'Right, Johnny,' Powerscourt murmured, 'up this little hill is the Temple of Apollo. Our first port of call, I think.'

Johnny Fitzgerald pulled a fearsome spanner from his pocket and proceeded to tap, softly at first, then more loudly, on the walls. They listened. Nothing moved in the woods around them. No noise came from inside. Fitzgerald tried again. There was a faint echo from the blows, the sound dying among the trees.

'No good, Francis,' whispered Fitzgerald. 'Nothing doing here.'

They went carefully down a rocky path that led to the edge of the lake. On the far side they could see the outline of the Pantheon, its six columns standing to attention in the dark. Powerscourt dislodged a small boulder which rolled down the hill and splashed into the water. The ripples made their way across the surface of the lake, fading as they went.

'Temple of Flora next,' muttered Powerscourt quietly, leading the way on the path by the water's edge. Just beyond the little temple Powerscourt could see the boathouse and the rowing boat that had carried him on his mission to the island. The island was sitting perfectly still in the water.

Fitzgerald peered carefully through the windows. He motioned Powerscourt to be still. He tapped slowly on the glass. There was no answer. Fitzgerald tapped again. Silence ruled once more over the Blackwater lake.

'Blank again, Francis,' muttered Fitzgerald. 'Do you think we are on a wild goose chase?'

'No I do not.' Powerscourt was defiant. 'Two more places to try, at least.'

They walked across the little path that separated the two lakes. To their left they could hear the noise of the waterfall, cascading down its rocks into the water below. The moon had come out from behind its clouds. The Pantheon was bathed in a ghostly light, beckoning them on across the water. Powerscourt felt for his pistol in his pocket. Johnny Fitzgerald was rubbing his spanner. They passed under the columns and looked at the great door that guarded the statues within. Powerscourt thought he might go mad if anybody locked him in there, surrounded for the night by Hercules and the pagan deities.

'Do you want me to force this door open?' Fitzgerald whispered. He was inspecting its hinges carefully. 'If I could get some leverage on it I think it might give way.'

'There's another door inside, Johnny. A bloody great thing made of iron bars.'

'Very good,' said Fitzgerald, and began knocking on the wooden doors. Then he walked round the temple, tapping loudly on its walls. Powerscourt saw a fox had come to join them, standing at the water's edge, a look of astonishment on its face at the nocturnal practices of its human neighbours. Fitzgerald climbed up a tree and scrambled on to the roof There was a domed rotunda at the top. He knocked once more on the roof, then slid back down to earth again.

'No humans in there, Francis. Only those bloody statues. Gave me the creeps, all standing there in the moonlight as if they're waiting for somebody.'

'Just one place left, Johnny. There's a little cottage up here that's been converted into a summerhouse.'

Powerscourt led the way. The fox had trotted off. Two owls were sending messages to each other across the trees. The Temple of Flora was now reflected in the moonlight on the other side of the lake, the pillars rippling in the water.

Suddenly Powerscourt realized they should have started here.

He stopped suddenly, holding Johnny Fitzgerald by the arm. He pointed to the path ahead.

'That leads up to the house, through the trees over there to the left. Can you see anybody coming?'

Once again he had the sensation of being watched, of eyes following his every move. Maybe the statues are restless, he said to himself. Maybe the Roman gods themselves come out at night, prowling round the lake, seeking out the unpurified spirits and banishing them to the underworld.

'Nobody coming,' whispered Fitzgerald, who was now making his way round the back of The Cottage.

'Look, Francis.' He pointed to some heavy footprints in the ground by the back door. 'It rained quite hard when we were in the train. Somebody's been here very recently. Very recently indeed.'

Powerscourt went back to the path to keep watch for any other visitors to The Cottage. Fitzgerald began tapping very softly on a window. He tapped again a little louder. There was a scraping noise coming from inside now, as if a hand was scratching on the wall. Fitzgerald summoned Powerscourt from his vigil. He tapped again. Again the scraping sound came back.

'Right, Francis. I'm going in there.' He checked the doors. He checked the windows at the front and the back. Powerscourt felt suddenly afraid. There was a muffled tinkling of glass. Fitzgerald had placed his coat above the middle lock on one of the windows. A dark patch was spreading across his hand. Maybe he had hit the window harder than he intended. He reached inside and lifted the window pane up as far as it would go. It creaked loudly as it went. A small colony of spiders hurried quickly away. Then he was inside. The first room was empty.

The second room was not. Tied to a chair, his mouth gagged, with dark marks on his face, was a young man Fitzgerald had not met. To hell with the introductions, he said to himself as he untied the gag.

'Name's Fitzgerald. Friend of Powerscourt. Friend of William Burke. Rescue mission.'

The knots were naval ones, he noticed, the rope drawn tight along the young man's arms and legs. Fitzgerald carried him back out through the window and dumped him on the grass. The young man looked very frightened indeed. He whimpered on the turf rubbing at his arms and legs.

'Who are you? What are you going to do with me now?'

'We're friends, Richard,' Powerscourt whispered, 'Powerscourt's the name. We met at the cricket match. Sophie Williams told people you hadn't been home.'

He tried to lead his little band away from The Cottage to safety. But Richard could hardly walk. Fitzgerald picked him up as if he were a sack of coal and set off towards the Pantheon.

'I've got to tell you something,' croaked the young man, 'something terribly important.'

Richard Martin's voice was very faint. Fitzgerald sat him on the ground. It was dark again, the moon hidden behind the clouds. The fox was on patrol once more, lurking outside the temple. A slight wind had risen, whispering through the tops of the trees.

'I lost track of time in there,' Martin said, 'I must have been inside that place for over a day. But they said they were coming back for me at midnight. If I didn't tell them what they wanted to know then, they were going to seize my mother and bring her to join me.'

'What time is it, Francis?' said Fitzgerald, staring at the blood that was drying on his arm.

'It's ten to twelve.' Powerscourt peered at his watch. 'We've got ten minutes to get out of here. I don't fancy going back to the station. It's the first place they'll look for us. There's a path behind the Pantheon that leads down to the river. There's a couple of rowing boats down there.'

Powerscourt stopped suddenly. Far off, beyond the lake, coming down the track from Blackwater House maybe, they could hear voices. Three of them, thought Powerscourt, stifling the urge to run.

'Follow me,' he whispered. 'Try to be as quiet as you can.'

He took the path behind the temple. It was not much used, brambles lying on the ground, the route sometimes invisible through the dark wood. They passed the lower lake with the waterfall and began going downhill. Once Johnny Fitzgerald, still carrying Richard Martin on his shoulder, stumbled and nearly fell. Powerscourt made them stop every now and then to listen for the voices. They heard nothing, but the owners of the voices could not be far from The Cottage now and would realize that they had been cheated of their prey.

'Where is the bloody river, Francis?' Fitzgerald was panting heavily. He looked as if he couldn't go on for much longer.

'Just there, Johnny,' said Powerscourt. He realized that his left hand had been wrapped round the pistol ever since the discovery of Richard Martin.

They clambered into one of the rowing boats. Richard was bent almost double at the stern. Fitzgerald cut the rope.

'Do you want me to put a hole through the bottom of this other boat here, Francis? In case we have company a little later on?'

'No,' said Powerscourt. 'I am sure they will check the station first. I think we should get out of here.'

The little boat had two seats in the centre for the rowers and further seats at the bow and stern. Powerscourt settled himself in the central seat and began to row as quietly as he could. Soon they rounded a bend in the river and Blackwater passed out of sight. Fitzgerald was keeping a watchful eye behind.

Captain Powerscourt banned all speech for the first ten minutes of their journey. Then it was only in whispers. They were on a long straight stretch now, trees lining both banks. A barrel overtook them rolling from side to side as it went. They could see a town approaching on their left.

'The lights begin to twinkle from the rocks,' Powerscourt muttered to himself,

'The long day wanes: the slow moon climbs: the deep moans round with many voices.'

There was a scuffling at the back. Richard Martin was sitting upright at last, rubbing sadly at the bruises on his face.

'Push off,' he said, smiling through the pain,

'and sitting well in order smite
The sounding furrows; for my purpose holds
To sail beyond the sunset, and the baths
Of all the western stars, until I die.'

Fitzgerald was peering back down the river, straining to see what other craft might lie behind. They shot under the centre arch of a great railway bridge.

'It may be that the gulfs will wash us down,' Powerscourt went on,

'It may be we shall touch the Happy Isles,
And see the great Achilles whom we knew.'

'To hell with Achilles for now.' Johnny Fitzgerald sounded very worried. 'The gulfs or the Happy Isles would do me fine at this moment. The only thing is, there's another bloody rowing boat behind and they're gaining on us. We might meet Achilles sooner than we think. We're going to need him.'

He leapt into the central thwart, grabbed a pair of oars and pulled for all he was worth.

'Richard, there,' said Powerscourt, 'can you see the others? The other boat I mean.'

'Yes, I can, sir. They're about two hundred yards away.'

Nobody spoke as Powerscourt and Fitzgerald tried to widen the gap. They had left the little town behind and were in wide open country, fields and pasture spreading out beside the Thames. The only noise was the splashing of the oars and the ripple of the water beside the boat. Powerscourt was feeling stiff again from his cricket. Twenty-five years have gone since I last rowed a boat in anger, he said to himself. Maybe we'll reach Henley. We could have our very own regatta in the middle of the night.

'I'm terribly sorry, sir,' said Richard Martin squinting back up the river, 'I think they're gaining on us.'

Far off to the left a puff of smoke announced the arrival or departure of a late night train. They had entered a long sharp bend so the pursuing boat was lost from sight. Another town materialized out of the gloom, nestling along the river's edge.

'Steer over to the bank, Johnny, quick as you can. We could get out on the towpath over there and vanish into the streets.'

'That won't do you much good,' said Fitzgerald, 'once they realize this boat is empty they'll come back and look for us in there.'

'We don't have much time, Johnny,' said Powerscourt anxiously.

'Tell you what,' said Fitzgerald. 'You and Richard get out right now. I'll keep going. They won't know you're not on board any longer. Quickly now. I'm sure this boat will go better with only one person. And I'm sure I can row faster than those other buggers.'

Powerscourt and Richard Martin leapt on to the towpath. Powerscourt gave the boat a huge shove and ran into the side streets. Johnny was making good speed, shooting through the central arch of the town bridge. He sounded as if he had begun to sing. Powerscourt thought he recognized the drinking song from *La Traviata* as Fitzgerald serenaded himself on his night flight down the Thames.

26

It was three o'clock in the morning when Powerscourt reached Markham Square. He brought with him not only Richard Martin, but his mother, wrapped up in her best coat and very apprehensive about going to stay at a grand house in Chelsea.

'I'm not happy about leaving your mother here,' Powerscourt had said to Richard when they reached his little house in North London. 'I'm going to ask the cab to wait. You go inside and tell your mother to get ready.'

Mrs Martin thought she was dreaming. First of all here was Richard, back home in the middle of the night with bruises on his face. Now he was telling her to pack a bag and come to Lord Powerscourt's house at once.

'I can't do that, Richard. What will the neighbours say to me disappearing like that in the small hours of the morning? I'll never be able to raise my head in the street again. People will think I'm a criminal being taken away by the police.'

'Just pack your bag, Mother,' said Richard, 'and please hurry. There's a cab waiting outside the door.'

Richard wrote a note to Sophie while he waited. Powerscourt had told him they could drop it off on the way so she would know he was safe and well in the morning. 'Dear Sophie,' he wrote, 'I am back in London after some very exciting times. I can tell you all about it tomorrow. Lord Powerscourt says you are to call at his house after you finish teaching. That's 25 Markham Square in Chelsea.' Richard paused briefly. Then the elation of his escape took over, the dramatic row down the Thames with the enemy in pursuit. 'Love, Richard.'

Richard had given Powerscourt the details of his incarceration on the train from the Thames Valley to Paddington. He told how he had been summoned to Mr Charles Harrison's office, how two men had seized him and bundled him into a waiting cab and on to the station for Blackwater.

'They blindfolded me before we got to that big house, my lord, so I wouldn't remember where I had been, I suppose. Then they tied me up in that little house where you found me. They used to come and ask questions every couple of hours or so. If I didn't answer them they would hit me sometimes. Every now and then they would bring me food and a glass of water.'

'What did they want to know, Richard?' said Powerscourt, his eyes never leaving the far end of the carriage where any new passengers would appear, his hand deep in his coat pocket.

'They wanted to know what I had told Mr Burke,' said Richard, grimacing at his memories. 'I said I hadn't told Mr Burke anything. They didn't believe me. They said I had been seen talking to him at the cricket match. Then they wanted to know if I had talked to anybody else. I said, No, I hadn't. I wasn't going to tell them I had talked to Sophie, was I?'

'Sophie did very well, you know, very well.' Powerscourt smiled at Richard. 'If she hadn't come to tell Mr Burke you had gone missing you could have been locked up in that little cottage for days, if not weeks. She was very brave.'

Richard grinned back at Powerscourt. 'So you think she might care for me, my lord?'

'Well,' said Powerscourt, 'I'm not sure that a slow train, currently passing Slough if I am not mistaken, at two o'clock in the morning, is the best place for a discussion of your prospects. But I should say that she cared for you very much, possibly more than she realized before. Now tell me, Richard, was there anything else they asked you? Did they mention any dates in the near future? Any events they might have wondered if you knew about?'

Richard was lost in thought, more concerned with his next meeting with Sophie than with the questions he had been asked at Blackwater.

'What was that, my lord? Sorry, yes, they did ask me if I knew anything about next Monday, the day, they called it. They muttered something in a foreign language I didn't understand. I think it was German, my lord. It sounded like Der Tag, Der Tack, something like that. I'm going to start on the German next term, my lord, at my evening classes. I've nearly finished French.'

Powerscourt stared out of the window. The river was just visible in the moonlight. He wondered where Johnny Fitzgerald was, if he had shaken off his pursuers.

'Next Monday, Richard. That's the big day. It's now Wednesday morning. We've got five days to stop them, whatever they're trying to do, one of them a Sunday. Just five days.'

'What do you make of it all, Francis?'

Powerscourt and William Burke were sitting by the fire in the upstairs drawing room in Markham Square the following morning. Downstairs Lady Lucy was looking after Mrs Martin, offering her round after round of toast and a flood of tea. Richard was still asleep.

'On one level, William,' said Powerscourt, 'it's kidnap pure and simple. I'm sure the police would be able to arrest Charles Harrison and his associates at Blackwater without any trouble at all. But I'm not sure we should set any of that in motion just yet.'

'Why ever not, Francis?' said Burke, growing indignant at crimes committed in broad daylight in the heart of the City.

'I am certain,' said Powerscourt, 'I am absolutely certain that the most important thing just now is to frustrate their plans. How we do it I do not know. But I feel very sure that any arrest would bring publicity and publicity is what they want for their main purpose. Have you found the figures I mentioned to you yesterday afternoon, William? The ones that would confirm my theory of what has been going on all these months?'

'I have some of them, but not all.' Burke reached for a paper in his breast pocket. 'I need to talk to young Richard when he wakes up. I have no doubt that your theory is correct, Francis. I cannot tell you what I think about it. It is the most monstrous thing I have ever encountered in the City of London. And I do not know how we can stop it. I fear it is already too late. Next Monday, did you say, is the vital day? Just three full working days away. God help us all.'

Powerscourt rose from his chair. The grey cat slid from behind the place he had just left. Faintly, from upstairs, there came the sound of Olivia crying.

'William, you must wake up young Richard and see what details he can fill in. You must send a message to the Governor of the Bank of England asking for a meeting this afternoon. Maybe he should come here.'

'I am certain he should come here,' Burke said. 'Every time the

Governor calls on an office in the City the place is filled with rumours within the half-hour. Such and such a firm is going bankrupt, such and such a bank has defaulted on their loans, such and such a broker is about to get hammered. Rumour travels faster than the wind. I shall ask the Governor to meet me here at two o'clock. Where are you going, Francis?'

'I am going,' said Powerscourt, 'to build a bridgehead with the world of politics. I fear that only they may be able to solve the problem once they realize how serious it could become. I am going to call on my friend Rosebery. He may be out of office now but he knows how to pull the levers. God knows, we may have to pull a lot of those.'

Michael Byrne was saying goodbye to one of his travellers in a small flat in one of Dublin's many slums. Three leaves in a shamrock, Byrne said to himself, three messengers to cross the sea to England. Three messengers to carry a message of hatred from one island to another. Three messengers to announce to the greater world that the cause of Irish freedom had not been extinguished by Victoria's Jubilee. Three messengers to carry packages across the Irish Sea. Three messengers to deceive his enemies.

'Go safely now,' Byrne said to Siobhan McKenna, the second of his envoys to set out on the boat to Liverpool. 'You know the story?'

'I know it as well as I know my own name, Michael Byrne,' replied the girl. 'It would be too dangerous for me to come and wave you off.' Byrne was apologetic, worried that his absence at the quayside could be interpreted as cowardice.

'Don't you worry. Don't worry at all.' The girl gave him a quick kiss on the cheek and set off on her journey. In her pocket she carried an invitation to an interview for the position of assistant teacher at the Convent of Our Lady of Sorrows in Kensington. Byrne hoped that her visit would multiply the sorrows.

Rosebery's formidable intellect was turned on to the racing papers. He was making notes as he read, as if preparing a memorandum for the Cabinet.

'Powerscourt!' He rose to greet his friend. 'How very good to see you. You find me deep in the study of form on the turf. One of my

253

most expensive animals takes to the race course tomorrow. But come, Francis, sit down, you do not look like a man who has come to talk of horseflesh.'

'I have not, I'm afraid.' Powerscourt sank into a deep red armchair at the side of the fire. A series of paintings of Rosebery's horses adorned the sides of the mantelpiece.

'Why don't you tell me the story from the beginning, Francis. The last I heard you were looking into a strange death in the City, a headless man found floating by London Bridge.'

'Very well,' said Powerscourt. He suddenly realized that he was incredibly tired after the exertions of the previous evening. He paused while he arranged the facts in his mind.

'Let me begin with the headless man,' he said at last. 'He was found, as you say, floating in the Thames with no head and no hands. I didn't know it at the time, but it was the start of the unravelling of a very great conspiracy.

'The dead man was Old Mr Harrison, founder and senior partner in Harrison's Bank, a private bank in the City. He was not the first Harrison to die in strange circumstances. His eldest son perished in a boating accident off the Isle of Wight eighteen months before. There were rumours, never substantiated, that the boat had been tampered with.'

'Why did he have no head, Old Mr Harrison?' asked Rosebery. 'And no hands?'

'I'm not sure about that,' said Powerscourt. 'The head was cut off to make him unrecognizable, I think. I'm not sure about the hands. Maybe the murderer had heard about this new thing called finger-printing. Johnny Fitzgerald told me the German police are quite advanced with it. You can identify people by their fingerprints. Every one is different. The Army have been using a system like it in India for years to identify people.' Powerscourt looked down at his thumb for a moment before he continued.

'They lived in Oxfordshire at a place called Blackwater, these Harrisons. Old Mr Harrison's sister still lives there. It seemed from talking to her and to the head groom that Old Mr Harrison had grown very worried in the last year or so. He used to ride round the lake on a pony and read and write letters to and from Germany. He got the groom to post the letters he was sending to Berlin and other places to avoid them being seen in the big house. He talked to his sister of conspiracies involving the bank, of secret societies in Germany.'

'What sort of conspiracies? What sort of secret societies?'

'I'll come to that,' said Powerscourt, 'I'm just trying to tell the story in the right order. Shortly after that, and after my learning of the secret societies, there was a fire at Blackwater. The fire experts are sure, though they would find it hard to prove, that it was started deliberately. Old Mr Harrison's other son, Frederick Harrison, was burnt to death in his bedroom in the inferno. The door of the room had been locked from the other side. Nobody ever found the key.'

'My God, Francis,' said Rosebery, 'this is frightful. It's like one of those Greek plays where there's nobody left alive at the end.'

'It may yet come to that,' said Powerscourt. 'It was a very strange house, Blackwater. The original owner had constructed the lake with classical temples all around the side. Hercules and Diana and Apollo peered out at you as you walked round the water. There was a very strange butler who had dealings with the Harrisons before they left Germany and came to London. He could have had motives for revenge.'

'Don't talk to me about butlers,' said Rosebery with feeling. 'Do you remember that fellow I used to have before I found Leith? Villain by the name of Hall?'

'The fellow who looked as if butter wouldn't melt in his mouth?'

'The same,' said Rosebery, nodding his head. 'The fellow had been cheating me for years and years. All kinds of bills were grossly inflated. Hall took a cut from every single one. A bad business.'

'I did wonder about the Blackwater butler,' Powerscourt smiled at the eccentricities of butlers, Jones' walls lined with shells, his cupboard lined with empty whisky bottles, 'but in the end I didn't think he could have done any of these murders. My attention was drawn, always, to the youngest member of the family, Charles Harrison, great-nephew of Old Mr Harrison, who is now in charge of the family bank. Four people have died to put him there. But I did not think that control of the bank was sufficient motive for all these murders. All he had to do was wait and control would have come to him naturally as the others died off or retired.'

'So what was going on? Is going on?' Rosebery was leaning forward in his chair like a jockey rising in his stirrups.

'There are two other relevant facts, I think.' Powerscourt was feeling very tired. 'The first is that I asked my brother-in-law William Burke to find out what was going on inside Harrison's

Bank. One of his young men made friends with a clerk in Harrison's by the name of Richard Martin. Last Saturday Martin and Burke and I were all at a cricket match at Rothschild's place in Buckinghamshire. Charles Harrison overheard Burke asking Richard to come and see him in his office in the City on Monday morning. Harrison must have thought Martin was going to tell William Burke about the strange goings on in the bank. But before he could do so Richard Martin was abducted. He was taken to Blackwater and locked up in a little house by the lake. Johnny Fitzgerald and I rescued him from there last night, or this morning. We had to row down the river pursued by another boat before we made good our escape.'

'God bless my soul. This is frightful, Francis. What is the other thing you spoke of?'

'The other thing is this.' Powerscourt rose from the chair and began pacing up and down Rosebery's library. 'All through this case I have had the feeling that somebody had been looking at the same questions as me. Old Mr Harrison, endlessly going round his temples, muttering to his sister about conspiracies, sending his letters secretly, had been on the same voyage of discovery. On Monday I found a box of his papers hidden on a little island in the middle of the lake. There were letters from Germany in which he was asking if somebody belonged to a secret society in Berlin, a society attached to the Friedrich Wilhelm University. And there were two separate articles about the fall of Barings Bank seven years ago. I didn't take them as seriously as I should have done.'

Powerscourt sat down again. As he made his series of points he crossed them off on the fingers of his left hand.

'Now we come to the denouement, Rosebery, or almost the denouement. Point One, Charles Harrison went to the Friedrich Wilhelm University in Berlin. I am certain he belonged to a secret society there. Point Two, the society was founded by the followers of a historian called von Treitschke. The historian died last year but the society lives on. Point Three, von Treitschke was a fanatical German nationalist. He believes that the true enemy of Germany is not Russia or France, but England. Point Four, I sent Johnny Fitzgerald to Berlin to see what he could find out about secret societies. He warned me that a shipment of weapons was being sent to Ireland from Germany, presumably by this secret society. Then, just as he was getting close to his quarry in Berlin, a young man calls at my front door in London asking where Johnny is and whether he is a friend of mine. The butler tells the caller that Johnny is in Berlin and confirms our friendship. Immediately Johnny is frozen out in Berlin. Whether the high command is in Berlin or in London I do not know, I am not sure it matters. Point Five is that all the members of the society have to swear to further Germany's interests by whatever means they can. Point Six . . .' Powerscourt paused. There was a faint shuffling behind the wainscoting as if mice were trying to break through to read Rosebery's books.

'Point Six is why I am here today. Our young man in Harrison's Bank reported that the money was being taken out of Harrison's Bank very fast indeed. The people who questioned him in Blackwater referred to next Monday as being the important day, the day that counts. A week before the Jubilee.'

Powerscourt looked at Rosebery, as if he was reluctant to complete his story.

'Out with it, man, out with it,' said Rosebery.

'I know this sounds incredible, Rosebery. William Burke could scarcely believe it. But he does now. Charles Harrison is trying to do a Barings in reverse. Barings collapsed because of imprudent lending to Argentina. They didn't want it to happen at all. But Harrison is trying to make sure his bank fails. Deliberately. He is trying to make sure his bank fails in the week before the Jubilee. He is trying to make sure that other financial institutions come down with him. In the days before the Jubilee London will be full of newspapermen from every country on earth, all of them having trading relations with the City of London. There will be financial collapse as the Queen prepares to ride out in glory to St Paul's. One of the sentences that Old Mr Harrison highlighted in the articles about Barings in his strong box was this.'

Powerscourt pulled a battered copy of the *Economist* from his pocket.

'It is a quote from Lord Rothschild, a key participant in the Barings rescue, I seem to remember. "If Barings fails, it will bring to an end the custom of all the world of drawing their bills and doing their finance in London."'

Rosebery turned pale. He went to the long table in the centre of the room and poured himself a large drink.

'Drink, Francis? Drink before the catastrophe? Monday, you said, next Monday. What happens then?'

'Next Monday is the appointed day for the second payment of

Harrison's Venezuelan loan. They brought it out two years ago with a syndicate of other banks. It didn't do very well and Harrison's were believed to have placed it with a consortium of other European banks. They haven't asked for any assistance for this second tranche.'

'How much is it for,' Rosebery spoke very quietly,' this second tranche?'

Powerscourt looked again at the racehorses on Rosebery's walls. Maybe it would be safer to invest in them than in Venezuelan bonds sponsored by Harrison's Bank.

'Four million pounds,' he said, 'but this is what matters. If Richard Martin is to be believed, and I am sure he is, Harrison's won't have the money to pay it. The money has been shipped abroad. And God knows how many other bills they may have engineered to come due on the following week.'

'Was the loan underwritten?' asked Rosebery. 'That's what did for Revelstoke in the Barings crash, you know. The arrogant fellow thought he didn't need to underwrite his Argentine adventures.'

'It was underwritten, by a variety of other financial institutions,' said Powerscourt. 'William Burke is trying to find out who they are. Some of them may go under as well.'

Rosebery stared into his glass as if financial rescue might be found in the crystal.

'It is impossible, Francis, to underestimate the seriousness of the situation. It is like a dagger pointed at the success of the Jubilee itself. Barings, as you well know, were saved by the Bank of England going round with their begging bowl and by the fact that enough of the money people felt it was in their interest to bail them out. But they might not feel that with Harrison's. When that discount house Overend and Gurney went down forty years ago nobody lifted a finger to save them. Nobody liked them. And, Francis, think of this. It is almost as bad for the Jubilee if they are rescued or if they fail. You mentioned the newspapermen. The ambassadors and other representatives of the world's powers will be here as well. Think what they will make of the week before the Great Imperial Pageant if our own papers are full of crisis and collapse in the City of London. Think of the national humiliation if we have a second banking disaster in seven years. Think of the flight of business out of London to New York and Paris, all of them wringing their hands as they go, of course, but going all the same. The Jubilee will not be a celebration of the greatness of Victoria's Empire, it will be a funeral, the beginning of the end of Rule Britannia.'

Rosebery sprang from his chair and headed for the door.

'I must see the Prime Minister at once. You'd better come too, Francis. Maybe the Government can save the day. But I doubt it. I very much doubt it.'

27

There were over two hundred passengers on the Dublin to Liverpool boat. It had been a rough passage. Many of them had not slept, walking round the decks all night until dawn greeted them over the dull grey coast of England. Pale-faced and tired, they carried themselves and their luggage down the gangplank and off to the waiting trains.

At the bottom of the gangplank were two burly constables, and behind them two agents from Dominic Knox's secret intelligence department in the Irish Office. The policemen changed. The secret agents did not. They had watched thousands and thousands of Irish travellers take their first steps on to English soil. Some of them they stopped. Always they were female, usually between twenty and thirty years old. 'They'll be young. They may well be pretty,' their chief had told the two agents. 'They will certainly look as innocent as newborn babes. For God's sake, don't miss them.'

Siobhan McKenna had attached herself to a large family with children ranging from four to seventeen. She hoped she wouldn't be noticed in that company. But something different about her clothes, slightly superior to the dress of her companions, made her stand out to the watching eyes below. As the family came down, dragging the youngest reluctantly by the hand, the first agent tapped the police sergeant on the shoulder.

'That girl, there, with the black hair.'

'Excuse me, miss,' said the policeman, 'these gentlemen here would like to ask you a few questions.'

The senior agent drew the girl away from the rest of the passengers. His companion stayed at his post, scanning every new arrival as they left the boat.

'May I ask where you are going, miss?' said the agent.

260

'I'm going to London,' replied the girl, smiling brightly at the agent. Smile at them, flirt with them, charm them, she remembered Michael Byrne's instructions on handling questions from the police.

'And what is the purpose of your visit, miss?'

'I'm going for an interview for a job at a school,' said Siobhan McKenna, tossing her curls in the way that usually worked with the young men of Dublin.

'Do you have any papers to back that up, miss?' The agent gave nothing away. But he could feel his heart racing as he closed in on his prey.

'I have a letter here from the Convent of Our Lady of Sorrows in Kensington,' she said, taking a letter from her bag and handing it over with a smile.

Sister Ursula was delighted to hear from Miss McKenna. She looked forward to seeing her for an interview on Monday morning at eleven o'clock. She provided instructions on the easiest way to reach the school.

'Thank you very much, Miss McKenna,' said the agent. 'Have a good journey now, and the best of luck with the interview.'

The girl thought she was going to faint with the relief of it all. As she set off for the train to London she was too elated to look behind her. Twenty yards behind, the other agent was following her every step.

'I don't want the messengers,' Knox had told his agents, 'I want to know where they are going, who they are going to see. We don't want the minnows in the pond, we want the bloody sharks because at present we don't know who they are. But the minnows can lead us to them. Then we will strike.'

The Prime Minister saw Rosebery and Powerscourt in the upstairs drawing room in 10 Downing Street. He had grown old in office. He had also expanded from fifteen stone at the start of his administration to over seventeen stone at the time of the Jubilee. He blamed the lack of time for exercise. The Prime Minister, unlike many of his opponents, did not believe that the function of politics was to make the world a better place, to be constantly bringing schemes for improvement in the nation's life. He believed that change was almost always bad, that it should, wherever possible, be resisted, that when necessary some small concessions might have to be made for the purposes of winning elections, but that was all.

'I presume your business must be urgent, Rosebery,' said the Prime Minister. 'Lord Powerscourt, good day to you. I can give you gentlemen fifteen minutes before I have to meet a delegation of ministers from the Empire. New Zealand today, I think. There are so many of them who have to be seen.'

Rosebery sketched out the nature of their business. It took him just over six minutes. The Prime Minister made one note of only a few words on a piece of paper in front of him. Reading it upside down Powerscourt could see that it said: 'Monday, four million pounds + + +.'

'That is the crux of the problem, Prime Minister,' Rosebery concluded. 'The Chancellor of the Exchequer is out of town. Mr William Burke, a leading City financier who knows the situation, is talking to the Governor of the Bank of England this afternoon. Time is very short.'

The Prime Minister looked at them gravely, stroking the long black beard that flowed down on to his chest.

'Thank you, Rosebery. Let me try to sum up the difficulties we face.' Outside the windows they heard a series of carriages arriving. The New Zealanders had come early.

'It is not and cannot be the business of Government to bail out financial concerns whose imprudence or wickedness has left them unable to meet their obligations. I do not need to tell you, Rosebery, the outcry that would erupt in the House of Commons if members felt that taxpayers' money was being used for these purposes.'

There was a knock on the door.

'The New Zealand delegation is waiting for you, Prime Minister,' said the private secretary.

'They're early, for God's sake,' growled the Prime Minister. 'I shall be with them in five or ten minutes. Give them some tea, show them round the bloody building, just give me a little time.'

The private secretary backed quickly out of the room.

'In one way this business is very like Barings,' the Prime Minister went on. 'I myself played a little part in the resolution of that crisis. But this time there is a difference. Barings was saved by a rescue package put together in the full glare of publicity. The newspapers were full of it for weeks. We cannot afford any publicity at all at the present time, not one word, not one paragraph. The effect would be devastating.' The Prime Minister nodded towards the presence of the invisible New Zealand delegation who could be heard clattering around the building.

'An earlier Chancellor, Powerscourt, told me once that he had conducted an experiment in the speed of rumour in this great city of ours. It took about five hours to get round the Foreign Office. It took three hours to get round the House of Commons. But it took less than half an hour to get round the City of London. Maybe it's because they deal in little else over there. But if word ever got out, then the damage this German person wants to cause would have been done. We cannot let that happen. We cannot.'

Powerscourt saw from the clock on the wall that their interview had lasted nearly twenty minutes.

'You say this banker fellow is with the Governor this afternoon?' said the Prime Minister.

'So we believe, Prime Minister,' said Rosebery.

'Then we must all meet again early this evening. I might be able to avoid another of these damned receptions. Perhaps I shall be indisposed. Might I suggest that we reconvene, with Mr Burke and the Governor, here at seven o'clock. And pray give some thought to how we smuggle four million pounds into the coffers of Harrison's Bank before Monday. I must go and make conversation with these New Zealanders. Bloody sheep, I expect.'

It was nearly five o'clock when Sophie Williams finally reached Markham Square.

'You must be Miss Williams,' said Lady Lucy, as the girl was shown into the Powerscourt drawing room. 'How very kind of you to call.'

'How do you do, Lady Powerscourt, how very kind of you to invite me here after all the trouble Richard has caused everybody.' Sophie was smiling at her new friend.

'Not at all,' said Lady Lucy, smiling back at the young teacher. 'But it's Richard you'll be wanting to see, Miss Williams, I'm sure.'

'Is he all right, Lady Powerscourt? He's not hurt, is he?'

'He's fine, just fine, a few bruises here and there.' Lady Lucy spoke as if a few bruises were a regular part of a banker's daily life. 'At this moment he's closeted with Mr Burke, who you know, upstairs. I'll just go and bring him down. Would you like some tea?'

'That would be very kind, Lady Powerscourt,' said Sophie, 'it's a long way from North London.'

Lady Lucy departed upstairs to see her brother-in-law. As Richard Martin made his way downstairs she had a brief conversation with William Burke.

'William,' she said firmly, 'whatever happens, however much the nation is in peril, you are to stay here for the next half-hour. If, by any chance, you have to leave, please do not go into the drawing room.'

'Here I am,' said Burke plaintively, 'trying to resolve great affairs of finance that endanger the future prosperity of this country, and you tell me I cannot go in to your drawing room for half an hour?'

Lady Lucy smiled again. 'Affairs of the heart, William, are at least as important as affairs of state, particularly when the people involved are young.'

Sophie had just time to notice a copy of *Jude the Obscure* lying on a side table when Richard appeared.

'Hello, Sophie,' he said shyly. He thought she looked perfectly at home in this luxurious house.

'Richard,' replied Sophie, 'I am so pleased to see you all in one piece again.'

He told her of his adventures, of his incarceration in the summerhouse at Blackwater, the last-minute rescue, the desperate flight down the Thames and the early morning journey to Markham Square.

'And there's another thing, Sophie,' he went on. 'Mr Burke has offered me a job in his bank. It pays a little more than I was getting at Harrison's.'

Sophie felt that insufficient attention had been paid to her own role in the rescue of Richard Martin. 'It's just as well I went to call on Mr Burke the other afternoon, Richard,' she said firmly. 'If I hadn't, you might still be locked up down there by that funny lake.'

She didn't say that she had broken down in tears, but Mr Burke had already told Richard that. Sophie felt that her relations with Richard must be on a new footing now. She stood up and went to the window. Maybe we always have to take the initiative, she thought. Maybe these feeble men would never do anything if women didn't give them a lead.

'Richard . . .' She turned back to face him, her eyes dancing. 'Richard, give me a kiss.'

The Governor of the Bank of England was a very worried man. He rubbed his ample stomach as if for reassurance. He fidgeted with his small beard. His eyes flickered restlessly round the room.

Burke had told Powerscourt before the evening meeting that the Governor was not facing up to the crisis well.

'He's never seen anything like this in his whole life, Francis. His only idea of a commercial crisis is two bad tea harvests in a row. Even then he probably had enough of the stuff stockpiled somewhere to raise his prices and make a killing. But of bankers and bankers' follies he has no idea, no idea at all. I fear he will not serve the City well tonight.'

The Prime Minister, fresh from his conference with the New Zealanders, looked tired. By seven o'clock in the evening he had normally fled by train back to his beloved Hatfield. Rosebery looked anxious. Powerscourt wondered how much money Rosebery and the Prime Minister would lose personally if there was a great crash in the City. Burke had put on a clean shirt for the occasion, remarking to his wife that one might as well go to Armageddon in a fit state to meet God or the Devil.

The Prime Minister called the meeting to order. They were seated at a small square table in the study of Number 10 Downing Street. The Governor was on the Prime Minister's left, with Burke on his far side. Rosebery and Powerscourt, representing forces other than Mammon, were on the other flank, Powerscourt feeling slightly out of place.

'Very well,' said the Prime Minister. 'I hope we can find a way out of this sorry imbroglio this evening. Governor, what do you have to report?'

The Governor was breathing fast. His fingers beat a small tattoo on the table as he spoke.

'I believe Lord Rosebery has already acquainted you with the facts, Prime Minister. The position, I understand, is more serious than we first thought. As well as the Latin American loan obligations, there are a number of bills due next week, amounting to another million pounds, bringing the total obligation to five million pounds. We believe that the total available capital of Harrison's Bank at present is less than one hundred thousand pounds. The rest of it has been transferred abroad. I do not have to tell you, Prime Minister, that our hands are tied. If we approach any of the private or joint stock banks in the City for assistance, I believe they would refuse. Nobody liked the Harrisons. The Bank of England's total reserve at the present time is just over one million pounds. We cannot effect a rescue. We cannot try to mount a combined operation, even if that were likely to succeed. The only solution,' the Governor looked desperately at the Prime Minister, 'is to let Harrison's Bank fail, with all that means. Or for the Government itself to intervene.'

The Prime Minister looked at the Governor as he might have looked at the senior steward on his estates, bringing him news of a bad harvest.

'I see, Governor. Mr Burke, let me ask you two questions. If a combined rescue operation were attempted, what in your opinion would be the chances of success? And what would be the chances of keeping it secret?'

Burke paused for a moment before he replied. 'Let me answer your questions in reverse order, Prime Minister. I do not believe it would be possible to keep such an operation secret, were it to be mounted. Too many people, too many boards of directors would have to be consulted. I do not believe the secret could be kept for as long as twenty-four hours. As to your first point, people are prepared to rally round, to pass the hat if you like, for one of their own, for people they like. It is an almost indefinable thing in the City. People who have been to the same school or belong to the same clubs will always have a sense of fellow feeling with their own kind. The Harrisons were outsiders. They were tolerated, but not welcomed. Some of our foreign bankers have made every effort to wrap themselves in the garments of Englishness, if I may put it that way. They join the clubs, they hunt or shoot with their colleagues in the financial world. They try to become insiders. The Harrisons were outsiders, necessary outsiders probably, performing a useful function in the business life of the financial community, but not really belonging. I do not believe anyone would lift a finger to save them.'

The Prime Minister nodded. He looked, Powerscourt thought, strangely unperturbed at the terrible tidings passing across his table. There was worse to come.

'Tell me, Governor,' he said, turning to look the tea importer straight in the eye. The fingers continued strumming nervously on the table. 'Leaving aside the question of the Jubilee, now almost upon us, what would be the impact of the crash of Harrison's Bank on the reputation of London as a place of business?'

The Governor's eyes looked wilder yet. 'Catastrophe, Prime Minister.' The Governor said the word catastrophe very slowly, dragging it out so the full horror could sink in. 'There is no other word. The City's reputation would be ruined, coming so soon after the near collapse of Barings seven years ago. Business would disappear to the Continent, to New York. It would be a catastrophe, Prime Minister. Could I just refer back to Barings?'

'No, you may not at this moment refer to Barings!' The Prime Minister was very firm. 'I have my own thoughts on Barings as I was in office myself at the time. Lord Rosebery, as a former Foreign Secretary and Prime Minister, could you tell us your view on the impact of such a collapse so close to the Jubilee?'

Rosebery looked surprised. The Prime Minister himself had been Foreign Secretary for a far longer period than he had.

'It would be a very great blow to the prestige of Great Britain,' Rosebery began. 'The foreign press, come to report on the glories of the Jubilee, would report instead on the weakness of what had been one of this nation's greatest strengths. They would glory in our discomfiture. We would be humiliated abroad. It would be as though some great Roman general were to be told, on the eve of his triumph through the streets of Rome, that the armies had mutinied and the colonies had raised the standard of revolt. The prestige and authority of the nation overseas, invisible but invaluable, would be greatly weakened. The Titan would still be a Titan, of course, but it would be a wounded Titan, limping on its passage, with blood dripping on the floor as it passed by.'

The Prime Minister managed a menacing smile.

'Thank you, Rosebery. Tell me, Governor, why do you not appeal to the patriotism of your colleagues, swear them to secrecy in your dealings, persuade them to save Harrison's Bank for the honour of their country?'

The Governor stopped drumming his fingers on the table. He looked as though he might be about to cry.

'Prime Minister,' he said, 'I have considered that. Of course I have. But I do not believe that such an appeal would work.'

'Is there no patriotism left then?' The Prime Minister was almost shouting now, turning the full authority of his office and his personality on the man beside him. 'Does profit come before the honour of the country? Does it, Governor?'

The Governor was on the ropes now. Powerscourt didn't think he would get up again.

'I don't think the people in the City would put it like that, Prime Minister. But if it came to a choice between preserving their own houses and their own balance sheets, and some misty notion of the honour of the country abroad, I have no doubt how they would react. They would choose to keep what they had, rather than throw it away. Please may I return to Barings, Prime Minister? On that occasion it was the Government itself that led the rescue. Surely it is up to the Government to do so again.'

The Prime Minister banged a very large fist on the table. The pictures shivered on the walls. 'Do not speak to me of Barings in that false fashion. The Government did give certain guarantees, but only when we were sure they would not be needed. Your predecessor had his rescue mission already in place when we gave our undertakings. They merely underwrote the confidence that the rescue would succeed. You do not have any rescue mission in place. You sound, forgive me for saying so, incapable of putting any rescue mission in place. Not a canoe, not a paddle boat, do I see about to set off from the quays of Threadneedle Street. You in the City are incapable of rescuing this wretched firm. It is politically impossible for the Government to commit itself to such sums without asking Parliament. Harrison's must sink, and the reputation of the City and the prestige of the British Empire will sink with it.'

Silence dropped on the room. Powerscourt was thinking, not of the impact of the crash on the City of London, but of Lady Lucy and her tragic family, the Farrells. He remembered Lucy telling him that the eldest child had also died, that the father was at death's door. The rooms they lived in were owned by Harrison's Private Bank. Burke had told him on the way to the meeting that the flats would have to be sold, whatever remained of the Farrell family thrown on to the cruel streets of London once more. One more widow, three more homeless children. He wondered how many more families would lose their homes if Harrison's failed, more statistics to be added to the enormous totals of the capital's poor.

The Governor was wishing he was back in the peaceful company of his teas and his warehouses. His firm had made a fortune out of Jubilee Tea, a new blend, produced specially for the occasion, combining the finest flavour of the finest teas in the empire. It would have a bitter taste now. Rosebery was feeling relieved, not for the first time, that he was only a visitor and not the occupant of Number 10 Downing Street. William Burke wondered if the Prime Minister had deliberately forced the meeting to crisis point, only to pull a rabbit from his hat at the end. Powerscourt was looking at the portraits of previous Prime Ministers looking down on them from the walls, Melbourne looking avuncular, Pitt looking exhausted, Liverpool impassive.

'Powerscourt!' The Prime Minister at any rate had not given up yet. 'It is thanks to your efforts that we know of this terrible plot. We are grateful to you. I know that you are not a man of finance, but have you any counsel to offer us now at the eleventh hour?'

The Prime Minister thought it would be only polite to hear from Powerscourt before he closed the meeting. He didn't expect to hear anything of substance. He was already contemplating the diversion he would have to invent to draw attention away from the problems in the City, the immediate despatch of troops to some remote part of Africa, a revival of the Russian menace on the frontiers of the Raj perhaps. India would be best, he decided, the threat from the Russian Bear would play well on the patriotic feelings of the Jubilee.

Powerscourt was to tell Lady Lucy afterwards that the Prime Ministers on the wall had come to his rescue. Directly opposite him was Disraeli, dressed in pomp and splendour as Earl of Beaconsfield in his last days, but still with something of Shylock or Svengali about him, conjuring ancient mysteries from the East to dazzle a mourning Empress.

'I was wondering about the Suez Canal,' he began slowly. The plan was still taking shape in his mind.

'The Suez Canal?' the Governor said scornfully. His fingers were tapping remorselessly on the table once more. 'What in God's name has the Suez Canal got to do with it?'

The Prime Minister was gathering his papers, his left hand searching automatically for his train ticket to a more peaceful world.

'I was thinking of the way it was bought actually,' said Powerscourt, refusing to be put off by the Governor. 'It had to be done in secret. The Government could not ask for help from the Bank of England in case word leaked out and the shares went up in price or were bought elsewhere. So they asked one man for a loan. Just one man. Rothschild. It was all done in less than half an hour, I believe.'

'Are you suggesting that we ask Rothschild's again?' said Burke, anxious to assist his friend.

'No, I am not,' said Powerscourt, 'But it was the principle I was thinking of. In this case the Bank cannot ask for help from the wealthy houses in the City, either because it would not be forth-coming, or because approaches to a variety of houses could not be kept secret. The Government cannot employ the taxpayers' money on such a scale at this notice because the House of Commons would not stand for it. But if the Government were to borrow the money from just one individual, then those difficulties might be overcome. I have only just thought of this scheme, gentlemen, forgive me if it is not properly formed.'

The Prime Minister looked hard at Powerscourt. Maybe he wouldn't have to organize a trumped-up row with the Russian Ambassador after all.

'Do you have anybody in mind, Powerscourt?' he said.

'I am not sure about specific individuals, Prime Minister,' Powerscourt replied, 'but I have a very clear idea of the type of individual who might be prepared to give assistance. Mr Burke was talking earlier about outsiders who want to be insiders, some-body who wants to be embraced into the bosom of the English upper classes. My candidate would not be a peer, but he would be eternally grateful for a peerage.'

'Bloody expensive for a peerage, five million pounds, even these days,' said the Prime Minister, laughing for the first time that evening.

'No doubt there are other inducements that could be offered,' Powerscourt went on. 'Some of our more fashionable clubs are very desirable for the simple reason that they are so hard to get into. I was thinking of the MCC or the Royal Yacht Squadron at Cowes for example. Some of the Pall Mall establishments may have been too quick in the past with their blackballs. That could, no doubt, be corrected. The Garter might be out of reach, Prime Minister, but surely the Chairmanship of a Royal Commission on some subject of little importance would not be. Invitations to spend the weekend with the Prince and Princess of Wales at Sandringham perhaps? Dinner with the Queen Empress herself at Windsor?'

Now it was Rosebery's turn to laugh. The tension was ebbing from the room.

'Come, Francis, you must have somebody in mind, surely?' said Rosebery. 'I am not a financier,' said Powerscourt, secretly amazed at how quickly the plan had unfolded in his mind, 'my only qualifica-tion is that when I began the investigations into Harrison's Bank I read the back copies of the *Economist* and other financial papers for the past three years. I was thinking of one of those diamond people, not Rhodes of course, but one of the more shadowy ones who must have made more money than he ever did.'

'Messel!' Burke broke in. 'Franz Augustine Messel. He might be our man. Or that other fellow, Sprecker, Hans Joachim Sprecker. They have both made enormous fortunes out of gold and diamonds in South Africa, Prime Minister. They are both resident in this country. Neither, to the best of my knowledge, has yet been elevated to the peerage.'

'What do we put on the recommendation, Burke?' asked the Prime Minister. 'Even nowadays you have to say something about charitable good works or help for the deserving poor.'

'Services to the financial community?' suggested Powerscourt. 'That could cover a multitude of sins. Usually does, I believe.'

'Let us be serious, gentlemen.' The Prime Minister's hand had stopped looking for his train ticket. Maybe he would have to remain at his post a little longer yet. 'Do either of you financial gentlemen believe this scheme to be possible? Governor?'

The Governor had turned pale. Life with Darjeeling and Earl Grey, Assam and Lapsang Souchong had not prepared him for this.

'I think it is a most, a most interesting proposal,' he spluttered. 'I could not commit the Bank to saying whether it would succeed or not. I'm afraid – '

'Mr Burke?' the Prime Minister cut the Governor off brutally.

'Well, Prime Minister . . .' Something told Burke that bravery, even recklessness, might be better than prudence and his banker's caution at this moment. 'I think it could well work. It could get us out of all our difficulties. There is only one problem, now I think of it. I spoke a moment ago as if we had two possible candidates. I fear, with the time at our disposal, we have only one. Sprecker has made huge investments in some Central European railroad. Unlike almost all his contemporaries in the City he goes out in person to check on the progress of the schemes he has funded. We could not get to him in time.'

'But Messel?' said the Prime Minister. 'Where is he?'

'I believe he is at his place in Oxfordshire, Prime Minister. They call it the Chiltern Versailles. We could reach him tomorrow morning. We have nothing to lose.'

'We have nothing to lose,' said the Prime Minister grimly, 'but the interest rate. What do you think he would charge for a loan in these circumstances?'

'I fear we would have to pay over the odds, Prime Minister, however many inducements we were able to throw into the pot.'

'Never mind.' The Prime Minister was gathering his papers once again. 'Bring him here. Bring him here tomorrow. On second thoughts, don't bring him here. The place is full of these foreign persons and their reporters at present. Where do you suggest we meet, Mr Burke?'

'Well,' said Burke, 'the Bank of England is out of the question. So is any office in the City. I would offer my house in Chester Square but my wife is having it repainted for the Jubilee.' He smiled an apologetic smile. 'Could I suggest, Prime Minister, that we meet in Lord Powerscourt's house in Markham Square? Number 25. We could let you know when Messel is expected to arrive.'

'Excellent,' said the Prime Minister. He looked round at his predecessors on the walls, his gaze coming to rest on Disraeli's wicked eyes. 'I'm going to take a leaf out of Disraeli's book, gentlemen. He sent his private secretary Montagu Corry to handle the negotiations with Rothschild about the Suez Canal. I shall use my equivalent. Schomberg McDonnell may look like a junior clerk in a solicitor's office, but he bargains with straying backbenchers and rebellious members of the Cabinet as though he had been born in an Oriental bazaar.'

'Does that mean, Prime Minister,' Powerscourt was taking his duties as host very seriously, 'that you won't be coming to the meeting yourself?'

'Don't be ridiculous, Powerscourt!' The huge frame shook with laughter. 'McDonnell can talk to the fellow downstairs. Then he reports back to us upstairs. I don't care if you have to hide me behind the arras, Powerscourt, I shouldn't miss it . . .' He paused suddenly and looked balefully at the Governor of the Bank of England. 'I shouldn't miss it for all the tea in China.'

28

Michael Byrne was a very superstitious man. He had never lost his faith in the Roman Catholic Church. Years of exposure to its teachings had left their mark. Nobody who had attended the Christian Brothers' school in Clontarf, the prayers and religious instruction reinforced with regular communion with the strap, could ever truly escape. So he had decided to send his last messenger to London disguised as a nun. With wimple and crucifix, rosary and prayer book, he believed his envoy would surely avoid detection if the agents of the British Government were watching the ports. The nun would always get through.

But the susceptibilities of Ireland were not shared by the policemen of Liverpool. Sister Francesca, like the two previous emissaries, was followed all the way to London.

Lord Francis Powerscourt was feeling cheerful as he walked back to Markham Square. The sun was still shining and the warm weather had brought the crowds out into Hyde Park and Kensington Gardens, young lovers lying happily on the grass. It looked as though this difficult case was nearly over. Tonight, he decided, he would take Lady Lucy out to dinner. A new restaurant had opened just off Sloane Square, specializing in fish. Lucy was very fond of fish. Then, when the Jubilee celebrations were complete, he would take her away, maybe to Naples and the ruins of Pompeii.

The front door was open when he arrived. Powerscourt had a sudden premonition that something was wrong, something was terribly wrong. He called for Lady Lucy. There was no reply. He hurtled up the stairs to check that the children were safe. Thomas and Olivia slept the deep sleep of the very young. Robert was nowhere to be seen. He looked in all the bedrooms for his wife. Perhaps she has gone for a walk in the park, he said to himself. But he knew that was not very likely. Lucy had said to him before he left for his meeting with the Prime Minister that she would be waiting for his return. She was anxious to hear the news.

Then he saw the letter. It was lying innocuously on the little table by the front door. 'Lord Francis Powerscourt', it said, in a handwriting that had not been learnt in an English school. Powerscourt tore it open. He noticed that his hands were shaking slightly.

'Dear Lord Powerscourt,' it said, 'We have your wife. If anything is done to save Harrison's Bank between now and Monday, you will never see her again. If events are allowed to run their course, she will be returned unharmed. But if Harrison's are saved, she will be dead within the hour. And if we see you or any of your associates, or any policemen, in uniform or not, we shall begin by cutting her face open.'

Lady Lucy had been kidnapped.

There was no signature. Powerscourt felt his head spinning. Christ in heaven, he said. Christ in heaven. He looked again at the envelope. He inspected the notepaper for any clues. Both were perfectly normal and could have been purchased in any stationer's shop in London. Or in Germany. He looked at them again. He wanted to scream. He began walking up and down the room, blinking back the tears. Christ in heaven, he said again. The bastards. Strange memories of Lucy danced across his brain. He saw her as she had been in this very room in the early evening a couple of days before. She was sitting in her favourite armchair by the window, reading. The late afternoon sun was pouring through the windows casting a glow, almost a halo over the blonde hair. One side of her face was in deep shadow. As she read, little smiles or slight frowns would cross her face. When she realized he was looking at her, she had blushed a bright pink. 'Francis,' she had said, 'I didn't know you were watching me like that. I'm not one of your suspects, am I?' And then she laughed as she rose to embrace him.

Now she was gone. The bastards. Hold on Lucy, Powerscourt sent his prayer out into the pagan air of Chelsea, hold on. I'm coming, Lucy. I'm coming.

He had no idea how to find her. He knew he wasn't thinking very clearly. He wrote a note to Johnny Fitzgerald and signed it

Excalibur. Excalibur meant drop everything, whatever you are doing, come as fast as you can. He had only used it once before. He started walking up and down the room again, his anger rising inside him in waves of fury he couldn't control. Then the door was flung open and an exhausted Robert collapsed on the sofa. His face was very red and he was panting heavily.

'Francis,' he gasped, 'they've got Mama. The bad men.'

Powerscourt sat down beside him. 'Let me get you a glass of water,' he said, 'you look as if you need it.'

Robert drained the glass in one long pull.

'Tell me what happened,' said Powerscourt. 'Take your time. Take it slowly.'

'It must have been about an hour ago.' Robert's voice was breaking as he spoke. 'I heard this great row going on down below. I came out of my room and peeped round the stairs. Two men were pulling Mama along the hall. They were shouting at her to be quiet. She was shouting back. I think she was saying, How dare you? Let go of me. Then she screamed. One of the men put something over her face and she went quiet. They pulled her out of the front door. I think they had a cab waiting outside.'

The boy stopped. He took a couple of deep breaths. Powerscourt thought the tears weren't very far away.

'I came down the stairs as fast as I could,' Robert went on. 'And I saw the cab up at the corner of the street so I ran after it. I couldn't think of anything else to do.'

'Did you see where it went, Robert?'

The boy nodded and pulled a rather dirty handkerchief from his pocket. Blowing his nose seemed to calm him.

'You know how bad the traffic is at that time of the day,' he said, looking to Powerscourt for confirmation. His stepfather nodded. 'If I ran as fast as I could, I could just about keep up with them. I kept some way behind them. I didn't think you would want me to get too close in case they saw me.'

Powerscourt nodded. 'You were right, Robert, absolutely right.'

'They went up the King's Road as far as Sloane Square,' Robert went on. Powerscourt had a sudden vision of that new restaurant he had been going to take Lucy to, just off Sloane Square, the white linen crisp and clean on the table, the candles glistening in the evening light, the wine sparkling in the glasses. He dug his nails very hard into his palms to stop the tears.

Hold on Lucy, I'm coming, hold on.

275

'Then they went down towards the river for a bit,' said Robert. 'Over into Pimlico Road – the traffic was quite light there, I had to run at full speed for about two hundred yards, I was worried I was going to lose them – and then they got stuck turning into Buckingham Palace Road. They ended up at Victoria station.'

'Did they get on a train?' Powerscourt was really worried now. Victoria was where people went if they wanted to go to Dover and the Continent. If they have left England, he thought, he might never find Lucy again.

'I thought I'd lost them there, the crowds were so big,' Robert continued. 'Then I saw them. Mama looked as though she was drunk or drugged or something like that. The two men were pulling her along. Nobody took any notice. I suppose they thought she was ill. They took a train to Brighton. I know it was Brighton because I asked the ticket man after it had left if the train stopped at all. He said it didn't, it went direct.'

Then Robert broke down completely. He cried for his lost mother, sitting on the sofa in her house in Markham Square, dusk slowly falling over the streets of London. Lady Lucy's favourite clock was ticking quietly in the corner.

'Robert,' said Powerscourt, 'I am very very proud of you. You have done magnificently.'

It didn't work. The tears flowed on. Powerscourt was close to tears himself as he looked at the boy, twelve years old and you could see his mother in his face, the same eyes, the same nose, the same fair hair.

'The thing is,' Robert went on' 'I should have got on the train. I could have followed them to Brighton and seen where they went, then come back and told you.' Robert shook his head. He reached for his handkerchief again and wiped his eyes. 'But I didn't have any money. I hadn't any money at all. I did have the money Mama gave me but I'd been to buy a new cricket bat. It's upstairs in my room. I think I'm going to throw it away now. If only I'd waited until tomorrow.'

Robert wept, the tears falling onto the new cushions Lady Lucy had bought the week before. Powerscourt felt desolated.

'You mustn't throw your new bat away,' he said very gently. 'You must tap it in and then when your mother comes back we will come and watch you score a hundred.'

'Do you think she will come back?' asked Robert through his tears.

'I'm sure of it. Thanks to you, we know where she is. All we have to do now is to find her.'

'Can I help? Can I help you find her?'

Powerscourt wondered what his mother would have thought about Robert missing school. He felt sure she wouldn't approve. He had seen Robert packed off to his lessons with colds that would have kept lesser men in bed for the day.

'I don't think your Mama would want you in any danger, Robert,' Powerscourt said. 'You've done most of the work already, now we know where she is.' He sat down beside Robert and held him very tight. 'We're going to find her,' he said. 'We're definitely going to find her.'

Hold on Lucy, I'm coming, hold on.

29

Lady Lucy didn't know very much about what was happening to her. Those horrid men kept putting something over her face. Fragments of hymns and prayers from her childhood floated through her mind. Defend us from all perils and dangers of this night. God be with us in our waking and in our sleeping. The day thou gavest Lord has ended, the darkness falls at thy behest. One thought never left her. Francis will find me. Francis will find me. Then she would drift off to sleep.

Johnny Fitzgerald arrived shortly before nine o'clock, clutching a sinister-looking black bag. He took one look at Powerscourt's face. The joke he had been about to tell dried on his lips.

'What's happened, Francis? Christ, you look terrible!'

Powerscourt told him about the abduction of Lady Lucy, about Robert's heroic pursuit of the villainous pair, of their departure with a drugged Lucy to Brighton. He handed Fitzgerald the note they had left behind.

Johnny Fitzgerald read it quickly. Then he read it again. He looked at his friend, his features drawn now, lines of worry etched across his forehead.

'Jesus Christ, Francis. The bastards. They'll pay for this. They bloody well will.'

Fitzgerald helped himself to a monstrous glass of whisky from the sideboard.

'We must make a plan, Johnny. We've never got anywhere without having some sort of idea of what we were trying to do.'

Powerscourt thought bitterly that he and Johnny had never had such a difficult task in all their years together.

'I don't think I can go to Brighton tonight, Johnny.' Powerscourt sounded very sad. 'I've got this meeting here tomorrow morning with the Prime Minister and a man who may save Harrison's Bank. If that fails, then Harrison's Bank will fall in a few days time and the reputation of the City of London will be ruined for years to come. But if that happens, Lucy should come back, if those fellows keep their word.'

'Francis, Francis, do you know what you are saying?' Fitzgerald was drinking his whisky very fast. 'You sound as if you want that meeting to succeed. Surely you want it to fail. Otherwise you may never see Lucy again. Can't you persuade the Prime Minister to call the whole thing off, to let the bank fail and to hell with the consequences?'

'I've thought of that, Johnny,' said Powerscourt bitterly. 'I seem to have a choice, don't I? Professional success means personal failure. Professional failure means personal success, don't you see? Success in this case could mean death for Lucy. Failure could mean that Lucy lives. So it looks as though I have to choose between the failure of the bank, the collapse of the Jubilee, and my precious Lucy, mother of my children. But I don't think it works like that. I know which course I would pick, of course. But I also know which course the Prime Minister would take. If he has to choose between one life and national humiliation, he will sacrifice a life. That's the kind of choice Prime Ministers have to take. Think of the number of lives they throw away when the nation goes to war. One life, just one, isn't even going to keep him awake at night.'

'So what do we do, Francis?' Fitzgerald could see the torture in his friend's eyes.

'There's only one thing we can do,' said Powerscourt. 'We've got to find Lucy in the next four days, that's all we've got before the final showdown at that bloody bank. I think you should go down to Brighton this minute. There may be somebody left on duty at the station who may remember them, maybe even a cab driver who took them wherever they were going.'

Fitzgerald was looking at a portrait of Lady Lucy, hanging by the fireplace. Whistler had painted her in a pale evening gown against a dark background. Her eyes looked as though she was teasing the painter. Fitzgerald took another medicinal dose of his whisky.

'I would think they must have gone to a hotel, Francis,' he said. 'Think about it. They can't have known before they started that they were going to have to pull off a stunt like this. They can't have rented a house in Brighton or anything like that.

'We do have a problem, Francis.' Fitzgerald was still staring, as if hypnotized, at Whistler's version of Lady Lucy's face. 'They will have a good idea of what we look like, you and I. I may even have met one or two of our kidnapping friends in Berlin. We can't use the police. If they see a policeman they may do something to Lady Lucy. Sorry, but it's true.'

Powerscourt started shaking as he thought about the razors. Another wave of uncontrollable anger was surging through him. He knew he would just have to wait till it passed.

'And if we send in the policemen in plain clothes,' Fitzgerald went on quickly, 'they'll be recognized. I don't know what it is about policemen in plain clothes, but they're even more recognizable than if they had their bloody uniforms on.'

Powerscourt was lost in thought. Uniforms. Something to do with uniforms.

'Johnny,' he said, pacing up and down the room again, 'uniforms can make you almost invisible. If you're a fireman or somebody like that people don't really look at you at all. They look at the uniform.'

'You're not suggesting, are you,' Fitzgerald said, 'that we turn into the Sussex Fire Brigade? Not that I wouldn't like climbing up those big ladders and waving the hosepipes about.'

'No, I'm not, Johnny.' Powerscourt was deadly serious. 'It was the principle of the thing I was thinking about. Army officers.' Powerscourt said triumphantly. 'I've still got my uniform. You must still have yours somewhere. We could be a couple of heroes home from the wars.'

Powerscourt looked at Lady Lucy's favourite clock. He wondered yet again where she was.

'It's nearly half-past nine, Johnny,' he said firmly. 'This is what we should do. Off you go to Brighton with your uniform. Do you have any medals? Ask at the station about any sightings of Lucy earlier in the evening. In the morning, Captain Fitzgerald begins making discreet inquiries of the hotel managers in Brighton. Begin at the Kemptown end and work your way along the sea front. I shall see you at the railway station at one o'clock tomorrow. I'm going to talk to the Police Commissioner here later on. We may not be able to send the police out into the front line but we shall have a substantial body of reinforcements to call on. God speed, Johnny.'

Fitzgerald fled into the night, whistling the Londonderry Air as he searched for a cab in the soft evening air of Markham Square.

As he tossed in his bed that night, the space beside him empty and cold, Powerscourt sent out another message. He directed it down the Brighton Line.

Hold on, Lucy, I'm coming. Hold on.

'What in God's name is keeping him? McDonnell's been downstairs for nearly half an hour.'

The Prime Minister was growing impatient. An improbable quartet waited nervously in the upstairs drawing room in Number 25 Markham Square. One floor below, in Powerscourt's study, Mr Franz Augustine Messel, millionaire many times over, was closeted with Schomberg McDonnell, private secretary to the Prime Minister, and the finest tea the Powerscourt household could provide. Messel had travelled down from his Oxfordshire mansion, arriving in Chelsea shortly before ten o'clock.

'We just have to be patient,' said William Burke, poring over a book of accounts.

'We don't have that much time, you know,' said the Governor of the Bank of England. 'We really need to have that money today to make sure we can cope with all the necessary particulars of transfer and so on.' The Governor was, if anything, even more anxious and uncertain than he had been the night before. He paced up and down the room, wringing his hands. Rosebery was reading the racing papers.

Powerscourt was standing by the window. Two policemen were stationed discreetly among the trees. Some stray American tourists in London for the Jubilee were admiring the houses in loud East Coast accents and wondering if Boston could offer anything finer. He felt weak from lack of sleep and sick with worry. He thought he had drifted off a couple of times in the night but terrible visions of Lucy being ill treated left him exhausted. He had resolved not to say anything to the Prime Minister or anybody else until this meeting was over.

There was a rush of footsteps up the stairs.

'Right, Prime Minister.' Schomberg McDonnell was a mild-looking young man with an innocent face and fine brown eyes. 'Sorry that took so long. I had to explain to Mr Messel that we could not, under any circumstances, tell him the reason why we wanted the money.'

'What's the score?' asked the Prime Minister, rising from his recumbent position on the sofa.

'Five million pounds at five per cent, payable over ten years,' McDonnell replied.

The Bank of England looked aghast. Rosebery turned pale. The Prime Minister seemed unconcerned.

'We couldn't lose that much in the Treasury accounts over ten years. We need a longer payback time, McDonnell.'

'I understand, Prime Minister.'

'Peerage,' said Lord Salisbury firmly.

'Set against the interest rate or term of loan?'

'Both,' said the Prime Minister.

'Christ!' said McDonnell, and fled downstairs to do his master's bidding.

'I was never very good at mental arithmetic at school,' said the Prime Minister, turning to William Burke. 'Don't think I could ever have managed the Exchequer. But something tells me that we should have to find two hundred and fifty thousand pounds a year in interest charges alone on that deal. Couldn't have managed it.'

Burke looked up from his account book.

'You are absolutely right, Prime Minister. Perhaps you would like me to do the calculations for you as further bulletins emerge?'

'That's uncommon civil of you, Mr Burke. I'm much obliged.'

With that the Prime Minister sank back on to the sofa and closed his eyes. My God, thought Powerscourt, he's not going to sleep at a time like this. The Governor of the Bank was looking desperately at his watch. Burke had opened a new page in his book and was writing five million in large figures at the top. He drew a line a third of the way down the page and put another heading of five million pounds.

Powerscourt wondered how much a human life was worth. Just one. Just Lucy's. He thought of the other human lives, the Farrells and the thousands like them whose prospects would be ruined if Harrison's Private Bank were forced to sell off all the properties they held for charities. He looked again at the portrait of Lady Lucy. He felt the tears starting in his eyes and thought of other things. He thought of Johnny Fitzgerald checking out the Brighton hotels, he thought of his meeting with the Metropolitan Police Commissioner late the night before, the Commissioner looking pale as he sat drinking brandy in Lady Lucy's favourite chair.

'My God, Powerscourt, this is the most terrible thing I have heard in all my days. I shall speak to my counterparts in Sussex. The resources of the Brighton force will be put at your disposal.'

Powerscourt had expressed his gratitude. 'But don't you see, Commissioner,' he said, 'how difficult the thing is. First we have to find her. But the kidnappers must not know we have found them. You have seen what they say in their note.'

Even the Commissioner shuddered.

'If we find them,' said Powerscourt, pacing up and down the drawing room like one of Nelson's captains on his quarterdeck, 'we have to work out a way of getting Lucy from their clutches. And, believe me, I cannot see how we do it at present.'

Out in the square a plain-clothes man was talking to the two policemen. A delivery van arrived and began unloading cases of wine at a house with a red door across the way. Life in Markham Square went on, even as the Prime Minister of Great Britain tried to negotiate the salvation of the City of London in Number 25 and Lord Francis Powerscourt was closer to despair than he had ever been in his life.

There was another rush up the stairs. A distant corner of Powerscourt's mind automatically noticed that Schomberg McDonnell was not out of breath at all. Perhaps it keeps you fit, he thought, working for the Prime Minister.

'Four and a half per cent,' he announced, 'fifteen years.'

'Christ, he's going to make even more money out of us that way,' said the Prime Minister, opening his eyes.

'Royal Commission, Prime Minister?' asked McDonnell.

'Not yet, not yet, dammit. Try him with some of that fashionable stuff. You know the sort of thing.'

'Weekend at Sandringham with the Prince and Princess of Wales?' said McDonnell. 'Dinner in their London home at Marlborough House?'

'Not weekend, McDonnell, weekends. Plural.'

'God help him!' said the private secretary, and shot back down the stairs. They heard a faint click as the study door closed on the floor below.

'Interest charges would run on that deal at two hundred and twenty five thousand a year,' said William Burke. 'That's not including repayment of the principal.'

The Prime Minister subsided on to the sofa once more. Burke prepared more sections of his book with headings of five million pounds. Powerscourt noticed that there was now a subsidiary row of figures labelled one per cent, half per cent, quarter per cent. Burke was preparing for all eventualities. The Governor wished most devoutly that he was somewhere else.

So did Powerscourt. Suddenly he could hear Lucy's voice echoing in his mind. She was reading a bedtime story to Thomas, her tone soft and quiet in the hope it would send the little boy to sleep. It was a fairy story about a princess locked up in a tower. Only a handsome prince could rescue her from her prison on the top of the mountain. He went to the window to blink back his tears.

This time the negotiations seemed quicker than before. The Governor had only looked at his watch once before McDonnell was back.

'Four per cent over fifteen years,' he reported.

The Prime Minister snorted as though he had expected better tidings. 'All right, McDonnell. Royal Commission.'

'Member or Chairman?'

'Start with member,' instructed the Prime Minister, 'see how you go.

'Very good, Prime Minister.'

'You're down to two hundred thousand pounds interest charges a year now, Prime Minister,' said Burke cheerfully. 'Total interest charges of three million. Three to catch five.'

'Could be worse,' said the Prime Minister, 'could be worse.'

Where is she? Powerscourt asked himself. What are they doing to her? He wished the meeting would end and he could tell his news to the Prime Minister and rush off to Brighton. He felt completely detached from this meeting, as if it were all a dream. It's a Greek tragedy, he thought. McDonnell is the Chorus, forever coming back on stage with fresh news of atrocities and the unburied dead. Hold on, Lucy, I'm coming. Hold on.

Rosebery had ringed a number of entries in his racing paper. Burke was now marking out further pages of his notebook ready for new calculations of interest charges. Powerscourt saw that he now had a separate heading called Repayment of Capital, underlined twice.

'Maybe we should open a book on how long each negotiation will be,' said Rosebery, inspired by his study of the turf. 'I say he'll be back inside three minutes.' There was not time for anybody to reply. Just inside the Rosebery timetable McDonnell returned.

'Three and three quarter per cent. Twenty years,' he announced.

'Member or Chairman?' asked the Prime Minister.

'Chairman,' said McDonnell. 'I thought it was worth it for the extra five years.'

'What have we left now?' The Prime Minister was still lying back on his sofa.

'Let me try him with clubland, sir,' said McDonnell. 'I talked to a man last night who said Messel had been very disappointed when he was blackballed by the Coldstream.'

'Carry on, McDonnell.'

'Very good, Prime Minister.'

'I hope we can deliver these bloody clubs for him, Rosebery,' said the Prime Minister, turning to his predecessor. 'Never cared for them much myself. But you belong to one or two, don't you?'

'Rest assured, Prime Minister, the clubs should be fine.' Rosebery smiled. 'The last time I counted I belonged to thirty-seven.'

'God bless my soul!' said the Prime Minister. 'How ever do you find the time to go to them all?'

One of the stairs at the bottom of the hall was creaking, Powerscourt noticed. There was a small but noticeable squeak that heralded the return of the private secretary.

'Three and a half per cent, Prime Minister, over twenty years. It seems Mr Messel is very fond of clubs even though he doesn't belong to many. That's the MCC, the Royal Yacht Squadron, the Coldstream, the Warwick, the Beefsteak, the Athenaeum and the Jockey Club.'

'All gone?' asked the Prime Minister.

'All gone,' McDonnell nodded.

'Christ, that's a lot of clubs. Can we cope with that lot, Rosebery?'

'We can, Prime Minister. But somebody should have warned him about the Warwick. The food is disgusting.'

'We're running out of bait,' said the Prime Minister, rubbing his eyes.

'A position on government committees, Prime Minister?' McDonnell seemed to have taken the measure of Franz Augustine Messel. 'I think he'd go for that, Mr Messel.'

'Any damned committee?' asked the Prime Minister. 'Forestry? Technical Education? Maritime Shipping?'

'Something like that, Prime Minister.'

'Use your judgement, McDonnell. Off you go.'

The Governor of the Bank of England joined Powerscourt by the window. The Americans had left. The policemen still guarded

Number 25. Rosebery returned to the racing pages, marking out some more winners for the afternoon. Burke was now writing his own name over and over again in the last page of the account book. The Prime Minister closed his eyes once more. Powerscourt was thinking again about professional success and personal failure. He thought again about the Farrell family, thrown out on to the unforgiving streets of London. He thought that he might never see Lucy again. I've just got to find her, he said to himself, clenching his fists very tightly. I'm bloody well going to find her. Hold on, Lucy. I'm coming. Hold on.

That squeak again. McDonnell's face never changes every time he comes back, Powerscourt noticed. Nobody looking at him could have guessed what sort of tidings he was bringing with him.

'Three per cent over twenty years. No interest payable for the first two years,' he reported.

'What's that, Mr Burke?' asked the Prime Minister from his sofa.

'One hundred and fifty thousand a year, sir,' said Burke.

'Done,' said the Prime Minister. 'I'll settle for that. What did you have to offer the fellow for the extra half per cent, McDonnell?'

'I'm afraid I said it was likely that there would be a joint committee of both Houses looking into the whole question of foreign loans.'

'Did you, by God,' said the Prime Minister.

'I thought,' said McDonnell, looking his most innocent, 'that Mr Messel might have useful things to say on the subject. And I only said it was likely, Prime Minister. Nothing definite. Nothing we couldn't wriggle out of later on, if we had to.'

'Powerscourt,' the Prime Minister rose from his sofa at last, 'we're obliged to you for the loan of your house. I'd be even more grateful if you could manage some champagne. Governor, Mr Burke, could you attend to the financial paperwork and so on with Mr Messel? Soon to be Lord Messel, God help us all. Bring the fellow up here, McDonnell. We must drink a toast! To the salvation of the City!'

Welcome, Mr Messel, thought Powerscourt bitterly, welcome to the higher hypocrisies. Welcome to the insider's world. Welcome to the club. Welcome to the Jubilee. Welcome to Britain as it is in the year of Our Lord 1897.

'Could I just have a private word, Prime Minister?' Powerscourt closed the door on the departing financiers. He told the Prime Minister what had happened. He showed him the letter from the kidnappers, already slightly crumpled from being taken out and read so many times. He wondered what the Prime Minister would do. He knew that men said he was one of the most ruthless political operators of the century, that the corridors and the committee rooms of the Palace of Westminster were littered with the corpses of his political opponents. His first response was not what Powerscourt expected at all.

'My God, Powerscourt,' the Prime Minister said, 'the last hour and a half must have been torture for you, listening to these negotiations and McDonnell running up and down the stairs. It must have been hell. Why didn't you tell me before?'

'I didn't think it was fair,' said Powerscourt sadly. 'You can see that if these negotiations had failed, then Harrison's Bank would have fallen and Lady Lucy could have been back in this house this evening.'

He looked quickly round the room as if his wife might just float in through the window.

'By God, you must find her, Powerscourt!' The Prime Minister paused, stroking his beard. The Powerscourt cat had made an unexpected entrance. It curled up happily on the Prime Minister's lap, purring loudly that it had found a new friend.

'Let me tell you what I can do,' he went on, scratching the cat's chin as he spoke. 'I can put the resources of the State at your disposal. If you want a regiment or two, you can have them. If you want a couple of destroyers moored off the coast of Brighton you can have them. If you want Brighton sealed off by the authorities, we can do it.'

He paused. A look of distaste passed across his features. This was going to be the bit Powerscourt dreaded. He knew what was coming.

'Let me also tell you what I cannot do, my friend.' The cat seemed to sense that its new friend was false. It leapt off the Prime Minister's lap and settled at Powerscourt's feet. 'I have had the honour to serve Her Majesty as her Prime Minister for seven years now. In that time I have done whatever I thought necessary to preserve liberty and the constitution at home and the power and reputation of this country abroad. But one thing I cannot do, however much personal circumstances might work on my heart.'

He looked rather sadly at Powerscourt.

'I cannot give in to blackmail, wherever it comes from. Government would become impossible. Thanks to your skill, this wicked plot has been uncovered and repulsed. I cannot have that victory thrown away. They say, Lord Powerscourt, that you are the most accomplished investigator in the land. I have no doubt that you will succeed in rescuing Lady Powerscourt from this contemptible gang of sordid blackmailers. Let us know if there is anything you need.'

'All I need,' said Powerscourt bitterly, 'is the one thing I haven't got. Time. I've got less than four days to find her now.'

'With all my heart I wish you Godspeed,' said the Prime Minister, rising to extricate himself from a difficult situation. 'We shall all pray for your success.'

30

The train was full of families going down to Brighton for the day. Powerscourt noticed that his uniform acted as a magnet for the small children. They stared at him shyly, peering out from behind their hands, hiding round the backs of the adults. He was sharing his compartment with a family of six, accompanied by their parents.

'Can I have a ride on the donkeys, Papa?' asked a small girl of about seven.

'Can we go on the pier, Papa?' – this from a boy of about ten.

'Can we go out in a boat?' said a future sailor, then about eight years old.

'Yes, yes and yes!' laughed their father, gathering three of his brood onto his lap. 'We're going to have such a good day!'

Powerscourt smiled the complicit smile of parenthood. It was, he realized, the first time he had smiled in the last eighteen hours. He hoped that he too would have a good day, but he rather doubted it. Hold on, Lucy, he said to himself as the train roared through the great tunnel a few miles from Brighton and the sea. Hold on Lucy, I'm coming.

He found Johnny Fitzgerald eating a steak pie and drinking lemonade in the hotel by Brighton station.

'Are you feeling all right, Johnny?' asked Powerscourt.

'I'm fine,' said Fitzgerald, 'but I've had a terrible morning.'

'The lemonade, Johnny.' Powerscourt pressed on. 'I've never seen you drink lemonade before in all my life. And I've known you over twenty years.'

'I tell you what, Francis.' Fitzgerald had turned serious now. 'I went for a walk along the sea front late last night when most of the citizens had gone to bed. And I said to myself that I'm not going to take another drop until we have found Lucy. Not another drop.'

A tall man of about forty, wearing cricket whites, approached their table.

'Forgive me,' said the cricketer, 'would you gentlemen be Lord Francis Powerscourt and Lord Johnny Fitzgerald?'

Powerscourt froze. His hand went automatically into the right-hand jacket pocket of his uniform. Surely they could not have been identified so soon? Johnny Fitzgerald's hand tightened on his lemonade glass as if he would turn it into a weapon. You could cut somebody's face open with a broken glass of lemonade.

'We are,' Powerscourt said quietly. The man in the flannels, he saw, had watched them both very carefully.

'Chief Inspector Robin Tait of the Sussex Constabulary,' said the man. He showed them a piece of paper with his credentials. 'We have been warned about your problems. I have a team of six men at your disposal, sir.' He bowed slightly to Powerscourt. 'Most of them, like me, are in cricket clothes to look as unlike policemen as possible. More officers, the entire resources of the Sussex Constabulary, are on standby for your call, if we need them. I understand we are looking for a party of three or four people, one of them a woman. Do you by any chance have a photograph of the lady so we know who we are looking for?'

Powerscourt produced a recent photograph of Lady Lucy and handed it over reluctantly. He always carried it with him. He felt that in some irrational way he was losing Lucy yet again, giving her over to the care of the Brighton police force. Still, at least they wouldn't kidnap her.

'Let me sum up our thoughts, Chief Inspector.' Powerscourt managed another smile in the direction of the white-flannelled Chief Inspector. 'We know that the party boarded a train from London to Brighton last night, two men and a woman. My first instinct was that they would stay in a hotel as I did not think they would have had the time to make earlier plans which could have involved renting houses or other accornmodation. We have three days to find them. If we do not, Lady Lucy will be killed. If either Johnny Fitzgerald or myself or any police officers in uniform or plain clothes are seen looking for them, they will start to mistreat my wife. I think you should read this.'

Powerscourt took out the kidnap note and handed it to Tait. He swore softly as he read it.

'There's a problem with these hotels, Francis.' Fitzgerald had finished his steak pie. 'I found a porter who had seen them arrive at Brighton station. He said Lucy looked unwell. But I haven't been able to find anybody who drove them to wherever they were going. And these hotels aren't very co-operative at all. I've tried six of them so far. But they have people checking in and out all the time. They don't remember anybody very well.'

'Lord Powerscourt,' said the Chief Inspector, handing him back the message, 'I have the manpower to check out all these hotels by the end of the day. I should be able to do so with the men under my command, and these are all hand-picked for tact and discretion, and, if you will allow me to say so, for not looking at all like police officers. Now we have a description of the lady, it should be easier. I think you gentlemen should keep out of sight for the hours of daylight at least.'

'It breaks my heart, Chief Inspector,' said Powerscourt sadly, 'that I should not be able to take part in this search. But if I were spotted, and anything were to happen to Lucy, I could never forgive myself. And I think that applies to you too, Johnny.'

The Chief Inspector rose to his feet. 'I propose to begin the search immediately. There is a quiet hotel not two minutes from here called the Prince Regent. We have already checked that the people we are looking for are not there. Could I suggest that we meet there in a few hours' time. If we have any luck before then I shall let you know.'

Lady Lucy knew they were drugging her. She thought they put something in the tea. She felt very dazed all the time. She thought at first that she was in a private house until something impersonal about the furniture and the pictures suggested she was in a hotel. The curtains were kept half drawn. Her captors spoke very little, sometimes in German and sometimes in English. One was always on duty, watching by the windows, scanning the passers-by, inspecting the pavements. Lady Lucy thought she could smell the sea. As she drifted in and out of sleep she wondered where Francis was. She saw him pacing up and down the drawing room in Markham Square, she saw him just a few days ago at the cricket match, marching back to the pavilion after his long spell at the crease, his bat tucked under his arm.

Francis will find me, she whispered to herself. Francis will find me.

From the window of his room in the Prince Regent, Powerscourt could just see the sea. Johnny Fitzgerald had gone to buy himself some really disreputable clothes.

'My own mother won't recognize me when I've finished with myself,' he assured his friend.

Over to the right the West Pier was thronged with visitors. Sailing boats were taking parties of visitors for trips around the coast. Overhead the seagulls made their patterns and their arabesques against a blue sky flecked with small white clouds. Powerscourt had always thought Brighton was a rather raffish place, a magnet for confidence tricksters and hucksters of every description. He thought of Lydia Bennet in *Pride and Prejudice* for whom a visit to Brighton comprised every possibility of earthly happiness, rows and rows of tents stretching forth filled with young and handsome officers and Lydia herself tenderly flirting with at least six of them at once. But Powerscourt was not thinking of young and handsome officers. He was racking his brains for memories of a siege or a sudden assault where the defenders held captives who had to be taken alive or the war was lost. For he knew that his problems were by no means over if and when they found Lady Lucy. How did they get her out? They could storm the building with the Prime Minister's regiments or the massed ranks of the Sussex Constabulary but one of the ruffians could cut Lady Lucy's throat before they surrendered. Powerscourt and his forces could try to climb in through the windows, if the windows were big enough, but there would still be time for Lady Lucy to suffer. Shortly before six o'clock he thought he had found the answer. He tried to find flaws in his scheme. He was sure it wasn't perfect, but it was the best he could do. He hastened to the telegraph office and sent two messages to London, asking for a special kind of reinforcements.

At seven o'clock the Chief Inspector returned. 'No luck so far, my lord,' he said to Powerscourt, who was sprawled across one of the Prince Regent's better sofas. 'We have worked our way along the sea front and have nearly reached the end. Then we are going to begin working back into the town.'

'Damn, damn, damn,' said Powerscourt. Suddenly he had an idea. 'Can you get me a boat, Inspector? I would like to take a sail along the sea front and look at the hotels.'

'A boat? Of course we can get you a boat. We make occasional use of one or two of the fishermen's vessels. But I would not recommend you boarding one right on the main sea front, there are too many people about. If you walk out past Kemptown towards Rottingdean over there,' Tait pointed out Powerscourt's route from the hotel window, 'we shall pick you up there. I'll get you a fisherman's jersey, my lord, you'll look less conspicuous.'

One hour later Powerscourt was sitting beside Tait as they made their way out into the English Channel.

'How far out do you want to go, sir?' asked the fisherman, a bronzed young man with tattoos down his arms.

'Hold on a minute and I'll tell you,' said Powerscourt, pulling a pair of binoculars from his pocket. 'I want to be so far out that I can see everything but nobody on shore could see me.' He fiddled with the lenses. 'About one hundred yards further and that should be fine.'

'Very good, sir,' said the fisherman. Powerscourt noticed that many of the tattoos showed warships of Her Majesty's Navy.

What an extraordinary sight it was, Powerscourt thought, as the boat made its way slowly along the Brighton shore. There were elegant Regency squares, some rotting now with the wind and the spray, others gleaming happily in the light. There were military rows like Brunswick Terrace over towards Hove where the houses were lined up in orderly precision, standing shoulder to shoulder like privates on parade. There were other grander buildings, hotels in the Second Empire style, that looked like architectural equivalents of Lydia Bennet, dressed up in frills and furbelows to the height of fashion to capture the hearts of the military buildings nearby. And in the centre of it all, set back from the sea, one of Europe's most improbable constructions, the Brighton Pavilion with its domes and echoes of the Orient improbably transplanted into the mundane earth of Sussex.

But it was the hotel windows that interested Powerscourt most. He locked his glasses on to three of the larger hotels in turn. He made his way along the frontage, down to the ground, floor by elegant floor. One of the hotels, he noticed, had the curtains almost completely drawn on the very top floor.

'Suppose you were the villains,' he said to Tait. 'You would suspect that an attempt might be made to rush your position with soldiers or policemen. So you would want to be able to see what was coming towards your hotel along the sea front. If I'm right you wouldn't want to risk one of those hotels in the town itself because you couldn't see what was coming as easily. The streets are often very narrow. But put yourself in one of those top floors on the front, preferably one with a view both ways, and you would be well warned.'

He handed the glasses to the policeman.

'Four hotels have rooms that fit your description,' Tait said. 'But we have checked them all. And we have drawn a blank in every one. Nobody remembers three people, one of them a woman, checking in last night.'

Late that night there was a melancholy conference in Powerscourt's rooms. All the police reports were in. All were negative. Johnny Fitzgerald had walked about the streets, looking remarkably like a recently released jailbird, trying to see if he could spot anything. He had found nothing at all. They resolved to meet again the next morning.

As Powerscourt leaned out of his window once more, staring at the deserted sea front and the empty elegance of the West Pier, the Town Hall clock struck midnight.

They had seventy-two hours left to find Lady Lucy.

31

At two o'clock in the morning four of Dominic Knox's agents called on a thirty-five-year-old chemistry teacher of Irish extraction who was famous for his ability to make fireworks at his school of St Michael and St James. Declan Macbride was dreaming when the officers called. He dreamt he was sitting at his desk marking an enormous pile of exam papers. However many he corrected, the pile never grew any less. It was, he had decided wearily, the educational equivalent of Sisyphus pushing his rock uphill for all eternity.

The agents were very polite, but insistent. They wanted to search his rooms. They knew, as did he, that Declan Macbride had been visited in the last few days by three messengers from Michael Byrne in Dublin. They searched his small desk. They went through his clothes and his books, they went through his cupboards. Shortly before three o'clock they started on the floorboards.

Two other officers called on a Catholic hostel off the Fulham Palace Road, well known for its links with travellers from Dublin. Three young women had to submit to the same treatment.

At four o'clock in the morning Lord Francis Powerscourt tiptoed out of his hotel. He made his way slowly down to the sea front. A wind had risen off the sea. Small breakers beat feebly against the pebbles of the beach. There was no moon. He walked past the ruins of the old Chain Pier, gazing sadly at the great hotels, their front doors now locked, curtains drawn against the night air. A lone fisherman was setting out on Brighton's oldest occupation. The pursuit of fish had been happening here centuries before the pursuit of fashion. Somewhere behind these windows, he told himself is

Lucy. A frightened Lucy, perhaps a drugged Lucy. The bastards. The bastards. He could hear the fisherman's boat scraping along the beach as he pulled it down into the water. He wondered if he should offer to help him. The first very faint hint of pale grey was appearing on the horizon. Dawn was coming to Brighton, another day for him to find his beloved. He felt hungry suddenly. He wondered if Lucy felt hungry too. Then it struck him. There might just be another way to find her. He hurried back to his hotel and waited for Inspector Tait and his policemen to arrive.

They came at seven o'clock, a disconsolate bunch, their spirits down after the fruitless visits of yesterday. But Powerscourt was in cheerful form.

'I think we may have been asking the wrong question yesterday. In the hotels, I mean. I'm not sure we could have asked the right question until today.'

'Francis,' said Johnny Fitzgerald, 'you're speaking in riddles. Explain yourself, man.'

'My apologies, gentlemen.' Powerscourt looked round his little audience. 'My assumption was that the three people we are looking for would have gone to a hotel. I still think they have gone to a hotel. But it doesn't necessarily follow that they checked into the hotel as a threesome. One German could have checked in with Lady Lucy posing as his wife. Or he could have left Lucy sitting on a chair in the hotel reception while he checked in for them both. The other fellow could have checked in later or gone for a walk, anything like that. It's quite possible that nobody in the hotel has ever seen them together. So, when we asked about a threesome, the hotel people said they didn't know, because they actually hadn't seen a threesome.'

Chief Inspector Tait was still dressed in cricket flannels, topped off today by a straw hat. 'So what is the right question, my lord?'

'I think the right question is this,' said Powerscourt. 'But before I come to it, let me say one other thing. I think our German friends will be very anxious about being followed, or discovered, or rushed by a party of policemen or soldiers. They kidnapped somebody earlier in this case, Chief Inspector, and they did not succeed. Johnny and I rescued him. So they will want somewhere where they have a good view of all routes in and out of where they are. One of them will have to watch Lady Lucy all the time. That means,

296

it seems to me, that they cannot leave their rooms. If they have meals in the hotel dining room somebody may spot Lady Lucy. If they leave the building they themselves may be recognized. So while they have Lucy as their prisoner, they are, to a large extent, prisoners themselves in Room 689 of the Duke of York's Hotel, or whatever it is called.'

'For God's sake, Francis.' Johnny Fitzgerald was growing exasperated. 'What is the bloody question?'

'Simple,' said Powerscourt. 'Do you have any guests who have all their meals sent up to their rooms? All of their meals.'

Chief Inspector Tait grinned. He looks ten years younger all of a sudden, Powerscourt thought.

'Excellent, Lord Powerscourt,' said Tait. 'When did you think of that?'

'Just before five o'clock this morning,' Powerscourt replied. 'I couldn't sleep. I went for a walk along the sea front. I suddenly felt hungry and wanted some breakfast. Then I wondered if Lucy felt hungry too. Then I asked myself how she would get her breakfast.'

'Right,' said Tait. 'They go on serving breakfast until about ten in most of these places. Shortly after ten we can begin our inquiries. Do you suppose, Lord Powerscourt, that we have to begin all over again and revisit all those hotels we called at yesterday?'

'I'm afraid you do, Chief Inspector,' said Powerscourt.

'I shall go and organize things immediately. No harm in getting our men back in position nice and early. But may I ask you one question, Lord Powerscourt? How do you propose to effect the rescue? I have been thinking about that and there are terrible risks whichever way we do it.'

'I think there may be a way of lessening the odds.' Powerscourt felt almost cheerful now. 'But I don't yet know if it will work. Let's find them first.'

'Christ Almighty! God in heaven!' Dominic Knox seldom swore, but the news from his agents at eight o'clock that morning left him in despair. His agents had searched all night and found nothing apart from a few trivial gifts in the schoolteacher's little kitchen. Nothing. Whatever Michael Byrne was plotting, whatever his schemes for the disruption of the Jubilee, Knox had been sure that these three young women were crucial. They would be carrying explosives or bits of rifles to be assembled in London. That was why he had been so careful not to intercept them until he knew where they had been, who they had visited in the capital. Now his strategy was in ruins. He had been tricked by his Irish opponents. Were the three messengers merely decoys to throw him off the scent? And if they were, what was Michael Byrne really planning? Knox realized he had been looking in the wrong direction, that all his plans had failed. Suddenly he remembered the rifles, buried in their coffins in Wicklow. He sent a telegraph to Dublin to open those graves at once and check the contents of the coffins. Pray to God, said Knox to himself, pray to God those bloody rifles are still there.

Powerscourt was pacing up and down his living room in the Prince Regent, pausing every now and then to gaze out to sea. Fitzgerald, looking even more decrepit than the day before, had gone to patrol the streets of Brighton. Powerscourt was turning his plan over and over in his mind, looking for flaws. They would only have one chance, just one chance to rescue Lady Lucy and restore happiness to both of them. Shortly after ten, just as the first of Tait's policemen were interviewing their hotel managers, he spotted a flaw in his plan. Damn, he said to himself. There must be a way round it. He stared at the West Pier, fortune tellers and Pierrots already getting into position for the day's work. The chambermaid knocked on the door and asked if she could clean the room.

'Later, please, later,' Powerscourt said abstractedly, looking at the prints of Regency Brighton on the walls. What had the Prime Minister said to him two days before? 'I can put the resources of the State at your disposal. If you want a regiment or two, you can have them. If you want a couple of destroyers moored off the coast of Brighton you can have them. If you want Brighton sealed off by the authorities, we can do it.'

Powerscourt sat down at the writing desk in the corner and composed a telegram to Schomberg McDonnell, private secretary to the Prime Minister.

The hotel managers of Brighton have always been a world-weary and rather cynical body of men. They felt cheerful that morning. Bright and sunny weather was always good for business. But on this day, as on the day before, they were visited again by the local police, asking a different question this time. No, we have no guests taking meals in their rooms, said the man from the Bristol. His brothers in Christ at the Worcester, the Old Steine, the Sea View and the Royal Exeter agreed. We do have one guest who takes meals in her rooms, the manager of the George told the policeman, who looked up with great expectations in his eyes as he heard the news, but she is eighty-seven years old and is not expected to live long. The Suffolk, the Royal Brighton, the York and the Oxford all shook their heads sadly and wondered what on earth was going on. In a quiet conclave later that afternoon they suspected that some terrible London murderer had fled to the worldly delights of Brighton. A man from the Burlington wondered if Jack the Ripper had come for a holiday by the sea.

At eleven o'clock Lord Francis Powerscourt had a visitor.

'What a splendid day to come to the seaside!' said a young man of about thirty years with laughing blue eyes and tousled fair hair.

'Mr Hardy, you were very prompt in answering my telegram from yesterday,' said Powerscourt, shaking him warmly by the hand. 'How very good to see you.'

'You didn't give me very much detail,' said Hardy, the fire investigator who had helped Powerscourt at Blackwater, 'but life always seems to be interesting when you're around, Lord Powerscourt. I've brought a few things with me but I forgot to pack my bucket and spade.'

Powerscourt told him of Lucy's kidnap. He showed him the kidnap letter. He explained that the police were talking to every hotel owner in Brighton. He explained to Hardy what he wanted.

'I see, I see. What fun! What a lark, Lord Powerscourt!' Hardy was rubbing his hands together in delight at the challenge ahead. 'I did take the liberty of sending a wire to the local brigade. Am I right in thinking that you don't yet know precisely which hotel we may be talking about?'

Powerscourt assured him that he did not yet have that intelligence.

'I think I'll take a walk down to the sea front,' the young man said, 'and have a look at the type of building we may be dealing with. But I tell you this, Lord Powerscourt. It's all a lot more fun than those insurance claims back in London!'

At twelve o'clock the cannon on the West Pier boomed out for midday, a secular and seaside Angelus for the holidaymakers promenading up and down the front. The seagulls protested loudly and flew out to sea in angry battalions. Even after years of the gun tolling twelve they still hadn't learnt to expect it.

The hotel managers of the Rottingdean and the Kemptown told the policemen that they had no guests taking their meals in their rooms. The Piccadilly did have such a guest but he was a young man who had broken his leg the day before. The Piccadilly's hotel manager assured his visitors that the young man expected to be mobile in a couple of days. The policemen were half-way up the front by now and were almost opposite the Royal Pavilion.

Powerscourt stood staring out of the window at the sea front. One o'clock passed, then two. Joseph Hardy had not returned from his inspection of the hotels. Johnny Fitzgerald had departed once more in his tramp's uniform to see what he could find. Maybe I've been wrong all along, Powerscourt thought bitterly. He looked at his watch. He could now calculate from any given hour of the day exactly how long he had to save Lady Lucy. At this point there were fifty-eight hours and eighteen minutes left. There might be a bit longer while the messages came down from London that Harrison's Bank had been rescued. But then?

There was a sudden pounding up the stairs to his room. Chief Inspector Robin Tait burst in. 'We've found them!' he panted. 'I've run all the way from the hotel to tell you! They're in the King George the Fourth, not far from the West Pier!'

'Well done, Chief Inspector!' Powerscourt shook the policeman firmly by the hand and pumped it up and down. 'I cannot tell you how pleased I am. This is fantastic news. How did you find them? Is there any news of Lucy?'

Tait slumped into a chair and wiped his brow with a perfectly ironed handkerchief. His wife likes to see him well turned out, Powerscourt thought.

'It began as a perfectly routine inquiry, my lord, the normal sort of thing my officers have been doing for the last two days. At first they only got the assistant manager and he looked at them rather suspiciously, demanded to see their papers and that sort of thing. It's amazing the difference not having a uniform makes to the way people see you. I'm sure we'll find that very useful later on. Anyway, the assistant manager went off to speak to the kitchens. That took about ten minutes. Then he came back and said he just needed to check with the manager.'

'Did your men know by now that they had found what they were looking for?' asked Powerscourt.

'I think they did,' said Tait, proud of the efficiency of his officers, 'there was something in the assistant manager's face, as if he felt guilty. This is what happened. One man booked two adjacent suites on the sixth floor of what you might call the west wing of the King George the Fourth Hotel two nights ago. There's an interconnecting door between the two suites. The other two, a man and a woman, came later. The woman looked pale and tired, as if she'd had a fainting fit or something like that. They all disappeared into Rooms 607 and 608. They haven't been seen since. All their meals have been sent up. They haven't even let the chambermaid in to clean up.'

'Didn't anybody think that was suspicious?' asked Powerscourt, his mind far away now with Lucy in her prison cell on the sixth floor of the King George the Fourth. Did she have any clean clothes? He knew she hated not having fresh things to wear every day.

'They might have done, my lord,' said Tait, aware suddenly of just how fragile Powerscourt was at that moment, 'but quite a lot of money kept changing hands.'

There was a loud knock at the door. Joseph Hardy, fire expert and fire investigator had returned.

'Mr Hardy, allow me to introduce Chief Inspector Tait of the local constabulary. Mr Hardy is an expert in fires of every sort. Let me tell you, Mr Hardy, that the Chief Inspector and his men have worked a miracle. Lady Lucy and the two villains are on the sixth floor of the King George the Fourth near the West Pier.'

'Splendid, splendid!' said Hardy cheerfully, rubbing his hands together. 'I did a few sketches when I was down on the front, my Lord. Including the King George the Fourth.' He produced a piece of paper from his satchel.

The hotel had a massive frontage, almost all of it looking out to sea. But on the west side, nearer to Hove, a turret-like structure jutted out, with one window looking straight out to sea, the window on its left looking west towards the pier, and a final window looking on to the street below and the other street running back towards the town.

'It's a perfect lookout post,' said Powerscourt. 'You could see people, or policemen, coming at you from three directions.'

Chief Inspector Tait was to tell his wife later that he knew even then how Powerscourt proposed to free the hostages. He didn't know if it would work.

'Gentlemen,' said Powerscourt, 'let me tell you how I think the rescue is to be effected. Any direct assault, either from the corridor outside or through the windows, might succeed. But the villains would have time to shoot Lady Lucy before they were overpowered. We could put something in their food, a powerful sedative of some kind, and then rush the rooms. But somebody might not eat the food. Lady Lucy might take two helpings and not wake up at all. If we had time, we could simply wait. But we don't have time. In fact,' he looked quickly at his watch, 'we have fifty-seven hours and fifty minutes to effect a rescue.'

Joseph Hardy was adding to his drawing of the King George the Fourth, the west wing in particular. Powerscourt could see sheets of red and great blobs of grey pencil moving up the side of the building. Hardy was smiling to himself.

'So, tonight or tomorrow night,' said Powerscourt, 'we have a fire. It won't really be a fire, of course, mostly smoke. The fire will be concentrated up the stairs and in the areas adjacent to the sixth-floor rooms. We will be able to make the fire fiercer, if necessary, to smoke them out. We can do that, Mr Hardy?'

'Yes, my lord, we can,' said Hardy cheerfully. 'That would be great sport.'

'At some point,' Powerscourt went on, 'they will have to come out. We shall have to make sure that there are no possible exits to the roof. We may need men with blankets, or whatever you fire people use, waiting down below in case they jump. Once they're out of their rooms and coming down the stairs, we seize them all. Especially Lady Lucy.'

Chief Inspector Tait looked sombre. Powerscourt suddenly suspected that he and his men might feel they were missing the fun. All the glory would go to the firemen.

'The role of the police, of course,' he went on, 'is absolutely vital. Your men, Chief Inspector, and there may have to be quite a lot of them, will have to be ready to break into the rooms if necessary. The hotel may have to be cordoned off. In the meantime I presume that you have posted a discreet watch all around the hotel in case our friends decide to cut their losses?'

Chief Inspector Tait nodded. He was fascinated by Hardy's drawings. The little blobs of grey pencil had now reached the sky. The top of the hotel was virtually obliterated.

'There are two things I must do,' said Powerscourt. 'I must send a telegram to the Prime Minister's office in London. I propose that we reassemble here at seven o'clock this evening. Mr Hardy, could you bring your colleague or colleagues from the local fire brigade? And could you in the meantime work out in more detail how our fire could work to the best effect? Chief Inspector, could you bring your Chief Constable with you to the meeting? And could you also ensure that the hotel manager attends?'

Both men nodded their agreement.

'And the second thing you have to do?' This time Tait had no idea what was coming.

'I presume, Chief Inspector,' said Powerscourt, 'that you can smuggle me into that hotel by the back door or through the kitchens? And I would be most grateful if you could find me the conductor of the orchestra who plays there in the evening. They do have a bloody orchestra, I presume?'

'They claim,' said Tait loyally, 'that it is the best one of its kind in Sussex.' He wondered if Powerscourt had gone out of his mind. Was he going to have specially selected music wafting up the stairs to Room 607, Music for the Royal Fireworks or something similar? 'Could I ask why you want to see the orchestral gentleman, Lord Powerscourt?'

Powerscourt smiled. Tait noticed that his eyes stayed cold.

'Of course you may, Chief Inspector. And no, I'm not going mad. I'm going to send a message. A message to Lady Lucy.'

Hold on, Lucy, he said to himself as Tait led him off towards the rear entrance to the King George the Fourth Hotel. Hold on. I'm coming.

He stopped at the telegraph on his way and sent a one-word message to London. 'Schomberg.'

32

The orchestral gentleman was a tall man in his late thirties, painfully thin. Like so many in his profession he felt that his abilities had not been properly rewarded. In his youth there had been so much talent. People had said that he would end up as a great conductor with a great orchestra in one of the great capitals of Europe. Even Paris or Vienna had not seemed beyond the realms of the possible. But his dreams had faded now. Here he was, on duty every evening with another collection of embittered violinists and mutinous sections of horn and brass, churning out waltzes and melodies to accompany the soup and the fish courses, the steaks and the crème brûlées of the Brighton holidaymakers. Sometimes, very late at night in the little garret the hotel gave him at the back of the building, overlooking the kitchen rubbish dump, he would dream again that he might escape from the King George the Fourth and find his proper station.

'How can I help you, sir?' he said to the man in the fisherman's jersey who had asked to see him. Powerscourt had avoided giving any name.

'I am staying in the hotel with my wife this evening and it is our wedding anniversary.' Powerscourt gave him a friendly smile. 'I would be most grateful if you could play this piece of music at precisely seven o'clock.'

He handed the conductor a piece of paper.

'Why yes, I think we could,' said the conductor. 'We played the whole thing at Eastbourne last year. I hope the orchestra haven't left their scores at home. They normally bring everything with them. Sometimes people ask us to play the oddest things, you know.'

Powerscourt handed over ten pounds.

'It's not the usual sort of thing we play here,' said the conductor defensively. 'I hope there won't be any trouble with the management or the guests.'

Powerscourt handed over a further ten pounds. The conductor looked more cheerful.

'There won't be any trouble with the management,' Powerscourt assured him. 'Don't worry about the guests. It'll be good for their souls.'

Powerscourt felt his arm being tugged as he walked back to the Prince Regent. He looked across. The tramp was speaking to him.

'Francis, for the love of God, I tell you, I'm sure they're in that hotel you've just walked out of.'

It was Johnny Fitzgerald. 'Johnny,' said Powerscourt, 'how very nice to see you. How in God's name did you find that out?'

'Well,' Fitzgerald went on, 'I've spent part of the last two days being a fortune teller on the West Pier. I gave the Great Mystic Merlin five pounds to clear off for a bit. I've been watching all these hotels from my pitch, just inside the entrance. There's a set of windows on the top floor of this King George place where somebody looks out every now and then. As if they don't want to be seen.'

'You're absolutely right, Johnny. The police have found them in Rooms 607 and 608. There's a conference in my suite at the hotel at seven this evening. We're going to plan the Great Fire of Brighton. We're going to smoke them out.'

The conductor looked around the great dining room. The room was nearly full. The conductor noticed that all the windows looking out to sea seemed to have been opened. He tried to spot the man who had asked for this piece of music but he couldn't find him. The conductor was running a little late. He nodded to his orchestra. He raised his baton. Very softly at first the third movement of Beethoven's Ninth Symphony floated out into the evening air of Brighton.

Four hundred yards away the manager of the King George the Fourth thought he was in the middle of a nightmare. Albert Hudson had served in the King George for nearly fifty years. Quite soon he would be able to retire with his wife to the little cottage he had bought near Ringmer, well away from the sea and well away from the ghastly tourists and what he saw as the crass vulgarity of modern Brighton. All afternoon people saying they were policemen had been skulking round his hotel. His hotel. Later on there was another collection of interlopers who said they were firemen. The worst week of his professional life up till now had been when two Indian Maharajahs had come to stay for a week; both with large retinues, mostly female, mostly from Paris. The two Indians had fallen out over one of the young women. The young women began fighting among themselves. It had been terrible. Now here he was in a meeting with a whole roomful of doubtful-looking people. There was a smart man who claimed to be the Chief Constable of Sussex. Albert Hudson thought he might have seen him somewhere before. There was a cricketer who said he was a Chief Inspector. There was a tramp who looked as if he should have been locked up. There was a man in a fisherman's jersey who pretended to be in charge. There was a very young-looking man who kept on drawing things. Hudson thought they were fire engines. There was another man who said he was a fireman and a mild-looking man at the end of the table who said he came from the Prime Minister's office.

Albert Hudson decided that he would defend the honour and possibly the fittings and the fabric of his hotel to his last breath.

'Forgive me if I have misunderstood you, gentlemen. Please forgive me. Am I right in thinking that you are proposing to burn down my hotel?'

Powerscourt sighed. His mind was four hundred yards away, on the Brighton sea front, listening to the noises.

The Chief Constable intervened in what his family privately referred to as his Reading the Riot Act voice.

'My dear Hudson,' he began, rubbing his hands together, 'this must all have come as rather a shock. We are not proposing to burn down your hotel. We are proposing to create an incendiary incident, mostly based on smoke rather than fire, in order to force a pair of villains who are holding Lord Powerscourt's wife hostage on the sixth floor to come out. This has to be done as quickly as possible, or they will kill her. Perhaps Lord Powerscourt would care to show you the note they left in his house in London a couple of days ago.'

Powerscourt felt in his pocket. 'You do not need to know anything about Harrison's Bank,' he said. 'That must be regarded as confidential. But you can see what they will do to my wife.' He handed over the note. Albert Hudson turned pale as he read the last two sentences.

The third movement of Beethoven's Ninth Symphony begins with a melancholy sound like a hymn. Then it moves off into a different world.

Lord Francis Powerscourt had proposed to Lady Lucy Hamilton during a performance of this very symphony at the Albert Hall in London five years before. Powerscourt remembered scribbling his proposal on a scrap of newspaper, not daring to speak in case God or Beethoven sent a thunderbolt.

The conductor was pleased with his orchestra. Maybe this would mark a turning point in his career after all. The diners in the King George the Fourth paused over the Sole Meunière or Lobster Thermidor as the music went on. Perhaps the man in the fisherman's jersey had been right, the conductor thought. It was good for their souls.

Up on the sixth floor Lady Lucy was straining to listen. She knew this was not something the orchestra normally played. This wasn't a waltz or a jolly piece of Handel. She strained in her seat towards the window. Her guardian of the moment was reading a foreign newspaper.

Powerscourt too was straining his ears towards the sea front. He knew the music should be well under way by now. He hoped Lucy could hear it.

Then Lucy knew. She knew the music. She knew when she had first heard it with Francis. She knew it was a message. She knew who it was from. She remembered that she had been crying softly in the Albert Hall when she had first heard this movement. She had cried till the end. I mustn't cry now, or they'll know something has happened, she said to herself. She wanted to sing, to shout, to perform once more her own Ode to Joy as she had wanted to in that darkened box opposite Kensington Gardens those five years ago when Francis asked her to marry him.

Francis has found me, she whispered to herself, blinking back the tears once more. Francis has found me. Francis is coming.

With a supreme effort of will, Lady Lucy Powerscourt turned slightly in her chair and pretended to fall asleep.

Francis is coming. Francis is coming.

'What about my directors? What about my shareholders?' said

307

Albert Hudson, manager of the King George the Fourth, defiantly. 'You are going to cause enormous damage to my hotel if you proceed with this madcap scheme. Who is going to pay for the repairs?'

As he looked round the room Albert Hudson thought this should have been his trump card. But he sensed that he was going to be proved wrong.

The man in the fisherman's jersey spoke to him very gently. 'All that has been taken care of, Mr Hudson. Mr McDonnell here has come specially from London. He is the private secretary to the Prime Minister.'

McDonnell too was gentle, trying to ease the pain of the old man whose hotel was to be sacrificed to the flames and the national interest.

'I have a letter here from the Prime Minister, Mr Hudson. He says that Her Majesty's Government will pay for any necessary repairs to any hotels in Brighton that follow any operations mounted by Lord Francis Powerscourt and the Chief Constable of Sussex. Here, you may read it.'

This was the result of Powerscourt's one word telegraph to Whitehall. He had explained the likely position in an earlier message. 'Schomberg' simply asked for McDonnell to come in person.

Hudson stared hard at the notepaper, as if he suspected that it might be a forgery.

'I too have had a message from the Prime Minister.' The Chief Constable was moving in for the kill. 'It gives me powers to take over any hotels I think fit in the Brighton area for the next forty-eight hours. Of course, I have no wish to use these powers. Co-operation will be much more satisfactory than coercion. If we can all work together then the final outcome is much more likely to succeed.'

Powerscourt wondered briefly what a hotel run by the police force would be like. Lots of minor rules and regulations, he suspected. Proper dress to be worn at all times. Drunkenness punished by a quick visit to the cells. Meals served exactly on time.

Albert Hudson looked round the room once more. Joe Hardy thought he might burst into tears, so sad had his face become as he thought of the flames and the smoke ruining the building he had tended for nearly fifty years.

'Very good, gentlemen,' he said. 'With great reluctance, great reluctance, I place the King George the Fourth at your disposal. If anything should go wrong with this operation I shall tell my directors that the blame cannot be laid at my door. I presume that I may evacuate all my guests in the course of this evening.'

The Chief Constable looked at Powerscourt.

'I'm afraid that would not fit in with our plans, Mr Hudson.' Powerscourt spoke in his most emollient voice. He was wondering if Lucy had got the message, sent up to her through the windows of the hotel. 'Most of this fire will take place on the upper floors of the west wing. The people we are concerned with are in Rooms 607 and 608 on the top floor, as you know. Mr Hardy here is a fire expert from London. He and Chief Fire Officer Matthews beside him from your local brigade will work out later this evening exactly how they intend to achieve the conflagration. But it is very important that the rest of the guests are evacuated at the time of the fire. It will make things look more convincing. With any luck – from our point of view, that is – there will be a certain amount of confusion. Maybe some of the women will scream. Maybe some of the children will cry. That is regrettable but it helps our purpose. These noises will carry up to the sixth floor. I hope they will help convince the two villains holding my wife that they have no alternative but to evacuate their rooms. Otherwise, they must feel, they will be burnt to a cinder.'

Chief Inspector Tait made a note in his book. Powerscourt wondered if he was going to hire some actresses for the evening to scream to police orders. Brighton had always been well supplied with actresses.

Albert Hudson knew when he was beaten. 'I see,' he said looking mournfully at his perfectly polished shoes. 'I see.'

'Now,' said Powerscourt, 'the more closely you are involved in the planning of the business, Mr Hudson, the greater our chances of victory. The police and the fire department here both need to return with you to your hotel for the detailed planning of this operation. I suggest this should happen at once.'

'I'm afraid, Lord Powerscourt,' Chief Inspector Tait sounded apologetic, 'that I should ask you and Lord Fitzgerald to wait here. Until it is dark, at least. I know it is unlikely that either of the two villains will come down into the body of the hotel but that is a risk we dare not take.'

Powerscourt smiled. 'Of course. We shall wait for the dark, Chief Inspector. We have often done it before.'

As Albert Hudson led his party of arsonists and police officers back to the King George the Fourth, Powerscourt saw Joseph Hardy showing his colleague a long list of calculations. Powerscourt thought they were talking about tar and pitch and other inflammatory substances. As they went down the stairs he heard Hardy talking about some other fiery potion whose name he did not catch. 'That stuff,' Hardy said with a laugh, 'it goes up like the fires of hell themselves. It's terrific!'

Powerscourt and Fitzgerald sat waiting for another battle, as they had waited together so many times in the past. Powerscourt remembered the terrible strain, waiting hour after hour in the roasting Indian sun for the enemy to unleash their gaudy cavalry on the thin lines of redcoats and their guns. He remembered waiting in the Piazza San Marco in Venice for Lord Edward Gresham to come to a fateful rendezvous in an upstairs room of Florian's restaurant. He remembered another Indian battle when he and Johnny had been surrounded in an ancient fortress near the Khyber Pass waiting for the Afghans to climb the slope and die in their thousands from the artillery.

'Francis,' said Johnny, I think I might take a little nap. Wake me in a couple of hours.' He looked at his watch. 'In six hours' time, I can have a bloody great drink. I hope that hotel man can open his bar for the celebrations.'

'One thing, Johnny, just one, before you go to sleep.' Powerscourt sounded very solemn. 'I realize that now may not be the best time to ask this question. It is after all a very personal matter. Forgive me for asking it. Feel free not to respond if you so wish.'

'Get on with it, Francis!' said Fitzgerald, draping himself neatly into the sofa.

'It's this, Johnny. What did you tell your customers when you were being Mystic Merlin on the West Pier?'

Fitzgerald laughed. 'It's terribly easy, really. Most of the customers are young girls. "Are you married, my child?" I would say, stroking their hands. "No, sir," they would reply. I would pause for a bit and start talking about lines of the hand meeting in particular places. Then I would say I saw a little house with a garden and three children playing and a husband just coming home from work. Some of them would give me extra money for that.'

Powerscourt thought of legions of Lydia Bennets, asking for

confirmation that the perfect officer was just around the corner, waiting at the ball in scarlet uniform.

'Did you give anyone bad news, Johnny?'

'No.' Fitzgerald was yawning now. 'Only one very pompous man. He looked very rich to me. God knows why he wanted to have his fortune told.'

'Maybe he too wanted a little house with three children,' said Powerscourt.

'Well, I thought he had plenty of houses already. I told him I saw a mountain, a very long time ago, and a great crowd on the slopes gathered to hear a preacher man.'

'What did the preacher man say, Johnny?' asked Powerscourt.

'The preacher man said,' Fitzgerald was laughing now, 'that the meek shall inherit the earth.'

Lady Lucy ate very little that evening. She wanted to stay alert for whatever the night might bring. She told her captors she had a very bad headache and needed to be left in peace. As she pretended to doze in her armchair she could almost hear her heart beating.

Francis has found me. Francis is coming.

Her husband spent much of the evening staring out of his window towards the West Pier. Various emissaries came from the King George with details of the plans. Chief Inspector Tait came with news that everything was going splendidly. He explained to Powerscourt that the police had evolved a system of sending each other messages by whistles for use in the smoke. They sounded very complicated. Powerscourt only remembered one. One long continuous blast meant that the fire could be stopped, the smoke engines turned off.

Joe Hardy came, looking very excited about the night ahead.

'We're going to have a proper fire in the rooms on the two floors underneath. Proper fire,' he went on gleefully, 'not just smoke like everywhere else. It should help them get hot in Rooms 607 and 608.'

He saw Powerscourt looking alarmed.

'Don't worry, sir. It won't be too hot. And we'll be able to put it out when we want to. It's going to be tremendous!'

With that, Joe Hardy departed into the night, whistling happily to himself as he went. As darkness fell over Brighton the Chief Constable himself appeared.

'I'm feeling rather nervous,' he announced. 'But I hope everything is under control. The inferno, as that charming young man from London keeps referring to it, is to start a few minutes after one o'clock.'

Shortly after midnight Lord Francis Powerscourt crept down to the front. There was a crescent moon and the stars were shining brightly over the sea. A slight wind came in from the English Channel. Powerscourt heard whispered greetings from the shadows and the doorways as he passed. 'Good evening, sir.' 'Good luck, sir.' Chief Inspector Tait must have his men posted everywhere tonight, he thought, as he saw a further posse of policemen lying on the beach behind the fishing boats. On the West Pier the moonlight was glinting off the girders, faint shadows reflected in the dark waters beneath. The great hotels lay sleeping on the sea front, like beached liners waiting for another voyage. A stray drunk was being escorted to a place of safety by yet more of Tait's policemen. A stray dog, watched by twenty pairs of eyes, trotted slowly along the front in the direction of the Royal Pavilion to guard the ghosts of the Prince Regent and Mrs Fitzherbert.

33

By a quarter to one Powerscourt and Fitzgerald were waiting in a room on the second floor of the west wing of the King George the Fourth. There were no lights. Hardy crept in and gave them both a collection of dampened handkerchiefs. 'Might be useful in the smoke,' he whispered cheerfully before departing to tend his flames.

Powerscourt knew the plan. He felt like a theatre producer who has given the stage directions for his final act but does not know what the actors are going to say. The smoke was to be increased step by step. The fire in the rooms below 607 and 608 was to burn very fast, helped by some of Joe Hardy's inflammatory liquids. The balconies were the key to the smoke. Each room in the west wing and in the section next to it had a small balcony overlooking the sea. All the guests in this part of the building had been transferred to another section of the hotel. They were told there was a temporary problem with the water supply. Tonight the balconies were occupied by barrels filled with a mixture of oil, tar and pitch, combined in a deadly recipe to produce the maximum amount of smoke. When the three residents of Rooms 607 and 608 finally came out a platoon of six was to take care of them. Two each for the kidnappers. Two for Lady Lucy, Powerscourt and Johnny Fitzgerald. Tait had tried to deter him, fearing that his personal involvement might make him hesitate when rapid action was called for. 'I'm the only one who will recognize her,' Powerscourt had said defensively. 'In all that smoke, sir,' Tait had said, 'you wouldn't recognize Queen Victoria herself.' Powerscourt had prevailed.

The Town Hall clock struck one. Powerscourt peered out at the sea front and the West Pier. Nothing moved. There was only the low murmur of the English Channel, small waves rolling in along the pebbles of the beach. Then it started. It started very slowly. Two floors beneath him the first of Joe Hardy's barrels began to pour a thick stream of smoke up the side of the building. That's nothing at all, Powerscourt thought, it's a drop in the ocean. Then other barrels began to join the chorus. Soon there were five, then ten, then fifteen, then twenty, then thirty, then Powerscourt couldn't see very much at all.

The front of the hotel was wreathed in smoke, the west wing almost invisible. The breeze from the sea was keeping the smoke close to the side of the building. Then the flames started. Two great sheets of flame leapt upward into the night sky from the floors above. Powerscourt learned later that the flames came from blankets soaked in Joe Hardy's most inflammable liquids. At thirteen minutes past one the hotel fire alarm went off. Hotel staff, supplemented by Tait's policemen, were running round the building, knocking on doors, shouting to the people inside.

'Fire! Fire! You must leave now!' Outside the first fire engine had arrived and hosepipes were being dragged into position. 'Ladders,' one of the firemen shouted, 'we need some bloody ladders. Now!'

At the front of the hotel a melancholy procession of sleepy residents was straggling out of the main entrance. The men were in dressing gowns. Women had thrown their coats over their nightgowns to face the night air. 'Move along, now, move along.' Powerscourt knew that the police were going to move the residents along the side of the west wing, directly underneath Rooms 607 and 608.

'Fire! Fire!' The shouts were everywhere in the hotel. There must have been about twenty or thirty men shouting now. 'Come along, come along please.' The voices of the policemen were more insistent and more irritated as the residents tottered out of the great doors. The hotel fire alarm was still sounding, a high and insistent note that wore away at the eardrums. A woman screamed very loudly just under Powerscourt's room on the second floor. Then another. Then a chorus of screams rose up along with the smoke and the flames to the sixth floor. The rooms above me must be an inferno by now, Powerscourt thought. Police whistles began to sound through the confusion.

Outside the hotel the firemen were raising great ladders, shouting encouragement to each other as they crept up against the side of the hotel.

Powerscourt opened the door. Great waves of smoke poured in. The smoke was getting thicker and thicker up the stairway towards the higher floors. After a minute Powerscourt could scarcely see the Praetorian Guard of policemen and firemen deputed to capture the kidnappers. Behind him another fireman had appeared with a hosepipe. 'Fire! Fire!' The shouts were still echoing round the rest of the King George the Fourth. They must come now, Powerscourt thought to himself. Surely to God they can't stand much more of this. They must come now. Maybe they would have to storm Rooms 607 and 608 after all. Maybe the people weren't going to come out. Maybe they were dead.

Hardy materialized out of the inferno. He pointed upwards. Powerscourt and his little band went up the stairs very slowly. He was straining for any noise coming from the upper floors but all he could hear were the shouts of the policemen and the instructions being bellowed to the firemen outside.

They were on the fourth floor now. Still nobody came down the stairs. Had they jumped out of the window? Powerscourt knew there would be a party of firemen below, waiting to catch anybody leaping from the windows. If they could. If they didn't miss them. If the fall wasn't too great. The thick smoke, dark grey, almost black, was still pouring up the stairway. The banisters on the far side had completely disappeared from view. Desperately Powerscourt reached for one of Joe Hardy's handkerchiefs and tied it round his face. He didn't think he could bear much more of this. Beside him, invisible in the murk, Johnny Fitzgerald was coughing in great spasms. Powerscourt felt dizzy. They must come now, he thought. Nobody could take this amount of smoke. More whistles sounded through the fumes. Powerscourt wished he had paid more attention to Chief Inspector Tait telling him what they meant.

Underneath the door of the fourth-floor rooms he could see flames dancing towards the ceiling. Outside there was a succession of screams and distant shouts that Powerscourt couldn't distinguish. Still the hotel fire alarm rang out into this smoke- filled night. They heard a noise above them. A crash, as if somebody had just fallen against the side of the wall. Someone was swearing loudly in German. They heard more noises. Powerscourt wondered if they should advance up the stairs. Wait for them to come down, Hardy and the firemen had said, wait for them. That way you hold the initiative. More noises were coming down the stairs. Hardy had explained to Powerscourt earlier how people come down stairs in the smoke.

'You try to hold the banisters with one hand. You try to touch the person next to you with the other hand.'

How many people were coming down the stairs? One? Two? Three? Powerscourt couldn't tell. Then phantom shapes could be discerned very dimly through the smoke. Powerscourt heard a whistle blowing very loudly on the upper floor. The fireman behind him suddenly advanced and turned on his hosepipe. The force of the water was a complete shock to the phantoms. They fell backwards, then rolled forward down the stairs. The Praetorian Guard moved in. Powerscourt saw that two figures had been apprehended and were now being bundled downstairs at great speed. There were only two of them. They were both men. The bastards, he said to himself, the bastards. Had they left Lady Lucy alone in that cauldron upstairs? Had they killed her before they made their stumble towards freedom down the stairs?

Panting, choking, spluttering, Powerscourt and Fitzgerald made their way up the stairs to Room 607. Behind them they heard one long continuous blast on the police whistle. It seemed to sound for nearly a minute. That's the ceasefire, Powerscourt remembered, or the end of smoke signal. As they reached the sixth-floor landing he could hardly move. The smoke seemed to have gone right down into his lungs. Quite soon, very soon, he thought to himself, I'm going to pass out. Johnny was in front of him now. Together they staggered into Room 607. The smoke was very thick. 'Lucy!' Powerscourt shouted. 'Lucy!' There was no answer. They crawled into the next room through the connecting door. 'Lucy! Lucy!' The only noise they could hear came from the street outside. Lady Lucy was not there.

A party of four firemen appeared in the doorway. 'Search the rooms,' Powerscourt said, and then he allowed one of the firemen, a giant of a man, to carry him downstairs. He met Matthews of the local fire brigade on the second floor. Johnny Fitzgerald was doubled up beside him. 'Please, search that room. Please,' said Powerscourt with the very last of his breath. 'They might have put her in a cupboard or under the bed or something.' Four more firemen raced upstairs. Powerscourt was retching now. It was very hard to breathe.

'You must go outside at once,' said the fireman. 'Otherwise you may do yourself permanent damage. I shall bring news to the main entrance if you care to wait there.'

Supporting each other like a couple of drunks, Powerscourt and

Fitzgerald staggered down the stairs. Perhaps this was their last battle, Powerscourt thought. Of all the battles they had ever fought this was the one he least liked to lose. As they left the west wing, the smoke abating now, great black marks on the walls, the carpets turned dark by the smoke, the hotel began to return to normal. The Palm Court where the orchestra had played Beethoven's hymn to love six hours before was undamaged. The dining room waited in the moonlight for its breakfast customers. Outside the front door, Powerscourt sat down on the pavement. He wanted to cry. He had failed Lucy. How high her hopes must have risen when she heard the music. Now he had let her down.

Matthews came back, looking sombre. 'We have searched everywhere in those rooms. So far we have found nothing. We shall go on searching. I am sending my men up in relays.'

Johnny Fitzgerald pulled his friend to his feet and led him to the other side of the street. There were policemen everywhere. The hotel residents seemed to have been brought back to the front of the George the Fourth to await return to their quarters. They were chattering noisily to one another, sharing in their reminiscences of escape from the fire. Powerscourt looked out to sea. The West Pier, the sea front, the beached hotels, the fishing boats lined up on the beach, were all the same as they had been an hour or so ago. But Powerscourt's world had changed for ever.

He turned to look back at the hotel. Only the west wing bore the marks of the smoke. He heard a whistle blowing somewhere far away. There was a lot of shouting from some distant place. The Chief Constable was about a hundred yards away, staring up at the roof. He ran back towards the main entrance. The whistle was still blowing, a series of short sharp bursts.

Just in front of the great doors of the King George the Fourth the Chief Constable stopped. He drew himself up to his full height. 'Silence!' he bellowed. 'Silence in the name of the law!' The crowd stopped talking. The firemen went on gesticulating to each other in sign language. Behind him Powerscourt could just hear the sea, rolling softly up the shore. The whistles continued, louder now. The shouting went on. Powerscourt couldn't hear what they were saying at first. He thought his hearing must have been damaged in the inferno. Then it came to him.

'Powerscourt! Powerscourt!' He couldn't see where the shout came from. Then Johnny Fitzgerald pointed up at the roof. At the opposite end to the west wing was a group of five people. One of them had a whistle. The whistling stopped. There was a much smaller figure in the middle of the group. Powerscourt thought he recognized Chief Inspector Tait as the man doing the shouting. The smaller figure was partly hidden by the policemen.

'Powerscourt! Powerscourt!' The Tait-like figure was pointing now, pointing at the smaller figure who was lifted forward to the front of the group.

There was another shout, a feeble shout, a thin shout, a shout with a weakened voice that only just carried down to the sea front.

'Francis! Francis!' The little figure waved at him. It waved as long as it could. 'Lucy! Lucy!' Tears of joy were pouring down Powerscourt's cheeks. 'Hang on, Lucy,' he shouted up at the roof, 'I'm coming. I'm coming.'

Lord Francis Powerscourt staggered across the road, waving as he went, on a last mission to the upper floors.

Johnny Fitzgerald went in search of the Chief Constable, still staring defiantly at the crowd by the front door.

'Congratulations, sir,' said Johnny, ushering the Chief Constable into the main entrance. 'Would you still be in possession of your emergency powers, sir? The ones that came from the Prime Minister?'

'Don't need them now,' said the Chief Constable.

'But they operated for a period of forty-eight hours, if I remember what you said earlier,' Fitzgerald went on.

'What do you want me to do?' asked the Chief Constable.

'Well,' said Johnny Fitzgerald, 'it would seem to me that you have the power to override the licensing regulations. Terribly restrictive they are at the best of times, if you don't mind my saying so. You could request our hotel manager friend Mr Hudson to open the bar. At once. Then Lord Powerscourt and Lady Lucy could have a drink when they come down from the roof, don't you see?'

The Chief Constable laughed. He clapped Johnny Fitzgerald on the shoulder. 'Splendid idea,' said the Chief Constable. 'By virtue of the emergency powers vested in me, I shall have the bar opened at once.' He strode off towards the hotel offices.

'Where is that man Hudson,' he shouted, 'when you need him most?'

Two grinning young policemen guided Powerscourt up the six floors to the roof. They brought him out just behind Chief Inspector Tait and his party. Lady Lucy was looking frail, her eyes dark, her face smeared with marks from the smoke. Powerscourt embraced her briefly.

'Chief Inspector Tait,' he said, 'may I thank you and your colleagues here from the bottom of my heart for saving Lucy's life. I shall always be in your debt. How did you manage it?'

There was an embarrassed shuffling about from the policemen.

'Well, sir,' said Tait, 'I thought we should have a position on the roof above Room 607. If the villains knew there was a way up to the roof, they might try to escape through it. They could have checked it out when they arrived, just in case.'

Tait paused and waved briefly to one of his colleagues in the street below.

'So we waited on the far side of the trapdoor. Once the smoke got thick in that corridor outside 607 we dropped a man down to hide behind the cupboards. He had a piece of string like that woman in the labyrinth in Crete or Rhodes or wherever it was. One tug meant they were coming up, two tugs meant they were going down. Once we felt the tugs that they were going down we went for those rooms. Lady Powerscourt was waiting for us. I think she thought I was you, my lord.'

Chief Inspector Robin Tait blushed. 'I got a great big hug, my lord. But Lady Powerscourt was in rather a bad way. She needed fresh air, so we brought her along the roof. I think she's better now.'

'I am so grateful to you all,' said Lady Lucy. Powerscourt was thrilled to hear the sound of her voice again.

'I think Lady Powerscourt needs to stay up here in the fresh air for a bit longer,' said Tait firmly. 'It's still very smoky down below. And you don't look too good yourself, my lord.'

Chief Inspector Tait smiled. As he led his men down the stairs each one was embraced by Lady Lucy. They're hers for life now, thought Powerscourt.

'Lucy, Lucy,' said Powerscourt, 'I'm so happy. I don't know what to say.'

Lady Lucy smiled back at him. She looked around at her strange surroundings, up on the roof with chimney pots and great wires and cables running everywhere. Just beneath them a grey and silver sea stretched out towards the distant horizon. It looked like polished glass.

'Just for the moment, Francis,' she said, 'up here on our own with the moon and the stars, you don't have to say anything at all.'

319

34

'Do you mind if I join you?' Powerscourt and Lady Lucy were taking a late breakfast in the Prince Regent the morning after the rescue. Powerscourt had not been able to get all the smoke out of his hair. He felt as if one of Joseph Hardy's barrels was still smouldering on the top of his skull. Lady Lucy looked tired. The long strain of her ordeal had not yet passed. The man asking to join them was the Prime Minister's private secretary, Schomberg McDonnell.

'McDonnell!' said Powerscourt with an air of great surprise. 'How very nice to see you. Some coffee? I thought you had gone back to London.'

Powerscourt didn't recall seeing McDonnell at the impromptu party in the King George the Fourth in the small hours of the morning the night before. Albert Hudson, the manager, had opened his bar in person, serving free drinks to the strange collection of policemen and firemen, departing from his post only to go down to his cellars and fetch more cases of champagne. Powerscourt particularly enjoyed overhearing Hudson asking the Chief Constable to whom he should send the bill for repairs to his hotel. Hudson had blinked several times when told he should post it to Number 10 Downing Street.

Johnny Fitzgerald had commandeered two bottles of the hotel's finest Burgundy. 'It tastes fantastic after a long period of abstinence, Francis,' he had assured Powerscourt and Lady Lucy. 'Nearly thirty-six hours without a drop. I think I might try this abstaining business again. But not for a while yet.'

The Chief Constable knew a remarkable collection of seashanties. Surprisingly the policemen knew all the words. Joe Hardy had wandered round the undamaged sections of the hotel, delighted at how well his plans had worked. 'Wonderful!' he had said to all and sundry after a couple of glasses. 'Wonderful! Best night of my life!'

'I'm afraid,' said Schomberg McDonnell, looking carefully at Powerscourt, 'that when I came down from London last night I had three letters from the Prime Minister in my possession. One was for our friend Mr Hudson. One was for the Chief Constable.' He paused to demolish part of a kipper. 'The third one is for you.'

Powerscourt opened the envelope. He felt sick.

'My dear Lord Powerscourt,' he read, 'May I add my congratulations to those you must have already received on the successful liberation of Lady Powerscourt. I always knew you would succeed.

'But I fear your country has more to ask of you yet. We have a major security crisis over the Queen's Jubilee Parade. I am not au fait with all the details myself but Mr Dominic Knox of the Irish Office tells me that some German rifles have gone missing. Mr Knox tells me that you know of these rifles, that you were indeed instrumental in tracking them to their place of concealment. Knox thought he had intercepted the people he believed were bringing this weaponry to London. Now he thinks the messengers were merely decoys, designed to throw him off the scent. He believes that one or more of these rifles may be in London where an unknown assassin may be waiting to kill Her Majesty on Jubilee Day itself.

'I would like you to return to London immediately and assist Mr Knox in his endeavours.'

Powerscourt handed the letter to Lady Lucy. He remembered that terrible night in the Wicklow Mountains where he had feigned death to put his enemies off the scent, two coffins filled with German rifles buried in the grave of Thomas Carew, two more interred in a windswept cemetery high up in the hills where Martha O'Driscoll shared her eternal rest with Mausers or Schneiders.

'Francis.' Lady Lucy's voice was very firm. Many of her vast tribe of relations – enough, Powerscourt had once said, to fill two rotten boroughs in the days before the Great Reform Bill – had served in the military. Maybe the sense of duty passes down the generations. 'I know it's terrible,' she said, 'but there is no choice. We must go back to London at once. I so much want to see the children anyway. It's only a few more days.' She smiled bravely at him. Schomberg McDonnell had nearly demolished his kipper.

'Can I ask you two questions, McDonnell?' said Powerscourt thoughtfully. 'Of course I shall come. But what does Dominic Knox think should happen if he doesn't find these rifles?'

McDonnell drank some of his coffee. 'He has a very devious mind, that Dominic Knox,' he began.

God in heaven, thought Powerscourt. What kind of Machiavellian intelligence does the man possess if McDonnell thinks he is devious?

'We can't cancel the parade. One of his suggestions is to declare that the Queen has been taken ill. She does not ride through the streets of London at all but merely appears for the Thanksgiving Service at St Paul's.'

'And the other?' Powerscourt was fascinated.

'The other is that we have a substitute, an old lady of the same shape and size, dressed exactly like Her Majesty, who rides out from Buckingham Palace on the great parade.'

Powerscourt wondered briefly if McDonnell wished he had thought of that one himself. 'It's bit tricky,' he said, 'if she happens to get shot and the world thinks it was the Queen.'

'At least the Queen would still be alive,' said McDonnell frostily. 'You said you had two questions, Lord Powerscourt. What was the second one?' McDonnell sounded like a man anxious to get away.

'You said you brought three letters down to Brighton with you,' said Powerscourt. 'I just wonder if you didn't bring four.'

'What would the fourth one have been?' said McDonnell, taking refuge behind a large slice of buttered toast.

'I think the first paragraph with congratulations about Lucy's rescue would have turned into a paragraph of commiserations about its failure. But I think the second paragraph, bidding me come to London, would have been exactly the same. Am I right?'

Schomberg McDonnell, private secretary to the Prime Minister, confidant and colleague of the most powerful man in Great Britain, laughed.

'I'm afraid you're absolutely right, Lord Powerscourt. I tore the fourth letter into very small pieces first thing this morning.'

Powerscourt smiled. 'We'd better go,' he said.

As they made their way out of the hotel dining room they were greeted enthusiastically by Joe Hardy. He embraced Lady Lucy and shook Powerscourt vigorously by the hand.

'Just wanted to say, Lord Powerscourt, that I'm at your disposal for any further bonfires you may be planning. Gunpowder Plot, re-run of the Great Fire of London, burning down the Houses of Parliament again, I'm your man! Best night of my life!'

Dominic Knox was pacing up and down an office overlooking Horseguards. He was a short, wiry man in his late thirties. Today, Powerscourt thought, as they shook hands by the door, he looked at least fifty. Knox looked as though he hadn't slept properly for weeks.

'Thank God you have come, Lord Powerscourt. I fear it is too late. I fear we are all too late now.' He looked gloomily out of the window. The park was full of visitors for the Jubilee, staring in awe at the soldiers from all over the world who were enjoying the sunshine in St James's Park.

'I cannot believe it is too late,' said Powerscourt, sitting down on the far side of Knox's enormous desk. 'McDonnell said there was a problem with the rifles.'

'I have two problems, Lord Powerscourt,' said Knox, relieved perhaps to be able to share his problems with a fellow-professional. 'The first does indeed concern the rifles. You will recall, none better, that two coffins believed to contain rifles were buried in the grave of one Thomas Carew, south of Greystones, and a further two in the grave of Martha O'Driscoll up in the Wicklow Mountains. Both have been watched ever since you left Ireland. We opened one of them up in broad daylight the day after you found them and found four Mausers of the very latest make inside.'

Knox paused and rearranged some papers on his desk. Powerscourt said nothing.

'Two coffins are still with Thomas Carew. But there is only one coffin with Martha O'Driscoll. Four brand new high-powered rifles have left the Wicklow Mountains and gone I know not where. We only discovered that two days ago, while you were in Brighton.'

'Christ,' said Powerscourt. 'You remember I told you I did not actually see the rifles being placed in the grave? All I saw was the disturbed earth on the top. They could have placed one coffin in the O'Driscoll grave and taken the other one somewhere else.'

Knox nodded gloomily. 'Of course I remember you saying that, Lord Powerscourt. We checked the grave the following day. There were three coffins in it, one of the widow O'Driscoll and two more that came out of the sea in the night. We opened one of them and saw these four new rifles inside.'

'And you have been watching this place ever since, I presume?'

'We have.' Knox stopped to swat a fly that was advancing over his desk, trying to read his secrets. 'I don't know how they did it. Maybe the watchers got careless or fell asleep. But one coffin has gone. And the problem is this, Lord Powerscourt. Michael Byrne, the man I believe to be responsible for this conspiracy, has been sending messengers to London. Three young women have been apprehended so far. All of them have perfectly legitimate reasons for being here, of course. All of them have gone to the house of an Irish schoolteacher. I believed that Byrne was trying to smuggle one or more of those rifles into London. Broken into pieces, of course, so they could be reassembled. But no. All they brought the teacher was one bottle of Jameson's whisky, two pots of home-made marmalade and a large quantity of best Irish potato-bread.'

'So you think they were decoys, despatched to put you off the scent?'

'Absolutely correct, Lord Powerscourt.' Knox went over to his window and pulled it firmly shut. 'You remember Wellington before Waterloo, wondering which direction Napoleon's armies were going to come from? He thought the Corsican would go round his flank to try to cut him off from the sea. But he didn't, he drove straight between Wellington and Blucher's armies. When he found out the truth at the Duchess of Richmond's ball in Brussels, that Napoleon hadn't taken the expected direction, Wellington said, "Napoleon has humbugged me." I too feel as if I've been humbugged. Humbugged by Michael Byrne.'

'Wellington won in the end, though, didn't he,' said Powerscourt, smiling. He looked at a large print on the wall of Queen Victoria's previous Jubilee ten years before. Loyal crowds filled the streets. Garlands and banners hung above the route, festooned across lampposts or strung between the buildings. In a carriage a small figure rode in glory through her streets. Powerscourt stared at the windows overlooking the route. Was one of them going to contain an assassin, lurking behind the curtains until it was time to strike and a German rifle, the most deadly, the most accurate in the world, rang out to shatter the climax of an Empress's reign?

'The rifles,' he said suddenly. 'Did they take the rifles and leave the coffin in the grave, or did they move the coffin with the rifles inside?'

'They moved the whole bloody coffin,' Knox replied, 'there are only two coffins there now. Do you think that is important, my lord?'

'I'm not sure,' said Powerscourt. His mind was racing. 'I have always wondered why they put the rifles in those coffins, you know. At first sight, it looks as though it was a convenient way of hiding them. They could be buried in innocent Irish graves in the middle of the night, disturbing the dead, no doubt, but an excellent hiding place. But suppose that wasn't the only reason. Suppose there was another reason.'

Powerscourt paused. Dominic Knox said nothing. The silence lasted for twenty seconds or more, faint sounds of merriment forcing their way in through the window from the park outside. Another fly had begun a long march across Knox's papers.

'Suppose the real reason for the coffins was this,' Powerscourt went on. 'You want to send some guns from Ireland to England. You know the police and security people are watching everything and searching people and premises they suspect. Think how different it is with a coffin. Here we have an English visitor to Ireland, maybe an Irishman who had come to work in London and goes back to see his family. Let's call him Seamus Docherty. The unfortunate man falls ill in Ireland. He cannot be saved. He passes away. But it is the dearest wish of the Docherty family back in London that father Seamus, husband Seamus, be buried by their local priest in their local church and buried in their local cemetery where they can lay flowers on his grave after Mass on Sundays. So the body of the dead Docherty is put in its coffin and sent over to London. It must happen all the time. Except there isn't a Seamus Docherty, apart from on the name plate of the coffin. It contains four high quality Mausers, capable of killing man or woman at five hundred yards distance. The weight is presumably made up with bits of lead or some other heavy material so nobody would suspect there wasn't a body inside.

'What do you think of that, Mr Knox?'

'I think it is very plausible, my lord.' Knox did not look greatly encouraged by the news.

'Think of it, man,' said Powerscourt. 'It may take a lot of manpower to find the answer. But there must be records of the transhipment of a dead body in a coffin. There may be records in Dublin of such a passage. If Seamus Docherty comes into London by train there will be records, manifests or something like that at Euston station, which will show where its final destination was.

Once we find out that Father O'Flaherty of the Church of the Holy Cross performed the burial, we will know where the coffin is. If it came by sea, which I doubt, there must be records at the Port of London authority.'

Powerscourt paused. There was something Johnny Fitzgerald had said when he came home from Berlin, something that didn't seem to make very much sense at the time. Hotels, something to do with hotels.

'I believe,' said Powerscourt, 'that a hotel room was booked for the Jubilee by their German confederates a long time ago. Maybe eight months or more. That must be where the gunman is going to make his attempt, from the hotel. A room, or a suite of rooms overlooking the route of the procession reserved last year. Surely we can find that out. Even if time is very short, we still have several days left.'

Knox looked up and shook his head.

'I said when you arrived, Lord Powerscourt, that there were two problems. One was the rifles. The other is politics.'

'Politics?' said Powerscourt. 'For God's sake, man, this a Diamond Jubilee, not a general election!'

'Let me explain myself better,' said Knox. He went to stare out of his window. 'I work for the Irish Office. Security for the parade is in the hands of a very stupid general called Arbuthnot. When I told him about the missing rifles, he went apoplectic, my lord. He turned into a sort of human earthquake, face a vivid red, eruptions of bad language, hot molten streams of invective pouring forth about my incompetence. He, in his turn, told the Home Secretary who has overall responsibility for security in the capital. There can be few things, Lord Powerscourt, more guaranteed to bring a promising political career to an ignominious and inglorious end, than somebody taking a shot, maybe even killing the Head of State at a Diamond Jubilee.'

'Losing a war, perhaps, caught embezzling Treasury Funds,' said Powerscourt flippantly.

Knox smiled ruefully. 'The upshot of all this is that I have not been relieved from my post. But I have been relieved of my men. I had sixty operatives, many brought over from Dublin to work with me on this problem. They have all been taken away from me.'

'Where have they gone?' said Powerscourt.

'The Home Secretary and General Arbuthnot have decided that my methods are not to be trusted. No doubt even now I am being trussed like some dead animal in their minds to be turned into the sacrifice or scapegoat if things go wrong. They have decided that the only way to meet this threat is to have policemen or security operatives watching every entrance that leads into the route of the parade. Where the bus leaves to go to Temple Bar, there you will find my men, or at the entrances of every station in London, waiting to apprehend any person carrying a large package.'

'But what about the Prime Minister? What about Schomberg McDonnell?' said Powerscourt.

'The Prime Minister,' said Dominic Knox, 'has disappeared. He cannot be found. McDonnell has vanished with him. Perhaps they would feel it would be more politic if they were not in London at this time. But he placed great faith in you, my lord, the Prime Minister. He seemed to think you were some sort of miracle worker.'

Powerscourt contemplated walking on the water or raising the dead from their tombs. Not appropriate, that, just now, he said to himself. Maybe turning water into wine would gain him the eternal gratitude of Johnny Fitzgerald.

'All right, Mr Knox,' he said 'tell me the worst. How many people have we got to make these inquiries?'

'Five. Just five,' Dominic Knox replied. 'Myself, yourself, and three of my men I've managed to keep out of the clutches of that dreadful general.'

'Six,' said Powerscourt, thinking of the miracle at the wedding feast. 'There's Johnny Fitzgerald. I'm going to find him. He's worth a regiment all on his own, two after a couple of glasses. We're not beaten yet, Mr Knox, not by a long way.'

35

Lord Francis Powerscourt was surrounded by angels, angels with broken wings, angels with no arms, angels with no heads, angels in stone, angels in marble. He was waiting for Johnny Fitzgerald at three o'clock in the afternoon in Kilburn Cemetery in the north-west of the capital.

Knox's depleted forces had been remarkably speedy in their negotiations with the keepers of the records. Three coffins had indeed been sent from Dublin to London in the preceding month. Their destinations had been three different firms of undertakers, who had reluctantly told Powerscourt and Fitzgerald their final destination. Henry Joseph McLachlan, aged fifty-four, had been buried here with these angels.

Sections of the cemetery were overgrown. Weeds and brambles covered the bottom of the graves and giant creepers had entwined themselves round the statuary. Rooks and crows circled above the trees, protesting at the arrival of living humans. Through the foliage occasional crosses could be discerned, almost hidden from view. The other area was not very large, only a couple of hundred souls waiting here for the last trump.

Powerscourt began making his way round the graves, looking for McLachlan. He was wearing a pair of old trousers and the fisherman's jersey Chief Inspector Tait had found for him in Brighton. The grave would be clean and fresh, the passing seasons yet to leave their slow marks of creeping decay. Johnny Fitzgerald materialized, in his Mystic Merlin clothes, a spade in his hand, a large bag of tools on his back. He had been very cheerful since Brighton, drinking only the finest wines to compensate for his brief period of abstinence.

'What's this bugger called, Francis?' said Fitzgerald.

'McLachlan,' said Powerscourt, 'Henry Joseph McLachlan. The

earth won't have settled long enough for him to get a proper tombstone yet. There'll be a small cross or a stone with his name on it for now.'

'Wouldn't it be grand,' Fitzgerald was looking down at a bunch of dead flowers, 'if people actually said what they meant on these bloody tombs.'

'What do you mean, Johnny?' asked Powerscourt.

'Delighted he's gone,' said Fitzgerald cheerfully, 'Thank you, God, for taking the old bastard away. Gone but not remembered. The Lord giveth and the Lord taketh away, not a moment too soon. May her life be as miserable where she's gone as she made mine here on earth, that sort of thing.'

'You're a bad person, Johnny,' Powerscourt laughed. 'They'll get their own back on you, all these people here. I expect they'll leave a message with St Peter that you're not to be let in. You're blackballed from heaven, Johnny. Hard luck.'

Powerscourt stopped. The afternoon sun lit up a row of graves not ten feet from where they were standing. One of them was new, very new with a small cross at the head.

'Here he is, Johnny. Henry Joseph McLachlan. Gone to his Father in Heaven, May 1897.'

'Do we open it up now, Francis,' said Johnny Fitzgerald, 'or do we wait till it's dark? That'll be bloody hours away.'

'We've got to do it now,' said Powerscourt, glancing uneasily round the cemetery. There were no gardeners on duty. No relatives had come for a late afternoon communion with their dead. They were alone.

Powerscourt borrowed a spade from an open grave nearby, the preparations apparently left half-finished. In a couple of minutes they had removed the earth on top of the coffin. Something moved behind them. Powerscourt and Fitzgerald turned quickly, hands going automatically into trouser pockets. A squirrel eyed them coldly and vanished up a tree.

'I think, Francis, we can open the coffin without taking it out of the grave. Give me that big screwdriver. You keep your eyes open up top.'

Fitzgerald lay down beside the grave. He began undoing the four great screws that held the lid in position.

'I don't suppose,' he said, panting slightly with the exertion, 'that you would recognize the coffin we're looking for? That would be too much to hope for.'

'It was very dark,' said Powerscourt, his eyes fixed on the main entrance to Kilburn Cemetery, 'all I could tell was that they were coffins.'

He was hoping more than anything that this would be the right coffin, if there was a right coffin. He remembered that night in Greystones, following the coffins on their journey from the sea. He wondered if the man with the pipe had been Michael Byrne. Maybe all three were full of dead bodies, not deadly rifles. Maybe he had got it all wrong. Maybe the deadly coffin had been sent to Guildford or Reading, not to London at all.

'Three screws out, one to go,' Fitzgerald reported. 'I think I could do with a drink.' Powerscourt thought of the other corpses he had met in the course of his investigation, Old Mr Harrison with no head and no arms, floating by London Bridge, Mr Frederick Harrison, burnt to death on the top floor of his mansion. Ordeal by Water. Ordeal by Fire.

'Give me a hand here, Francis. We can just take a peep inside.'

Fitzgerald made the sign of the cross. Powerscourt lay down beside him. Together they tried to lift the lid. It was stiff. It didn't want to move.

'Bugger it,' said Fitzgerald, 'is there another bloody screw somewhere?' Anger seemed to give him extra strength. Slowly, with a faint creak, the lid of the coffin came up.

There were no rifles. Only a white face that looked surprised to be dead, the eyes closed, the hair carefully brushed across the forehead, the hands folded in pious expectation of the second coming.

'Sorry, Mr McLachlan,' said Fitzgerald quietly, 'very sorry. We'll put you back where you belong in no time.' He replaced the lid and the screws, lying on the ground beside the grave. Powerscourt was whispering to himself. 'Lord now lettest thou thy servant depart in peace according to thy word.' Johnny Fitzgerald was hurling the earth back on top of the coffin as fast as he could.

'For mine eyes have seen thy salvation, which thou hast prepared before the face of all people.'

Fitzgerald had moved on to the turf now, laying it out in neat rows. He stamped on it to make it flat once more.

Powerscourt was still whispering. 'To be a light to lighten the Gentiles and to the glory of thy people Israel.'

Johnny Fitzgerald jumped off the grave of Henry Joseph McLachlan. He brushed the earth off his clothes. 'Where now, Francis? I don't suppose you passed the Gravediggers Arms on your way in here? The Last Trump perhaps? That would be a good name for a pub.'

Powerscourt was looking at a piece of paper. 'We've got a choice here, Johnny. There are two coffins left. One is in the North London Cemetery somewhere near Islington. The other is the West London Cemetery near the river in Mortlake. Do you have any aesthetic preferences for either of these locations?'

'To hell with Islington,' said Fitzgerald firmly. 'There are lots of good pubs near the river in Mortlake. Mortlake gets my vote. I presume your carriage is still waiting near the entrance, Francis? We must be the only grave robbers in Britain to have their very own carriage to carry them round their targets. To horse! To horse!'

The streets were very busy. Every cab, carriage and brougham of the capital seemed to be full of visitors, inspecting the sights of London before they watched the Jubilee Parade. Powerscourt looked at his watch. It was now twenty minutes past four. He had noticed a sign at Kilburn that said the cemetery shut at five o'clock. If they arrived too late at Mortlake they would have to wait for a quiet moment to climb over the wall. It didn't look as if there would be any quiet moments in London this evening.

They made it with fifteen minutes to spare. They picked up their spades and Johnny's bag. Powerscourt took out two huge fisherman's bags and hid them inside the entrance.

'One blast on this whistle,' he said to Wilson his coachman, 'means come to the entrance as fast as you can. Two blasts means Help.'

Chief Inspector Tait had given Powerscourt some police whistles as a memento of the night in the King George the Fourth. Powerscourt had asked for three more for the children and regretted it deeply within twenty-four hours. Robert said it would be very useful for refereeing football matches with his friends in the park. Thomas and Olivia blew theirs once to universal delight. But they didn't stop blowing them. Powerscourt thought their lungs must collapse under the weight of blowing, from the top of the stairs, in the drawing room, in the garden. They crept into the kitchen and blew them right behind the cook and her assistant, causing panic and near mutiny below stairs. They dashed out into the street and frightened little old ladies taking a quiet afternoon walk in Markham Square. Lady Lucy only separated Thomas and

Olivia from the whistles by pointing out that she and Francis wanted to play with them as well. Even then Powerscourt had to invent a whole new vocabulary of police whistles. One blast on the whistle meant Go and get into the bath. Two blasts meant Get into bed. Three blasts meant Go to sleep.

'Look at this place, Francis, would you just look at it.' Johnny Fitzgerald was leaning on his spade, for all the world like a workman taking a well-earned rest, and looking at the vast expanse of cemetery. Well-ordered rows stretched almost as far as the eye could see. North towards the river, west towards Kew, the West London Cemetery was enormous. Thousands, if not tens of thousands of dead must be interred here.

'My God!' said Powerscourt, horrified at the prospect of searching for one grave among so many. 'It looks to be about the same size as Hyde Park, Johnny.'

To their left was the Belgravia of this country of the dead. Avenues of great stone catafalques, temples to the departed, stretched out towards the rear wall of the cemetery. Even in death, Powerscourt thought, the rich had to be better housed than the poor. If you had money in this life, then you had to show it when you were gone, neo-classical temples with shelves and closed chambers to contain the dynasties of the wealthy. Iron grilles barred the entrance to these last resting places of London's better postal districts. Inside spiders wove their webs very thickly. The air was musty. Bats no doubt came out at night to guard the money and the dead.

Powerscourt pointed this necropolis out to Johnny Fitzgerald. 'In here, Johnny. We can wait till the place closes up. Nobody would find us in here.'

Crouching down beside the catafalque of the Williams family of Chester Square, five of them interred in their five star luxury, Powerscourt and Fitzgerald waited in silence until they knew the cemetery was closed. Powerscourt felt claustrophobic, choked. Fitzgerald was drawing something with his finger on the dust of the side wall. Powerscourt thought it was a wine bottle. At last they heard the bolts being pulled and the keys turning in the great locks of the main entrance. Until the morning they were alone. Alone with thousands of the dead, one of whose coffins might not contain a corpse.

'We'd better have a plan, Johnny,' said Powerscourt as they emerged from the dank air of Belgravia. 'Should we start at the middle and work out, or begin round the edges and make our way into the centre?'

'Maybe there's one section where they put all the new arrivals, Francis. Like new boys at school. What's this bugger called anyway?' Johnny Fitzgerald pointed his spade into the middle distance as if the newest graves were there.

'This bugger is called Freely,' said Powerscourt, checking his piece of paper again, 'Dermot Sebastian Freely.'

The sky was mostly blue. Small clouds drifted overhead. The tombstones were warm from the late afternoon sun. 'Let's begin round the edges,' said Powerscourt, 'and work our way in towards the centre.'

'All right,' said Fitzgerald. 'Dermot Sebastian Freely,' he muttered to himself, 'where the hell are you?'

By seven o'clock, after an hour and a half of searching, they had found nothing. Powerscourt reckoned they had covered less than a tenth of the territory. He began to worry that they might not find Dermot Sebastian Freely before it was dark.

The whole century is enclosed here, in this enormous cemetery, he thought. He passed the grave of a man born in the year of Trafalgar, 1805, when England was saved from invasion. He passed the grave of a woman born in 1837, the year of Victoria's accession to the throne. He passed an ornate headstone commemorating a man who had been born in the year of the Great Reform Bill in 1832 and passed away in the year of the Second Reform Act of 1867. He passed the last resting place of men who had been soldiers, who had fought in the Crimea or in Africa or in India, servants of the Queen who had turned into an Empress and whose dominions now stretched across the globe. He doubted if they had been heroes, these bodies sleeping peacefully in the evening sun, but as it said so frequently on the tombstones, they had fought the good fight, remembered most often by the loving tributes of husbands and wives, sons and daughters. Powerscourt thought of the ending of *Middlemarch*, Lady Lucy's favourite novel: 'for the growing good of the world is partly dependent on unhistoric acts: and that things are not so ill with you and me as they might have been, is half owing to the number who lived faithfully a hidden life, and rest in unvisited tombs.'

By eight o'clock Johnny Fitzgerald was getting thirsty, muttering to himself the names of the pubs he knew along the river, the Dove, the Blue Anchor, the Old Ship as if it were a final blessing on the dead.

'Who the hell was Zachariah?' he asked Powerscourt at one of their occasional conferences. 'I've seen quotations from the old bugger about five times in the last half an hour.'

'Old Testament,' said Powerscourt. 'Prophet. Long white beard.'

Fitzgerald looked at him doubtfully but returned to his stretch of tombs. There was a breeze coming off the river, rustling the leaves of the trees, whispering its way through the tombstones. At nine o'clock they failed to notice a small boy who had climbed into the cemetery by a tree at the southern end and hid himself in its branches, keeping a careful eye on the two interlopers.

Powerscourt was thinking about Lucy and the journey they would take when all of this was over. Maybe the Italian Lakes, he said to himself, remembering Old Miss Harrison in Blackwater House describing her holidays there all those years ago. Charles William Adams, he read, Mary Nightingale, Albert James Smith, beloved husband of Martha.

Maybe the Italian coast, Portofino in its fabulous position right on the sea's edge. Somebody had told him about Corsica, wild and mountainous but with magnificent scenery and great peaks rising out of the very coastline itself. Anne Louisa Jackson, Catherine Jane O'Malley, Thomas Piper, Gone but not Forgotten.

Maybe we shouldn't go abroad at all, he thought. Maybe we should just go about our lives very quietly rejoicing in each other and the fact that we're still alive and not in a place like this. The roll call of the dead went on, the names tolling in his head as he passed them by.

Peter John Cartwright, Rest in Peace, Bertha Jane Hardy, George Michael Simpson, Gone to his Father in Heaven.

'Francis, Francis!' Johnny Fitzgerald was beckoning to him from about two hundred yards away. Powerscourt ran the whole way, his spade over his shoulder, hoping that the long search was over at last.

'Here he is,' said Fitzgerald softly, 'Dermot Sebastian Freely, born 18th February 1820, passed away 30th May 1897. I am the Resurrection and the Life.'

Powerscourt looked carefully round the cemetery. He saw no living soul, only the birds rising and swooping over the rich pickings of Belgravia. In his tree the small boy snuggled into his branches, scarcely daring to breathe.

Resurrection was coming early for Dermot Sebastian Freely. In a few minutes Fitzgerald was lying on top of the grave, great piles of earth on one side of him, screwdriver in hand.

'One,' said Fitzgerald, placing a large screw between his teeth. Powerscourt was gazing round the four corners of the West London Cemetery.

'Two,' said Fitzgerald. Powerscourt turned from his inspection and peered down into the open grave.

'Three,' said Fitzgerald rather indistinctly as the third screw was clamped between his teeth. The small boy saw that the two men had their backs to him now. The fisherman's jersey wasn't looking round the place any more. He knew what they were doing, opening up the grave. The Christian Brothers at school had told him this was a mortal sin. Very slowly, very quietly, he began to make his way down the tree onto the path outside the walls.

'Four,' said Fitzgerald, placing the screws carefully on the ground beside his spade. Powerscourt made his way to the other end of the coffin. They began to pull at the lid as hard as they could.

The small boy had reached the ground. He looked around him quickly. Then he began to run as fast as he could to find his father. His Pa and his new friend from Dublin would be pleased with him.

'Heave,' said Fitzgerald, panting hard. 'Heave for God's sake.' Powerscourt put his feet on the bottom section of the coffin and pulled with all his might. Very slowly the lid came off, inch by tantalizing inch. The coffin did not want to reveal its secrets. Then it came off completely, throwing Powerscourt and Fitzgerald back on to the grass. Dermot Sebastian Freely was not inside.

36

Platoons of pink clouds were drifting across the sky, floating gently towards the west and the setting sun. Powerscourt and Fitzgerald looked at each other. Then they stared, mesmerized, at the contents of the grave. Dermot Sebastian Freely's coffin contained no mortal remains, but four long packages, wrapped in brown paper. At the bottom were a number of small boxes. Mauser Gesellschaft, Berlin, said the legend.

Here, thought Powerscourt, here is the final, the conclusive proof of the links between the German secret society and the Irish revolutionaries. He had watched these coffins come ashore in the middle of the night in the little harbour of Greystones, borne into land by muffled oars from a great yacht out at sea. He had followed them on their sinister journey into the Wicklow Mountains just a month ago. Now he met them again, sent from Ireland to this enormous cemetery to lie among the English dead, before being collected and sent on their deadly mission.

Fitzgerald opened one of the boxes. The bullets looked sinister in the gloaming, the dying sun glinting off the tips as Fitzgerald held them up to the light. Powerscourt opened one of the packages. The rifle was shorter than the ones he had seen so often in India, but beautifully made.

'Right, Johnny. The most important thing is to get these rifles away from here. Somebody can watch over Freely's grave later to see who turns up. Let's get these damned things out of the cemetery. We can put the coffin back in the grave later.'

Carrying two rifles each, Powerscourt and Johnny Fitzgerald set out for the entrance to the cemetery, some two hundred yards away. The light was fading fast now, the long shadows from the tall tombstones fading into the ground. Suddenly Powerscourt saw a tree moving by the rear wall. He tapped his friend on the arm and put two fingers to his lips. They were no longer alone. Two men were climbing slowly down to the ground.

Powerscourt and Fitzgerald ducked behind a pair of ornate gravestones. It may have saved their lives. The first shot sounded very loud, echoing round the dead. The bullet whipped into one of the tombstones and ricocheted off towards the opposite wall.

'Christ!' whispered Fitzgerald to Powerscourt, pulling a pistol from his pocket, 'these people aren't very friendly. Must be colleagues of the late Mr Freely.' With that he crawled off into a long patch of shadow to the left.

Powerscourt saw that the opposition were still advancing. He dropped to the ground and took careful aim with his gun at the man closest to him. He heard a scream. He didn't wait to see how badly hurt the man was. He gathered up the rifles and sprinted half-way towards the rabbit warren of Belgravia and its mausoleums.

There were another two shots. Johnny Fitzgerald must be firing, Powerscourt thought, covering my position. Another bullet sang into a tombstone a few feet to his left. This was getting too close for comfort. He peered round the side of his tombstone and fired at his opponent, less than fifty yards away. He missed. He gathered the rifles again and set off. Belgravia was only a few feet away when he heard the shot. Then he felt the bullet pass through his left shoulder. Blood was pouring down the fisherman's jersey. He staggered into the shadows of one of the mausoleums and let the rifles drop to the ground. He peered out through the iron grille at the cemetery in front of him. Bats were squeaking all around, flapping dementedly at the night air. The rooks and the crows were fleeing the cemetery of the dead and the dying as fast as they could.

Powerscourt sat on the ground and tried to staunch the blood. He looked out. His adversary was advancing very slowly towards him, unsure which mausoleum he was in. Powerscourt took careful aim and fired. Damn, Damn. He had missed. The wound must be upsetting his aim. He had given his position away. I'm damned, he thought to himself, if I'm going to end my days in a bloody cemetery. I want to die in my bed. He worked his way backwards, inching slowly, painfully away from his previous position.

Where was Johnny Fitzgerald? Had he been wounded too? Was he dead? But the man knew where he was now. Powerscourt saw him raise his pistol and point it very precisely at where he sat. The man was taking his time. He was going to make certain. Then another shot rang out into the west London twilight. The man toppled forward and crashed on to the ground. At the far end of the cemetery a pair of owls were having a conversation, loud and insistent hoots that echoed the sound of Fitzgerald's pistol.

'Just making sure this bugger's dead, Francis.' The voice of Johnny Fitzgerald sounded very close. 'Are you all right?'

Powerscourt winced as he rose to his feet in the mausoleum of Jonathan Sanderson of Richmond. The shoulder was very painful.

'Delighted to hear from you, Johnny,' he said. 'I've stopped a bullet with my shoulder. There's a lot of blood but I think it's only a flesh wound.'

'The other one's dead too, Francis,' said Fitzgerald, tying a large handkerchief round Powerscourt's wounded shoulder. 'That's one each. One for me, one for you. The bugger here was a pretty good shot.' Fitzgerald laughed suddenly.

'I've got a great idea, Francis,' he said happily. 'Why don't we bundle the two of them into the coffin of our friend Dermot Sebastian Freely? Then we could give them both a decent burial in Freely's grave.'

'So then we picked up the rifles and got out as fast as we could.' One hour later Powerscourt was back in Markham Square, telling Lady Lucy what had happened. A local doctor had bandaged his shoulder. The guns were safely locked up in the nearest police station. Johnny Fitzgerald had gone to tell the glad tidings to Dominic Knox.

'You look pale, Francis. You must have lost a lot of blood.' Lady Lucy was looking at her husband very carefully.

'What do you say to Sorrento, Lucy?' said Powerscourt.

'Sorrento?' said Lady Lucy incredulously. 'It's late, Francis. You've had a very tiring few weeks. You must rest.' She peered at him anxiously.

'Sorrento as a place to escape to, Lucy, once this shoulder is better. We could go for a week or so. Spectacular scenery, dramatic walks round the coast. You can look at the Bay of Naples. On a good day you can see Capri.'

'I think that is an excellent idea, Francis.' Lady Lucy smiled at him, relieved that his brain was still working normally.

'You see,' said Powerscourt, moving on the sofa to find a more comfortable position, 'I am sure this affair is over at last. So many times I have told myself the business has finally ended only for some other problem to occur, your kidnap, the missing rifles. Harrison's Bank is safe. Mr Knox has no problems now with Irish terrorists. The Queen can ride out in glory on her great parade as safe as if she was in her own garden. It's over.'

37

Powerscourt had never seen anything like it. Neither had anybody else. Stretched out before him in five long lines lay the British Fleet, or some of it. Eleven first class battleships, five first class cruisers, thirteen second class cruisers, thirty-eight small cruisers, thirty new torpedo boat destroyers, one hundred and sixty-three warships of the Royal Navy spread out across the Solent, thirty miles of Victoria's sea power manned by forty thousand men and carrying three thousand naval guns.

Three days before one million Londoners had cheered themselves hoarse as a small great-grandmother, dressed in sober grey, had crossed the streets of her capital to a service outside St Paul's Cathedral with an escort of fifty thousand troops from around her vast empire. Sophie Williams' class of six-year-olds had been to a Jubilee dinner in the Town Hall and had gorged themselves on cakes and jelly. There had been no incidents along the route. Dominic Knox of the Irish Office had taken himself off to Biarritz for a celebratory holiday and a flutter on the tables.

But of Charles Harrison, wanted by the police in connection with the abduction of Richard Martin and the kidnapping of Lady Lucy, there had been no sign. The Commissioner of the Metropolitan Police had told Powerscourt that Harrison might have left the country by private means or be hiding somewhere remote like the north of Scotland.

If the Jubilee in London was a celebration of the length of the Queen's reign and the size of her Empire, the celebrations at the Naval Review at Spithead were about the might of the Royal Navy. Without calling home a single vessel from the overseas stations, the Admiralty had assembled the most powerful fleet the world had ever seen. Powerscourt, his left shoulder still in a light sling, and

Lady Lucy and Johnny Fitzgerald were guests of Rosebery aboard the *Danube*, the vessel carrying members of the House of Lords, one of a flotilla of boats that followed the Royal Yacht *Victoria and Albert* through the lines of warships, all manned by sailors in regular lines along the length of every deck. Salutes rang out over the water, clouds of smoke drifting towards the land. As the Prince of Wales in the Royal Yacht, flying among its five huge flags the Royal Standard of Great Britain and the German Imperial Standard, a black eagle on a gold background, moved through the fleet, bands played the National Anthem. The sailors cheered and waved their caps in the air as royalty passed by.

'What are those ships over there?' said Powerscourt to Rosebery, pointing to the most distant line, the one furthest from the land.

'Those are the foreigners,' said Rosebery, 'Americans, Italians, Russians, Norwegians, Germans. They've come to see what the British Empire can put on the water.'

'And what is that old ship with the two red stripes around her funnel at the end of the line?' asked Powerscourt, raising his telescope to his eye.

'That is SMS *Konig Wilhelm* of the Imperial German Navy.' Rosebery too was peering at the foreign vessel. 'Fellow from the Admiralty told me on the way down that she was actually built at Blackwell's Yard in England nearly thirty years ago now.'

'Why would the Kaiser send such a hulk to this parade, Rosebery?'

'The admiralty man said it was very significant, that it was all done for public opinion at home.' Rosebery was squinting through his glasses. 'Bloody Kaiser wants the Germans to feel ashamed so they will vote him lots of money to build new ships. He's just appointed a new Naval Secretary too, a man by the name of Tirpitz.'

The Royal Yacht was drawing abreast of the pride of the American Navy, the USS *Brooklyn*, painted not in black like the British, but in a gleaming white. More cheers rang out across the Solent.

'God bless my soul!' said Powerscourt suddenly. 'I don't believe it. Johnny, take a look at the party on the German deck, next to the Captain.'

Fitzgerald raised a telescope to his eye.

'I don't see anything unusual, Francis.' He fiddled with the aperture. 'Can't see anything strange. Oh my God. I see what you mean. God in heaven, Francis, this is too much, it really is!'

'What are you looking at?' asked Rosebery

'It's not what we're looking at Rosebery, it's who.' Powerscourt had turned pale. Standing on deck, chatting cheerfully to the Captain, dressed in an immaculate white suit that was almost indistinguishable from the uniforms, was Charles Harrison, former banker of the City of London, suspected of multiple murder, the man who tried to ruin Britain's world-wide reputation for financial probity, the man whose secret society had sent the Mausers from Germany to Ireland to spoil an Empress's Jubilee.

The Royal Yacht had reached the *Konig Wilhelm*. The German band broke into the British National Anthem. Some of the elderly peers on board the *Danube*, well fortified with champagne by now, began to sing.

> 'Send her victorious
> Happy and Glorious!'

The Prince of Wales looked particularly pleased with the reception from his cousin's fleet. He bowed stiffly to the party on the deck.

'That fellow in the white suit, the one not in uniform, Rosebery, do you see him? That is Charles Harrison.' Powerscourt pointed to the bridge of the *Konig Wilhelm*.

'Is he, by God,' said Rosebery. 'He's got well away. He's back among his own people now. That's German territory, that ship. British police have no jurisdiction on board there.'

The German band had moved on to 'Rule Britannia'. The peers were singing heartily.

> 'When Britain first, at heaven's command,
> Arose from out the azure main . . .'

Powerscourt was remembering the conversation with his old tutor in Cambridge. Had Brooke not said that the leader of the secret society was an officer in the German Navy? Perhaps he was the Captain of the *Konig Wilhelm*.

> 'This was the charter of the land
> And guardian angels sang this strain . . .'

And then Charles Harrison saw Powerscourt. The same look of

astonishment passed across his face that had crossed Powers-court's a few minutes before. He scowled. He shook his fist at them across the water. He shouted something in between the verses.

Powerscourt thought it was 'One day we'll get even with you, you'll see.' Johnny Fitzgerald thought the parting message was slightly different: 'One day we'll send you to the bottom of the sea.' With a final shake of his fist he disappeared below the decks of the *Konig Wilhelm*.

'Rule Britannia, Britannia rule the waves . . .' Some of the peers were stamping their feet on the deck as they bellowed out the chorus. 'Britons never never never will be slaves.'

For a split second Powerscourt didn't know what to do. He looked round suddenly to make sure Lady Lucy was safe. She was chatting happily to an elderly peer. Harrison was escaping back to Germany. He could never be brought to justice now for all his crimes. But then, Powerscourt realized, he had won. Harrison's plans had been thwarted. The City of London had been saved. The Irish rifles had been intercepted. Lady Lucy was safe.

He waved back across the water, as if saying goodbye. Fitzgerald and Rosebery joined him in the salute as the Royal Yacht passed on to the end of the line and turned back towards Portsmouth. The *Konig Wilhelm* band had fallen silent. 'Rule Britannia' had finished.

'I tell you one thing,' said Rosebery cheerfully, looking at the contrast between the old German ship and the assembled might of the Royal Navy. 'They say he wants to build a fleet to rival ours, that Tirpitz and the bloody Kaiser. Well, just look at the difference between what they've got and what we've got. It's going to take them a bloody long time.'

Suddenly, in the midst of this vast Naval Review, Powerscourt and Lady Lucy found themselves completely alone on one side of the boat. The other passengers had gone to inspect the flagship of the Imperial Russian fleet on the other side of the *Danube*.

'Lucy,' said Powerscourt, in a voice she hadn't heard for weeks, 'I've been thinking.'

'Yes, Francis?' said Lady Lucy, her eyes sparkling brighter than the shine on the ship's polished brass.

'It's just that with all this charging around and about,' said Powerscourt, trying to sound grave and serious, 'we've hardly had any time to ourselves at all.'

Around and behind them the vast display of naval pomp and arrogance, the cruisers, the destroyers, the battleships might have been in the Pacific Ocean rather than the peaceful waters of the Solent.

Lady Lucy teased him. 'I do hope your shoulder's better,' she said with a mischievous smile.

'I think it's almost better now.' Powerscourt removed the sling and put his left arm around Lady Lucy's waist in a trial run. He held her tight.

'What were you going to suggest, Francis?' His wife gazed innocently up into her husband's face.

'Let's go home, Lucy,' said Powerscourt.

'Francis,' Lady Lucy replied, 'that would be delightful. I'm rather tired of hotels just at the moment. Let's go home.'